## SIL

Devin dragged her close to him, his hand twisting sensuously through the russet waves of her hair, forcing her head back until his gaze scorched deep into hers. "No danger from the sea will come to you, I promise."

His face slowly bent toward hers, and with a small moan, Nanon raised her face and surrendered her lips to his, clinging and tasting the sweet questing, afraid it would not last.

She was right, for he wrenched away from her. Shaken, she throbbed with a chaotic mingling of alarm and unleashed desire. A silver flame burned in his eyes as they searched hers. "I had no way of knowing the danger to you that I spoke of might be myself, and not the sea."

"Devin, I could never fear you," Nanon answered in dulcet tones.

He took her in his arms again, and kissed her deeply, passionately. Her mind whirled with excitement. How warm and fragile and incredible it was to share such tender intimacy with Devin. She knew now that no matter what happened, he was her love for now and forever. . . .

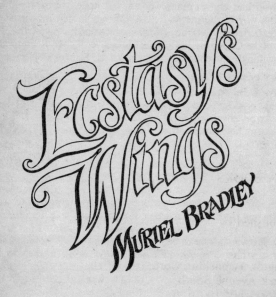

# Ecstasy's Wings

## MURIEL BRADLEY

ZEBRA BOOKS
KENSINGTON PUBLISHING CORP.

ZEBRA BOOKS

are published by

Kensington Publishing Corp.
475 Park Avenue South
New York, NY 10016

First printing: November 1989

Printed in the United States of America

# Chapter One

She was late returning home and Théo would be furious
with her. Whipping her full red skirts to midthigh, Nanon
began to run, the long wet grass sparkling the lengths of her
brown legs with early-morning dew. Her slippers were worn.
Age had molded their leather to her ankle, arch, and sole
with such delicate comfort that she might have been barefoot.
So she fairly flew, and if she hadn't had the small travel case
in one hand, she felt that she could have spread her arms
wide and soared across the meadow. It struck her that if her
brother knew what she was thinking, feeling, at this giddy
moment, he might shut her up in the turret room instead of
trying — belatedly — to marry her off.

Earthbound she ran, peering ahead to the de Cavanac
stables until her eyes widened with surprise and she ran even
faster. Out of breath, a catch in her side, she was within
hailing distance. "Théo, stop! What are you doing?"

He continued to back her chestnut mare between the
shafts of the small shabby rig. "So, you're finally here. Have
you finished doing servants' work at Malmaison? Have you
draped the furniture for the mistress's departure, hidden the
silver in the garden, scrubbed the chamber pots?"

She caught her breath, decided he was being beastly
again, and almost bit her tongue upon remembering her
father's counsel that she ignore his soldierly bluntness. To
speak to her this way, Théo must be truly provoked, for he
was usually courteous, though brusque and secretive. He'd
cautioned her the night before to behave in a more ladylike
fashion and to guard her speech, otherwise no man would
have her. As if she wanted a man! Or if she did, he had to be

someone so notable that it was unlikely her brother would bring them together.

She dropped her skirt to below her knees and spoke, an instant later regretting her pertness. "Of course I'm here. I said I would be. But what are you doing with Dominique? Why aren't we taking the team and the big carriage?"

With his back to her, he growled. "I doubt its springs would hold up even for the short distance we have to travel. Are you objecting to your saddle mare being used in this manner? Think, Nanon, it was you who boasted she could pull any light vehicle on the estate."

"I said I'd trained her to do that here on our own land because sometimes it was convenient. Whatever you plan, eight miles to Paris is too far for Dom."

"She's fast, she's strong, and this single rig is light. We need her. Come on, Nanon. Don't pout."

He swung around to face her, a handsome man, taller than the average, his hair the same bronze shade as hers, his eyes as dark as amber though opaque and unreadable whereas hers were full of light and expressive of her every mood. She studied him closely. In homespun breeches and plain double-breasted jacket, he could fool no one in Paris if that was his intent. His bearing was too imperious, the set of his shoulders and the sheen of his boots, which he hadn't thought to change for plainer ones, more than hinted at what he was.

He put out a hand to retrieve the travel bag. "And how is the beautiful Creole? Did you wish our former empress Godspeed for me?"

Nanon's face flushed. She made a move as though to stand arms akimbo and let her tongue lash out at him. Then, she remembered. Father had said Théo was bone-weary, exhausted from the years of fighting. She must be careful with him and mind her temper, no matter the provocation. She chose her next words with care.

"I know you don't mean to sound disdainful of Joséphine's birth on the island of Martinique. But she is my godmother—though admittedly in secret—and as kind and generous as she is beautiful. Have you forgotten what she meant

6

to France in the beginning? That the Old Guard called her Notre-Dame des Victoires? They always said Napoléon's luck deserted him when he put her aside for the Austrian. Which he wouldn't have done had she been able to give him an heir. She was always his tenderest friend."

Théo shrugged, a faint smile tracing the curl of his sensual lips. "I do remember. I also remember that her gross extravagances put him and the country into such debt that the army could barely be clothed at the last. And I remember the gentlemen who constantly surrounded her. There's more I can say, but I won't — it's not for your innocent ears. You're a loyal Bonapartist, that's agreed."

She was startled at his last remark. "Aren't you?"

"I'm faithful to France, and to Bonaparte when he serves France well. Which he isn't doing at the moment. And as for Joséphine, I don't believe in a cult, never have — no matter how kind and how generous she is, as you say. But come . . . we're wasting time. Why must you talk and argue and probe! Other young women don't do this. And that red skirt of yours . . . For God's sake, Nanon! We're supposed to blend into the crowd today, and you're like a flaunting banner."

Silently she agreed with him. However, as she continued, her expression did not betray that she had heard his criticism of her. "But today's journey to Paris . . . it's something you're doing for *her.*"

"No, for France. There's a difference. You mustn't confuse the two. Joséphine and France are no longer one."

She said suddenly, stubbornly, "I'll drive Dominique. She knows my hand."

He pretended to be thunderstruck. "A woman at the reins of a coach? Are you mad, little sister? We'll be stared at all through the city, and the last thing we want is to call attention to ourselves. Forget what they may have allowed you to do during your frivolous hours at Malmaison. That's over. Speaking of that, did they never seek to find you a husband? There must have been suitable gentlemen who flocked around the Empress?"

Nanon glared at him. "Is it so objectionable that I am

7

eighteen and unmarried? I don't find it so."

"There's no one else but me to look after you. I want to see you settled. Father's condition is grave, and I may have to leave here at any time. You know my commitments." Coldly he continued. "You've changed, Antoinette-Élise. . . ."

She noted this time he refrained from using her pet name, Nanon.

"I have," she agreed. "But I was a child when you left us, so you don't remember me at all. And you're not yet the head of this family and in a position to tell me what to do." She stopped, realizing she was not obeying her father's injunction to mind her tongue with Théo.

"Don't you think you'd be wise to listen when I do tell you what to do?"

As he leaned against the side of the coach, his eyes brooded down at her and she wondered . . . was it her sun-darkened skin that had caught his attention, since he'd left behind a child with a porcelain complexion? He'd probably noticed that she was slender and strong, not as pleasingly curvaceous as she would have been had she dined well and lolled about on cushioned settees. Instead, during these past years she'd churned butter in their dairy—her firm arms attested to that—and she'd scythed wheat in the fields when the able-bodied were conscripted from the land during the disastrous Russian campaign.

Concerning her appearance, he'd remarked only that she'd grown taller during his absence. Now, as though touched by a quiver of vanity since his assessment of her as bridal lure had been so harsh, she ran her fingers through her curling, bright-brown hair, worn tousled and shoulder-length for convenience.

Observing that feminine gesture—a bit pathetic, he thought—the criticism in Théo's look faded. He opened the coach door. "We can discuss this later, Nanon. Get in. We're late. That red skirt—why must you wear such bright colors! Well, I have a cloak for you. That will cover you up."

"Oh, Théophile, you are . . . you are . . . Never mind!" She walked to Dom's head, scratched her mare's ears while

8

trying to control her exasperation. "For pity's sake, I'll run in and change. Then I must see Father before we leave."

"He's asleep. He's had a bad night—the pain doesn't ease."

"All the more reason."

"But we'll be back by evening." He glowered at her.

"No, it's been two days I've been away helping them pack at Malmaison. So I must look in on him."

"Dammit, Nanon!"

But she'd fled toward the house, forgetting to take the travel case he held in his hand. Scowling he watched her go, then tossed the small satchel into the coach. Because he and his close friend, Edmond de Laval, had fought in Napoléon's armies, neither could risk being seen when the Allies entered Paris. Yet they must confirm the presence of Devin D'Amboise in the city. Théo had described D'Amboise to his sister. A lot depended on her cooperation.

A downstairs room that adjoined the library had been rearranged into a bedchamber for General Philippe de Cavanac. Grievously wounded years earlier at Wagram, he still fought on. This time against pain, depression, boredom, and solitude—though he was well served by his servant, Simon, and by Georges Degrelle who had been his military aide.

Degrelle, a younger man, had sustained injuries in that same battle in Austria. By perseverance and exercise, he'd regained the use of his sword arm. And his splintered thighbone had healed; he now walked with only a slight limp.

Yellow window draperies and bed hangings lightened the invalid's room as Nanon tiptoed through the doorway past a dozing Simon. It was very early but Degrelle, alert as usual, sat at a table by the fire which burned briskly in the grate. He was pale-skinned, his almost classic features made more eloquent by the thin, lavender-hued scar which seared his face from jaw to hairline. The color of his eyes was a surprising match for his fair hair—hair as yellow as wheat, eyes as golden as a lynx's.

9

He started to rise from the light meal on the tray beside him, but Nanon signaled him back to his chair. He put down his napkin then, and watched her with the intensity of a cat stalking a nestling.

Always uncomfortably aware of his attention to her, Nanon, as usual, tried to ignore it. "How is he, *monsieur?*" she whispered.

"He was awake most of the night, but is drowsing now. He asked for you."

So, it was good she was here. Relieved that she had been right in insisting that she visit her father, Nanon smiled at Degrelle, more warmly than she'd intended, and then turned to bend over the figure in the camp bed. This bed distressed her, for it was not much more than a pallet with a wooden heading. Still, it was what her father wanted since it was similar to those used in the field. His head lay against a mound of pillows, which at least promised some degree of comfort, while others were propped beneath his shrunken legs.

She looked down at the aristocratic features defined by pain, and smoothed his covering, leaning over him. Sometimes, in a restless sleep, he would murmur her dead mother's name. Thérèse de Cavanac had been spared knowledge of the near-fatal wound her husband barely survived. And thankfully she would never know that two of their three sons had died in battle, or that Joséphine, her intimate friend, had been distressed by the divorce Bonaparte had insisted on.

Philippe came awake suddenly, startling her. "Nanon, you've returned. Is all well with you, child?" His voice was frail, his eyes hooded, but the love he felt for her shone out strongly. She nodded soberly as he continued. "And how is it at Malmaison?"

She knew that to him Malmaison meant Joséphine. And she was correct in her suspicion that his feeling for their lovely neighbor went beyond amiable devotion. Yet, it wasn't easy to regard one's own father as having once loved passionately and outside the marriage bond. Her mother, a wise

10

woman, possibly would have understood, though Nanon found that degree of sophistication a bit difficult to comprehend.

She sighed and answered. "The Empress is safe, and as cheerful as one can be in times like these." She paused. He was still listening, so she thought about what else she could tell him. "It's not serious, you understand, but she coughs slightly."

He nodded, his smile pale but tender. "Because she still waltzes and wears those thin frocks and leaves a heated ballroom to step out onto cool balconies. . . ."

Nanon almost said, "Is that what she did with you, Father—you, a distinguished hero, so handsome in your uniform?" She was aware that Joséphine—now in her fiftieth year—still slipped away with gentlemen who found her irresistible. But these days she was using her seductive influence only in attempts to reverse the dwindling fortune of Napoléon.

"Tomorrow she'll depart for Navarre. I wouldn't have left you, but Hortense wanted me there before her own leavetaking." She knelt close to her father and lowered her voice, conscious of Georges Degrelle's dim presence in the room. "Do you know what we did? Hortense and I sewed diamonds into the hem of her mother's traveling skirt for safekeeping. She wouldn't trust any of the ladies-in-waiting."

"True, true. A lazy and disloyal lot most of them. She's fortunate to have a daughter like Hortense, as I'm fortunate in having you, Nanon. Does she speak of *him?*"

"She no longer deludes herself with false hope. He's defending Fontainebleau . . . hopelessly, I'm afraid, in these last days." There were already some rumors of abdication, even of exile, but she wouldn't tell her father that.

"Whatever happens, she'll receive fair treatment from the Allies since it was their enemy who divorced her." His voice trailed away. "They allowed her to retain rank and title in any event. Even though some call her the Duchess of Navarre."

"Father, I must go. Théo's waiting for me. And impatiently, I might add. We're off to Paris. You remember . . . ?"

She wondered if he did, for so often his mind wandered, the present meaning less to him than the past.

He surprised her. "I remember. Be careful of D'Amboise if he is there. He must be kept away from Joséphine. They're distant cousins, did you know that? His father's family is also from Martinique, that little island way off somewhere, and the British want her back in the West Indies. Without her, you see, Napoléon can be more easily snared, placed in a cage." His eyes closed.

How much more he knows than I assumed he did, Nanon thought.

She was pensive, not having been aware of the kinship between Joséphine and D'Amboise. Her only knowledge of Devin D'Amboise had been Théo's suspicions of him, and the little he'd told her of the man's unusual background. Anglo-Irish on his mother's side, he was rich now, with powerful connections. His talents were being used by the British Foreign Office, but he had never been quite accepted due to the intermingling of blood, which was considered to result in a curious heritage. She recalled Théo's disdain when he'd wondered aloud where the rogue's loyalties really lay?

Suddenly she felt older than when she'd raced through the meadow earlier that morning. History's sinister shadows plucked at her, and she wished they wouldn't. Still, she was grateful for her father's insistence that she affix maps to the library walls, the better to follow France's progress in the days when the Corsican was changing Europe's boundaries at his whim. She was glad to have this knowledge now, though Théo would scoff and say she was certainly not adding to her feminine allure by having read to their father the weekly war bulletins!

Ah, Théo! Saints and angels defend her! She'd almost forgotten he was waiting for her. She sprang to her feet, whirled about, and butted directly into Georges Degrelle's chest. How silently he'd come upon her, carrying the cup whose contents had spilled onto the floor. Winded by the impact, Nanon hung onto his supporting arms for a moment while staring at the spreading puddle. Then she was astonished. Was he inadvertently touching her bosom? He'd wrapped one of his arms around her — to assist her, of course. But as she looked down between them, his hand was pressed beneath the swell of her breast, where it didn't belong. It seemed to cling there as though magnetized to the print muslin of her bodice. His pale skin flushed scarlet for that one awful moment that he seemed unable to release her, overcome by the temptation of her flesh beneath the flowered material.

Her own cheeks reddening, Nanon hastily retreated a step, but the backs of her knees hit the camp bed and involuntarily she swayed forward. Once more it seemed they would grapple, but he fell back, mumbling. "Forgive me, Mademoiselle Nanon. I was bringing this broth to your father. . . ." He knelt and began to mop at the floor.

Instinct told her to disregard the tension between them. They had to share a roof, for Georges was indispensable to her father's care since he was familiar, as she and Théo were not, with the contents of the drug cabinet and their uses in relieving pain.

She glanced over her shoulder at her father, who'd drifted into sudden sleep. Then, with an innocent look at Degrelle, she told him, "There's nothing to forgive. I am so clumsy. Good-bye, *monsieur*. I leave my father in your good hands." She stopped, chagrined at using that unfortunate phrase. But he was bowing, and she was unable to see his expression. She managed to keep her own severe.

But only until she reached the corridor outside. There, she leaned back against the door and fell into a fit of silent laughter. It might be much more to the point for Théo to busy himself finding Georges a wife, rather than worrying about his sister needing husbanding. But now there was no time to change the red skirt into some more seemly garment. Nor could she insist on driving the rig as she'd planned. Her brother had had to wait too long for her to join him, and she knew his uncertain temper too well.

Nanon hastened along the hallway and out the front door. Skipping every other stone step, she reached the path in a

13

bounce and a flurry of red skirt and petticoats, grasped the neck of the stone lion resting on its pedestal, and swung herself around it to land on the driveway. Théo groaned at the sight of her, while Dom bucked delicately with excitement.

Then brother and sister exchanged a look of truce. Both had had a little time to reflect, and had decided it would be nice if they could learn to like each other. Still, Captain Théophile de Cavanac was finding it difficult to have his orders—no, his suggestions— questioned by his sister. He'd been away and out of touch with society, but he was certain other young women understood their place in life far better than Nanon did.

As he assisted her into the coach, she picked up the black cloak he'd left on the seat. "Is this sufficient disguise for me?" She shook it out, hopeful it would cover her red skirt. "Ah yes, it has a hood—it will hide my face. It's so voluminous . . . is it a man's?"

Théo gave her a sidelong grin. "No one will think you're a man. Anyway, for our purposes it might be better if they do." Not likely, he reflected, not with that feminine gait of hers which he had to admit was a provocation of which she was surely unaware.

He closed the coach door, lingering beside it, surprised at himself. She patted his hand which rested on the latch. "Take us to Paris, then. We'll find the man you seek. From your description I'm sure to recognize the scoundrel. I'll help you all I can, Théo."

"It's not only for me. You'll be helping the Creole, too, you know."

Immediately he was aware of his mistake. Her lips compressed; she'd detected that underlying scorn of his for anything or anyone not purely French, and Parisian French at that.

She retorted. "There's no ill fortune in having been born a Tascher de la Pagerie on the island of Martinique. They are an old and respected family of pure French blood."

It wouldn't be expedient to ruffle Nanon's feelings further,

14

so Théo replied hastily. "Forgive me. I'm unfair. Joséphine's been more loyal to the state than Talleyrand or any of the rest of them."

Which, he reflected, is precisely why the British will try to use D'Amboise to spirit her out of France. If, in truth, he had already arrived here as the message received through secret channels indicated.

As a little girl, Nanon was never one to sulk or bear a grudge, and she was rewarding Théo now with a smile of forgiveness that kindled a strange response in him. The smile emphasized details he hadn't noticed before — the dark red fullness of her lips making him think of the folded petals of a rose. And then there was the mischievous uptilt at the corners of her long-lashed eyes. This made him want to join her in laughter. Her delectable dimple flashed, disappeared. Why, she was a little beauty. There was spring fire in her smile. Thoughtfully, he climbed to his perch and gave expert attention to the reins. He knew he wanted to please her by handling Dom with care.

Guiding the mare around the circular driveway, past the woods whose solitary path led to the swamp pond, didn't lessen his concentration on his sister. She'd been isolated in the country with no *fêtes* to attend, no parties to dress up for, no gadding about except for occasional visits to Malmaison. And with no female members in the family to assist in seeking out suitors for her, how could a girl find a husband worthy of her?

Yet, he began to line up reasons why it might be difficult to secure her a husband. She was too independent, too self-willed. When she did attempt compliance he sensed it was only to soothe him. He knew he was bad-tempered these days. Rippling the reins across the mare's back, he pondered how it was possible he could be contemplating so frivolous a matter as Nanon's marriage when they were setting out on a journey whose consequences might be bloody. He'd better keep his attention on the road, he decided.

But then, like a wind vane, his thoughts veered back to this problem of Nanon. Perhaps marriage for her would not be a good idea after all. Wasn't she needed to oversee their household, to care for their father? Such a reflection on his part might be selfish, but it *was* realistic.

If only she hadn't smiled . . .

# Chapter Two

They secured the coach in a tight alleyway behind buff-colored buildings whose narrow rear windows seemed to be perpetually shuttered. From a distance the hum of the street crowds could be heard, but in this deserted lane, chosen earlier by Théo, there was silence.

Thinking to please his sister, he stroked the forehead of the spirited mare whose sides heaved nervously. But Dom shook her mane and, with square, yellow teeth grinding at her bit, snuffled hard, opened her mouth, and shot spumelike flecks of froth at him. In disgust he wiped the stuff off his face, and at that moment, Nanon slipped by him.

He called softly. "Wait. Let me see if that red skirt of yours shows."

"I took it off."

"You . . . ?" His jaw slacked.

She opened the cape a fraction. "I had another in the travel bag so I changed in the coach."

Feeling himself stabbed by this lack of female modesty, he grumbled. "Go on, then. Hurry yourself. And hurry yourself back here, too. I don't want to have to come looking for you. Remember now, when the Austrians angle their slow turn into the avenue, the British will be behind them and they'll have to wait. If he's in their contingent you'll have time to single him out. Then, come back here on the double."

She nodded her head emphatically, threw him an impudent salute, then pulled the hood over her coppery curls and disappeared. He muttered a mild oath. It was degrading to his rank, to the medals of valor he'd won on the battlefield, that he had to depend on a flighty girl.

. The raucous street throngs pressed around Nanon, but the atmosphere was not the doleful one she'd expected. The victorious enemy, known as the Allies and led by the Russian Tsar whose very own strategy had been preeminent in France's downfall, were entering Paris on this last day of March in the year 1814. And yet these French citizens appeared to be in a jubilant and welcoming mood! Believing that it was Bonaparte who was the author of their defeat, did they so detest him? Nanon wondered. Today the attitude was that of carnival. People sang and danced and waved white flags signifying their new allegiance to the Bourbons who would now rule France.

Nanon was pushed about, squeezed by, and hugged to strangers. Finally, while pummeled by the heels and elbows of dancers, she discovered the steps that would lead her above street level to an archway in which she could find shelter. From this vantage point, it was the splendid horses that at first caught her eye. After that, the marching soldiers; and then the distinctively uniformed officers. Some wore dark green dolmans and sleek white breeches that displayed every line and bulge of the male physique. Others were clad in bright blue and crimson, their buttons and facings gold. A man's height was frequently rendered more impressive by the tall fur busbys worn in certain ranks as headgear.

No matter their reason for being, the busbys added a touch of color to the spectacle Nanon would later describe to her father. Finally, when the crowd hushed, she rose on tiptoe. Before her strode the theatrical Austrian hussars, elegant in white-plumed helmets and magnificent pelisses. Close behind were the British, handsomely uniformed but a more somber-appearing lot.

As Théo had promised, the marchers were forced to stop and she was able to count through them, man by man, studying each in turn and each horse — since her brother had clearly described the mount that Devin D'Amboise was sure to be riding if he were here. Was this he? No . . . This next one? No.

Then she knew. The tallest, the most erect in bearing of

the mounted officers—the one riding a very large gray horse—paced to a halt almost directly in front of her. Nanon's trained eye admired the superb animal. A pity it was not a stallion so that it could sire others of its kind. Next, her attention shifted to the rider. But his helmet revealed little of his face; yet this was he, for Théo had told her of the legendary Irish pacer Boru that no man had ever ridden except his master.

These two are a match, one for the other, she reflected with a rising edge of excitement, the amber lights in her eyes darkening with the suspense of recognition. She could feel her body tensing, her heartbeat quickening; for today was a victory of sorts for Théo and herself. D'Amboise was *their* enemy. They were the ones who knew about him, but he did not know about them.

She moved down the archway and hastened, but in a not unseemly fashion, back to the alley where Théo waited. Away from suspicious eyes that might be watching, she began to run. At the sight of the coach and Dominique, hindered only by her heavy cloak, Nanon careened forward with a mighty leap.

Even Théo laughed at the flailing, long-legged jump that carried her from the cobblestones, over the coach's step, and through its open door into the interior. Breathless, she announced. "He's here!"

But instead of scrambling to the box and driving off with all speed, Théo continued to stand by the coach's door, staring in at her. "You saw him?"

"I did, indeed. Just as you said, the British had to halt while those prancing hussars took their time. I recognized him almost at once, though I couldn't see his face clearly. That horse of his is a fine specimen. And the man himself— as you described—is impressive. I mean, he knows how to sit a horse smartly."

"What else?"

"What else? I told you, he's the one. He was in British uniform atop that magnificent gelding."

Théo's brows slanted in amusement. "Ever the one for

19

barnyard details, aren't you, Nanon?"

*Damn his soldier's bluntness!* She replied sharply. "A stallion has endurance and power, but in war the gelded have the advantage since they can be controlled."

"I take it you are referring to beasts — not to humans."

Nanon tossed back the black hood and ran her fingers through russet waves of hair, her eyes sparking at him in exasperation as she spaced her words. "Why . . . are we wasting time this way? Father will be waiting to hear our news. And we have our own plans to make now that we know the man's in Paris and may come our way tomorrow, even tonight. No other road leads to Malmaison but ours. Will you run him through, or challenge him first?"

"By God, you're bloodthirsty. If we do away with him, will you claim his horse, is that it?" Théo slammed the coach door, sprang to the perch, and slapped the reins across Dominique's rump. It hadn't been easy to stand talking inconsequentials with his young sister, but it was necessary to use up the time agreed upon by Edmond, Luc, and himself. If Luc Ducloux performed the crucial deed he'd assigned himself, and if Edmond were quick enough in spiriting him back to the coach, no one would believe the youthful Luc was other than an observer at the scene. Not even Nanon, waiting inside the coach, would understand what happened when Edmond and Luc showed up. They could tell her some fanciful tale to account for their presence, and she'd believe it.

Carefully he backed the coach around, swore at Dominique who balked, and finally guided her out of the lane. Farther up the line he'd already staked out another solitary alley with only the one exit so that there would be no possibility of traffic passing by.

From within the coach, Nanon perceived they were traveling in an opposite direction from the one they should have taken. But now her concern was for Dominique who must be tiring, and who was being driven much too fast by Théo. Unaccustomed to slippery cobblestones, the mare could lose her footing. If Dom were lamed or worse, she would never forgive herself — or Théo!

They appeared to be heading toward the Champs Élysées and its review ground where the Allies were to receive a final welcome from the fickle French. She peered through the coach's small rear window at the people closing in behind them on the streets. Most were émigrés flocking back to the city now that the Bourbon flag had replaced the tricolor. It made her wish she were far removed from these Paris streets with their pervading odor of drains, bakeries, and opportunistic disloyalties.

The coach lurched, its jolt making her sprawl onto her knees. Before she could rise, the door flung open and she was confronted with Théo's handsome face, now contorted with hard lines. He seized her by the shoulder and jerked her upright. "Secure the mare and wait for me."

Her temper flared at the rudeness of his order, but she had no chance to respond. Instead she watched him stride purposefully into the crowd ahead. Earlier, he hadn't wanted to be seen in the city, but now he was off on some errand of his own. How could he expect his homespun clothing to disguise his military bearing? She'd get even with him sometime, somehow; but right now they had to work together.

She had no intention of remaining behind with the coach. She quieted Dom and gentled her down before tethering her to the rail surrounding a chestnut tree whose branches were decorated with tight buds that would soon unfurl into a frill of new leaves. Discarding the anonymous cloak, Nanon retrieved her own lavender and blue shawl from the travel case, looped it around her shoulders and over her head. She remembered to humble her own demeanor as she sauntered toward the avenue, passing the stalls of vendors selling wine, brandy, and sausages to the crowd.

Standing on tiptoe, she looked for Théo. If she found him, she'd have to avoid him. But he was nowhere to be seen. From her hard-won space on the street's edge, she continued to survey the crowd. He must have drifted farther down among the stalls on his mysterious errand. Perhaps she'd better get back to the coach in case he returned to it by another route.

21

Her decision was made too late, for all of Paris seemed to be at her back forming a barrier. As the congestion increased, Nanon knew she could never force her way through this crowd. Its temper, set almost at an ominous pitch, ran too high. The earlier merriment had vanished, leaving an edge of dark anticipation as the parade of men and horses continued by, awe-inspiring in its might.

Théo might be caught in a similar throng of spectators. She hoped this was so, for it wasn't difficult to guess what a dudgeon he'd be in if he returned to the coach to find her missing. Expectations appeared to be escalating as the men and women surrounding Nanon pointed toward the reviewing stand around which the military leaders had gathered. With the others, she started up the broad avenue, but as the unruly crowd began to push forward, she was left behind. Grateful for the freedom she now had to move about without shoulders and hips being thrust against her, Nanon looked up at the March sky where, overhead, a sturdy breeze was weaving the tree branches. The clash and movement of their swaying dance seemed an accompaniment to this strangely fateful day.

Again the rousing sound of passing drums and flutes, and the sight of flying banners, drew her attention. This time she was astonished to see their quarry mounted on his gray horse, which stood in a stationary position to one side. He was watching the crowd as though assessing its depth and its potential for danger. She thought excitedly, he mistrusts us. He thinks of us as the cynical French who have always been great compromisers. It's possible he even suspects this welcome could be a ruse to disguise the people's true feelings.

His cold look raked the front row of spectators, found hers, lingered, passed on . . . then slowly returned as though her startled gaze compelled him. For one riveting instant, Nanon felt a chill as his harsh, male stare seemed to touch her physically. The moment hung between them, then evanesced as he spurred his horse into a gallop that took him away from her sight.

From behind, someone gripped her shoulder. She felt a

22

shock of alarm, but it was Théo; and for once he didn't appear angry with her.

"You!" she gasped. "Were you here all the time?"

He nodded solemnly. "And D'Amboise saw us together just now. He's not aware of who we are, so it's all right. Come on, we can go now."

But something extraordinary was happening up ahead, at the spot to which D'Amboise had spurred his horse. She could see that the Allies' leader, the Russian Tsar, sat his horse like an icon in the sunlight, presenting a striking figure in that white uniform with gold epaulets across his wide shoulders. The sunlight now glinted on what appeared to be the shimmer of steel. Even from a distance, Nanon perceived the astonishing feat of the youth who propelled himself upward from the crowd, his raised arm holding the thing that glittered in the sun, a scimitar of death.

The Tsar's mount reared in panic, the assailant grasped the imperial saddle. Nanon stared, knowing sudden, great fear as she followed the shining arc of the knife. . . .

After its first howl of terror the crowd remained in shroudlike silence. Théo shielded his sister with his shoulder, but when she stood on tiptoe she could see mounted men spurring their horses into jostling contact with someone hidden from her view. A kind of sourness rose in her throat as she whispered. "What's happening? Where's the man with the knife?"

Théo's voice broke, recovered. "You don't want to know."

Angrily she turned to him but at the look on his face, one of anguish, she grew silent.

For Théo himself, it was as though his own body had been lanced, not by that knife but by the many weapons that had hacked at him in battle. He looked at his sister who could never comprehend. He said, "There's no time. . . ."

No time now to mourn his friend Luc for, of course, it was he who had tried, and failed, to kill the Tsar. No time to look for Edmond, who would now have to seek his own route of escape. Théo told himself no one could have dissuaded Luc, who'd lost father, brothers, and friends in the terrible winter

23

retreat from Moscow. He and Edmond had planned to help him escape, but there was no need for that now. Théo despised sentimentality, yet he knew that beneath the hooves of the Cossack horses, Luc Ducloux had escaped—forever.

Since he was taller than others in the crowds, he'd observed all that had occurred. Almost without thinking, he muttered, "That cursed D'Amboise was the one who grabbed the knife away." He almost said from Luc, but stopped himself in time. He looked down at his sister who stared numbly up at him. "D'Amboise was slashed by the assailant's knife. The army horse doctors will attend to him as he deserves."

The bright day seemed to have blurred, and Nanon felt dazed as she watched the people still milling around them. But the crowd appeared to recover quickly and, seeming once more ready to celebrate, began to race along the avenue to a new vantage from which to observe the ceremonies.

In the alley Théo untied the restless Dominique, opened the coach door for his sister. Then, to her surprise, he turned and climbed atop the perch, leaving her on the street below. Nanon realized he must have been far more affected by what had occurred than she had suspected. It was not that she needed assistance, but such an oversight was unlike him. Should she offer to climb onto the box and sit beside him on the drive home, or would he be offended by her concern?

At the very moment she puzzled over the question, he shouted down at her. "Nanon! Inside with you!"

Shocked by his tone, she looked to see if a coach-and-four could be bearing down on them in this narrow space. Or might he have seen a pack of murdering footpads on the prowl, searching for mischief, gold, or virtue? It was neither. An outsized gray horse—its rider with a bloody kerchief binding the hand that held the reins—stood motionless at the lane's end barring the path of the de Cavanacs.

It was too late to dodge and run. Her father had often said one should never display fear to the enemy, never allow him the advantage of knowing he's surprised you. Nervously Nanon clutched the fold of her dun-colored skirt, and attempting to assume an unhurried manner, she prepared to

tep up and into the coach. But with her first move, she made
disastrous discovery. Her legs were shaking and she felt
aint, as though she might topple at any moment.

Her brow beading with perspiration, she dared a sidelong
ook. The massive horse with its silent rider was moving
oward her, the huge creature curvetting in absurdly mincing
rances, closer, closer.

Once again she tried to scramble upward, but her foot in
ts flat-heeled slipper skidded from the step's metal rim and
he plunged forward, her forehead and nose coming in pain-
ul contact with wood and leather. She winked away tears of
ain as, behind her, there were sounds of a swift dismount-
ng. Involuntarily Nanon had pressed her palm to her aching
orehead; quickly she snatched it away.

"Are you hurt, *mademoiselle?* Allow me to assist you."

In dismay she heard herself mutter, "Well, do it then!"

This time, as she reached for the door handle, a strong
varm hand cupped her elbow while an arm half-circled her
vaist. With one powerful heave she was sped up and into the
oach.

Panting, her face crimsoned, she landed on the leather
eat. Anger, or perhaps fear, infused her with new energy.
he stared straight ahead, summoning a trace of that deport-
nent taught her years ago when she'd attended Madame
Campan's school.

"Thank you for your help, *monsieur.* And please tell the
lriver he's to move on." If only Théo would take the cue she
vas handing him and drive away at once . . . Archangels and
levils! It had never been part of their scheme to encounter
Devin D'Amboise face-to-face.

But the man's hands rested on the doorframe while he
:ontinued to look in on her. True, his expression revealed
:oncern, but Nanon would have none of it. She looked at his
ingers, long and graceful in their strength—quiet hands.
he shivered, raised her chin high, and at last stared up at
im, determined not to be intimidated.

Her catalog of his features was so swift and, yes, reassur-
ng that she was startled. She discovered she wasn't observing

25

the devil incarnate. He was a mere man, but of considerabl
height and width of shoulder. Rather handsome in a rugged
manner. His bronzed skin, taut over broad cheekbones, had
the look of having been scoured tight by wind and weather. It
was a look she understood.

He held his plumed helmet neatly within the crook of his
elbow, and she noted that his hair was thick, sable black, and
worn longer than she was accustomed to seeing a man's locks.
It curled against the collar of his tunic, lending him the air of
a cavalier. Yet she was hardly familiar with cavaliers. Her
gaze reached his eyes. They were of an indeterminate color,
set deep beneath his brow.

But those eyes warmed suddenly, changing from what
seemed to be gray — slate gray like his cape, like his horse — to
a hue that made her think of the green darkness of the
Cavanac forest. Now, they mocked her scrutiny of him. "I'm
your enemy, remember?"

Her rapt attention retreated into embarrassment. "I was
not admiring you, *monsieur*," she snapped. "In point of fact
quite the opposite." Then her voice lowered as she candidly
asked, "How is it that you know enough to believe we're
enemies?"

Before he could answer her, Théo jumped down from the
box. Stiff-legged and bristling like a mastiff, he was surprised
to find his tall stature diminished by the other man's size.
"Do you dare address my sister?"

"Your sister? I was told you were the coachman." He refrained from glancing at Nanon whose tawny eyes fired as
she glowered at him. "Considering your family's espousal of
revolutionary principles, it was my belief that ceremony no
longer prevailed among you. It *is* Captain de Cavanac with
whom I speak?" His gaze traveled the length of Théo, from
head to boot and back again.

Théo made an ungracious acknowledgment while he and
Nanon exchanged wary glances. How did this man know
their identity? Was he playing with them as a cat torments a
mouse? Both looked at D'Amboise's hand, the one bound in
a bloody rag.

26

His gaze followed theirs. "Word travels fast so I daresay I on't have to explain this to you."

"No, you do not. Good day, Colonel." Théo spoke dismissively, and Nanon could sense the hard glaze of his anger.

But D'Amboise didn't appear ready to withdraw at someone else's suggestion. Instead, his attitude grew more relaxed, a posture which Nanon knew Théo would regard as insulting. "I'm aware of your father's exploits at Wagram. I've long admired him, though he and I were on different sides of the field, so to speak. I'd like to pay my respects to General le Cavanac. Could it be arranged, perhaps today? We must remember the fighting's over and peace is here — so they tell me."

Nanon spoke. "That's ridiculous."

D'Amboise looked at her sharply. "You don't believe in peace, *mademoiselle?*"

"I didn't say that. What I mean is, you can't follow us to our château, if that's what you have in mind. My father is an invalid . . . he doesn't receive visitors."

Théo added icily. "Today's route is circuitous, you comprehend?"

"And if it were not, you would see to it?" D'Amboise's expression darkened ominously.

He wore a sword, her brother didn't! Nanon interrupted hastily. "You've lost blood. . . ."

"The slight cut can be attended to at Malmaison since I'm on my way there."

Sweet Jésus! There was no pretense here at all. He didn't care if they knew his destination.

She spoke again, her tone deliberately honeyed and inviting. "In our village the apothecary can treat your wound, which I trust isn't serious. But tell me, Colonel — won't you be missed by the Guards? Having saved the Tsar's life, you must be considered a hero."

"I'm not a hero to those who wanted the Tsar assassinated." A quicksilver smile appeared, then disappeared. "Don't concern yourself with my absence from the Guards. I'm due a leave, and since I'm in favor at the moment, this is the best time for me to take it."

Nanon's next words stunned her brother. "In that case we've reconsidered . . . and if you wish to pay your respects to my father, we'll be happy if you choose to spend the night as our guest."

"An imposition I fear, *mademoiselle?*"

"No, no . . . we shall be delighted."

Théo found himself forced to second his sister's extraordinary invitation, though he thought her mad. *What could she be plotting short of throttling the fellow in his bed!*

D'Amboise stepped back, saluted gravely. Nanon looked over his shoulder to see that behind him, all the while, had stood that great zombie of a horse — motionless, never champing his bit, not even once flicking his silvery tail at the bothersome gnats — whereas her own Dom was nickering and stamping her hooves, the reddish satin of her coat rippling in her haste to be off.

As Théo lifted the reins and turned the coach in a tight circle, Nanon once more looked back down the lane to where the tall, solitary figure stood beside his mount. Then she settled against the cracked leather of the old coach, feeling not weak but strangely languorous. It was the lassitude of the day, she told herself — its terrible events, its astonishments, its dangers. And there was the night ahead . . . for she knew she must ride at midnight to warn the residents at Malmaison.

On the coach box, Théo was aware that it was impossible for the mare to outrun the powerful gray. He was furious with Nanon, still he couldn't, at the moment, come up with a better plan than to lose the blackguard in the forest and run a blade through him. With only the dagger in his belt, it would be impossible for him to overpower D'Amboise . . . unless, of course, he and his sister used cunning. He was beginning to think cunning was not beyond Nanon and that in some way he'd underestimated her. Silent laughter began to ring inside him. He need no longer worry about her making some man an obedient bride. Let her remain at the family château. She was an excellent horsewoman and a bit of a rogue. He and Edmond could teach her to handle pistols and a sword; she night fit in with their plans. He had never before ventured to use a female as a decoy or a courier. Still, Nanon's first test would be tonight, for he had no intention of allowing D'Amboise to leave the neighborhood alive.

# Chapter Three

With an appearance of calm, Nanon stood in front of the library's green marble fireplace. To the two formally dressed men who observed her, she was a fetching picture in her frock of white muslin, its high waist emphasized by the coral-colored ribbon tied in a narrow bow beneath her breasts. A ribbon of the same shade wound through her bright curls, arranged in such a tumble by her own quick fingers that it appeared at any moment they might escape this attempt at a formal hairdress.

In her hand she held a glass — crystal, sparkling, globe-shaped — containing the liquid mixture laced with the laudanum Georges had provided from his secret store.

He watched her now. "For your father this would be the exact amount required. But for someone who is larger, younger, stronger . . . I'm not so certain of its potency. We may have to double it."

Théo spoke in a low angry voice. "See here, Degrelle, you must be sure of what you're doing."

"One can't always count on good intentions, Captain. If the event should turn out unhappily — you follow? — the final resolution may have to be the pond in your woods. It's close at hand behind the house. I'm told in the past that's where mistakes were conveniently disposed of."

"That's an untruth!" The words burst from Nanon, and her hands shook with anger as she walked to the table and placed the glass between them. "We won't even discuss what Monsieur Degrelle appears to be suggesting. I'm not proud that it was my idea to use a strong draft to put D'Amboise to sleep, but it's a less bloody plan than either of you have explored. And remember, I only want him safely asleep until the Empress leaves Malmaison. Do you hear, both of you?"

Degrelle's catlike eyes assessed her coolly, his glance shifting from her mouth, to her bosom, to the gauze-thin fabric below her waist, through which the outline of her limbs could be traced. It seemed even the dark relief of her femininity was visible to his lingering look. The dress was a gift from Joséphine, a gown Nanon had never before worn. She knew now she'd never wear it again, but it was too late to change.

Stung by the sensual significance in his gaze, she flared. "I would never have believed that you had such a murderous streak in you, *monsieur.* I'm extremely disappointed."

"I was speaking only of the possibilities, a kind of rude eventuality if you will. And concerning my 'murderous streak' as you term it . . . Nanon, have you forgotten I'm a soldier?"

Nanon . . . ? At what juncture had he dropped formality. Yesterday he had seemed meek spirited where she was concerned. Today he was aggressive, taking liberties. She could see that Théo's downturned lips expressed his disapproval of that. But hadn't they themselves effected this change in the relationship by making Georges a partner in their intrigue? She ventured a self-mocking smile, while both men stared at her, bemused by the unintended invitation in the warm up-curve of her lips.

"Since we haven't reached a true conclusion on this matter, I suggest we dine . . . and then decide." She waited for Théo to second.

But Théo's keen gaze fastened on Degrelle. "If we serve brandy in the library, isn't it possible a man's taste could detect an . . . unusual flavor?"

"Not if he's told what he's drinking is an unfamiliar import from the vineyards of, say, Spain."

There was something going on; something clandestine in their remarks, something roiling beneath the surface and not meant for her to know. Increasingly anxious, Nanon studied the two of them, observing Degrelle's bland countenance

31

grow secretive, watching her brother's expression darken and become brooding. There were warning signs here, so once more she emphasized her point. "The potion must not be lethal—there must be no chance of that!"

Degrelle bowed. "I shall behave punctiliously toward your guest. He'll be in no danger. Do we confer later?"

There was a pause; finally she nodded, noting that he didn't again call her Nanon. She took Théo's arm, and together they left the room. In the corridor she whispered. "By taking him into our confidence, have we opened a Pandora's box?"

Théo laughed softly. "I think *you* are the key that opened it, sister, not our furtive little plottings. It's possible the man's in love with you. In his heart he may be thinking of you as his Nanon. We were both aware of the slip when he called you by your familiar name."

Théo's arresting face bent closer to her own. "He's well born; fine featured except for that scar won honorably in battle. What are your feelings toward him? Has there been romantic play between the two of you while I was absent these years? All this time spent together under the same roof . . . propinquity I think it's called."

Her voice rose. "Théo, I know you want to rid yourself of me. But you can't do it by trying to make me Degrelle's responsibility."

"You haven't answered me." He took her arm, examining its rounded fullness between his thumb and forefinger. "Do you care for him?"

"I . . . do not. And I don't care for what you are implying, Théophile. I may lack suitors, but I don't feel the need to fall into Georges' nuptial embrace." She paused, partly amused. "There, you see—you have *me* doing it. Think what I just called him—Georges! We now seem to be Georges and Nanon. And all your fault, brother, with this nagging of yours."

"You're too outspoken, *mademoiselle!*" Yet, at this particular moment, she was so engaging that he wondered why he persisted in baiting her. So, instead, he bent down and kissed her cheek. "Will you forgive my carping?"

Abruptly she pulled away from him. "This is the second time today someone has asked me to forgive him. There's nothing to forgive unless some guilt, of which I'm unaware, is present in your mind. Now, I must see to dinner."

Their conversation had not proceeded as she'd intended. She'd planned to question Théo closely concerning the fate of their guest. She'd hoped by his answers—if she could trust them—to allay her own uneasiness. But the right moment seemed to have passed. So, her posture erect, she walked swiftly down the corridor, leaving him staring after her.

On a darkened upper landing, a tall figure watched with interest. From the high-ceilinged reception hall below, sounds carried in eerie fashion. He'd heard, as well as seen, the exchange between brother and sister. Feeling blameless for eavesdropping—in perilous territory one protects oneself by any means—he remained still for an interval, pondering the scene just witnessed.

She was a minx, and the brother was a man of ambivalences—an interesting and dangerous family. It hadn't taken Devin long to make up his mind about them, especially since he'd examined their dossier in the file Lord Castlereagh had handed him in London. It had been his good fortune to recognize the two of them as they stood together on the Champs Élysées just before the fateful incident with the knife-wielding assassin. That he'd not been delayed too long, and had been able to follow them into that lane with its one egress, had been better luck still.

Deciding to wait before attempting another sortie down the staircase, he returned to his room and paced the chamber. Upon reaching its far end, he confronted the French doors leading to the balcony. He stared out through the glass, though he'd already studied the landscape and knew exactly what he would have to do. But he had time, for his plans had been well laid.

Earlier, the family's manservant Simon had assumed valet duties, bringing herb-scented soaps and basins of steaming hot water to fill the hip bath here in the guest quarters. The man had removed all traces of blood from Devin's dress uniform, had pressed it and restored it to spotless condition; and Devin's high boots now gleamed like black mirrors. A razor of Birmingham steel had been provided to erase the beginning stubble of beard. What's more, Simon had bandaged his injured hand, noting with satisfaction that the slash was minor and appeared healthy enough.

It had been a long day so, yawning, he collapsed into an armchair, stretched his legs onto a shabby ottoman, and crossed his booted ankles. Briefly he admired the sheen of the leather. Then, relaxed, he briefly reminisced about his English mistress. He rather missed Clare, but at the same time he knew relief that they'd reached a comfortable understanding before his departure from London. They'd agreed she would no longer be waiting for him at his town house, particularly since Lord Carney was paying her serious court. A bit restless now — it had been two weeks since he'd secretly visited Clare and she'd opened her winsome mouth for their final delicious kiss — he surveyed the bedchamber.

The most impressive of the room's pieces was the four-poster bed resting beneath an ancient brocaded canopy which, he'd warrant, was more heavily embroidered with cobwebs than with time-encrusted gold thread. Candelabras were set about, but their tapered flames, quivering and uncertain since the wax was burned down, did little to relieve the gloom surrounding him. He could guess the château was understaffed, and it was apparent the family lacked wealth.

With a wry expression, he thought back to that single coach so incongruously pulled by a riding mare. In the area where Boru was presently stabled, he'd observed a larger carriage which had seen years of service, its interior leather cracked and its springs sagging. However, to the de Cavanacs' credit, the four carriage horses, as well as the black belonging to Captain de Cavanac, appeared well cared for.

Simon had hinted that there was neither a competent chef in the kitchen nor a proper majordomo to run the household, and that the daughter had managed with only village help during the war years. Devin didn't expect a gracious meal or scintillating company. He'd already met the surly brother and, later, the father's aide-de-camp. That man reminded him of a tightly leashed greyhound ready to course.

But it would be a pleasure to look at the girl again. It was obvious she wasn't one of Society's young ladies — which made her the more appealing. He could see that her shimmering skin had known sun and rain and the good outdoors. He'd never casually lusted after women; therefore it was interesting to him that she'd caught his attention. He mocked himself. *Really it has nothing to do with the two weeks since I've shared Clare's bed. . . .*

He unhooked his long legs from the ottoman; rose to his full height, which was considerable; tugged down his tunic and strode to the door. As a revolutionary-bred young woman, she was probably untrustworthy; doubtless she was as passionately indiscreet as her mentor, his cousin Joséphine, still . . . Curiosity concerning her continued to disturb him, and for all his solid common sense, his grasp of reality, he knew he must see this Nanon again.

The dining hall was a dark-paneled room containing ornate chests and family paintings as well as two massive oak sideboards. It was centered by a table large enough to seat forty. With the help of Sylvie, a former field companion borrowed from the village for the occasion, Nanon had placed silver candelabras at intervals down the length of that table. With the white damask, the silver service, and the bowls of early daffodils brought in from the garden, the effect was a festive one.

But Nanon, mistrustful of her brother and Degrelle, was fearful that their guest might not live to see morning. Her concern was simple enough, only that the stranger should not reach Malmaison. But she knew her brother's motives went deeper and involved the forces operative in their country, which was presently in turmoil.

Since Théo's return from Spain, there had been secret meetings in the château late at night. She was aware that couriers had arrived in darkness to be met with torches and then sent on their way. Often she'd watched from her window embrasure until sleep overtook her. Yet, in the morning, with Théo in his usual black humor, she couldn't bring herself to question him. His colleague Edmond de Laval, a member of the powerful Montmorency family, would appear at odd hours, always teasing her and trying to steal a kiss. But she knew she was never the attraction for his visits, to him she was a child to be flattered and played with.

It was the British—and by extension D'Amboise—who menaced Théo's schemings, of this she was almost certain. Thus, when their guest descended the staircase and approached the three awaiting him, she felt apprehension for his safety. This sensibility toward D'Amboise annoyed her; still, she was unable to set it aside. To herself she opined that, were a stray ox in their midst, she would save it from slaughter and return it to its owner's field.

Motioning D'Amboise to follow her, Nanon placed him to her right, seating him closer to her than she had first intended. While doing this, she declined to trade glances with the silent Théo and Degrelle. She was pleased to see that Simon had fulfilled his valet duties. Their guest appeared to be immaculately groomed, his uniform pressed and clean, his boots shining. His black hair—she was becoming accustomed to its length—curled at the top of his tunic collar, and she noticed his muscular neck and broad shoulders before she looked away from him. His lean, powerful body was none of her concern.

Around the large table, the flickering candlelight outlined each presence, yet disguised individual expressions in a manner that was disquieting. Her brother and Georges appeared intent on wine and food, in that order. She cleared her throat. As that slight sound broke the silence, D'Amboise looked to her so immediately, she was startled.

"Colonel D'Amboise, it's regrettable that my father is weaker tonight and thus unavailable for your promised meeting with him."

"And mercifully so, *mademoiselle*. To a patriot like your father, an unexpected visit from someone he thinks of as an enemy of France could be devastating. I now understand this."

Nanon raised a linen square and dabbed at her lips to conceal a smile. Yes, truly upsetting, she thought dryly, but hardly devastating. France can take care of herself, it is Joséphine that is my father's true concern. And mine. Deciding she'd better get on with her night's work, Nanon frowned upon directing a glance toward Théo and Degrelle; both were glumly imbibing too much wine. Are they fortifying themselves for their own night's work? she wondered. Whatever it was, they were no help with conversation.

D'Amboise looked at Nanon expectantly. The candle flame burnished the tawny skin of her throat and bosom, her profusion of curls shone almost russet in the dancing light, and the simplicity of her low-cut gown she was wearing was appealing. Slender-waisted and with high breasts, she seemed to have a strength and directness about her that told him, in his most private thoughts, she'd accept a man's hard arousal with a passion equal to his. There'd never be mere passive surrender here or silent enduring of a lover's caresses, he'd warrant that.

He was surprised to find himself sensually stirred by her, but when she said nothing further to him, he looked down at his plate. He'd assumed that at this provincial table the food would be simple and nourishing. To his surprise, he was being served pheasant stuffed with truffles, and the wholesomeness of the garden greens was disguised by a complicated and delicious sauce.

Her brother and the other man stolidly ate the food set before them by an aged manservant. They drank their wine and said little. He was here on sufferance, at his own invitation in a manner of speaking, and they were letting him know he couldn't expect them to entertain him.

The girl was eating delicately and watching him now in a way that amused him. But he mustn't be too intrigued by her, for he knew in this house he must sleep — if at all — with his sword as his close companion. Still, it would have been pleasant to have shared his bed in another way. Feeling a rush of innocent good will he raised his wine glass to her. Her eyes followed his gesture with a look so feverishly intent that he abruptly set down his glass. Could there be something wrong with this excellent *cabernet?* Poison . . . He hadn't thought of that.

Seeing his reaction, Nanon stiffened. During her attentive glance at him, she'd thought of a solution far better than the use of drugged brandy. He appeared to relish his wine, and he was drinking deeply, as men will who are exhausted by the day's events. Continuing to watch him, she began to devise a plan involving only D'Amboise and herself. And Sylvie, of course. She must get to Sylvie and ask for her help.

# Chapter Four

Nanon had no head for wine and she knew it. So, raising her half-filled glass to her lips, she only pretended to drink from it during the remainder of the meal. At her whispered suggestions, however, the elderly Bertrand replenished the glasses of the others.

The dessert arrived—a glorious spun-sugar confection that was Sylvie's specialty. It was for this she'd been pressed into service tonight, promised three francs and an almost-new bonnet. Shortly after the delicacy was eaten, Degrelle was called to assist Simon in attending her father.

Then, as Nanon and D'Amboise rose, Théo excused himself, casting a meaningful stare at his sister to remind her that when he returned, he and their guest would take brandy in the library.

She hung back, a smile so lightening her countenance that D'Amboise, who was beginning to feel the strain of the day, immediately revived. He offered her his arm. "Will your brother be offended if I retire without partaking of his further hospitality?" His brow quirked humorously. "I really don't think he'll mind, do you?"

She lowered her lashes, not knowing how entrancing a picture she presented at that moment. Elation and decision mingled, and unconsciously she wet her lips and looked up at him with such intelligence and challenge that once again he felt the tug of sexual tension.

"I shall explain to him for you. But if you'll excuse me, I must speak to Sylvie." She turned away. How adept he was at spinning an intimate cocoon to surround just the two of them. Somehow, by his remark, he'd made them into fellow

39

conspirators. It seemed all was working well for her.

"Ah yes, my compliments to Sylvie, too." He inclined his head and strolled on slowly.

Nanon caught Sylvie at the pantry entrance and whispered. "Sylvie, the dessert was sublime. Now, two bottles of our best wine — to our guest's room. Quickly. With a tray and the crystal glasses and a plate of biscuits. Then you may leave. Do it immediately and without anyone seeing you. Use the back staircase."

"The bonnet?" Sylvie was practical.

"In its round box in the pantry behind the sugar bin."

"Three francs?"

"Oh, for goodness' sake, hurry yourself! In the bonnet box, of course."

Sylvie rolled her black eyes expressively and departed. Whatever young Nanon was up to was her own business. Since they'd shared work together in the summer fields, she had conceived a great liking for this enlightened family. She was glad they were no longer a part of the decadent aristocracy. It was only just that most of those had been sent off to visit Madame Guillotine.

What was it she was supposed to do before she left? Yes, a tray, wine, glasses . . . for that guest at dinner. Not that he hadn't had enough already, though he showed it less than the captain and that aide. He was big and fit — a devil of a fellow all right! No Englishman he, no matter what country's uniform he wore. She gave a lustful shake to her overendowed bosom. He was what she called *sauvage*, a man wild and unruly — particularly so in bed. She could tell. . . .

D'Amboise reached the bottom of the staircase. With his back to Nanon he did appear tired, even a bit unsteady with drink and fatigue. She was no longer doubting that she'd be able to coax him into indulging in more wine. She could slip away after seeing him sufficiently befuddled. Then she'd wait in her room, and as soon as she was certain he'd fallen into heavy slumber, she'd be away and riding for Malmaison. At least her way of doing things would spare a man's life.

When she came to the stairs to stand beside him, he looked down at her. That she was up to something crafty was clearly mirrored in that pretty face of hers. Still, while he was in the house these few hours why shouldn't he enjoy looking into those lustrous eyes, even let himself be beguiled by that enchanting mouth. To look, that was all he required; he wouldn't dream of demanding liberties. He was a guest under her father's roof.

But then, in complete contradiction of such high principles, he heard himself. "You're much too young for me, *mademoiselle,* so if you're considering assisting me up these stairs, you had better not."

"And why not, *monsieur?*"

"Because, you see, when we reach the top of our climb, I'll have to repay you. And all I have with me at the moment is . . . a kiss."

As though she hadn't heard that last, Nanon made a pert riposte. "I'm eighteen, and you're really not so old, *monsieur.* Fifty years, perhaps?"

He roared at her. "Thirty-six, *mademoiselle.*"

She repressed a grin. "Ah, forgive me. That isn't so ancient an age, is it? Thirty-six . . ." She mused.

They watched each other, their gazes mingling and holding a fraction too long. Once again she seemed caught alone with him inside that golden cocoon. It was a feeling that was tremulous with an emotion she couldn't name. Then, as though to relieve the tensions of the moment, they laughed together—a strange, soft laughter. Once more they looked at each other, this time measuringly.

She murmured. "Perhaps we should mount the stairs quickly before Théo returns."

Swaying a little, his good hand gripping the banister, D'Amboise was enormously intrigued. He reflected. Théo, the jealous brother . . . "Upstairs, you say . . . you and I . . . together?"

41

"I'll see you to the door of your bedchamber."

"And then? Will you see me safely into my bed for the night?"

"Yes. I mean . . . no, certainly not. No! It's just . . . Oh, hurry."

"I'm flattered." He appeared ponderous and slow in his movements as though he did require help. Tentatively, nervously, her hand touched his waist. She felt a thrill, almost of fear, as she encircled that hard, unyielding body with her arm, slipping as far around as she could reach.

He held to the railing, and up and up they went. She hadn't realized that the bandaged hand resting on her shoulder for support could be so heavy, and she tried not to sag under its pressure. The length of his strongly muscled right leg moved against her own while she attempted to match him stride for stride, worrying them up each step.

At the top of the landing, she was breathing hard with the effort to get him that far. Below, a door opened, closed; and she heard footsteps — Théo's — at the far end of the lower hall. Taking a deep breath, she gave D'Amboise a tug which enabled them both to make it up the last rise. Though still on his feet, he appeared to be nearly asleep with drink and exhaustion. She propped him against the bedchamber door to allow his weight to swing it wide; thus she could, with caution, lower him to the carpeting inside. He'd sleep there.

She'd find Théo, tell him . . . what? She'd think of something later. But for now . . . She groaned despairingly — he appeared to be stirring, coming awake. His mouth twitched. She watched in fascinated suspense as his tongue moistened the corner of his upper lip, then paused in its sensuous lick as, beneath half-closed lids, his eyes turned darkly green assaulting hers.

With his next move, an easy and powerful one, he pulled her high in his arms. As her feet left the floor, Nanon curled her arms around his neck in a distracted embrace, staring into eyes level with her own — eyes alert and filled with humor to match that rakish grin!

Ah, bastard! The palm of one hand now flattened against

42

his chest in stiff anger. Nanon pushed herself back from him and glared. But dignity was difficult with the tips of her toes still held inches from the floor. "You tricked me . . . unforgiveable . . . let me go!"

"Mmmm . . ." he hummed. "Why should I? You assisted me up those confounded stairs. I did promise payment." As a ripple of amusement crossed his lips, his mouth came close to hers.

Along with that marvelous, musky scent, a delicious quiver held her in thrall. His jaw rubbed her face, slid against her cheek in an intimate manner that made her very bones shake. She closed her eyes, feeling like a small, hypnotized rabbit. Then, warmly caressive, his mouth came down with slow assurance on hers.

"I don't want —" The exclamation was a mistake. Her lips had barely parted when his tongue moved swiftly to explore hers with an intimacy she'd never dreamed could exist between man and woman. After circling the sensitive inner rim of her lips, it plunged gently, incredibly, within to take possession. She no longer seemed to breathe. Her heart pounded, her thighs trembled.

He kept his mouth on hers moments longer while he lowered her gently until her feet touched the floor. "There! I've let you go as you demanded. You aren't hurt at all, are you?"

Before she could reply, he swung open the door — his movement carried her inside with him. Over his shoulder, she caught sight of a table with the tray, the crystal goblets, the wine. How absurd her plan had been — how awkward, how naïve.

He saw the repast at the same moment as she, and guessed at its invitation. "What is this?" he asked, and then began to laugh with great exuberance, making her cringe with embarrassment.

From below, they began to hear Théo's voice calling. He sounded less drunken than she'd expected, more menacing. "Nanon, where are you? Answer me!"

They met each other's eyes and between them there was a conspiratorial silence. He swung her deftly inside the room, quietly closing the door, and she perceived that he was no longer laughing. His expression, serious at first, grew grim while he listened to Théo's bellowings.

And she knew he'd forgotten the kiss.

But she hadn't. She drew herself up and away from him. She couldn't allow his presumption to pass. She spoke coldly. "I'm waiting for you to apologize."

"For what, my dear?" He didn't understand her meaning.

Her lips tightened in anger, she turned away from him. But the distance between them was more than these few steps. Now, she could hear her brother thudding up the stairs, his military dignity forgotten in his search for his sister and their guest. D'Amboise moved in front of her and shot the bolt across the door. She could have called out; Théo would have heard, forced the door, and released her. There would be hell to pay between the two men, what with Théo seeking to defend his sister's honor.

Was that what she wanted?

She kept silent.

"I'm sorry for this," D'Amboise finally whispered while they both stood waiting for Théo to cease his curses and threats and leave the upper hall. "But not truly sorry," he emphasized as the sounds of Théo leaping down the stairs faded. "Fortunately for all of us, your brother's gone off in the wrong direction. Now . . . will you share that glass of wine with me? And, oh yes, a biscuit."

In truth he had no bold intentions toward her. He was curious, her lips had seemed so cool, chaste. And she'd reacted in such an extraordinary fashion to his kiss, not surrendering to it as . . . well, as eventually he'd expected she would. He wondered if it were possible that this had been her first experience with a man? She was eighteen, in full and lavish bloom. But if she were virginal, he knew he would never storm the garden.

She had begun to tremble in reaction to him, to the unfamiliar experience, to the knowledge that she was with her enemy. He was so obviously in command of all his senses that her feeble plan to ply him with wine seemed ridiculous. She should have left him to the library and the laudanum-laced brandy. But never, she knew, to his death . . .

"Good night, Colonel D'Amboise," she said severely. To herself she added, Don't think about that kiss or how it made you feel. She'd have liked to sweep tray, glasses, and wine to the floor, but of course she couldn't give way to the impulse. It was their only crystal, and the best of the few superior bottles of wine remaining in their cellar.

He did seem somewhat apologetic. "If you won't join me in a glass and a biscuit, then good night, Nanon. I hope we meet again." They couldn't, he knew. Hastily he amended. 'In the morning I'll try to make up for my behavior tonight. You see, I didn't know. . . ." He paused. He would not be there in the morning to express his regrets. The expression in his eyes deepened into a curious warmth, its mysterious message almost, but not quite, reaching her. He finished lamely. "It was only a game. . . ."

The kiss was a game, then. It was just as well. This experience was something she really didn't want to know about. It had not been pleasant, she told herself, the heat of that thrust and capture inside the tender privacy of her mouth. Unconsciously she put her hand to her lips.

He saw and smiled.

"Good night, Colonel!" she repeated furiously, and releasing the bolted door, she rushed from the room.

# Chapter Five

Midnight. In the distant corridor she could hear the clanging of an ancient clock, the sound she'd been waiting for. With the wine consumed at dinner, and with all his raging around the halls in search of her, by this time Théo must be snoring in his bedroom on the third floor. Degrelle, in his quarters that adjoined the invalid's, was the lighter sleeper. She'd have to chance waking him. Keeping close to the wall where she knew the floorboards wouldn't creak, she tiptoed past her father's room.

Closing the side door that led to the garden, she hastened down a pathway, pausing only to look back as a film of clouds drifted across the moon's last quarter. The château appeared to be sleeping, its stone entrance a ghostly blur in the night. And that wink of light in a window far up could only be the moon's reflection in its panes. Nevertheless, she intently studied the dark turrets, feeling a swell of love for her birthplace. Since romantic expectations seemed to have passed her by, she would always live here—even when Théo married as he was bound to do someday. She'd never quite understood Joséphine's cryptic remark: we all believe we have a *someday*.

On her way back to fetch Dominique, she passed the stall containing D'Amboise's huge gray. From their conversation at dinner, she'd learned that this Boru was of Arabian and Barbary stock and stood nearly seventeen hands high. She'd remarked that Boru resembled the drawings she'd seen of the "great horses" that had carried medieval knights in armor.

When he'd seemed surprised and pleased by her comment, she'd capped it with the further remark that her knowledge and love of horseflesh probably equaled his. The amusement in his smile was a reminder of Théo's criticism of her. But with D'Amboise, what did it matter how forthright she was?

She coaxed the great gray beast. "Ah, Boru . . ." But he was indifferent to her overture, only skirling a white eye at her. Hastily she backed away.

After bridling her own Normandy-bred mare, Nanon lifted her brother's saddle from its rack, hefted it up and onto the mare. Tonight she must ride astride. Beneath the shabby velvet of her riding habit, she'd pulled on breeches left behind by a stable boy who'd gone off to the wars. Reaching under Dom's belly for the girth band, she cinched it tight, tested it, and then shortened Théo's stirrups to match the length of her own legs.

Snuffing the candle's wick, she led the mare toward the mounting block. On the way she halted, listening uneasily to a sound that resembled the scattering of grain across a floorboard. Feeling the nervous quiver of the mare's satiny skin so close to her cheek, she turned to quiet her.

It was only then, at the flick of an eyelid, that she saw the figure detach itself from the shadowed doorway. This time, the footstep that had shifted the pebbles outside made no effort to be stealthy. Who else but D'Amboise . . . ? And she must deal with him; family tradition demanded courage, but she was damnably scared.

Spooked by the stranger's step in the darkness, the mare backed off, stripping the reins from Nanon's grasp. A man's hand reached to retrieve them, and an arm, with ugly strength, dragged the mare back on her haunches. Her neck twisting sideways under the pressure, the bit cutting into the tender mouth, Dom gave a whinny of pain.

In the half-dark Nanon recognized the intruder. "Théo! What are you doing to Dominique? How can you treat an animal like this!" She rushed at him in fury. "Let her loose, give her back to me."

He held the reins high and away from her, chuckling at her

47

assault, but then the chuckling stopped and he slapped her smartly on the cheek. It was a light blow that barely stung, but she sensed the force withheld. She stood, one hand on her cheek, her eyes widened in shock.

He handed the reins back to her, and, partly recovered from her outrage, she soothed Dom. Her words were bitter. "I shall never forgive you for this."

"And I shall never forgive *you*, my own sister. You knew very well what Degrelle and I had planned tonight, and you deliberately thwarted the . . . arrangement."

She looked at him over her shoulder, her eyes erased of all expression. "And you were drunk enough, Théo, not to think of the consequences to all of us if the British discovered that he died under our roof."

"It didn't happen, so it's of no import. You succeeded in steering him away from the library and up to his room. God's truth, girl, have you no shame? What inducement did you use? No, I don't want to know. But of this I'm certain. He sits there in his bedchamber at this very moment— waiting and well armed. What did you say in warning him? What secrets did you disclose?"

"I said nothing." Her face was impassive while within she raged.

"You lie, Nanon . . . and you lie well. Good. We can make something of that and your stubborn spirit. You have courage and a wit we can enlist." He reached out to curve his fingers beneath her chin and drag her closer to him. "I've observed you spying from your window on many nights. Next time, dear sister, you'll no longer be merely a curious girl wondering what her big brother's about. My colleagues meet again in a week's time. I'll require your presence among us; we can use a female like you."

She was dumbfounded by his words as he leaned closer. "Remember, we Cavanacs stand together." He left her then, took the reins, and led Dom to the entrance. "What is this?" He was staring at the flat saddle that belonged to him. "Nanon, where's your proper sidesaddle?"

Disdaining the hand he'd held out to give her a boost up,

she stepped into the stirrup, settled herself atop Dom, and glared down at him. "You need someone like me, do you, Théo? Then accept me as I am. If I need to ride astride, I do. And remember, I can deal successfully with a knife or gun to protect myself, again if need be. These capacities were forced on me by the rigors of life here while you men were fighting Napoléon's wars!"

A long hard stare passed between them, neither gaze dropping first until he threw back his head and let out a bellow of laughter. "I see another need I'd rather not have — taking on the responsibility of you for life, sister. It's a certainty no man would marry such a presumptuous lass . . . you're arrogant, insolent and meddlesome. Though much of it is bravado, I'm beginning to entertain the idea of our partnership. Shall I ride with you to warn Joséphine?"

Astonishingly, Nanon was able to deliver a quiet reply. "I haven't said yes or no to being a part of your schemes with de Laval and the others — oh yes, I've guessed he's with you — and it isn't necessary for you to accompany me to Malmaison. Remember, there's D'Amboise waiting for you upstairs with gun and ready sword. If you attend to him, let it be in subtle fashion unless you want the British on our doorstep."

Though taken aback by her calm reaction, he recovered. "Thank you for your sage advice, wise woman. Now . . . off with you!" He gave a brisk slap to the mare's rump, and Nanon heard another short bark of laughter. Its undertone of irony seemed to accompany her like an echo in the night as she galloped down the dark path beneath the dense overhanging boughs.

She's lost too much time, and she bent her head close to Dom's flying mane, urging the mare on. Her brother was a strange and difficult man. Valorous in war, he'd saved lives; yet he'd denied life to others in hand-to-hand combat. He was principled in some ways, not at all principled in others. She had not needed Joséphine to assure her that no perfection exists, nor total villainy either, in the manner in which human beings are put together and in the actions they take. She wondered if there would ever again be time to talk intimately with her godmother as she had done in the past. . . .

The first raindrops splashed on her face as she cantered her mare into the Malmaison forest, the thudding of Dom's hooves blurred by the wet pine needles. A branch had snatched away her cap, so wet curls clung around her forehead and ears, her hair's length barely shielding the back of her neck from the insistent streams of water. Within the forest the dark was total, though in less than three hours' time the sky would lighten. As the rain continued to slash down, she held Dom to a more cautious pace. She'd forgotten her gloves, and the reins were slippery in her bare hands. When Dom stumbled, she eased the mare to a walk. She'd risk her for no one.

In the midst of the explosion of rain that beat against his balcony, D'Amboise reconnoitered the corridor. Finding his passage safe, he silently departed the château, wondering that his leave-taking was without incident. There must have been a happening here tonight to change the plans his enemies had for him. He entered the stable with caution and quickly saddled Boru, at the same time noting the absence of Nanon's mare which he knew she doted on. Since it was hard to believe that a female would ride out in such a storm, and since a sidesaddle remained on the peg, he was certain that her brother or the other fellow would be waiting for him on the road to Malmaison.

But he'd had time for careful prearrangement. Twenty-franc gold pieces had tempted the most venal of the grenadiers standing guard at Malmaison that night. And his own plan of action had long since included his accomplices. Of course, now there'd have to be an earlier start for the coast; still, he could take care of that. He derived a cynical pleasure from the knowledge that he didn't have to depend—as did his cousin Joséphine, a former Empress of France, no less—on the uncertain loyalties of those who were supposedly guarding her from harm. He swore softly, looking at his palm. A bit of blood had seeped through the small bandage. But that would not interfere with his use of a sword if there was need for it.

A grizzled veteran of the Grande Armée was on guard tonight, a local villager who'd known Nanon since her childhood. He stepped sleepily out of the sentry house at the end of the driveway leading to Malmaison. Hunching his greatcoat up around his ears, he listened suspiciously to her explanation for her unexpected presence at this late hour.

Grumbling but waving her on, he retired to the partial warmth of his shelter while wondering what urgent message Nanon de Cavanac could be carrying to the Empress. At a distance, several of the grenadiers on night duty stared curiously as a young female, scandalously riding astride, disappeared in the direction of the château.

Nanon dismounted below the entrance steps that led to the massive front doors of the country house. So many memories . . . Barely seen through the gloom were Joséphine's gardens with their crocuses and beginning daffodils. Beyond were grape trellises and a greenhouse containing exotic palms and ferns, as well as rare blooms brought from Egypt and Arabia. And over there was where they'd all played their games. Even Bonaparte had joined them in leapfrog and prisoner's base.

Marcel, Joséphine's trusted caretaker and servant, had recognized Nanon's mare. He ran down the steps to take the reins. "Mam'selle de Cavanac, what is it? Why have you come out at this hour on such a night? Is it your father?"

"Father's as well as he can ever be. But I must see your mistress at once. I've a message to convey. It can't wait."

He surveyed her dripping state and shook his head disapprovingly. "You've ridden here on a man's saddle. I've known you long and well, but I shall never understand you, Mam'selle Nanon."

"Well, I wouldn't try to just now, Marcel. You can puzzle out my behavior at another time. For now you'd better alert the grooms to wake the drivers and bring around the traveling carriages."

Marcel was astonished. "I can't give orders until the Empress herself tells me to! I'll take your mare to the stable, and you wait here for me."

But she swept by him, running up the steps to burst through the front doors into the foyer to find that someone else was about this late at night. Two ladies-in-waiting, in flawless makeup, yet wearing night robes, were on the staircase.

Nanon greeted them while they exchanged curtseys with her, their eyes bright with curiosity. She, in turn, wondered what they were doing up at this hour.

She sped by them, at the same time looking down into the familiar rooms below. The chandeliers were encased in linen bags, the furnishings covered with dust sheets. Those hampers down there were packed with objets d'art, while the usual bowls of flowers, the cushions, paintings, and books had all disappeared. Low fires burned in the grates, and the windows were shuttered, their valances and draperies removed or covered. Nanon glanced back at the two ladies who were pretending not to watch her as they whispered to each other.

From the landing she scurried down a long corridor, only pausing to catch her breath outside the Empress's door. Adjusting her skirt and her jacket, she raised both arms and combed her fingers through damp curls to bring some order to her appearance. It was necessary that she seem competent, courageous, and firm—qualities demanded by the Empress—in order to convince her godmother to leave this warm house at once.

Now, almost ready, Nanon straightened, then smartly threw back her shoulders, assuming an attitude of authority. The forward thrust of her breasts in two rather enticing crescents didn't add to the commanding impression she was striving for; nevertheless, she held to her brave stance, raised her hand, and prepared to rap on the door.

From behind her, a man's deep voice spoke in amusement. "Nice, very nice, indeed. I always knew you'd grow up to be a properly fetching young lady."

She felt an unholy wrench of surprise. Those suggestive tones were not unfamiliar. But not here, please, not tonight! Slowly she turned around.

# Chapter Six

Théo's friend Edmond de Laval stood in a doorway; even in its deep shadow she could recognize that elegant bearing. "I did surprise you, sweet child?" He moved forward to stand close to her. Above a youthful countenance on which fine lines had been incised by experiences both in battle and in the boudoir, his thick hair, prematurely grayed, was the shade of pewter. His eyes searched hers guardedly. "Did Théo send you with a message for me? We missed our rendezvous in the Paris stalls after that bloody business today. I came directly here to the country as planned."

She knew that her brother and de Laval belonged to the Bonapartist secret assembly. And she had guessed that this man was a frequenter of those even more secret midnight meetings at the château. If he and Théo had arranged to meet in Paris, and then here later, instinct told her it was better to pretend ignorance.

She shook her head. "I'm not privy to my brother's plans." An unexpected rush of tears filled her eyes. "It's horrible . . . what occurred in Paris. A man's life stamped out under the hooves of horses."

"Come now, Nanon, chin up. You're more resolute than this. You know what can happen. The Allies are not friends of France, and what the Cossacks did to that poor fellow was not a pretty sight. Still, life goes on. But tell me what are you doing here?"

She saw no reason to mislead him. "I've come to warn the Empress. She must leave at once for Navarre and not wait until morning. A relative of hers, one who may wish to do her harm, is very near here."

Edmond looked thoughtful but made no direct response. "It's a bleak night for you to be out."

"You, too, owe an explanation, Edmund. Théo would never come to Malmaison, so what are *you* doing here?"

An impish expression dipped into the dark blue eyes. "I'm in love, is it so difficult to surmise that? Since you won't have me, I have to admit I'm enamored of one of the ladies staying here."

"Oh pish, Edmond . . . this is nothing new for you. But I'm surprised my brother didn't mention your being in the neighborhood." Sweetly she concluded. "Or is it that he doesn't know with whom you bed this week?"

"That's unworthy of you, Nanon." He caught her hand, raised it to his lips, and lightly ran his tongue across the tips of her fingers. "And you may have done me great harm. You made so much commotion on bursting into this house that my lady has gone to investigate, leaving me in a sorry state."

She pulled her hand away. "Then don't let her return to find you at dalliance. I'm sorry to have disturbed your pleasures." A sudden smile dimpled her cheek. "I hope your state will be improved when she returns, and that all is not lost."

"By God, I think you've grown up. Come here to me!"

She backed away, suddenly understanding the fancy dressing robes and lovely maquillage of the two ladies on the staircase. With Edmond she'd just pretended to be more knowing than she was, but . . . *two* of them, at one time? She regarded de Laval curiously as, with an exaggerated bow to her, he stepped inside the bedchamber opposite. With the opening of the door, a rush of perfume and feminine body scent filled the corridor. Nanon shrugged, then turned and rapped softly at the Empress's door.

A melodious voice that faintly betrayed the accent of Martinique called, "Godchild, is it you? My maids told me you'd arrived. *Mon Dieu,* what a night! Come in, come in. . . ."

Nanon stepped inside, knowing that everything in this exquisite suite of rooms would remain in place until its owner's departure. Bowls of exotic fruits, vases containing hothouse roses, jeweled boxes on pearl-inlaid tables. Not until the leave-taking for Navarre, when Joséphine stepped over the threshold for the last time, would all these objects be laid away, a prerogative of rank.

The surroundings were examples of Joséphine's taste—walls covered with apple-green silk, a handwoven carpet with its chosen design of roses, furniture constructed of gracefully scrolled wood, small paintings by Fragonard and Boucher, silver lamps, silver trays containing crushed petals; and everywhere one could breathe in the odor of the occupant's alluring womanhood.

Nanon's heart fell as she crossed the foyer to the inner chamber. Atop a carved chest was set a great gilded cage containing a flamboyantly feathered parrot. Truly a huge bird, beady-eyed, red-beaked and disagreeable, yet a favorite of Joséphine's.

Wearing a white dressing gown that floated gracefully around her still slender body, her silky, chestnut-colored hair ruffled from the bed pillows, the former Empress hastened to greet her visitor. She drew Nanon near to her, kissed her fondly, then held her at arm's length to study her appearance.

"Tell me, why are you here in the middle of the night? Has something terrible happened to Philippe? No? Thank God, then. But you're drenched from the rain. What is going on at your house that they'd let you ride out at this hour? And you must take off that wretched riding skirt and jacket you're wearing, it looks like the habit I gave you when you were fourteen—it's out at the sleeves." She shuddered prettily and raised a thin, curved eyebrow. "It is the same? Well then, dear child, it should have been disposed of in the rag bag long ago!"

Maidservants appeared, and in the hallway's open door, a band of ladies clustered, sleepily peering in at Nanon. The lilting voice continued giving orders, adding a request that tea be brought. "And warm dry clothes for my godchild."

Tears almost surfaced once more, and Nanon did tremble with emotion. "There's no time for tea, madame—but thank you for your thoughtfulness. And the clothes I'm wearing are almost dry now. There's a matter of great importance that I must relate to you."

The Empress remained standing, the hazel eyes beneath her arched brows appearing to change to deep blue as she listened to her godchild detail the day's events.

"So you see," Nanon concluded, "the carriages must be brought around immediately, and you and your ladies must leave here as soon as possible. Certainly before daybreak."

"A remarkable tale," the older woman murmured. "You say I've much to fear from this Devin D'Amboise who's on his way here, and that he means me mischief?" She tilted her head reflectively, and Nanon was astonished to observe a dreamy bemusement in her expression. "I recall meeting him at my old home, Trois Îlets, when he was a youth. We're somewhat related. He was a bit of a rogue then; I'd be interested in seeing him now since he's made a name for himself both in London and in Ireland. A feat that's difficult to achieve these days, I should say. And he's very, very rich, you know. That's always an appealing characteristic in a man when it's accomplished through his own efforts." She sighed. "Oh yes, I keep abreast of such matters. He must be twenty years younger than I. I'm forty-eight . . . if you will, fifty. And he's a grown man now."

"Actually he is rather old . . . thirty-six."

"Old? I'd say that was ancient." Joséphine burst into bell-like laughter, her pleasure-loving nature still evident despite her anxieties. "How droll you are, Nanon. I'd forgotten what it is to be your age. Ah, but first come and see the new puppies that arrived after you left. *He* sent them to me from Fontainebleau for safekeeping. They must go along with us, too. As well as my beloved Paco—you saw him in his cage."

"Puppies you say?"

"Come with me."

Joséphine led the way into the dressing room, where two enormous, rough-coated wolfhounds lay side by side on an Aubusson rug. They lifted their heads in concert and looked stolidly in her direction.

"Oh!" Nanon tried not to groan at the sight of five great, snuffling puppies nursing at the female hound's teats. She spoke quickly. "They're beautiful, all of them. But . . ."

"Nanon, don't be concerned. We can manage. And I'm ready to do as you suggest, pack and leave immediately. I believe that the rumors you've brought me are true. There may well be a plot to cause me scandal, and through me to hurt *him*. It may be that in the future the Allies will not regard me too unkindly, but for the present, I shan't remain here to find out." She paused thoughtfully. "Later . . . we'll see how it all turns out later."

She began to issue orders in a manner that Nanon knew belied her reputation for Creole indolence. Her ladies scurried to dress themselves and to alert the others who were still asleep. A maid brought in her mistress's traveling dress, and Nanon recognized the sweeping skirt into whose hem she and Hortense had sewed the diamonds.

Throughout the château candles glittered bravely. There was a great surge of movement. Hampers, jewel cases, Joséphine's small trunk containing part of her favorite wardrobe, and even boxes of tulip bulbs that couldn't be left behind because they were the Empress's favorites, were carried out the front entrance.

Standing before a long mirror, Joséphine smoothed the fabric of her traveling skirt over her rounded hips as she looked into the glass at the younger woman's reflection. "Don't be so brooding, my dear. I'll travel in a fast campaign coach that Bonaparte gave me for my personal use. Rather ironic that, don't you think?" She fastened a jeweled earring in each earlobe. "In the sturdiest coach in my fleet, we'll put Paco's cage and the dogs and the two basketfuls of fine puppies. More frequently of late I find my pets mean more to me than human friendship, which is so often a passing quality. But not your family's, of course! You and your departed mother and your father—dear Philippe, he was so handsome as a young man—have been as close to me as my own daughter Hortense and my grandsons and my wonderful son Eugène."

Nanon's head was aching, and she shivered from the chill of the rain as well as from her despondent feelings at this hurried departure. For a fleeting moment Joséphine held her close; then she swept forward imperiously, leaving her suite of rooms without a backward glance, only motioning over her shoulder that Nanon must follow her.

The faithful Marcel appeared on the stairway with tears in his eyes. Nanon was relieved that the house was being left in his hands. She promised herself she'd ride over each week to see that the gardens, the greenhouse, the château itself were kept in proper order until their owner's return.

At the last, the carriages lined the driveway, the horses pawing the earth in their eagerness to be gone. With the pale melon color of dawn in the eastern sky, Joséphine clasped the younger woman's hands in both of hers.

"I dislike those dank Normandy forests I'm bound for, but I've never lacked the courage to meet any situation that I must. Your mother was my intimate, your father my dear friend. I know they've told you my story, that when I was newly widowed and thirty-one years old, I was within two days of having my head sliced off by the guillotine."

Nanon nodded soberly as Joséphine continued. "When I was readying myself for that final day in my life, the fearful Robespierre was himself attacked and killed. Those of us still left alive in the prison were freed. So, you see, I've had practice in facing these reversals of fortune." She smiled, mischievously this time. "And it was only a year later that I met the young Napoléon. I shan't tell you which of us made the first move." She sighed. "I became an Empress. And now you see what has happened. It's been this way for me all my life."

She turned and stepped into the campaign coach, within which one of her ladies waited, and then looked through the window. "Now, my dear, smile for me. That long face of yours will never do, for you're really quite lovely when you smile. If you strive for a cheerful mien, life's difficulties will ease a bit because the world is kinder to a pretty face with a happy gleam in the eye." Leaning out she tapped Nanon's cheek. "Do you think what I've just said is a simplicity?"

"Yes . . ."

Her laughter sparkled as she withdrew inside the coach. "You've always been candid, godchild. I like that."

The signal was given; with the crunch of the turning wheels, the lilting voice faded. Numbed by fatigue, Nanon watched as the procession continued its slow pace forward, the big coaches laden with boxes and goods and passengers. The armed grenadiers rode ahead, the veterans forming a guard as all of the carriages rolled in a caravan down the driveway toward the far gate.

A sudden commotion to her right brought Nanon to attention. A horseman rode swiftly from the rear of the country house, in the direction of the woods. A familiar voice called out mockingly, its sound echoing back to her as its owner disappeared in the path among the trees. "Farewell, Théo's little sister. . . . We'll meet again."

Tired as she was, she couldn't help but smile as this jaunty rider, the lady-loving Edmond, vanished. No doubt he was on his way to seek out her brother and make excuses for his tardiness.

She transferred her attention to the line of carriages as a new maneuver occurred. The six mounted men at the head of the procession reversed their direction to circle back and approach Joséphine's coach.

Perplexed, she watched the leader signal to the horsemen riding guard at the rear of the caravan. They hesitated, but then, in obedience to orders, trotted smartly forward to take their place in the lead position.

The campaign coach was being deliberately slowed, the six horsemen wheeling in formation to force it toward the high yew hedge. The coach horses reared as the vehicle began to tilt into the planting. It was now at a dangerous angle. The grenadiers swiftly dismounted and, working without sound, levered it back into position before dragging the struggling driver and his groom from the box.

Shocked by this action, Nanon felt a dreadful foreboding. And then she knew!

She raced forward, keeping behind the shadow of the yew. As she dodged into its dense growth, branches caught her hair and raked the backs of her hands. Still, she plunged recklessly on in an attempt to push through to the other side. If she could come abreast of the coach at the place where it leaned inside the stickery yew she would . . . well, what *would* she do? She had no real strategy, only instinct working for her as well as the strong arms and legs propelling her body through the woody barrier.

When she groped and clawed through the last coarse mass of shrub, she saw that fortune had guided her. She'd arrived parallel to the coach; its door was now within easy reach. This had been her hope.

Her limbs were shaking as she crouched down to listen to the men's voices coming from the far side of the equipage. How could she, an exhausted young woman, cope with six men? She couldn't. And she had no doubt she was seeing the unfolding of a scheme concocted by D'Amboise and the British to kidnap Joséphine.

But there was one thing she could do. She levered herself and gave the door handle a hard twist, at the same time pushing shoulders and head to the floor level of the coach. As she tumbled through the door, Joséphine's companion uttered a terrified squeal, which the Empress hushed with a hand across her mouth. The woman stared, wild-eyed, over the palm that gagged her. Joséphine, almost without surprise, gripped Nanon's shoulder with her free hand, and she pulled her godchild the rest of the way inside.

She then gave her lady companion a shake and let her go. 'Well, child—it's you! Let's waste no time, I've been at the heart of too many conspiracies. We have traitors here. And look at you—blood all over your hands from the thorns. But worse on theirs out there . . . they've bled a country, dishonored a noble leader." She spoke grimly as she sent a swift glance through the window to her right. "They've cut us away from the others. This is Devin's doing. It is what you swore to me might happen. But I've no intention of remaining to find out where they intend to take me!"

The lady-in-waiting was whimpering as Nanon leaned across her, whispering to Joséphine. "What can I do?"

"Don't talk, girl. We'll act before these stupid swine can." She shoved her wailing companion through the door into the hedge. "Quick . . . out and be still! Get yourself through that hedge, lady. I'll need you later or I'd leave you behind. I'll be right in back of you, so don't falter—we'll lose ourselves in the garden's maze. *You*, godchild, be alert and do this for me. Take my place in the coach for a short while only. You can escape them at the first stop, wherever it is—I vow you can. I'll reach Marcel in time to have him find men to follow you at a distance. Here, take these."

She flung shawl, scarfs, and veils in Nanon's direction. Her companion had already vanished into the green darkness. Joséphine followed, gathering up the hem of her traveling gown as she slid within the protection of the yew hedge. Watching the hem of that skirt disappear, Nanon was reminded of the hard glitter of its mistress's courage, as well as the hidden jewels.

"Farewell, godchild. . . ." The voice was little more than a breath in the paling night. And both women were gone, their passage concealed by the strident military orders being given in the continuing attempt to pull the coach out of the embracing hedge.

Nanon curled herself into a far corner, terrified that the grenadiers would look in upon her. But since no one bothered, she presumed even these men flinched from facing the one they betrayed. She looped cashmere over her head and shoulders, pulled folds of silk across her face. The situation and her panic were chasing away the exhaustion that had assailed her earlier.

The coach rocked and jolted while being pushed onto the roadway. The horses whinnied and balked, and as something banged, Nanon wondered if they were becoming unhinged from the coach. It would mean her own discovery if this happened; and worse, an inevitable search for the missing Empress on the grounds surrounding Malmaison.

Finally they seemed to be on level ground. Whoever the new driver was, he was whipping the team into a gallop that took them hurtling past the line of halted carriages. She

62

raised her head, peered around the curtain to look out. Only frightened faces stared at her as the team thundered by. And from somewhere far behind, she could hear the bay of the wolfhounds and the parrot's eerie scream. They plunged on beyond the lead carriages, through the gates, onto the open road. Malmaison was left behind.

How had D'Amboise bribed these faithless French grenadiers? Or had this skulduggery been arranged by others? For Joséphine who'd long survived the deceptions of the Court, today's experience was merely another in the long list of intrigues. Except that, in this instance, it wasn't Joséphine — it was she, Nanon de Cavanac — riding in Bonaparte's campaign coach! How long would it be before she was unmasked, and what would happen to her then?

By dawnlight the coach was traveling at great speed along a road that was unknown to her. Only occasional drays could be seen — wagons, teams, and sometimes a single horseman bound for . . . where? Back to Paris or on to the Channel, to Calais? Or to some hidden lair in some nameless place? The horses would soon tire. They would have to be exchanged for others. Had Joséphine been able to alert Marcel to send rescuers? If not, Nanon must slip away on her own. She went through her pockets. She hadn't a centime on her; and Dominique was stabled at Malmaison just when she needed her most.

The early morning continued to disclose terrain that was unfamiliar — meadows with flocks of sheep, stands of poplar trees, and grassy pasture rolling toward low-browed hills — while the forests had been left far behind. Resting her feet on Joséphine's hand trunk, Nanon found, tucked beneath the leather seat, a food basket and a water flask. There was even a chamber pot. All had been prepared for the journey to Navarre.

The escorting horsemen were keeping to an even gallop alongside her vehicle. From the little that she could see, the riders were in plain, dark clothing. Either their grenadiers' uniforms had been discarded — which was unlikely — or this was a different band of accomplices. Her spirits sank even further. If this were so, it could indicate a degree of strategy which might make escape more difficult. At least with the grenadiers, she knew with whom she was dealing.

Doubling the veil across her face and raising the felt curtain, she peered ahead. A horseman on a gray was riding parallel to the lead horses that drew her coach. Her heartbeat began to race in tempo with those pounding hooves. He, of course! The knowledge quelled the little hope she'd had that someone other than D'Amboise was responsible for her predicament. It did not help to remind herself that it was Joséphine's predicament she'd assumed.

By now her godmother's journey to Navarre would have been resumed posthaste. Every link seemed coupled except her own, and this filled her with further outrage at D'Amboise. Still, they'd fooled him, she and Joséphine. . . .

The wheels' steady rhythm, the rocking of the coach, and exhaustion claimed her. Winding the Empress's cashmere shawl around her shoulders, she nodded, then slept.

Her dreams were fitful. A young girl's dreams, innocent . . . but not entirely so. They concerned a man, his leg hard against her own as they matched strides mounting a staircase. A man who raised her up in his arms until her mouth was level with his, her breath strangely smothered due to her nearness to the fine sculpture of his lips. A man whose gray gaze, silvered in the candlelight, caressed her face, admired her form as no one else ever had. He'd scanned her from head to foot without seeming to . . . but she knew.

He'd made her aware of herself in a way that Edmond de Laval with his stolen hugs and fleeting kisses on the cheek never had. The dream reminded her that she'd known a nibbling of satisfaction in wearing the frock that Joséphine had given her, though when Degrelle's gaze had searched out her body through the filmy material, she'd vowed never to wear it again!

And in the dream she remembered how she'd provocatively swayed her breasts, arched her slender back, moved her small rear in insolent rhythm when she'd guided him toward his bedchamber and the wine. Awake, Nanon could never make such an admission, but in her dream she knew these things. . . .

It was much later that the slowing of the coach, and finally the complete cessation of all movement, disturbed her sleep. She moaned softly, keeping her eyelids closed, trying to drowse on and thus cling to the entrancing dream.

But, with a rasp of metal, the coach door opened. Dazed, Nanon came awake, shielding herself within the shawl's voluminous folds. Almost too late, she twitched the veil across her face. A breeze from the door set its silk to fluttering as the intruder spoke.

## Chapter Seven

The eyes were an English blue, the face as bland as an eggshell, while a very new brush of mustache bristled above an awed smile. The young officer had identified her as the Empress. She was safe for the time being.

Impossible as it seemed to Nanon that she could assume an identity other than her own, she knew she must strive for Joséphine's mellifluous tones as well as her guile. She thought, I must get rid of him; and raised her hand in imperial dismissal. Upon catching sight of her own frayed cuff, she hastily tucked her fingers beneath the shawl.

He blurted out, "Is there no lady accompanying Your Majesty . . . you are alone?"

She murmured through her veil with soft emphasis. "I have been alone since the day I left Fontainebleau. Always alone." Was that sigh, that meaningful pause, sufficient to gain his sympathy?

Her playacting did have an effect, the young man's composure appeared to wilt before her eyes. This was *the* Joséphine whose alluring reputation had reached throughout Europe and to the far side of the Channel.

"Your Majesty . . ." He regained a degree of control. "Madame! I'm to ask you if there's further accommodation that you require before we go on to our destination."

"And that is . . . ?" She spoke quickly, hoping to catch him out. He was trying not to stare, yet she knew he was eager to define her features through the silk. "Our destination, sir!" she demanded.

He flushed and replied hesitantly. "There is a possibility we may be bound for the seacoast."

Her heart pounded so loudly that she wondered if her masquerade could prevail. She was no longer tempted to exploit Joséphine's reputation for charm in an effort to discover exactly where they were bound. She'd heard enough.

"Your name, sir?"

The fellow did seem flattered by her interest. "Andrew St. Giles." He bowed very low. As he withdrew, she heard him murmur, "At your command . . ."

The impression Nanon made on St. Giles would have been comical except for the seriousness of her situation. If she'd truly been able to convince herself that Joséphine was safe, she wouldn't hesitate to jump out of the coach and make her identity known. She'd have to face D'Amboise's wrath when he learned he'd been tricked, but her real fear was that, upon discovering the ruse, he and his men might change direction and ride in pursuit of the Empress's caravan. Despondent, Nanon decided she'd have to bide her time awhile longer.

There was a booted footfall outside the coach. "All well within, I trust?" She recognized that voice!

How dare he! The jauntiness in his tone infuriated her. She could see him standing there as though well aware of his own formidable presence. A bully no less! And the assurance in his smile . . . never mind that it was a compelling smile which had had an effect on her the night before.

Her answer was a withering, "Go away, sir!"

He stood thunderstruck outside the coach. Had he heard rightly? He supposed he couldn't blame Joséphine for the ill temper of her reply; however, he'd expected her to treat him cordially in an attempt to gain her freedom. She was wily and seductive and a great chess player. It was said that she had beaten even Napoléon at this game. He'd looked forward to matching wits with her.

Finally D'Amboise walked away, pensive. Knowing Joséphine, he figured it was likely she was making plans to have his head. He looked around him to see that the men were changing their mounts. These were his own followers; the disloyal grenadiers had been left behind and good riddance. Up ahead, that young aide of his was mooning about. "St.

Giles . . ."

"Sir?"

"Tell me, what was the attitude of the ladies when you asked if they required any courtesies? They've been silent and quite docile considering what's happened. I confess to being curious."

"The Empress is the only passenger in the coach, Colonel. I was about to tell you this."

D'Amboise's gaze scorched him. "You were about to! And why didn't you? You mean there's no companion with her, the Empress travels alone?" Good Lord, no wonder she'd snarled at him. Her solitary status would make it awkward aboard ship, doubly awkward for him who must find her a proper maid. Since St. Giles was watching him intently, a bit fearfully, he merely nodded. "I see. Move the men out at once."

"We're waiting for you, sir. You've not yet exchanged your mount for the fresh animal we have ready."

"No need, Andrew. The limit of Boru's endurance has not been reached." He didn't feel it necessary to explain his sentiment in regard to his horse. On the morning of the day her son Devin was born, Fenella D'Amboise had ridden the stallion who was Boru's grandsire. The almost supernatural strength of that equine line was a family legacy. Indeed, D'Amboise seldom spoke of what had occurred ten years back when a stable doctor's tragic mistake had deprived the newborn foal Boru of his right to carry on his noble lineage.

There were many hours of travel before dusk closed in. On the outskirts of Morlaix a stop was made. This time the mounted men were left behind at lodgings while a fresh team and driver were readied for the final miles of the journey. Only D'Amboise and St. Giles would ride escort this time. The smell of wild grass and the salt tang of the sea freshened the air. Both men were revived by this and by the expectation of the good food and sound sleep soon to come.

D'Amboise deliberately kept his thoughts from the woman

in the coach, who'd remained silent since that one outburst directed at him. As for St. Giles he could think of nothing else but the veiled lady.

The veiled lady herself was miserable knowing the anxiety her father must feel over her absence. She hoped Théo and Degrelle had succeeded in concocting some plausible tale to explain it. She'd slept—not very well—no sensual dreams this time; had nibbled on a chicken bone, quenched her thirst from the water flask, and bathed the scratches on her hands. The coach had jolted up and down deep ruts, sped along smooth roads, and strained through the mud swamps left by a rain squall. And no Marcel had ridden to rescue her.

She hadn't given up the scheme she'd devised to secure St. Giles's help. He'd be disillusioned when her true identity was revealed. Yet, to attempt to keep up this ridiculous pretense of being someone else with only the aid of scarfs and veils was impossible.

She breathed in the scent of the sea as it blew across the bracken. She could only guess how such a great body of water might look. At any rate, her curiosity brightened her spirits. She'd removed the veils that made her feel like the inmate of a seraglio. The Empress had worn them while traveling to preserve her exquisite skin from the elements, but this was something Nanon had never worried about. Her own golden complexion had never suffered from being bathed by the sun. The dampness in the sea air caused her bronze waves to curl more tightly until they sprang into a halo, and rosy color returned to her face. She felt invigorated, which had to be a favorable sign under the circumstances.

Twilight. And the horses pulling the coach had slowed to a walk. For some time now Nanon had been aware that travelers and horsemen were following close behind. Now, carriages going at a great clip dashed by as they neared a town, its torches visible in the distance. She peered around the edge of the curtain, noting the positions of D'Amboise and St. Giles who rode ahead of the coach.

The wheels clattered as they entered a cobblestoned

square, and once again Nanon craned to see all that she could. The streets had widened and were crowded with shops and passersby on foot. Far below, down a steep hill, she perceived the dark rim of a harbor, its wharves lined with small boats while larger ships loomed in the gray distance. Sea and horizon seemed to blend, the water's huge expanse almost indistinct, hidden by the fast-falling night and the mist rolling in.

The driver braked the coach, then made a reverse turn which sent her clinging to the back of the seat for safety as the vehicle plunged precipitately down a road leading to the level of the docks. As the coach rocked from side to side, a suspicion that had lurked in Nanon's mind since they'd entered the town continued to grow.

She had seen a painted sign that signified they were in Brest. From war bulletins she was aware that this was a port with barracks and vast naval fortifications, and that it was also a point of departure for commercial shipping.

The fears she'd entertained increased. If Joséphine were not to be held here on the continent, could the plot be to put her on a ship bound for . . . Africa? Even America?

But she was Antoinette de Cavanac, unimportant to France, to the Allies, to anyone at all for that matter. D'Amboise might be a blackguard willing to abduct a woman for political reasons, but presuming he was a civilized man — after all he was partly French — she should be able to appeal to him. If properly approached, he might arrange to have her sent back to her father's house. Yet, how could she be sure of this? She had conspired to trick him, and since this flawed kidnapping must discredit him in the eyes of the British, he might be disposed to take revenge.

These docks, on which sailors and stevedores were milling about, and where there was much shouting and much movement of crates and barrels, might be the ideal place for escape. There must be a sailing scheduled for tonight; otherwise why were so many people hurrying toward the docks? The crowds would make flight easier. She could lose herself among them. Nanon closed her eyes and wished for the impossible. If only Dominique were here, she'd jump on her mare's back and gallop fast and far!

Once more she became aware of the sound of hoofbeats as she first had outside of Morlaix. But it could mean nothing. Even though Joséphine had promised that if it were possible Marcel would have a party follow her, she'd given up hoping for this.

Now she knew what she had to do. She shrugged her shoulders out of the confining shawl and pulled a scarf over her hair, tying it securely beneath her chin. The confusion of wagons, teams of horses, and milling men was slowing the coach until it was now at a near standstill. Ahead of it, D'Amboise and St. Giles were attempting to clear the way. Nanon was frightened, her mouth was dry, and her limbs were trembling; but she knew that when she opened the coach door, she must time her leap to the turning of the wheels. No matter if she did fall in the street, she'd be up and running fast!

One, two . . . make ready! she thought, and reached for the door latch. As she did so, her heart tumbled in shock for the handle itself turned sharply under her hand. And it was not she who had turned it! She drew back as though stung by a scorpion. These street crowds were full of toughs and roust-abouts so someone — a robber, an attacker? — was pulling the door open from the outside.

This time, when she lurched forward it was to secure the door on her side. But instead it flung open in her face, and, losing her balance, she fell through it, legs flailing, arms outstretched. At the very last she heard herself scream. "Devin! Devin, help me!"

Two powerful arms seized her, and she heard a voice roar. "Why the hell should he, sister?"

She was being borne upward, up and up and — thanks be — out of danger. She gasped, cried out, and looked into Théo's blazing eyes as he propelled her out of reach of the rolling wheels. He swung her high, and she found herself gripped by another pair of hands that pulled her higher still, onto the back of a horse.

71

Holding her tightly against him, the rider reined his mount and wheeled it in place. "You're safe, you know." As de Laval's arm wound closely around her, he laughed softly in her ear and then pressed his mount into a gallop that took them through the tide of vehicles streaming behind the coach.

After going a short way, he sharply reined his horse into an alley entrance. They came to a thudding halt in front of a tavern—the most disreputable Nanon had ever seen, but what did it matter? Her brother and his friend had ridden after her—and they'd found her!

With Nanon still in his arms, de Laval swung down from the saddle. Her arms clasped tightly around his neck, she cried. "Sweet Lord . . . it is you!"

"No . . . only Edmond." He kissed her full on the mouth as he'd never done before. But when he set her on her feet, she continued to cling to him, barely believing in her good fortune.

"Where is Théo?" Nanon looked around.

And with a great clatter he was there, leaping out of his saddle, the reins of his black stallion looped over his arm. In his relief at seeing her, he swore convincingly as he took her in his arms and shakily smoothed her hair.

Helping her retie her scarf, he asked, "How did this come about? Are you all right . . . did anyone hurt you? Heaven and hell, Nanon! If Edmond hadn't seen Joséphine's coach cut off from the others and found her in the garden, then ridden straight to the château and told me, we couldn't have followed you in time. We twice took a wrong turning before we caught onto your trail outside of Morlaix!"

She was jubilant, breathless. "You were behind me?"

"We couldn't make the attempt to pry you out of there while the escort was with the coach, but when they were dropped behind in Morlaix—"

Edmond interrupted, clapping his friend on the shoulder. "Stop babbling, Théo. They'll be after us. Here . . ." He tossed the reins of the horses to the boy from the stable next to the tavern.

Standing between the two men, Nanon was at last able to speak coherently. "Why should they care? I'm not their victim. It was Joséphine they wanted."

"You mean that all this time they truly thought *you* were the Empress?" Both men burst into roars of laughter, Edmond finally adding, "They may still think so, and try to hunt us down. Though there are only two of them, and we're more than their equal." She could see he spoke with his usual swagger, but it was easy to excuse him now.

Théo pushed them both ahead of him. "Inside, quickly. I know this place. The tavern keeper's a knave and a law-breaker — and a friend of Edmond."

Edmond grinned. "Of you as well."

Nanon knew exactly what that meant. The man might be a rascal, but he was a Bonapartist rascal whom they could trust.

Once settled inside, the trio sat in a dim corner of the smoke-filled taproom while Nanon answered their questions and verified that it was D'Amboise who'd led the abduction. When the men ordered wine, she shook her head. There was nothing she required, she was too dazed with excitement to eat or drink.

Finally Edmond pushed back his glass and said, "Since we have to start back to Morlaix tonight, I'd better find a mount for Nanon."

He disappeared, and Théo signaled a serving maid. "Is there a room where my sister may rest briefly?"

The wench tittered knowingly. "No sleeping chamber is available, *m'sieu,* but there's a small place that can be used for a little while."

Théo raised an eyebrow and looked at Nanon with amusement. "Is it satisfactory?" She nodded, and he rose at the same time she did.

About to follow the girl, Nanon glanced back at him and spoke feelingly. "I'm grateful for a place to retire until Edmond returns. In fact, gratitude fills my heart at this moment. I shall never, never forget this, Théo. I'll make a proper speech once we're home again. And if I've ever been rude to you—which I have—I apologize and swear I'll make it up to you." She thought for a moment. "And for anything rude or violent you've done to me or to Dominique, I forgive *you.*"

The bow he gave her was exaggerated. "Those are very pretty words, and I'll hold you to them."

When she reached the doorway, she looked back. He was seated, calling for another bottle of wine. She hoped he'd order the roast duck as well. He needed sustenance, and that food's delicious odor permeated the room.

The maid showed her upstairs, to a chamber that was little more than a loft. The one window was on a level with a shoulder of hilly earth that sloped down to the alley outside.

The girl explained. "This is for a little rest and a wash only, *mam'selle.*" She leaned close. "You're not really his sister, are you? He's such a handsome man."

"I am his sister, and I agree, he is handsome." Nanon gazed around her in dismay. There was a cot with a mattress and near it a stand containing a basin and a pitcher full of water. Nothing else. She understood. The room was used— after a whiskey-soaked sojourn in the taproom below, followed by a tipsy climb up the stairs—for a tumble on the mattress. Finally, a pitcher of water was poured over two heads blurred by drink and by the appeasement of passion.

The serving girl departed after much lingering about, but Nanon hadn't a coin to give her. She filled the basin and splashed water on her face, then combed her hair with her fingers and arranged her scarf over the damp curls. After smoothing her jacket, she shook out her skirt and looked around for a chair to sit on. There was none. She wouldn't go near that stained mattress, so she stood next to the window wondering how long it would be before a horse could be hired for her.

Thinking back to the miraculous appearance of her rescuers, her heart leaped and warmed once more, and she knew that she loved them both and would be forever grateful.

She grew restless with the waiting, but finally a knock came at the door and Théo called out, "Edmond's still on the search for a decent mount for you. I expect we'll be off soon."

She opened the door. "Come in, though I'd rather we waited below." She glanced around the loft in distaste. "May we do that?"

"This is a seaport town, and you've seen the patrons here — not a pretty mannered lot. By this hour they're more boisterous than when we first came in."

She walked over to her brother's side, feeling an unwonted tenderness for him. His face had lines in it which should not have been there. But this was not surprising, considering more than a day's hard riding lay behind him. At least she had been inside a coach and had had some rest.

Nanon gave his arm a hug. "Dear Théo, when you swung open that coach door, I've never been so glad to see anyone. I told you, I'm saving my real speech of gratitude. I intend to make it in front of Father." His eyes no longer seemed tired, but almost too brilliant as they studied her. She continued. "You haven't told me how Father really is."

"Believe me, I didn't try to spare your feelings. I did tell you the truth. He suspected that something had happened to you, but he put on his face of courage. So, he's as usual, not better, not worse — and being well taken care of by Degrelle. I thought we'd have to tie Georges down, he was so insistent that he ride with us to find you. I tell you, the man's in love."

To this she made no comment. It was a dilemma that would have to be resolved if Degrelle were to remain under their roof. But where could they find someone as devoted and as knowledgeable in caring for their father? And it meant so much to him to reminisce with Georges about the days on the Wagram battlefield. There! She, too, was calling him Georges. . . .

"But you're not in love with him!" Her brother stepped close, and it was then she could smell the brandy on his breath. He and Edmond were entitled to stronger drink than wine if that were their preference, but she was concerned. "Did you have your dinner, Théo?" He shook his head. "But you must eat before we start out."

Beneath the sensuous slant of black brows, his eyes

watched hers, an unreadable expression in them. "You do have thoughts for my well-being, don't you, Nanon? You care what happens to me."

He was so often sarcastic with her that now she was puzzled as to his exact meaning and how she could reply to him. "Certainly I care, and others care for you, too, Théo. Edmond for one, and those who join you in the assembly, as well as your old comrades . . ." She faltered. He was looking at her in such an odd manner, studying her so intently. . . . Was it that he didn't want to recall those comrades of his because too many of them lay dead in Spain and in Egypt? Perhaps she was being thoughtless; her father had warned her to watch her tongue.

"Look!" He spoke so suddenly that he startled her. "I've been extremely concerned for your safety. The real truth is that I've been terrified . . . *me!* Scared out of my damn wits by Edmond galloping in to tell me you'd been abducted. He knew it was you; he saw the whole affair from the woods and he talked to Joséphine, as you know. But you're safe now, here with me—you're wonderfully safe."

"Oh, I am . . . I know I am! I'll always be safe with you." Not even the pungent smell of the liquor bothered her now. Her eyes were shining into his. How kind he is, she thought . . . how fortunate I am to have a brother like mine.

Yes, she was smiling at him. He looked down at that whimsical smile that so captivated him and seemed to persuade his heart that all was well with his world. He didn't understand this tormenting swell of affection he felt for her, particularly since he hadn't been able to watch her grow up. In that way, she was a stranger to him. Yet, in contrary fashion, it was as though she'd been with him always, like this . . . close.

Wonderingly, he reached out to her. Haltingly, he tried to explain. "I've never had someone to return to . . . as Edmond has had—oh, he's had many. I only wanted one person, do you understand, Nanon? I've treated you badly, but I wish . . . I think . . . you are that person."

"How could you treat me badly? You were harsh some-

76

times, impatient often . . . but then I probably deserved it. I'll do better in the future."

"Did you hear me? I said you are . . . that person I want." His fingertips lightly touched her cheek, traced that vagrant dimple, trailed to her lips, lingered. . . .

He was barely aware that her warm smile had disappeared under his caressing hand, that she'd stiffened as their sibling gazes mingled in poignant shock.

# Chapter Eight

Confused Nanon drew back, reminding herself that men who'd been years in battle were sometimes scarred in their minds and hearts, ever subject to strange moods. Just now, his intimate caress of her face had repelled her. It was not brotherly. But if not that, what was its meaning? And his words had not made sense to her.

"Théophile, this has been a difficult and dangerous time for all of us, and none of it is over yet. Surely you and Edmond need sleep, and the horses require rest as well. Perhaps we shouldn't start for the château tonight."

A flush stained his face from forehead to jaw. His voice thickened. "You mean you and I should stay right here?"

"There must be an inn, even a farmhouse, outside of Brest that will take us in, a place where no one would think to look for me. They'd find shelter for you and Edmond, too. And we could start out before dawn."

He answered as though at random, his voice dark and making no connection with what she'd just proposed. "On the quay when I pulled open the coach door why did you call out for D'Amboise?"

She regarded him with dismay. "I didn't."

"Your exact words were 'Devin, help me.'"

"I couldn't have . . ." She hesitated. Had she called out for D'Amboise involuntarily? Making up a small joke to relieve the tension between them, she gently insisted. "I must have said 'Heaven help me!' Yes, that's it. I'm not a fervid believer, as you know, but we all call upon the Lord and his minions willy-nilly when it suits us. And since you did arrive as my answer, I'm probably on my way to becoming a believer — in miracles," she rattled on. "If I did call out as you say, it's because I thought some knave was breaking into the coach. Who else was there to assist me except D'Amboise or his aide?"

"Had you given thought to that brawny driver on top of the coach?"

Her lips tightened at his sarcastic retort. She would refuse to get into a warfare of words with him; the atmosphere between them was strained enough. She ducked around him and started for the door. "If you stay with your decision to ride tonight, then we must purchase cheese and bread to take with us. We can attend to it downstairs right now, before Edmond returns."

But his leather-sleeved arm barred her path.

Her face clouding, Nanon looked sidelong at him. He was drunk, and she'd had enough of this childish game.

Then it became not quite so childish.

With a smoothness that gave no warning, his hands reached out and caught her beneath her arms, tightening and hurting her as his fingers slid down her sides to capture her waist. She tried to evade him, but not quickly enough. With a groan he swiveled her in close to his body. She could feel his heavy belt with its buckle, its dagger; the hard length of his legs, straddled and pressing against her own.

"Others must have told you you're bewitching when you smile. Don't pout at me now, Nanon." Placing his finger under her chin, he turned her face up to his.

She was shaking, her own breathing as unsteady as his but for a different reason. The pounding within her was parented by a grotesque fear of him that she was attempting to hold in check.

She assayed an easy laugh that came out a dry kind of croak. "My godmother tells me that a woman's smile improves matters. It seems for once you agree with her." Continuing to speak to that child she sought in him, she tried once more. "Tell me you're jesting with me, that you're sorry you gave me a start. And remember, Edmond will be here momentarily, so let's be off."

As though she were a recalcitrant filly under his hands, Théo whispered. "Stop now . . . not so fast."

Relieved by what she took to be a sobered reaction on his part, even a good-natured one, Nanon tossed back her head. But that loosened her scarf and it streamed to the floor, freeing a mass of curls to touch her shoulders and cheeks and to gleam like ancient bronze in the candlelight.

Partly releasing her, he leaned down from his height to wind one of those burnished strands around a finger and then, with drunken and rapt concentration, tuck behind her ear. It was when he relaxed his fingers and let his hand glide slowly, lovingly, down the side of her throat to linger at its pulsepoint that distrust became real and panicking fear.

Nanon opened her mouth to protest but she was mute. He closed her lips with the pressure of his fingertips and, cupping her chin, drew her face to his. His countenance seemed to enlarge before her eyes. It was a stranger's face, male and quite beautiful in its sensuality. This was someone she did not know at all.

"Please . . ." she whispered to this man she didn't know.

"No! You . . . please," he countered thickly, painfully. And the pupils of his eyes—Théo's eyes?—seemed to dilate, to bore almost unseeingly into hers from depths of a savage license that she could never plumb. She struggled to pull back from him while searching for some potent phrase to use to stop this, to save them both. She saw his face become distorted, its expression grow tragic. If she hadn't been so frightened herself, she could have felt for this stranger.

It was too late. She stood frozen in terrible surprise as he lowered his head to nuzzle her cheek, and then, with the greatest delicacy, he fastened his lips to hers, his tongue scrolling with unhallowed passion across her mouth. Her teeth clenched tight against him as his hand roved to open her jacket.

The scream started, but no one except herself could hear because it was deep inside her. Horror, like a cold sweat poured through her, and Nanon broke from his grasp by exerting strength she didn't know she possessed. She whirled

80

and bolted from the room and down the stairs, dodging past a roomful of astonished gapers before stepping into the damp April night. Sea-fog mists closed around her as she fled. . . .

She found shelter in a doorway, folded her arms across her midriff to stop the shuddering. Had it all really happened? Could she have misinterpreted the scene in the tavern loft? When his hand gentled her cheek and throat, when his gaze locked deep into hers, could she have misread the significance? Was it mere brotherly affection, no matter that it didn't seem so at the time. Had she read dark meanings into innocence?

Feeling faint she pressed her knuckles against her lips. If those excuses she sought were true, then why didn't she return and ask Théo's forgiveness for her wild flight?

She shivered. How could she explain his fingers opening her jacket, his lips slaking across her mouth. And what would have befallen her if she hadn't fled? She covered her face with her hands. She could not bear to imagine it.


St. Giles found the campaign coach, its unlucky driver standing beside it and staring into the empty interior. At his approach, the fellow trembled. "Sir, she's gone! Two horsemen pulled her from the coach . . . she's been abducted!"

And not for the first time, St. Giles thought, stupefied. Then he exploded, angry at himself as well as at the unfortunate man. "You footling idiot, to let a thing like this happen! Stay here! I'll find her, but if I do come back without the lady, you'll swing for this!" Or I will, he said to himself. His orders had been to remain close to the vehicle and guard it at all times, but, diverted by the harbor and its ships, he'd ridden far ahead.

His eyes glistening with fierce resolve, he set out at a canter to question whoever might have observed a lady being forcibly removed from a coach. The crowd had cleared and fog was settling in when, several queries later, he spied the creature in the doorway of a shuttered shop.

His attention being caught by the woman's attitude and

her interesting garb, he slowed his mount and sidled it closer. Her head was lowered, her hair a tangle of mahogany-colored curls. She was clad in an obviously well-made riding habit, its tightly fitted jacket defining a small waist and pleasant bosom, its ankle-length skirt fashionably overlapping in front and edged with black braid. All of this didn't fit with the anguish she displayed.

Abreast of her now, he could see that the velvet was well worn but unmistakably some aristocrat's garment that had been handed down to the wench. But was she a wench? Curiosity prodded him, and he dismounted and drew close. The fingers covering her face were slim and tapering, and as she seemed to peer at him through them, he became even more curious as to the reason for her misery. Had a gentleman wronged her? He might be able to ease that. Better still, though confounded by her own wretchedness, she might have seen something of what had occurred in the streets. There was really no one else about. . . .

"*Mam'selle,* have you perchance observed—?"

He was as shocked as she appeared to be when she lowered her hands to exclaim. "Andrew St. Giles, it's you!"

"You're correct in naming me, but God's truth how is it you know me?"

Nanon cut him off. He was an idiot, she'd known it from the start. "I haven't time to explain. Could you extend a small loan so that I may find a public conveyance that will take me to Paris? If you'll tell me where I can address you, I'll return the sum with my gratitude and a full explanation."

Bewildered, he replied. "But who are you?"

There was no use dissembling further, it would only waste time. "I was the passenger in the coach you escorted from Malmaison."

His response was a bleat; then he said, "Are you telling me it was you—whoever you are—and not the Empress Joséphine?"

"I took her place when the grenadiers surrounded her coach. She escaped you, it seems." It gave Nanon pleasure to impart that information. "I'm Antoinette-Élise de Cavanac, the Empress's goddaughter."

"Joséphine has no goddaughter—only her own daughter Hortense."

"History may agree with you, St. Giles . . . but here I am."

He was furious. It would have made a far better story at his club if he'd escorted the glamorous Joséphine to the coast. He abruptly said, "I require no further explanation from you. I'm convinced you were the woman in the coach."

She was relieved. "Then you'll help me?"

"Listen carefully to me, *mademoiselle*. You've put us all in a very bad place. The driver tells me ruffians absconded with you from the coach. What they did to you, why I find you weeping here, and how you've now escaped them, I don't want to know. I'm going to see that you get back inside that coach. Colonel D'Amboise is aboard ship, and he expects me to bring you to him . . . I mean, he expects the Empress will be brought to him. Since you've played the role thus far, you'd better continue in it so that he can see the grave error he's made. It is his responsibility and not mine."

Since she was no longer Joséphine, he was no longer the shy young officer impressed by an Empress. She saw him signal the driver of a coach standing at a distance down the road. Instantly the equipage came on at a fast pace. Sword of vengeance! He meant what he'd just said!

She faced him in anger. "Why should you want to detain me? If this incident is as unfortunate for your own career, as you indicate it will be for the Colonel's, I shan't tell anyone about it. Think now, how could you have been expected to fulfill your duty when I'm not the person I'm supposed to be. No fault lies with you!"

"Don't attempt to engage me in conversation, Mademoiselle de Cavanac. I want no complications." And with that he slung an arm around her shoulders, placed another under her knees, lifted her shoulder-high, and set out to meet the coach, his horse trotting amiably behind.

She struggled, scratching at his face, pulling at the hair his cap didn't protect, and pummeling his chest. Though she kicked and squirmed, he marched on, enfolding her so tightly it was impossible to break free. The coach arrived, and the driver scrambled down to tether St. Giles's horse to the rear of it. He then assisted the younger man in pushing Nanon inside.

St. Giles sprang in after her, shouting. "To the sailing dock, driver—and remember, the devil's behind you!"

When Nanon made a feint for the opposite door, he reached out from behind her and cruelly pried her fingers from the handle. Pressed hard against him, she resisted frantically, but he was the stronger. Holding her with one hand, he snatched the shawl from the seat and quickly wound its length around her from shoulder to heel. Thus swaddled, she was propped against the seat while he stretched one long leg across both her knees to hold her prisoner.

She opened her mouth to cry out, but his palm sealed her lips. Though encased like a trussed mummy, she struggled with him until her head slammed hard against his elbow, the blow sending light prisms dancing before her eyes.

The rest was a blur of fast-moving coach, black night paled by mist, hollow sounds of dock traffic, then lapping water. St. Giles's arm restrained her as dark shapes surrounded the coach and then proceeded to haul them both aboard ship.

Her head began to clear as she was supported across a deck and assisted down a companion ladder. But when she again attempted to cry out, a hand gagged her. She was pushed through a door into a small cabin lit by an oil lamp, and fell forward across a table that was braced to the floor. When she straightened and turned around, St. Giles had closed the door. He stood with his back to it, glowering at her.

"This is where I bid you farewell. As I was ordered to do, I've delivered a lady and her trunk to this ship. Now I'm off to rejoin my regiment." He made her an extravagantly deep bow. "Henceforth, I disclaim responsibility. I leave you to our friend D'Amboise. I see this as his error not mine, as you have so carefully pointed out to me. So, you can explain for me why the baggage delivered is not quite as promised." He winked. "A nice baggage just the same."

Unable to retaliate with a name rude enough to match this

insult, Nanon reached behind her, seeking a weapon with which to retaliate against his insolence. Since he'd called her a baggage, she'd behave like one. She grasped an object and hurled, but her aim was too far off for her to do him harm. He saluted smartly and escaped through the closing door. Englishmen . . . barbarians all!

She leaped across the floor to the door latch, but he'd secured it from the other side. An imprecation sprang to her lips. Unfortunately, it reminded her of Théo from whom she'd learned it, and she sagged dispiritedly against the door.

Finally, Nanon looked at her surroundings with a thought as to how she could escape. There was the small trunk, which a seaman must have brought in earlier. The cabin was scrupulously neat, even luxurious in a sense. The carpeting was a deep blue—she slid the sole of her boot across its texture—and thick. Matching cushions covered built-in seating, and a sleeping bunk was set below mahogany-paneled walls. She ran quickly to a brass-framed porthole, stood on tiptoe, looked out. There was nothing out there but fog, not even the lights of Brest could be seen.

Once again she tried the door. Many questions assailed her. Do ships sail at night? Could she get away before they went to sea? What was the sea like? She'd never gazed upon an ocean. What would D'Amboise's reaction be when he discovered she was not Joséphine? She didn't want to think about that, so she hastily stooped to retrieve the fragments of the object she'd thrown, a small globe depicting the world. It had been shattered.

While her head was still bent to the task, a knock on the door brought Nanon upright. She pushed the broken pieces beneath a cushion and spoke with intentional irony. "You may enter."

A lad of about thirteen peered around the door at her, his awed expression turning into one of surprise. "Your supper tray . . . mademoiselle?" He gave the cabin's occupant another quizzical look.

She guessed correctly that he'd been told to expect a regal older woman. Instead he was looking at a disheveled young person only a few years older than himself. Nanon smiled weakly, and immediately he grinned back. Good! Perhaps she had won herself an accomplice. Wondering at her own unpracticed deceit, she continued to smile, this time her face was glowing, its dimple deepening, her eyes shining with humor.

He returned her look admiringly and, placing the tray on the table, whisked off the white cloth atop it. She knew she was hungry when she caught sight of roast chicken, biscuits and a mound of butter, a pitcher of milk, a pot of tea, oranges, and honey.

There was the honey of guile on her tongue as well. "Ah, this does look delicious, thank you . . . and what is your name?"

The boy backed away, staring at her with eyes that were almost sea green in color. "I am called Claude, and I'm to tell you that for a time there is no one except me to serve you. Later, there will be a maid here, but for now, I'm to bring a basin of water for you to bathe yourself . . ." His face flushed scarlet, and he slipped through the door before she could question him further.

Again she tried the doorknob; it didn't yield. Despairingly she turned back and seated herself at the table. Thinking she would need all her strength for whatever lay ahead, Nanon shook out the linen cloth, placed it on her lap, and picked up the knife and fork. She proceeded to eat everything set before her. The tea was good; she drank it with a generous pouring of milk. The thin cup was from Limoges, she noted. Of course, since all this was intended for Joséphine.

When she finished, she looked longingly at the bunk bed and its soft coverlet, but there would be no time for sleeping.

As if in answer to that thought, there was a knock, followed by a familiar, deep voice. "Devin D'Amboise . . . may I have your permission to enter?"

Nanon continued to sit on the built-in seating opposite the door, her knees drawn up beneath her velvet skirts, her arms hugging them. Her head with its untidy halo of sherry-colored curls, was resting against the blue cushions. Soon,

86

she would be seeing his face, and that sight — *when he saw hers* — would be worth almost all the travail she'd come through.

Using her most lilting tones, she spoke. "Enter, m'sieur."

# Chapter Nine

D'Amboise had plotted this first meeting with Joséphine, going over it in his mind, seeing it as a scene played out between them. It was natural that she'd perceived him to be an enemy and a base conniver. But using his best persuasion, he would hint at the support she might anticipate when they reached Martinique. There were many on the island who remembered her, who loved her and were loyal to her.

Walking the narrow passageway he'd rehearsed words, attitude, deportment. Having discarded uniform dress before the journey to the coast, he'd given thought to this first impression. Now, upon hearing the invitation to enter, he glanced down, a trifle nervously, at the sheen of his Hessian boots, at the superb fit of his buff-colored English trousers, at the immaculate shoulder line of his formal, single-breasted coat. At least he wouldn't offend her with the appearance of a brigand. Joséphine was a woman to whom outward manifestations of style and demeanor meant much, and he hoped to appease her somewhat by his show of respect.

He was also determined to prevent any outburst of imperial temper. She was a warm and generous woman — whimsical, not truly imperious by nature. She might listen to him. He hoped so, for his curiosity concerning her was great. With a correct and sympathetic approach on his part — who could tell? — as distant cousins they might become good friends. Thus, he squared his shoulders and stepped inside the door, his expression calm and in control.

Holy God in heaven!

There *were* two of them, after all! St. Giles had been mistaken. She did have a maid of sorts with her, a careless-appearing lass who was, at this moment, taking her ease among the cushions.

He glanced around in astonishment. "Where is your mistress?" He looked back at the reclining wench, her arms linked cosily around her velvet-skirted knees, her attitude one of outrageous disrespect.

The possibility that began to confront him was so outrageous in its own right that he flushed darkly and was unaware that he spoke aloud. "I don't . . . believe what I see here!" His eyes, with their glint of gun metal, narrowed in ferocious concentration. *"You* are the young de Cavanac . . . that wily female from the château, the general's daughter!"

She uncurled herself from among the cushions and, patting her skirt in place, rose to confront him. "It is I, not a wraith." Since to her he no longer presented a figure of uniformed authority, she concluded wickedly. *"M'sieur* Devin D'Amboise, I see — without helmet, boot, or sword!"

Though it seemed to her the ague was shaking her, clicking her teeth like castanets, Nanon stood, outwardly resolute, and allowed her gaze to absorb the virile length of him, as well as his stylish attire. As she'd promised herself she would do, she stared long into his face; and, as she'd hoped, that face was a landscape of stupefaction and fury.

The sensual outline of his lips thinned in rage. "Where is the Empress Joséphine? What have you done with her?"

"What have *I* done with her?" Oh, she cherished the sight of his astonished face! *"I* have done nothing. But *your* plans have misfired. The Empress escaped the grenadiers at Malmaison. She's on her way to Navarre. It was I who took her place in the campaign coach." How incredulous and bewildered he looked, oh joy!

She leaned forward, her fingertips resting on the table between them, and tantalized. "And what do we have here, Devin D'Amboise? Only you, only me! Since this is the predicament, don't waste any more of our time. Set me ashore immediately and I . . ." She stopped, listened intently, and then looked down at the carpeting that covered the floorboards.

There was a barely perceptible roll of movement underfoot, but that hint of motion had been there for some time. It was the crackling noise from far overhead that arrested her attention. It sounded as though a giant hand had seized a huge piece of fabric and was aimlessly tattering it.

*"What is that sound?"* But just then the movement beneath her feet became a discernible heaving.

His own emotions were running amok now while he watched her eyes widen and her gaze rove in dismay from the floor to the low ceiling above their heads, then to the open porthole.

Instinctively, he lunged to close it. With his back to her, his palms flattened against the brasswork, his arms extended to support his weight, he remained without moving, his head dropped between his shoulders as though he'd been poleaxed. Christ! He knew the ship had begun to ease out of the harbor nearly an hour before to take advantage of the twilight breeze and thus be in position to catch the favored wind at dawn. And here he was with no Joséphine, but with a French general's young, strong-willed daughter who was, recalling that failed kiss, possibly a maiden.

Overwhelmed by this calamity, he could think only of hard fact, so he answered. "It's the ship's canvas you hear."

She interrupted excitedly. "You're saying that the sails are set to catch the wind?" She knew nothing of ships, but she did know that the wind billowed and stretched their sails as it propelled them across vast stretches of water.

"They've been unfurled for some time." He did sound unhappy about that.

"We can't be sailing . . ." Her voice trailed in disbelief. "And if we are, this ship must turn back." She stalked close to his shoulder, jabbing a punctuating finger at him. "Are you listening to me? You must put back to the dock. However it's done, *you must see to it!*"

Still facing the porthole, and with disaster hard upon him, Devin had already decided which course he would have to navigate with her to regain any kind of advantage. He inhaled deeply, lifted his head, and stared at her. "*Mademoiselle . . . Nanon . . .* it is you who have brought this upon yourself. You placed yourself in the Empress's coach, I didn't. Had you not played such a foolhardy trick you would be safe in your own bedchamber at this moment. Neither the captain, the crew, nor I had anything to do with your presence here . . . you think about that!"

He allowed his gaze to rake her coldly as he increased his attack. "Let me further inform you, there is no turning back. This is a merchant vessel bound for Martinique, carrying cargo, passengers, and you. Had the Empress been aboard as planned, she would have accepted the situation with grace."

"She would not. She would have found a means to circumvent you!"

A flicker of a smile crossed his mouth. "It's true she might have plotted against me, but in subtle fashion. Strolling beside her on deck, I might have to be cautious not to approach too close to the rail. But she would never have demanded the impossible."

"To be put ashore you mean?" Nanon was thinking rapidly.

"Exactly."

"How do I profit you by remaining on board?"

"You don't. I'll have to look at that defiant face of yours almost daily, but I vow I shall send you back to France on the next vessel that leaves Martinique."

Hearing this, Nanon's hidden anxiety and dread, as well as the painful stiffness in her neck muscles, subsided somewhat. "I don't know that I can trust your vow, but I shall certainly keep out of your way. I have no desire to look into your face either, *m'sieur.* I find this a deplorable situation." She gestured as though she held a bold banner in her hand. "It cannot continue."

He shrugged, and moved around the small center table to stand opposite her, his presence rugged and threatening for all his fine attire. "It has to, Nanon. And if it gives you satisfaction, this . . . misfortune we're involved in may well have blackened my career."

"I know that." Her smile was acid-sweet.

"But in any event, I had already concluded my obligation to the British Army; and besides, I saved them their ally, the Russian Tsar. Joséphine's cunning in eluding me at Malmaison, as unfortunate as it is, will be balanced against my long and, may I say, dutiful service with the Foreign Office."

He might have said "valorous," but due to the curious legacy of his birth, his particular deeds would be buried forever in Castlereagh's file. He was bemedaled for great courage in the field, but an Englishman bearing Irish and French bloodlines could never be officially acknowledged as having been entrusted with dangerous state missions.

"That all sounds very nice. Except that it has nothing to do with me. Before you leave — one question. What is the significance of all this . . . peacock finery of yours?"

He followed the direction of her withering gaze to his garments and replied dryly, "Perhaps the British style in gentlemen's attire is in advance of that worn in the French countryside. Days ago my man in London sent my chests aboard ship. You'll recall that tonight I believed I was paying a visit to a civilized person, the fascinating and fashionable Joséphine, and therefore I dressed accordingly."

At that Nanon was silent, unsure whether there was an insult here or not. Finally, she gritted out, "I believe I do prefer a soldier's uniform to a sprigged vest and dandified frock coat. But it's not my concern, *m'sieur.*"

He kept a smile from tugging at his lips. When she challenged him this way he wanted to shake her or, more often, to enfold her in his arms and subdue that pretty mouth with his own. Was she truly a maiden he wondered? In his experience shy virgins were . . . well, shy!

"I agree, Nanon, it isn't your concern."

She paced away from him. "*My* concern is to remove myself from this ship. But if I must remain aboard, how long will it be until we reach Martinique. More than a month?

Then a wait for a vessel returning to France, and another six weeks after that to make the return voyage? In this time my beloved father might die. And it might well be that grief over my absence will kill him. Your fault, do you deny it?"

She waited testily for him to reply. Somberly he watched her, and said nothing. She paced on. "I see you cannot deny this. And let me tell you another great flaw that I observe in you — and like a cracked mirror you have many! For all your supposed devotion to your fine horse, where have you left him? In some hired stable in that odious barracks town back there." She paused, a brow arched caustically. "Or have you made arrangements with *your valet* to retrieve him as though he were another piece of luggage?"

"You *are* a thoughtful lass, Nanon. But Boru is not your concern, either; still, to answer your kind question, he's being brought to my property in Ireland by a trusted friend who, at this moment, is on his way to Brest."

She crossed her arms and faced him. "All of this was long in planning, then?"

He nodded, and began to inspect the riding habit she was wearing. She became aware, in dubious fashion, of the interest in his gaze as it followed the arms she crossed over the swell of her bosom. That gesture had strained the snug fit of the velvet around her small waist and over her shapely thighs.

"Since you possess only the clothing you have on, it's fortunate your godmother's hand trunk is here. You'll appear a rare charmer dressed in her sheer frocks. Or is the correct word . . . "transparent"? It seems I've heard Paris style so described."

Indeed he had, since some of Clare's chatter had lingered with him. His mistress had been envious of the Parisian ladies who'd renounced undergarments in order to achieve a classic silhouette. Though it was well known that Napoléon disapproved of the exposed bosom and the limb-revealing draperies. As for himself, Devin rather wished he'd been around to see them.

Nanon spoke coldly, answering what she rightly perceived to be a rakish gleam in his eye. "I will not fall into a discussion of fops and fashion."

"When we reach southern waters, sheer cotton will cool and soothe your skin, Nanon."

She flared. "I shall not open that trunk! If I must continue this voyage, what I'm wearing will do very well."

"The tropical warmth has a way of melting resolute statements such as yours. I speak from experience."

"I'm sure you do, but please take your experience elsewhere, I should like to be alone, now."

The humid air would dapple and glisten that silky skin of hers. The tumble of hair, the bronze of pear leaves in autumn, would be scented with island spices as the wind blew through it. She was bright, she was courageous, an expert horsewoman. She was everything he liked. And she was perfect with that tawny complexion of hers, only a little darker than was fashionable in Paris. She was clever, sensitive; and was pretending to be unafraid. She was perfect . . . for him. He wanted to take her in his arms and reassure her, but he knew she would claw him like a tiger cub, so he would have to wait.

"M'sieur D'Amboise! Are you dreaming? Must I repeat that I prefer solitude—even in this cabin—to your company?"

He bowed gravely. "I understand your distress, Nanon, and I forgive you. And . . . my name is Devin."

"My rudeness was intentional. Please do not think of forgiving it . . . D'Amboise."

"That's a *little* better." He spoke wryly; then added, "I trust you'll be comfortable tonight. After tomorrow, confinement in this cabin won't be necessary. We'll be far from shore, with the sea fathoms deep, you understand?"

She nodded, her steady gaze revealing nothing. He went on. "The boy Claude will attend to whatever needs you have until someone more suitable can be found."

"Truly, I can fend for myself."

94

"Perhaps." He moved toward the door. "We have several ladies aboard. They are rejoining their husbands. I'm sure you'll find congenial companionship among them. Some have daughters near your age—"

"*Good night,* D'Amboise!"

He closed the door and left swiftly, striding along the passageway, and in his haste thwacking a shoulder, striking his head on a low beam, and swearing, while the full impact of this calamitous night descended on him. "Disaster" was a gentle term for it. St. Giles must have known it was not Joséphine he'd brought aboard. Now, Devin understood why there'd been no farewell when the younger man had departed the ship.

The burden of this bungled affair would haunt him; especially if the general died before father and daughter could be reunited. It was impossible to turn back, either the calendar or the events. And he was finding it even more impossible to accept the tenderness he felt toward this young woman whom he'd known only briefly and under extraordinary circumstances. No one, not even Clare with whom he'd shared five, almost domestic years, had so touched his imagination or entangled his heart.

With Nanon it was all different. With Nanon . . . he wanted to talk, walk, ride, share, know, instruct, make love, taste her; *have her* in the deepest sense. And if it turned out well, then who could tell what their future together might be. . . .

His eyes darkening, he paused at his quarters, his shoulder brushing the hanging lantern outside his door, sending its light aswing so that shadows seemed to race and pursue, back and forth, back and forth. He glanced down the short passageway to her cabin. At the château when he'd crushed her mouth beneath his to search it with desire, he'd been so certain of her response to him.

But he'd been wrong, and it wasn't just that drunken brother of hers blundering his way through the upper hall that had discouraged intimacy between them.

"Colonel D'Amboise!"

Previously he'd not heard the footsteps. Startled, he swung around, his hand by instinct finding the place where his dagger should have been.

"It's been a long time since we've met. You're even more handsome out of uniform than in, dare I say that?" The high voice trilled into suggestive mirth. And he looked into the pert, blue eyes of Amalie Farrar.

"Madame." He bowed over her hand, his lips brushing it. "This is a great pleasure. I did see your name on the ship's listing . . . you are joining Charles?"

"At last I am. I could find no further excuses to keep me in Paris, and with your British army there, it was not exactly a festival." Her eyes twinkled knowingly. "How do you manage it, Devin? With blood ties to an ancient Martinique family, you, an Anglo-Irishman, slipping back and forth across borders. Oh yes, I've heard the rumors. And they'll kill you one day—one of your own compatriots surely will. What a misfortune that would be." She turned to her companion standing in the shadows. "Do you know—"

"Yes." The voice was as soft as water whispering. "Oliva Russo . . . you remember me?"

His face burned. "*Madame* Anton Russo?" He had seen the familiar Russo name on the ship's listing . . . but *Oliva* Russo?

Her laughter was as seductive as her voice. "Oliva Valinski when we met in Poland; it was winter. Sergei died the following year during the last siege."

Amalie interrupted fussily. "I was unaware you two knew each other. That winter must have been a memorable one, eh? Oliva's married to Anton Russo now, you know the family. This is her first trip to Martinique, she's a bit distressed about it all. I told her everyone will accept her even though she is a Slav. She speaks almost flawless French, and has a family title as well." She twirled her fingers at him, tiny opal and diamond rings sparkling. "You may escort us, my dear Devin." The two women whispered, and he could see Amalie looking at him with amusement. "There are two of us so you are quite safe."

The ladies' cabins were in an opposite passageway. He dispatched Amalie first, confirming his suspicion that the two had made this last-minute arrangement between them. Oliva swayed ahead of him, and as he followed her lissome walk, his thoughts were in exquisite turmoil. It was formidable to see her again. He wondered at the state of his stars since their paths had crossed at this fateful time when he'd mishandled the Joséphine matter and had begun to believe his heart might be captured by Nanon.

Pausing at her door, Oliva looked up at him over her shoulder. "This is not coincidence. I asked Amalie to plan it."

"I suppose I guessed, since Amalie enjoys games. It's extraordinary to see you here. You've been widowed—for that I'm sorry—and you are married again."

"Does that prevent our sharing a tête-á- tête for old times? I have my samovar with me. May I offer you tea in my cabin? It's been so long. Do all women say that to you . . . that it's been so long?"

He scowled. "You know that isn't true, but it is like a miracle seeing you on this ship."

"A miracle sacred or profane?" Her white teeth gleamed in the shadows.

"Oliva, tonight there's been a crisis in my personal affairs. I've had to try to solve it, which I've not done very well. May we talk tomorrow?"

She began to chuckle softly. "A headache tonight, Devin?"

She had always known how to make him laugh. Now as they smiled at each other, their eyes met—hers slanting and luminous, the color of quince; his slate gray, far, far back in them was the beginning kindling of silver fire.

She'd placed herself directly in front of him. He could smell the fragrance of that red hair, veiling each side of her face and pulled back in a loose knot at her nape. As she arched her back, and moved closer to him, the body scent rising from her low-cut bodice surprised him with its tradewinds' spice; he could almost guess its origin . . . star anise, cinnamon, clove.

"Why do you smell like this when you've never been to the island?" He was tempted to cup her face between his two hands and touch her lips, but he resisted.

"Anton has given me potpourri to sew into the hem of my bed pillow so that I may have sweet dreams all through the night. That is not easy for me. You know."

"I know." He kissed her forehead.

She had positioned herself against him so that no passerby could spy her, thus her hand now slid with slow and stealthy grace down the front of his coat. "You know my nightmare, my deepest fear," she murmured to him.

He knew that, too. "Traveling to a strange land . . . it is difficult for you Slavs." She nodded, and their gazes locked. "Why isn't Anton with you?"

"He departed for Fort-de-France several months ago, to open and prepare the big house on the plantation. He's been living in small bachelor quarters." Devin knew her husband had been living in the house of a beautiful quadroon, but his expression did not change as he listened. "I remained in France with his family. When Paris fell, they fled to the country and here I am, arriving sooner than expected on your island. Do you know Anton?"

"He's a good fellow, not the man I would have expected you to marry."

She didn't smile. "Nor I."

He placed an arm around her. "It's time for you to try to sleep. Perhaps the potpourri *will* help. I'll see you in the morning."

But she'd begun to weave the tips of her fingers beneath the edge of his coat, and they discovered the soft suede of his skin-tight trousers. Here, they paused. There was a long sigh shared between them, as though, at the moment, breathing was difficult for both. The arm he'd placed around her shoulders tightened involuntarily. Her head back, eyes half-closed, she watched him while her fingertips continued their sensual exploration. They slid delicately up his iron-hard inner thigh, and he shuddered at the intimacy of her touch. Then, both of his arms came around her, crushing her to him.

Dreamily, and with the back of her hand, Oliva stroked his manhood. "Don't let me be alone tonight, Devin," she said.

# Chapter Ten

With his arm still around her as she nestled against him like a small, languid kitten, they entered the cabin, the wedge of his shoulder nudging the door closed behind them. He surveyed the comfortable quarters, aware of the globes of her breasts, seductively familiar and firm, pressed against his side. Still, he knew he would leave her here, bid her good night, and go. There was no time for the samovar and confidences over tea. He looked down at her face, studying its perfect oval, comparing her lustrous eyelids to pale pearls. She had changed so little over the years.

With her eyes still closed, she murmured up at him, as though aware of his fixed regard, "Always, you gave me comfort, you gave me sleep. To one who can't sleep nights, this is a priceless gift. Take care of me, Devin."

He answered bluntly. "With Russo's wealth, you're well taken care of."

The pale green eyes snapped open. "I didn't mean in that way!"

He sighed. "I know you didn't." Again, he glanced around them. "A cabin to oneself is worth a great deal of gold on this ship where space is valuable."

The fine fringe of titian lashes lowered to subdue and soften her gaze. "I know you well, Devin. You are curious and you are wondering how Russo and I ever met, isn't that right?" His look continued steady. "When the French withdrew before the onslaught of the Russians, my family put itself under Napoléon's protection, and so we left and came to Paris." His expression didn't change so she added, "There was nothing else for me. *You* were all I ever wanted. . . ."

They'd been through this a long time ago, lying in front of the fireplace in the old Polish castle. He could never offer her the permanent allegiance she desired of him. Now he muttered uneasily. "Oliva . . . *don't!*"

Cannily, she retreated. "I ask only that you stay here with me until I sleep."

"Only until then," he agreed, but she sensed that his tone had deepened.

"At least, help me disrobe." She was daring Fate, but considered the venture worthwhile, since a quick downward glance at those powerful thighs in skintight trousers told her certain results were already being achieved.

His smile quirked. "I'm not a lady's maid."

"No, but you are an old friend."

He laughed outright, his fingers touching the collar of her embroidered pelisse as he noted that beneath it her gown was a froth of muslin and lace. "This is what old friends are for?"

"Yes—and why not?" She faced him and snuggled in closer to his chest. He let his chin rest thoughtfully on the top of her head while one arm continued to cradle her shoulders and the other soothed her, stroking down along her spine to her slender flanks. There his hand paused, comfortably cupping her beneath the buttocks until, finally, he began to gently massage and knead her flesh.

Her head fell back, and she uttered a soft moan of gratification while he looked down at the crushed velvet of open lips, soft and red and moist. And he remembered her touching him intimately in the passageway.

"Make me sleep, Devin. . . ."

His intent was merely to walk her across the cabin, lower her to the bunk bed, kiss her lightly, stroke her hair, and then leave her.

But her affecting cry recalled the pleasures each had once given the other. He felt compassion for her; her life had been difficult. And she had been kind to him.

"Until you sleep, then." To reassure himself, he, too, was repeating the litany. He would pat her hand, smooth her brow, and depart.

He walked her to the bunk, and with one hand on her shoulder, the other cushioning her hip, he made her face away from him and lightly kissed her nape. Then he removed her fitted coat and, with awkward fingers, began to unfasten the tiny, covered buttons at the back of her dress. Somehow, the knot of red hair came loose, and as her head drooped forward, it swept like a silken avalanche to the bedcovers.

It was then he grew conscious of the taut expectancy of his own body and of the air surrounding them, and of the silence that was almost tangible except for the ragged catch of two people breathing.

The buttons undone at last, with the palms of his hands he pushed the dress down from her shoulders and, carefully, as though she were a limp doll, he slipped her arms through each armhole. As the garment swooshed down below her hips, the air cooling her nearly naked skin, she relaxed farther over the bed, her arms barely supporting her body, her lovely backside within inches of his gaze. Beginning to feel fevered, his breathing uneven, he undid the lace-tucked chemise and calf-length drawers, allowing both undergarments and gown to fall to the floor.

It was considerate of her to keep her back to him so that he could resist temptation. For that, and for the sight of her rounded buttocks, he was grateful. He looked around him but saw no night robe to throw about her so, with one hand, he swept back the quilt, hoping she'd quickly cover herself. "Into bed, Oliva. I'll sit beside you a little while, and then I must leave."

But before he could prevent it, she disobeyed his order and turned swiftly to face him, her eyes slanted into a narrow glitter of desire. What she had begun in the passageway by sensuously stroking him, she intended to conclude to her own satisfaction and, of course, to his.

The eroticism of her naked form struck D'Amboise like a fist to the chest. He very nearly staggered backward under the attack of its full-blown sensuality. He's never quite forgotten, though tonight he definitely hadn't intended to remember, the astonishing contrast between her delicate shoulders and the heavy, brown-nippled breasts outthrust above her tiny waist. Nor could he deny those rounded hips that begged to be clasped and kissed, the curly, thick hair within tapering thighs that made the same demand of him.

She saw surrender stark in his face, and threw back her head in voluptuous relief, sending her auburn hair sliding in long, shivering splendor across her shoulders to hide her bosom. Unable to stop himself—not wanting to—Devin reached out to part the strands that hid her breasts so that his eyes could gloat over them once more.

"Stay with me, Devin." The plea was no longer needed. The straining bulge beneath the fine fit of his English trousers visibly betrayed that he would, he must, remain with her as she desired.

"Ah, let me. . . ." With accomplished strokings, she quickly assisted him in removing coat, linen, lacings, and boots.

As he pulled her to him, their nakedness melding, she asked, "Are you punishing me?" He answered, "Yes," and opened his legs, raising one to enclose and entwine her hips.

"It's good," she murmured, and they fell backward onto the bed. . . .


Nanon's hands clutched the rail, and her face was turned boldly to the wind; it seemed she would never gain her fill of just looking. Her gaze embraced all: the sweep and majesty of blue-green waters that rolled on without end, the sky a blue, uncluttered distance. Directly above her sails clattered and snapped and stretched and sang. And everywhere were the sounds of ship's bells.

Last night she'd barely closed her eyes, her anxious thoughts centering on her father and the manner in which his frail health would respond to her unexplained absence. Her one hope was that her brother and Degrelle would concoct some story to allay her father's fears for her safety. They might have the wit to say she'd accompanied Joséphine to Navarre. But how could they account for her mare being left so summarily at Malmaison? Her father would know it was out of character for his daughter to abandon Dominique in someone else's stable.

Staring at the sea, Nanon renewed her determination not to hide in the cabin and fret. It would do no good to let body and mind decline. She must be strong enough to face whatever might lie ahead in her uncertain future. With this in mind, she would exercise and walk the deck, eat well, and engage in conversation with the other passengers.

Sternly, she put aside all thoughts of Théo and the final hour in the loft at the inn. To replay in her mind what had occurred between her and her brother would deter her from her resolve. When she was safe once again in her father's house, she'd take out that frightening memory and try to understand it.

The captain, a rugged-appearing man in his forty-fifth year, passed her once, twice; each time intrigued and looking back at her. She was youthfully appealing with those bronze-colored curls blowing around her face, despite her eccentric garb, a riding habit. Undoubtedly she was part of the new French youth with which he was unfamiliar. He came to a halt. "Mademoiselle de Cavanac . . ."

Startled at hearing her name called, Nanon looked over her shoulder at him.

He bowed. "Captain Levreux. May I present myself? Yours was the name unexpectedly entered on the listing, and yours is the one charming face to which I've not been introduced. Do you find your quarters satisfactory?"

"Yes, captain—I do find them so." To forestall further questions which might prove awkward, she hurriedly added, "Since this is my first time at sea, I'm eager to learn everything there is to know."

His own charm at the ready, Levreux directed his black eyes full into hers. "It would be my pleasure to instruct you, *mademoiselle,* but I've many duties to fulfill as you can well understand. Yet, we might steal the time . . . little moments here, little moments there. Perhaps?" His sharp, black brows arched upward.

Unsure of how to respond to what she presumed to be a form of sophisticated banter, Nanon replied, "I do appreciate your responsibilities."

The captain was curious. Weeks ago, an aide to D'Amboise had reserved the cabin this young woman now occupied, and he wondered if there might be a connection between those two. There had been a rumor that an elderly aristocratic lady might come aboard ship. This, certainly, was not that one.

"Do you know a friend of mine, Devin D'Amboise, who's sailing with us? If you do not, I'll see that you two meet. I am sure he'll be delighted to share his knowledge of the sea with you."

She stiffened. There was nothing she cared to share with D'Amboise. In fact, she'd chosen to step on deck at this particular time because she'd expected him to be below indulging in the midday meal along with the other passengers.

"Please don't concern yourself, Captain Levreux, there must be excellent books of instruction that detail the art of navigation, the use of the compass, and so forth." To Nanon, who'd had her father's library always at hand, the remark did not seem unusual.

"Books?" Levreux frowned. "What have books to do with it? It's all instinct, my dear—intimate knowledge gained by many years of experience with the sea and her ways, the ways of a woman, I might say. The sea is a seductive mistress upon whose bosom—" He stopped abruptly. It was plain to see that his usual gambit would not work with this young woman. Her candid gaze, cool and direct, without the slightest hint of coquetry, skewered him. He gave an inward shrug and retreated.

"Certainly one must keep logs and such, but nautical lore doesn't come from the pages of books. It comes from here." He tapped his temple. "And here." His well-groomed hand rested on his heart. "There are manuals, of course, but they're too technical for you."

She interrupted this flow. "Your passengers are fortunate to have a man like you to put their trust in, captain."

He touched his mustache with his little finger, and considered her comment. He decided rightly that there was no flattery or flirtation intended. She was too straightforward. Feeling a bit uncomfortable with this female who had declared her inclination to read books—the new French youth?—he was relieved when his first officer appeared and beckoned him away.

Nanon sauntered back along the deck, restraining the first impulse to merriment she'd felt in three days. Having closely observed Joséphine and her friends, she was prepared for encounters such as this one with Captain Levreux. She'd learned that innocence was a mantle, virtue a protection. But what she had never been prepared for was the insinuating kiss of a Devin D'Amboise. . . .

And he was there, just ahead of her!

He stood, holding a rope taut with both hands, while staring up at the rigging where a seaman worked. It was too late to flee, and she was unable to withdraw her gaze from that tall, strong body. His long, muscular thighs were clad in tight black breeches, and his wide shoulders were covered by a shirt of coarse linen, opened to the buckle of his broad leather belt. Black hair curled to below his collar, and since he was turned toward her, she could see the dark texture of hair on his bare, sun-browned chest.

She hated him, of course. Her heart began to beat rapidly as defiant warmth pulsed through her.

And then he spoke, knowing she was there yet not looking at her. "Have you had enough of your cabin's solitude, Nanon? Are you here on deck to join me?"

She sputtered and, with very little grace, stamped her foot. "Believe me, D'Amboise, I wouldn't join you in kingdom come!"

At that he swung his head around and, still clutching the rope, looked directly into her eyes. "You will, Nanon—you will."

Her mouth opened, but she was mute. There were no words to do justice to her feelings at that moment.

From behind her a soft voice spoke. "You are making a

mistake not to accept his invitation, whatever it is."

Shocked by the change in D'Amboise's eyes as he looked just beyond her, Nanon turned around. A small woman with a mass of red hair pulled severely back from a quite beautiful face was standing near her. She reached out to place a gentle hand on Nanon's velvet sleeve. "You must be one of the passengers I haven't yet met. Let us walk and become acquainted, shall we?"

The younger woman was startled to hear D'Amboise's strangled cry. "No . . . !"

She whirled about to look at him again, but he couldn't release the rope he held for if he did, the seaman in the basket above would come tumbling down onto the deck. His face seemed suffused with rage and also a kind of alarm which Nanon didn't understand. She smiled, gratified that she could somehow get back at him.

Turning once more to the pleasant woman who was regarding her with great, slanting, green eyes she said, "I would like that very much. My name is Antoinette-Élise de Cavanac . . . my friends call me Nanon."

"Then may I call you that, too, Nanon? And I am Oliva Russo."

# Chapter Eleven

Discreetly Oliva linked an arm through Nanon's; at the same time she noted that this girl was wearing an exquisitely tailored, though well-worn riding habit. How extraordinary. And extraordinary, also, that she appeared to know D'Amboise. There did seem to be an interesting complication here.

"Since we'll all be enjoying a long voyage together, it's comforting to have women friends with whom to trade confidences. First, about myself. I'm of Polish birth, sadly widowed, but recently remarried. Is it not romantic to be rejoining a new husband and beginning a new life on a faraway island?"

There was a thoughtful moment before Nanon replied. "Yes, very romantic, and I'm sure your husband is to be congratulated." The words sounded stilted to her ears, but worse, the older woman was regarding her expectantly. She dare not divulge any personal information just yet.

The silence grew awkward until Oliva, with a dazzling smile, confided. "I carry my samovar with me, it's a Slavic custom. The other ladies and I are about to have tea . . . you'll join us, please?" Her laughter tinkled like breaking glass. "I think you must be ready for civilized company — other than that man's back there." As she turned to look over her shoulder, Nanon followed the direction of her gaze, but D'Amboise was not in sight. "Do you know him well?"

There was hesitation. "We have . . . a slight acquaintanceship."

The cat-green eyes studied the younger woman. "I know

him, too—somewhat." Oliva waited for some further comment, her pique and exasperation mounting. But the stubborn girl remained silent, so she forged on. "I understand he has many talents. Among them, he's a good sailor, and all hands are needed on this ship—even those of a gentleman and a soldier like D'Amboise."

Nanon's silence on this subject remained baffling; Oliva sighed, then lowered her voice. "It's said some of the crew fled our ship while in the harbor at Brest. It's rumored the men were followers of Bonaparte, and they're hoping to aid him in his hour of need."

With this, Nanon stopped short to stare at her. "I was unaware of this occurrence, Madame Russo." So, she mused, this is why D'Amboise is doing a seaman's task back there.

"Ah, please. I am Oliva to you."

Feeling tense as a bowstring being plucked by inquisitive fingers, Nanon was loathe to bracket herself with her abductor. Yet, the two of them should have contrived an explanation for her presence on the ship. D'Amboise must have told the captain some tale, but she didn't know what it was. Consequently, it seemed unwise to remain in Oliva Russo's company; she and the other ladies would expect to learn why Nanon was traveling alone to Martinique. That island was a small world unto itself, and this ship was a still smaller one. Distasteful as it would be, Nanon must seek out D'Amboise to discover what story he'd already related.

They'd begun to descend the companionway, Nanon ahead, Oliva following closely. Nanon was thinking furiously. She'd been too eager to go off with Madame Russo in order to cause D'Amboise distress. He'd startled her with his expression of shocked alarm when the red-haired beauty had approached them, and she'd wanted to spite him for shouting that harsh "No!" at her as though he had every right to censor her actions. Now she was in a fine fret.

At the bottom of the ship's stairway, Nanon looked over her shoulder. "I do appreciate your asking me to meet your friends. I hope they'll be my friends, too. Could I join you later? I've just remembered there's something I neglected to tell Claude, the cabin boy."

In a flurry of chartreuse-yellow skirts and ruffled petti-coats, Oliva whirled in front of her to bar her way. "I insist that you not run off and disappoint us. Whatever beckons you, it can wait; can't it? Please?" She refused to lose this Nanon. She must learn why the girl had clashed with D'Amboise on deck. There were ramifications here, and she intended to get to the bottom of them.

Her hand closed firmly on Nanon's wrist, and though she told herself she must be careful not to ask the direct question, still, she couldn't resist. "You must have ridden your horse to this very port before embarking!"

This blunt probe was met with such a somber look that, afraid of losing her quarry, Oliva hastily retreated. "Like the Hungarians, we Polish talk too much. We are too outspoken. Forgive me for trespassing when our friendship is still so young. You're so independent, though I've always admired the freedom accorded women in your country. And as for your former empress, I've known of her devotion to the genius Bonaparte. It's tragic that he's falling from power. Fatalistically speaking—remember I am a Slav—it may not be his downfall quite yet. But let's not dwell on things political. You *must* come with me!"

And why must I? Nanon asked herself. She would even have welcomed D'Amboise, had he arrived at this precise moment. Yet, if she continued to rebuff this woman, she would appear suspiciously ungracious, even rude. This could lead to speculation of an unpleasant nature. Though what could be worse than the truth, Nanon was unprepared to guess. Her father would have counseled, Go forth and meet the enemy. And Joséphine might have added, And while you're about it, Nanon, act as though you enjoy it!

110

The six women sat in a rosewood-paneled cabin so small that, of necessity, they were almost knee to knee. The fragrance of Indian tea rose from the samovar which Oliva had contributed, and Nanon noted that, with the exception of the Polish woman, the others were dressed in garb suitable to shipboard, high-waisted muslins set off by shawls or pelisses in muted colors.

Here, as in her own quarters, the furnishings were built in: the seats, the dresser, the desk, and the storage beneath the bunks. The great difference was that four occupants shared this space — two women, each with a daughter who was slightly younger than Nanon.

Nanon and Oliva, teacups in hand, silently compared quarters, both secretly satisfied with the privacy their own cabins afforded. But for very different reasons. To Oliva it meant that she could continue to have nightly assignations with Devin; while Nanon cherished her solitary cabin, because she thought it would be a buffer against intrusions.

A kind-faced woman spoke in concerned tones as she daintily forked a second slice of lemon into her teacup. "We are missing Madame Farrar and her great-aunt. Is there some difficulty there, does anyone know?"

One of the daughters, a robust girl, tittered. "I hear that the elderly lady suffers from *mal de mer*. The sea is so calm today, I wonder what would happen to her if a squall were to overtake the ship."

Her mother answered in dry tones that indicated to Nanon the two must often be at odds. "You sound as though you relish the thought, Marthe. In that case we should all have to see to each other, which is as it should be — in fair weather or foul."

The girl shrugged sullenly as her mother continued. "And you can thank the Almighty One for your strong constitution, my dear Marthe. During a bad storm, very possibly you will be the only one in an upright position, and thus you'll be able to attend to the rest of us. You can even see to Madame Farrar's great-aunt Flore when she has need of someone to hold her head."

Marthe made a mock-doleful face as her mother continued. "My daughter has a seafarer's ballast inside her, so her doting father says. Unfortunately, that blessing does not translate into respect for the weakness of others."

Marthe's lower lip began to jut petulantly, and Nanon hastily put aside her saucer. Good manners had prevented questions. Though she'd intercepted an occasional inquiring glance at her riding costume, no one had commented directly — yet.

She began to murmur thanks and excuses. "You've made me welcome, and I thank you for that. But I really must return to my cabin." She knew she owed her fellow travelers more of an explanation than this. And then it came to her. In the past, how many times had she noted Joséphine's attentiveness to her daily journals during the holidays at Malmaison. Hastily she concluded. "I must write in my diary . . . everything that happened today, for instance."

The circle of faces turned as one to stare at her, all eyebrows raised. Oliva clapped her hands enthusiastically. "A female journalist in the modern mode, that's it! How clever and close-mouthed you've been."

The Polish woman might well have shouted aloud that Nanon was a spy. The others looked shocked. Marthe's mother recovered first. "Your wit, Madame Russo, is quite madcap. I am sure Mademoiselle de Cavanac merely keeps a girlish diary as young ladies will. Oh!" She looked around. "She's left us. . . ."

Nanon had fled the cabin, then had paused for a moment at the foot of the companionway. Deciding not to ascend to the deck in search of D'Amboise, she pivoted and raced back to her own quarters. There she encountered Claude diligently lining up covered containers outside her door.

112

"Sea water, *mademoiselle*," he explained, blushing painfully.

All of this must be intended for her bath, which accounted for his crimson face. "Then, carry it in, please." Nanon swept in front of him while he placed the containers inside. With an embarrassed glance at her, he brought out a length of cord and secured it from hook to shelf, across the end of her cabin.

Scarlet as a turkey cock, he mumbled, "There's no laundry maid . . . you may need to . . . uh . . ."

Her straight face denied his confusion. She dismissed the boy, sorry that she had no small gift to offer him. Since her pockets were empty, she was truly dependent on that large, masculine presence she so detested.

She locked the door, grateful that a sliding bar had been placed inside it during her absence. Stripping off her skirt and jacket, she stepped out of boots, stockings, drawers, and chemise. It was chilly in the cabin, but after filling a large basin and using a handkerchief and soap to sponge herself from throat to toes, the toning quality of the salt water warmed her. She even doused her cropped curls and then shook them out; whatever the sea water did to her hair couldn't be helped. It was good to be clean all over.

Next, she sat back on naked heels to wash the limp underwear she'd been wearing since she'd left the château. On tiptoe she hung it on the line Claude had set up for her. All was well except that she had nothing to cover her unless she stripped a sheet from the bunk or wound herself in the cashmere shawl.

Realistically, she could no longer ignore the garments in Joséphine's hand trunk. Crossing the blue carpet, Nanon knelt and lifted the unlocked lid. As a faint fragrance of rose petals drifted up to meet her, she breathed in deeply; a swell of tears filling her eyes.

Then, impatient with herself, she shook aside nostalgia for Malmaison and its rose gardens—there was no place for it in her present circumstances. From beneath a layer

113

of frocks, she searched out underclothing as well the pair of slippers that nestled among Joséphine's belongings.

When she pulled a silk chemise over her head, it clung to her breasts far more sensuously than did her own cotton tops. Nevertheless, it was pleasantly cool, like the rippling caress of a silken breeze. She stood and slid one bare leg, then the other, into a pair of embroidered, calf-length drawers which were of the palest pastel shade, but upon looking down at herself, she was chagrined to discover that the lacework at the crotch was provocatively placed. Astonishment gave way to amused resignation. She was fortunate not to have a female cabin mate observe her embarrassment.

Due to the last few days of constant wear, her ankle boots had begun to chafe her heels. She and her godmother were a matching five feet, four inches in height, and though Nanon was slimmer, she knew Joséphine's wardrobe and sandals would fit her well enough. She'd received a dress now and then from Malmaison, but never underclothing! She'd supposed all such intimate wear was as plain and unimaginative as her own.

Earlier, along with the soap, young Claude had brought her paper, pen and ink, mirror, comb, and hairbrush. Now, wrapping a damp handkerchief around the bristles of the brush, she used it to smooth the wrinkles from the velvet material of her bedraggled outer garments.

Claude knocked at the door to ask if he could remove the empty containers. Hastily Nanon tugged on jacket and skirt, and when he entered, she immediately asked, "Have you seen Monsieur D'Amboise?"

The boy nodded. "He's on deck, *mademoiselle.*"

She wrote a note:

It is imperative that our stories agree as to the reason for my being on this ship. I shall meet you on deck before the dining call.

Suddenly she looked up from the paper. How many bells

was that? She couldn't remember.

"Please take this to Monsieur D'Amboise, and when you find him, if there's an answer, come right back here with it. Will you do this for me, Claude?" As she looked in his eyes, she knew she needn't ask. His gaze signified utter devotion. He nodded and sped away.

Once more she removed her jacket and skirt. Placing both on the small center table, she went back to the careful task of brushing the nub of the velvet to try to revive its freshness. While doing this, she began to compose what she'd say to D'Amboise. There had to be a truce between them, otherwise the voyage could turn into a nightmare of festering resentment and anger. Still, she must continue to maintain her own spunk and to be alert to what went on around her.

Though she was finding her immediate surroundings not too impossible to live with, at least for now — and the sky and sea were to her a serene enchantment — she must never, never be lulled into acceptance of the situation. She must keep up her guard at all times. Half-aloud, she muttered the phrases she would use when confronting D'Amboise on deck.

Within minutes there was a sharp, double rap on the door, signaling Claude's return. With a touch of impatience Nanon surveyed her outer garments spread on the table; then she glanced down at her impromptu chemise and drawers. It would only be necessary to open the door a crack. For this reason she reached for the cashmere shawl; as a modest covering it would do.

But through the partly opened door she looked not into a boy's sea green eyes but up, up to a man's broad chest, the linen shirt discreetly buttoned; to a strong column of sun-bronzed throat; to a rugged face with carved cheekbones beneath a flintlike gaze.

Seeing him suddenly in the guise of an unexpected intruder, her prudence vanished. She felt a blaze of anger as though a wild chord strummed through her making her desire to hurt him. *Hurt* because of what he had done to her in depriving her of all she loved. He'd taken freedom, family, home, country—even Dominique—from her. He'd set her on an enormous ocean, which might well chart her life in an unbidden direction.

She raised her fists, locking them together, bare knuckle against bare knuckle. It was as though, thus placed, her two hands held a poignard, its blade ready to pierce and kill . . . and *hurt*.

So graphic was her expression and so fierce her gesture, he reached out and seized her two hands, jerking her hard into the passageway and full against his body.

In their mutual display—hers of fury, his of self-protective astonishment—her shawl slid sideways to disclose a shoulder with skin so pearly lustrous, a curve of breast so silkily outlined, that he could only hold her and admire her with a kind of naïvety that belonged more to raw youth than to a man of his experience.

She contrived the release of one hand and angrily shrugged her shoulder back beneath the cashmere while winding its fringe across her breast.

Now gravely expressionless, he glanced once along the passageway to make certain there'd been no one to observe them; then he pushed open the cabin door, gesturing. "Please . . . let's go inside."

Some of her belligerence dissipated as she flounced ahead of him. "I shall. You stay out!"

His grip tightened; forcing her to look up at him. "I agree. There's been a certain lack of dignity here, Nanon. If you dress yourself properly, I'll meet you on the deck. That's the message I came to deliver."

Her eyes narrowed, hammering at him with tiny sparks. "I'll meet with you, D'Amboise, only because we must discuss what I said in my note. There must be an appropriate reason for my presence on this ship."

"Agreed, my dear—agreed," he soothed. "I'll wait for you by the longboat at the ship's stern." He paused. "Aft or at

116

rear end of the vessel, that is."

She slammed the cabin door on his suddenly ingratiating smile, then spun around and fell back against it, glaring as she recalled his own admission that Joséphine might have relished pushing him overboard.

# Chapter Twelve

By the time Nanon ascended to the main deck to meet with D'Amboise, her mood had softened. With civility they might — they must! — bridge their differences. Furthermore, she was determined to control her reactions, which would not be easy to do.

Candor forced her to admit that even when he provoked her, she was far too conscious of his physical presence. His ease of bearing, the disturbing attentiveness in his gray gaze, that powerful confidence so often tinged with deprecating humor — all these brought forth a simmering response that she didn't quite understand.

Still, the implication of her awareness of him did not entirely elude her. Joséphine had tutored her in the essentials of romantic congress between men and women. Though much had been left unsaid, it was these unvoiced matters of a personal nature that perturbed her. Besides, once they'd kissed. . . .

The last of the sunset faded as she made her way along the deck. Ribbons of crimson, on the horizon, were fast unraveling into the color of ashes. Yet there was still enough light reflected from the silver mirror of the sea for her to observe the sights around her.

The ship was a three master, doubling at the end of the war as cargo vessel and merchantman. Its decks were scrubbed, its masts varnished. Even the intricate web of rigging, with lines, ropes, and cables that stretched to the mast tops, had a discipline of its own. The ship's officers and the seamen she encountered were either neatly uniformed or dressed in seaman's blue. They would nod respectfully as they passed her with sure-footed glides that counterbalanced the swing of the planks. It was all strange to Nanon, but the ship's world seemed secure. By the time she reached the canvas-shrouded longboat, whale-oil lanterns were being lit.

D'Amboise stepped from beneath the longboat's shadow, looming even larger than she'd remembered. He wore a dark jacket, and the wind was blowing his black hair. Her own curls were being ruffled by the breeze, and she hadn't expected this twilight chill. She barely controlled an uneasy shiver. He saw and, without a word, reached out to draw her close to him.

When she resisted the shelter he offered, he growled. "Don't be foolish. I can't have you coming down with some ailment of the lung. There's no one to nurse you, except Claude or myself. You wouldn't like that, and we're much too busy, anyway."

She announced with fervor. "I shall not be sick. I am never sick. And remember this, I do have friends aboard. There's Madame Russo . . . Oliva. And I've met the other ladies. I'm sure if it were necessary, we'd care for each other"—she quoted Marthe's mother—" 'in fair weather or foul.' "

"Is that so?" He gave her a tantalizing, sidelong grin. "You've gotten on friendly terms very quickly, have you?"

She hadn't at all, and they both knew it.

Though she protested, he removed his coat and eased it around her shoulders to shield her from the wind.

"Thank you." Finally, primly, it was said.

"You're welcome." He was studying her intently which, somehow, made her blush. And though it was past twilight now, into dusk, she perceived his smile through the shadows. Obsessively she noted there was an ironic tilt to that sensually chiseled mouth of his, a crease of maturity in each cheek. His white teeth were a quick gleam in the darkness.

*What was the matter with her?*

She was even conscious of the sea-salt and leather scent

119

of him as she tucked her chin against the standing collar of his coat.

Shaking aside her preoccupation with the taut look of his cheekbones, as well as the handsome angle of his brows, she spoke up firmly. "Has the captain been given a reason for my presence on this ship?"

"He questioned me a short while ago, and I explained that you're to be a houseguest of the Pageries who know your father. He's been told that I'm escorting you to their plantation at Trois Îlets—it's little less than an hour from Fort-de-France."

She thought this over, and agreed. "That was adept enough, I suppose. However, you and I know that I'll not impose myself upon that family, even though my god-mother was born a de la Pagerie. I prefer to remain close to the harbor at Fort-de-France." He raised a querying brow, and she concluded. "This will enable me to be ready to board the first ship that will return me to France. There must be a respectable inn which will provide me with lodging."

"Do you realize that you'll require chaperonage, and my distant cousins might find that difficult?"

She interrupted crisply. "M'sieur, if I remain in an inn, someone can be hired and you will be recompensed."

He chuckled. "We won't let a few gold coins come be-tween us."

Her resolution very nearly frayed as she indignantly tossed her head. "We have concluded what we met here to discuss. The lie you've thought up is reasonable enough." She raised her hands to remove his coat from her shoul-ders before stalking off.

He checked her gesture. "We'll debate your living ar-rangements at another time because there's something else I must speak to you about. It concerns Madame Russo."

She shrugged off his touch on her arm. "I am not inter-ested." But she was, and she remained very still to listen. Amber-colored eyes, brilliant with pride beneath the fine bronze of her lashes, held him. She urged him on. "What

120

have you to say?"

He'd already determined this would be difficult. He tried to speak humbly, but also economically. "You'll be doing me a favor—which admittedly I don't deserve—if you will not . . ." He paused. How should he say it! "If you will not accept any courtesies this lady may offer you."

"I don't understand."

"Believe me, a gesture of friendship on her part will not be unselfish."

"How can you possibly judge another's motives? You astound me!"

"It's this way, Nanon—she comes from a very different, a far more sophisticated, milieu than your own. I can't say more than that. It's simply not in your best interest to pursue familiarity, or an exchange of confidences, with Madame Russo, no matter how generous-hearted she may seem to you."

Nanon's temper flared and her lips quivered. "How is it that you dare dictate with whom I shall be friendly? How do you know what my best interest is? You, of all people, who have certainly not contributed to it!"

"Believe me, I do know. I ask you to please keep your distance from . . . the lady I've mentioned. This ship is a closed environment."

"Indeed, it is! And, at least tonight, I shall keep my distance from all of you. I'll not go to the dining salon. I don't choose to share a table with you or with anyone else at the moment. Deceit is not part of my character, and I would be unable to hide my indignation or the reason for it. Wear your mask and be charming to the others, D'Amboise. Only remember, I shall be friends with whom I please. The arena of my life has not been so circumscribed that I can be easily led astray if that's what you're hinting at. After all, *m'sieur,* I am eighteen years of age, nearly nineteen!"

"Yes," he sighed. "It's easy to see how youthful you are. But I can't let you go hungry so I'll send Claude to your cabin with a tray."

He bowed politely to her, then surprised her by departing abruptly, thus leaving her to make her own prideful exit minus a spectator.

Or so she thought.

A figure darted out at her as she hurried across the deck toward the companionway; a voice called out, "My dear!"

She halted. "Madame Russo!"

"Yes, it's I." Oliva came closer and patted Nanon's arm in greeting. Then, casually, she fingered the lapel of the coat still flung across the younger woman's shoulders. "I came to search you out; someone said she saw you on deck. I thought we could sit together while dining. Have you made other plans?" With firm fingers, she tugged at the jacket's lapel.

The darkness hid Nanon's flushed cheeks. "No, I haven't, although it's kind of you to think of me. I've a headache, not at all serious, and I should go directly to my cabin. Perhaps, tomorrow . . .?"

"Hmm, I see. I'm sorry, and I hope you'll soon feel better."

As they entered the companionway, the light of a nearby lantern revealed the lack of expression on the other woman's face. It seemed to Nanon that Oliva's countenance was very beautiful and utterly immobile; how could a face tell so little? How long had she been on deck? What had she seen, heard? And how despicable of D'Amboise to plant suspicion of her friend, Oliva. . . .

Nanon's thoughts were interrupted by Oliva's gracefully swift move that swept the coat from her shoulders. The red-haired woman glanced thoughtfully at the garment, then tucked it over her arm. "Since you're on your way to your own cabin, I'll relieve you of this and see that it's returned to its owner. No, no trouble at all. Monsieur D'Amboise is a very old and dear friend of mine — and of my family's as well. And I believe he knows my new husband, Anton." Her smile was sudden and wide as her face came alive. "I did observe the two of you together just now. Tell me, has he upset you in some way? I seem to

122

sense this has happened."

A distressed Nanon had been very nearly holding her breath due to her dislike of subterfuge. Now she felt a long wave of relief. She hoped that Oliva wouldn't attach any importance to the meeting on the deck. It certainly hadn't been a tête-à-tête, yet she knew she must be careful to preserve the explanation she and D'Amboise had agreed upon.

"I barely know Monsieur D'Amboise. However, he and the Pageries are related to my godmother." At least, that much was the truth, though she was not revealing her godmother's identity.

Next came the fabrication which it was expected Madame Russo would repeat to the other ladies. "I'm to be the Pageries' houseguest . . . well, we shall see." Her voice trailed off, she then finished strongly. "There is no quarrel between Monsieur D'Amboise and myself." An outright lie this time! "As I have said, our acquaintanceship is slight. He lent me his coat against the wind, and it's most kind of you to see that it's returned. Until tomorrow, then . . ." And Nanon quickly ran down the stairs.

Oliva did not remain as calm as she appeared. Instead, she clutched D'Amboise's jacket to her breast, stood for a moment, and then held it aside to look at it as though weighing its significance. While standing in the shadows earlier, she had watched the two near the longboat, but had heard nothing of what was said.

And then — *enfin*, she mused — he had gone by her hiding place with so rapid a stride that she'd been unable to catch the expression on his face. But she knew him well enough to guess, seeing the angle of his head and the carriage of his shoulders, that he was close to laughter for some reason. Which, to her, did not bode well. Humor in a man like D'Amboise was . . . serious. No, "dangerous" was the better word. It could mean he was interested in that girl.

Truly, she would have liked to hurl his coat to the deck and slash her heels across it. Memory taunted her, reminding her of a time when a young captain had placed his cloak around *her* shoulders to protect her from a cold wind sweeping over a battlement on the castle at Pulawy.

How well she remembered that protective gesture, and what sensual entertainment it had led to. D'Amboise's eyes brooding into hers with silver fire while his strong fingers had curled inside her décolletage to lower it, his palms holding her breasts while, taut and excited, they seemed to thrust into his eager hands. His dark head had bowed, and his tongue had flicked the peaks of her nipples until she'd cried out. Together, within that cloak of his, they'd slid to the stone flooring, not feeling the cold, forgetting the guests in the ballroom below, forgetting everything except themselves and their passionate pleasures.

It was the first time they'd been together. His hand had moved beneath the furred hem of her skirt, had clasped her ankle, moved to span her calf, to round her knee, to explore with his fingertips' sensitive touch her inner thighs, and to find at last the curling hair that guarded her entry. Gasping aloud, *she'd begged him* — and his searching fingers had complied.

As she recalled those long-ago memories, Oliva's breath hissed out, and aware of the shudderings of desire, she sped down the stairs of the companionway. She would not permit herself to be distracted by the ship's bells summoning the diners. She must find Devin at once . . . to return his jacket to him, of course.

It was Captain Levreux who stopped her headlong passage. His experienced eye had marked the new Madame Anton Russo as less than bridal though exquisitely appealing. What was she up to, with her husband waiting for her on Martinique, rushing in to the passageway opposite her own, and with a man's coat hugged to her breast?

"Madame, allow me to relieve you of your burden."

They faced each other, a long, clear-eyed comprehension flashing between them. Madame Russo handed over the coat, then drew back her shoulders with stately dignity "How kind of you, Captain Levreux." Fastidiously she explained. "Mademoiselle de Cavanac and I were walkin the windy deck just now. M'sieur D'Amboise gallantly loaned his coat to the young lady, and she asked that it be returned to him."

"It shall be attended to, madame."

He bowed. She nodded regally and swept by him, this time in the direction of her own quarters. He looked after her, having noticed for the first time that her usually bell-like voice was husky and her accent less than impeccable. After all, he mused, she is not a Frenchwoman, merely a Polish aristocrat who married into Martinique society.

# Chapter Thirteen

On the main deck, he was watching Nanon from a distance. It was colder this morning, and he could see that she'd pulled a shawl around her shoulders, its length reaching to the hem of her riding coat. When he'd knocked at her cabin the night before, and she'd opened the door on a feeble crack, the fringe on this same shawl had outlined the enticing swell of breasts beneath that silken bit of underwear she'd had on. Which made him wonder. Had she relented and rifled Joséphine's trunk?

He groaned, damning himself for the teasing tenor of his thoughts. This was a young woman to be approached with dignity, not with a lustful itch. He was too old for that sort of thing; and to win her confidence and her friendship, great care was needed. Particularly so since he seemed to have done everything wrong since he'd met her.

As she looked out over the water, her profile was contemplative. But almost as soon as he'd determined he'd remain in the background and not intrude, he found himself striding in her direction.

He slid his hands along the rail next to hers. "Good morning . . ."

She looked up in surprise, sun-bright curls tumbling about her forehead. With the back of her hand, she whipped them aside. "Oh, it's you! Good morning." Catching the rail once more, she steadied herself.

It seemed to him that beneath those burnished wisps of

hair her eyes were full of sea light and great good humor, and he also detected a marvelous dimple deepening in the curve of her cheek. She's happy today, he thought, pleased. What a healthy, lithe creature she is — open and free of artifice. Life would be glorious in every way if they could be friends . . . *more* than friends, that nagging sensualist inside him urged.

She nodded amiably in the direction of the jacket he wore. "I see Madame Russo returned your garment to you as she promised."

He sent her a startled look. "One of the seamen brought it to my quarters last night. Why did you think she would . . . ?" He paused, his expression troubled. "You met her after you left the deck?"

She shook her head. "She was *on* deck and saw us together." Her tone softened. "You seem distressed, D'Amboise. She heard nothing of what you and I said to each other. And I was able to tell her that fable you contrived. She'll be sure to repeat it to the other ladies. I've been cautious in what I've said, and I've kept more or less to myself. Isn't that what you advised? Or is it Oliva Russo that I'm to avoid?"

His shoulder moved closer to hers. "You're being cooperative — I like that."

"I'm so glad you do!" she shot back; then, with a jot of acerbity, she declared, "D'Amboise, I'm discovering that some questions asked of you are never answered."

His gaze held hers. "Possibly my greatest fault."

"Oh, I can think of others." To rescue herself from the unexpectedly voluptuous sensation staring into his amused eyes induced, she hastened on. "Marthe's mother, Madame Lecourlaix, has invited me to visit her husband's plantation. I shan't accept." Nervously she pulled her gaze from his. "Though it might be instructive to learn something of plantation life — who knows? — as soon as we reach Martinique I may be able to board a ship returning to

127

France."

Facing her, Devin casually leaned back against the rail. "It won't be a ship quite like this one." Wanting to keep her with him, he continued. "Have you noticed its heavy deck and reinforced hull? No, I suppose you haven't, no reason to. But you do see the discipline of its men. These are the real core of the crew, not the few malingerers who were left off at Brest."

They both turned to watch the men at work. At first light, the hammocks had been stored away and the decks washed down. Now the crews labored furiously as, at a shouted command, they began to take in sail with a great fuss and noise.

Above them, Nanon could hear an eerie skirl high in the masts. There was the clatter of chains and the hiss of what seemed like fathoms of rope uncoiling. Her glance questioned him. "The wind does seem brisk this morning. I know nothing of ships and the sea but . . . yes, as I look around, it all seems solid and safe and the men appear to be well trained."

He nodded. "We're aboard a former man-of-war; it's the first to be refurbished to accommodate passengers as well as cargo. But keep in mind, Nanon, that not all ships are like this one. The West Indian merchantmen are less dependable. Their sailing schedules from Fort-de-France will be dictated by the wind alone. For this reason we'll be lucky if we find immediate passage for you. To pass the time before a sailing can be arranged, you might consider accepting a few invitations like Madame Lecourlaix's."

She studied him, wondering if he was trying to impress upon her the necessity of staying at the de la Pageries', which she had refused to do. But by now she was less intent on his words than on the proximity of his shoulder to her own.

His cleanly shaven face with its strong features seemed austere in the early morning light. But when she peeked

128

again, the careless length of his black hair and the enfolding warmth of his smile belied this first impression. Recalling the little she knew of his history, she supposed she shouldn't be surprised by any contradictions she saw in him.

She allowed herself a more personal scrutiny of him, indulging in quick, sidelong glances. Beneath his jacket, the thickly woven white shirt — this morning modestly closed — strained across his powerful chest. He was wearing dark trousers, their bottoms tucked into half-boots of Spanish leather, while his mid-torso was cinched by a studded belt with a heavy silver buckle.

He caught her watching him, and as she hastily looked away, she knew that his darkening gaze reminded her of the gray-green depths of the Cavanac forest. But there was a prowler there, barely concealed, taunting her with the memory of certain dangerous feelings she'd known that night in the old château. . . .

Confused by this thought, she glanced down at his hands. "Your knife wound . . . how is it?"

Disarmingly, he held out his palm. "Very nearly healed as you can see. But what's this?" He took her fingers in his and lightly traced her knuckles, discovering the few scratches that still remained.

Without thinking she replied. "Oh, those came from the branches of the yew at Malmaison."

He didn't try to hide his humor. "You fought your way through that terrible hedge to rescue Joséphine — and then she ran off and left you by yourself in her coach."

"That's unfair," Nanon blurted out. "It wasn't quite that way." Dismayed, she looked out over the water that was beginning to billow and froth with whitecaps.

Gently he touched her cheek. "If I misspoke just now, forgive me. We must be friends."

"Why must we?" she answered snappishly, staring across the railing. Surely the sea was in as roiling and restless a

129

state as she was.

His broad shoulder interfered with the view. He'd moved almost intimately close as though shielding her from the wind. "Let me say it this way, I would like to be friends with you. Look at me, Nanon. Together we're set on a course that can't be altered. At least, not at present. Could we make the best of it?"

"*You* make the best of it!" She knew it was a testy answer, but she felt she must put distance between them since his closeness was so exquisitely disorienting. Sweet sword of vengeance defend her! She looked toward the far horizon, trying to avoid the wedge of his shoulder. But scudding clouds were now appearing, and the sea had turned metallic in color. The wind was even colder. Still, and what an absurd admission it was under the circumstances, his presence did make her feel warm inside. And she was overwhelmed by a sudden desire to trust him. She'd never before known such ambivalent feelings, such lacings of pleasurable uneasiness, such melting within.

Thinking this, her eyes blazed up into his. "Very well, D'Amboise—we shall be friends and civil to one another. You guard your tongue, I'll guard mine."

"Agreed." With abrupt warmth his fingers closed over hers, and then entwined with them.

She looked down at their joined hands, and a smile twitched at her lips. "It's only common sense to declare a truce, but do we need to seal it quite so fervently?" Deftly she released her fingers from his. "I accept your offer of friendship."

His eyes kindled with silver fire far back in their depths, and for a passing moment she felt uneasy. But his next words were simple enough. "You won't regret our bond."

She nodded pensively. The touch of his hand had been as besieging to her as a caress, it still lingered across her skin with a sweet tingle. She hoped he'd never guess how his virility affected her. It was neither seemly nor maid-enly to yearn like this. Why, just now when he'd thrown back his head in laughter, she'd wanted to trace the strong line of his throat with the tips of her fingers. And worse! Shocked at her own immodesty, she knew she would like to have followed her fingertips' path with the heat of her open lips. . . .

Joséphine had once instructed her that ardent feelings for another could strike one at first sight. It was not unusual. She'd called it *le sport*—a playful and carnal lust-ing, and had said one should not be ashamed of this very human response.

Nanon could still hear that lilting voice: *Ah, but for the grandeur of true love, my child, one must wait. Love, like a golden storm with the sun's rays hidden behind it, moves slowly. This golden turmoil, enfolding one in its own good time, this alone is the reality of love.*

A great pang of sadness caught Nanon. She missed Joséphine and her impetuous little lecturings; missed the strong and constant affection of her father; the comforts of her old home, its gardens, her own room. In recalling her godmother's words, candor had forced her to admit that somehow she'd lost the protection of an earlier inno-cence. And she seemed to have lost the safeguard of the once-fierce anger she'd directed at Devin D'Amboise.

To be vulnerable in this way was dangerous, and now, understanding her feelings, she wondered what might have happened that night in the château when he'd lifted her high in his arms for that sweetly assaulting kiss. That is, if Théo had not come upon them. Reminded of her last confrontation with her brother in the loft, Nanon shuddered.

Tentatively she accepted the hand D'Amboise held out to her. He was saying, "We'll go below and have an early meal to start the day properly." He chuckled. "Or do you think this might give our island ladies something to cluck

131

about?"

She smiled back at him carefully; she did trust him on the score of her reputation—if only because of his own position in all of this. Amused, she reflected that it was apparent she'd learned to be a bit cynical.

Meanwhile, he was thinking that she appeared radiant though somewhat thoughtful. What courage she'd displayed in this damnable situation for which he was responsible. Now, in the rising wind, he sheltered her, his arm about her shoulders. "I'll win everything back for you, Nanon. Everything that you've lost through my doing. Your home, your father, your freedom. And that mare of yours, too. I promise, you'll see them all again."

Braced against the elements now beginning to pull furiously at them, she raised her face to his but remained silent. For above the line of his shoulder she could see long swatches of sodden clouds swallowing the sun while the ocean's surface seemed to be rumpling into great heaving swells. The wind's talons raked at them while the stout deck jarred beneath their feet with each sudden slap of angry waves against the ship's hull.

Losing balance, they staggered, but he quickly caught her and held her closer still. Nanon was shocked to discover she was aware of far more than the nap of his coat against her cheek and his strong arm surrounding her. There was much more . . . the hard-muscled length of his body pressing thrillingly against her own; his legs were straddled and the secret bulge of his manhood, at their juncture, was prodding her upper thigh. All at once she was wild with longing to embrace him as he embraced her against the raucous shout of the wind.

Her face scarlet, she looked up at him, but he was scowling at the morning's fast-retreating light as he growled. "There's heavy weather approaching, and this wind's not going to drop or change its course."

Abruptly, he swung them both about, and leading

Nanon across the deck to the companionway, he thrust her inside its shelter. "You go below. It will be all right, Captain Levreux's been alerted there's a storm on the way. It's arrived a little sooner than we expected, but the crew's prepared. They know what to do." He nodded encouragingly, though already his thoughts were with the men on the deck.

"Yes, it will be all right, I know . . . I am sure."

Looking down at her, he saw that her eyes were dusky-soft and unafraid, which made him want to lean down to that enticing mouth of hers—full-rounded and quivering, as deep a red as the heart of a rose. Later, he thought, later . . . and instead he touched the tip of her nose with his lips, gave a humorous tweak to one of those wildly blowing curls of hers, and then left her.

She looked after him, her heart careening at the exciting—perilous?—passion that she had glimpsed.


Swaying with the roll of the ship, Nanon entered her cabin, its timbers groaning and the floorboards swooping beneath her feet. Because of the cold morning she'd worn the stableboy's trousers under her riding skirts; now, she took them off, folded them and hid them away. The cabin boy, Claude, had been there for a canister of sea water stood near the door as did a small tray containing a pot of lukewarm tea, an orange, and a half-loaf of hard sour bread. It seemed like slim nourishment to her, but she appreciated his thoughtfulness. He must have assumed she was suffering from the pangs of seasickness as were some of the others. She sliced the orange with a pearl-handled knife and tore apart the bread to discover its center was soft and delicious.

Would anyone see her if she stole to the top of the companionway to observe what was going on? she wondered. Though she was aware of sailors' superstitions about women aboard ship—especially when there was danger— she decided to chance it. Besides, she would see D'Amboise again. . . .

# Chapter Fourteen

As she moved along the passageway near the place where the lantern was swinging, a cabin door opened and a tall figure stepped out, an unfamiliar tarpaulin jacket slung over his shoulders. With the heavy canvas collar turned up, he was in shadow. She hesitated. "Devin . . . ?"

"*Devin* . . . ?" he mocked, flattening back the high collar and looking down at her. "That sounds much friendlier."

Her eyes mischievous beneath the fine fan of her lashes, she agreed. "I recall the terms of our contract, so I'm striving for a certain amiability, *monsieur.*"

Standing tall above her, he breathed his next words. "This conversation has great promise it seems, but unfortunately I must resist. I have to be on deck." His gaze glittered. "And where are *you* bound, Nanon?"

She answered truthfully. "To view the storm from some vantage where no one can see me. You see, Father will be keenly interested when I tell him of this experience — I want to be able to describe everything to him."

He froze in astonished silence, wondering if he'd heard her right. Concluding that he had, he responded harshly. "A storm at sea is not to be viewed as a performance. It can demand unholy sacrifice — the lives of good men. Is this dramatic enough for you, Nanon? Sailor's lore tells of a terrible, mythical presence lurking in the deep, carrying a tolling bell above its heart. Sometimes it seems this fantasy might be half-true. The creature's demon waves have

135

been known to sweep the men in a watch overboard, to be lost forever. And in the wind's roar those who are left say they hear the bell. . . . I'm not predicting such an event will happen, but I am saying a high sea like today's is not to be watched as a performance."

She flushed at his reprimand, her eyes brilliant with hurt. His next words were spoken in a more conciliatory tone. "Did I speak too hastily? Perhaps so, because I can't look out for you up there. We'll be running ahead of the wind; and all hands are needed—even mine, though I'm far less a sailor than the others. Until this is over, you must stay below. I doubt there'll be difficulty in persuading the other passengers to do the same."

"But I didn't mean . . ." She halted, distressed.

He sighed. "I was impatient, and I know it's no excuse to say that I am uneasy." He shrugged off the heavy jacket and let it drop. "I'll walk you back to your cabin—will you please stay there?"

To reassure her, he lifted a hand as though to caress her cheek. But at the same moment, she turned her head aside and, by chance, her warm, full lips brushed into the palm of his upraised hand, her moist tongue tip crushing into his scarred and sensitive palm.

He stood there, shocked at the intimacy of that touch, and at the hot demand it sent racing through him. Such a small thing to happen, nothing really . . . no, *everything!* Her open lips against his palm undid reason and control and released the desire that was in his heart. . . .

Bewildered at his expression of wonderment and surprise, Nanon stepped backward a pace, but, gripping her shoulder hard, he dragged her close to him, his free hand twisting sensuously through the russet waves of her hair, forcing her head back until his gaze scorched deep into hers.

She heard his voice, husky with emotion. "No danger from the sea will touch you, I promise."

To her his face seemed a shadowed blur in the half-light, and she was so overwhelmed by a surge of desire, a sensation unknown to her, that she began to tremble like an aspen leaf, her very bones shaking. His face slowly descended toward hers, and with a small moan she raised her face and surrendered her lips to his, clinging to them and tasting the sweet questing with a fear that it could not last.

She was right, for almost immediately he wrenched away from her, cursing softly for there was no time to accept the feast her mouth offered him. With reluctance his hands fell away from her shoulders. As she stared, shaken, he left her to stride down the passageway, a tall, lurching, angry figure, who'd grabbed his tarpaulin coat from where it had fallen. He halted at the foot of the companionway ladder and then, tantalized by the fire of her unexpected response to him, slowly turned around.

Along the corridor's distance their gazes met and fused, locked together by the sensual force of the current that flowed between them. She couldn't move beneath the heat lightning of those silvery eyes as he slowly returned to confront her. Her astounded heart throbbed with a chaotic mingling of alarm and suddenly unleashed desire.

She wanted to flee, she wanted to stay; she knew she was hopelessly beguiled by him, and had been since that first night at the old château. As truly as she was her father's daughter, it was destined that Devin D'Amboise should become her life, that he should reach out from wherever his journeys took him, to whatever destination, to draw her to him.

So now, without resistance, she went into his arms, lured by the powerful emotion she saw etched in his face. She was awed by the expression in his eyes—he wanted her; by the fine cut of his lips—they craved hers; and awed by the tensed hardness of his body against her own. Even the heavy belt buckle that pressed beneath her breasts with a curiously desirable hurt was a breath-stealing excitement;

its cruel metal seemed as much a part of him as his lean, virile strength and the assurance of the strong hands that molded the narrow velvet of her waist.

A silver flame burned in his eyes as they searched hers. "I had no way of knowing that the danger to you I spoke of might be myself, and not the sea."

"Devin . . . I could never fear you."

With the faintest of smiles revealing a trace of self-mockery, he sighed her name while above the thudding of her heart, she was aware of his fingers holding her, spanning her waist, moving to encircle her. She held her breath as they stroked upward to pause for a tender beat above the wincing curves of her breasts. She could not keep back her startled gasp as his palms lightly traced their outlines beneath her velvet lapels sending quivers of hot sensation trembling through her.

He leaned against the corridor's wall, slanting her body up against his and lowering his head, his lips parting hers. She flinched only for a moment as he searched with a deliciously plundering tongue that probed and tantalized, curling into the secret recesses of her mouth. Then her response answered his intimate caress. And though she could barely breathe, instinctively she followed his intoxicating lead, her own tongue swirling across his, teasing with its pointed tip, then withdrawing to rim inside his lips; and she interspersed tiny bites and moist little lickings.

Their mouths clinging, his fingers brushed beneath her coat and thin shirt to glide across her naked breasts, sending a primitive message deep into her inmost core. Her thighs trembled against his, and she muffled a cry while his hand lingered, traced delicate circles around her tightening nipples. Then almost savagely he released her, immediately glancing along the passageway. He was not concerned that a straying passerby might see them; but now more than ever, he was aware of the groaning of the

138

ship's timbers and the swell of the sea.

Pulling the lapels of her jacket together, he kissed her throat, the magic warmth beneath her chin, the ravishing contour of her temples. . . .

Nanon's mind was whirling with excitement, but for one sober instant she was able to think clearly—and it was a sweet and imperishable thought. How warm and fragile and incredible it was to share such tender intimacy with someone . . . *with Devin*. She knew unbelievable joy. Why, he was her love for now and forever!

"I have to leave you now." Her lips and her intelligent eyes continued to tempt him, but with a wry whisper he promised, "No ship with you aboard shall be permitted to go down to the bottom of the sea, Antoinette de Cavanac!"

She didn't answer him. She couldn't. Love had muted her. Herald of happiness, she thought, *I love*.

At the end of the passageway, again disguised by the tarpaulin, he did not look back. Bemused by fantasy— folly?—as a youth might have done, he again pronounced her name to himself, but this time he said Antoinette D'Amboise. Yes, he liked its sound, and she was what he wanted—but here lay the peril.

There were those dangerous second thoughts. . . .

He'd lived too many years, she too few. She was virginal. And since she was without experience, didn't she deserve better than a man like himself, twice her age, hammered into his own ways, scarred by battle and killing, scarred by diplomacy's secrets? And, yes, something else— he could be passion-spent.

He grasped the companion ladder and leaped up three rungs at a time, all the while debating whether to turn his personal hourglass upside down to consider its other side. If he did so, what would he find? He was almost sure that he could love her deeply . . . and he had a fortune to offer her. But if that were all that was in his favor, was it enough? He didn't think so. He stepped out on deck, and

139

as he took the brunt of the first wave that swept across it, he concluded that he would fulfill his vow to return her to France, to her father's house, and then they would see. Perhaps the whimsical stars that guided his Fate might have one more measure of good fortune in store for him.

Gripping the sides of her bunk, Nanon stared up at the cabin ceiling, which appeared to rise and then descend upon her as the ship rode the troughs of the waves. She pulled herself to a sitting position, perspiration plucking at her body, sweat misting her forehead. Waterspouts of Hades . . . this cabin of hers was hot as the torments of hell. If water from the sea should seep under the door, the floor itself would sizzle.

Dangerous or not, she decided to pry open the porthole to let in cool air. But first she had to get out of her clothing. Tugging at its velvet collar, she pulled the jacket from her shoulders. Surprised by an unexpected weakness in making this effort, she paused to catch her breath, then patiently withdrew one arm at a time from the confines of the long, tight sleeves.

Dizzy, swaying, hobbled by the dragging skirts of her riding habit, she managed to stand. But suddenly her eyes glazed and her stomach seemed to rise inside her to send a gush of bile to her throat.

Great saints! So this was how it felt to be nastily, horribly sickened by the motion of the heaving sea. Clutching her queasy middle, she attempted to brace herself against the table. Then, with a groan she sank to her knees; her chin almost level with the carpeting, she scrabbled weakly for the retching pail left somewhere alongside the bunk.

There followed misery such as, in her days of wondrous health, she'd never imagined possible. She seemed to slide giddily from gray consciousness into a black doom. With an effort more of will than of physical empowerment, she finally reached for the table top and pulled herself upright, only to stagger forward and fall into her bunk.

She knew vaguely that something wonderful had happened to her awhile ago in the passageway, but what it was now seemed swept away. . . . So, waking, sleeping, she was only thankful for her solitary cabin. But eventually the time came — was it hours or days later? — when she sensed a wet cloth being passed across her face, along her throat, beneath her arms, and down her chest. As she nuzzled gratefully into the sensations of cool water, clean linen, and distant words of comfort, she wondered if she'd reached some unearthly plateau. . . .

Someone had restored order to the cabin; someone had propped up her limp body and changed the stinking sheets. When she was finally able to open her eyes and murmur her thanks, it was Claude's face that swam, through pale green light, into focus.

"Mademoiselle Nanon! You are yourself again!"

She groaned. "If you assure me it's so, perhaps I am." She turned to face the wall. "If this ship had gone down, and myself with it, I shouldn't have cared at all. I ache, I'm weak — and did you look out for me all this time? Thank you, Claude. . . ." Her voice faded. She hoped he'd go away for a little while and let her grope her way back to some resemblance to the living. But when she turned back and raised up on her elbow, he was still there. "Tell me, how did the ship fare? And how are the others — the ladies and the crew?" Her voice had become stronger. There was someone else she wanted to ask about, but Devin seemed so far and distant from her in her present state that she couldn't voice his name.

"This ship is stout, no fear. And the ladies . . . well, as you have done, they've remained in their quarters."

She tried a smile. "Alive, I presume?"

141

He nodded solemnly. "Oh, yes indeed. It was a heavy storm, but we've been out of it for close to three days now."

"Three . . . days?" Feebly Nanon sat up and looked around her, again wondering at the neatness of the cabin. She was aware that the surrounding air, though dank, was balmier than it had been before the storm broke. She looked down at the white sheet, at the daintily embroidered shift that covered her body. With curious fingers, she touched its sheer lawn fabric and asked, "Where is my own clothing?"

"He did his best to furbish it for you." She followed the direction of Claude's embarrassed gaze. The all-too-familiar, bottle green riding habit hung from the cord strung across the end of the cabin. It was in desperate condition, she could see that — the velvet shapeless, its nap ruined by the application of water and strong soap. She sniffed, realizing that the wretched garment must also be the source of that clammy odor.

"You said . . . *he?*" she questioned, her heart sinking.

"Monsieur D'Amboise had to open the trunk there to find clothing for you to wear. I'm sorry, *mademoiselle,* that it was necessary to call upon him when he was so busy. But I couldn't lift you by myself and change the bedding at the same time."

After a distraught moment, Nanon managed to get out, "I . . . see."

"When the winds calmed he was no longer needed on deck, so he came below to assist those in need. The ship's doctor left us at Brest to join one of the ships that was still fighting at the time. Monsieur made a sling for Michaud, the carpenter, who has a broken leg, and he taught me how to change the wrappings on the wounds of a sailor who was pierced by a falling spar." With downcast eyes, Claude concluded. "Five men were carried overboard; nothing could be done to save them."

Nanon's pallor intensified, and she uttered a soft cry as

tears filled her eyes. Claude was quickly at her side. "I'll fetch you a tray at once, with food and drink. You must regain your strength."

She shook her head. "I'm grateful for your concern, but I couldn't possibly swallow anything, Claude. Those men . . ." She wiped at her eyes with a corner of the sheet.

Claude continued to stand nearby, and she was touched by what she presumed to be his devotion to her. "There must be others who have greater need for your attention right now. Give me a little time, Claude, and I'll walk to the dining saloon myself, I promise."

She glanced at the trunk, hoping there would be a dress suitable for her to wear.

"I must take care of you as Monsieur D'Amboise did. He charged me with this." The boy's smile was shy. "I should like when I am older to be like him, even though my station in life will never permit it. He's strong and important and rich, but very kind."

Then she was not the object of Claude's dedication. Hero worship, that's it, she thought—and it was inevitable that an unsophisticated lad should feel thus. Though he was well spoken, and had been educated by a former patron, it was possible that in Claude's humble experience, those who were important and rich had seldom been kind and generous.

Claude continued to look expectantly at her, so it was inevitable that she ask the next question. "What did you mean—that you must care for me in the same manner as Monsieur D'Amboise?"

His eyelids fluttered disconcertingly as he looked away from her. Devils and archangels! She could guess his answer. A flood of scarlet flamed her cheeks.

"Now that you're able to bathe yourself, Mademoiselle Nanon, I'll bring in a hip bath and the sea water. . . ."

"That's enough!" She almost strangled on the phrase. "And you're quite correct; I must regain my strength immediately. I can lie abed no longer. When you fetch the dinner tray, I suggest you do make it fairly substantial, though I don't know how I can stomach food." She shuddered at the thought of eating, and Claude dipped his head at her and rushed away.

After he departed, Nanon merely sat, rigid and ashamed. Those gentle swipes of the cloth around her feverish breasts—now, she remembered it all!—and across her belly, and the cleansing attention to the intimacy of her sweating thighs. . . .

Undoubtedly, young Marthe Lecourlaix had been engaged in ministering to the females in the opposite passageway. Nanon was alone in the cabin intended for Joséphine, and for this reason was sharing a separate corridor with . . . him. It was only to be expected that he'd be the one to whom the cabin boy turned when help was needed in tending her.

The intense physical malaise she'd just been through seemed somehow to have altered her memory and to have subdued the magic of the passionate kiss they'd shared. She didn't think she could face him again. How many days would it be before they reached Martinique? How many times would she have to pass the swinging lantern outside his quarters to reach the companionway?

It had been wrong of her to act as she had, to lose her head that way; wrong of her to respond to the attractions of a man who'd so callously planned to kidnap the Empress and bring her to this far-off place. How could she have forgotten—forgiven?—this scoundrelly behavior of his? Where was her loyalty to her godmother—and to France? Sadly misplaced, no doubt about that.

She continued to brood. She'd behaved in an unruly fashion. It was as though she'd drunk enough tumblers of Théo's brandy to intoxicate her brain. As for her heart, how could she have believed for a single instant that she loved Devin D'Amboise?

How not? a small voice inside her countered.

But she disregarded that, pulled herself from the bunk, and walked carefully to Joséphine's hand trunk. Her body felt better, stronger . . . but she feared that her heart remained unhappy and insecure, a circumstance that she must do her best to overcome.

# Chapter Fifteen

Life on shipboard resumed its pace, the ladies praising the ship's officers and crew as well as praising D'Amboise for his skilled care of the injured. Nanon began to suspect the tributes to him were due more to his rugged and charming self than to his having stood in for the ship's doctor.

She continued to observe him, but only from a distance; there were no further passageway encounters. And he was never on deck when the ladies did their exercise turns, wearing broad-brimmed straw hats to protect their European complexions. She learned from Claude—but with no explanation as to why—that D'Amboise had been taking his meals in the galley annex with the ship's officers.

It occurred to her that he could be saving her from embarrassment. Or perhaps . . . himself? He, too, might have had second thoughts following the interlude in the passageway. She certainly had.

But she must be practical; they could no longer avoid each other. In less than two days' time the ship would reach Martinique, and since she was without funds, arrangements would have to be made for her to stay in some inn. She detested this reliance on D'Amboise. Now she'd have to accost the man, whereas she'd certainly expected it would be the other way around!

The night was moonless and she slipped away from the chatty companionship of Madame Lecourlaix and the other women to make her way to the upper deck. Hoping—planning?—for a chance meeting, she stopped beneath the shadow of the longboat station where they'd rendezvoused once before.

It was agreeable to be by herself, to breathe in the evening air and enjoy this respite from the day's fiery heat. She'd solved the problem of modesty by simultaneously wearing two of Joséphine's transparent frocks, one over the other. Even so, their style and diaphanous material outlined breast and limb—but not too outrageously. Oliva had sent Nanon inquisitive glances, yet had managed to check the questions that hovered on the tip of her tongue.

Tonight Nanon had on a white batiste, its revealing filminess disguised by an overfrock in the softest shade of mint. A silk fichu of the same pale green shade filled in the deeply scooped neckline which otherwise would have bared her high breasts.

With a deliberateness that she preferred not to admit, she's chosen the fetching hue. She knew that it complemented the rich bronze of the curls she'd threaded through with a narrow, matching ribbon borrowed from Amalie Farrar.

Her hair had grown in the weeks just past. In this humid atmosphere it continued to curl audaciously, skimming her shoulders and lending a sensuous, titillating aspect to her appearance, as though she'd just raised her head from a pillow. Her eyes were brilliant as she peered through the night. If he hadn't been so circumspect in avoiding her, this nocturnal ploy of hers wouldn't have been necessary.

At least in the darkness if her cheeks burned on confronting him, he couldn't observe this and she wouldn't be humiliated. She looked up at the stars, dimly seen through the rising mist. But then a movement along the deck alerted her. Among the shorter figures of the seamen on scattered watch was a tall form, walking in her direction.

She was astonished to discover that anticipation was sending her heart into beating a drummer's tattoo against her rib cage. Here he was! Walking so purposefully, covering the deck so fast, that in another second or so he'd pass by without seeing her.

"Devin . . . Devin D'Amboise," she sputtered. His name seemed to choke her, its sound almost flying away on the blowing breeze. Oh, dear God, she hoped now that he *wouldn't* hear her.

But he did, and halted. "Who is there?"

Had she abandoned all dignity, all pride? He was intelligent, he would guess this wasn't an inadvertent meeting. She pulled herself together, gulped in a deep breath, and stepped out from beneath the longboat's black shadow. "It's I, Antoinette." She rushed on, a trifle shakily. "It's necessary that we talk. . . ."

Even in the dark she saw that his look of surprise was instantly erased as he reached for her arm, patted it, and firmly slipped it through his. As though this were merely some social duet, he eased the situation by remarking, "Let's stroll awhile, Nanon, shall we? It's very pleasant on deck tonight." He inclined his head toward hers and spoke softly. "I agree we do have some talking to do."

She stumbled self-consciously and both of them reached down at the same moment to untangle the hem of her skirt. Their fingers touched, their heads collided, and hastily each reared back from the other.

"Pardon. . . ."

"Forgive me. . . ."

For a beat, she couldn't recall the words she'd rehearsed.

He took control of the awkward silence. "The other night I must have offended you deeply, Nanon. I'm sure you know which particular actions of mine I refer to. I overstepped certain bounds by forcing my attentions upon

148

you while you are temporarily placed in a dependent situation. Under the circumstances, you couldn't possibly welcome my advances." He concluded dryly. "Perhaps you would under no circumstances. I apologize. I want you to know I have concern for your feelings and I also feel a great responsibility for your welfare. This last week I've been preparing to tell you this."

This speech gave her an opportunity to recover her poise. If it hadn't been so dark, he might have detected the snap of humor in her eyes. "Really, D'Amboise, you've said everything there is to say. You said it well, and I understand."

As they now paused near the ship's rail, she continued. "I haven't thanked you for assisting Claude with my care during the storm. I certainly didn't anticipate what seasickness could do to a person." A blush threatened, and she was grateful for the night.

"I did what I could," he murmured. "And I'm sorry about ruining your riding outfit. However, I see you've found other attractive clothing." He refrained from reminding her of his earlier warning that in this heat Joséphine's sheer frocks would be welcome.

She looked directly at him. "We can't continue to avoid each other since we're nearing Fort-de-France and we must arrive with some plan for my shelter there."

"You still refuse to stay with the de la Pageries?" She nodded, and he sighed. "Very well, Nanon. I see you're being more sensible about all this than I was. I should have brought up the matter of finding you an inn sooner, and not made it necessary for you to waylay me on deck."

She wondered if she'd heard him right. "D'Amboise, need you emphasize that I had to ambush you? Particularly so, since this ambush was necessitated by your cowardly avoidance of me."

In his turn, he was stung and roared. "Damnit, woman! I've just done my best to explain to you in detail

149

why I thought it wise —" He stopped abruptly, then urged in a quieter tone. "I'm at fault. Nanon, let's remember our agreement to be civil to each other. And we do have some basis for a closer degree of friendship."

Was he being sly, reminding her of what had occurred between them in the corridor and in her cabin? Ah well, it was over, so none of it mattered. Neither her humiliation at his having tended and sponged her feverish body, nor her anxiety at having shared those kisses in the passageway.

What was saddening, and what gave her a feeling of desperate melancholy, was that for a brief time she'd really believed that he was her love. . . .

"Good night, D'Amboise, I'm going below now. No need to accompany me — certainly not. We've made our peace with each other; it's all that's necessary."

She pivoted briskly and disappeared almost immediately into the long dark of the deck, leaving him standing there to sort out the contradiction between what his heart whispered — that he wanted to love her and be with her — and the stern advice of conscience — that he was an unlikely suitor, in age, background, and experience.

Out of the pitch black, a voice spoke at his side. "Devin, you and that girl . . . it's absurd. She's a child. Why do you bother?"

He whirled around. "Oliva! Christ! When you sneak up on a man it's enough to send him over the side! How long have you been hanging about?"

"What an inelegant phrase . . . 'hanging about,' indeed! I was simply availing myself of a breath of cool air, it's so hot below. And I couldn't avoid observing the two of you. She did flounce away in a pique, didn't she? At least it looked that way. What on earth did you say to her?"

Coldly furious, he remained silent. But at the same time he was aware of the faint, star-anise aroma of her silken hair as she pressed her cheek against his arm.

"Oh Devin . . ." She half turned, her warm fingers stealing with delicate accuracy inside his open shirt to stroke insinuatingly the crisp mat on his chest until they discovered and wickedly tweaked the very tip of his nipple. Before he could stop her, she was leaning in to him, her face nuzzling inside his shirt, searching his hot, bare skin with her tongue to find and lick at that tiny, hard nub on his chest. He muttered angrily and shifted uncomfortably, disgustedly aware that there was a part of himself that was responding enthusiastically and in a most irresponsible fashion to her seduction. . . .

He awakened slowly, groggily—feeling replete and drained at the same time. Before he recognized his surroundings, a sense of drowsy well-being told him his sensual appetites had been sated, appeased in every possible and improbable and remarkable manner.

True, he didn't feel particularly uplifted this morning, or even tenderly loving toward his sexual partner, which would have been a pleasant token; he merely felt well serviced, ravished, seduced. His eyes still closed, he lazily shifted sideways; then, opening one eye, he discovered he was lying on a thick pile of silk fabric.

*On the floor . . . ?*

Abruptly he sat up, lean and powerful and naked, aware only of a minor twinge in his back. Next, he looked down to find himself shackled by a rope of red hair coiled around each ankle. Disbelieving, he turned; at the same time bumping his head on the side of the bunk next to him. He swore softly and stared at the voluptuous female body lying slantwise across the silken mats, her head touching his thigh.

Gently he reached down to release those braids of hair that trapped him. Without opening her eyes, their owner sighed, rolled over with a complacent smile, and unerringly put her hand between his legs.

He leaped to his feet, barely restraining the yelp that crescendoed to his lips. Now he remembered exactly how he'd gotten here, and precisely how the two of them had passed the night.

Oliva's eyes — the green of muscat grapes — opened. She yawned — her small teeth exceptionally white within the pink enchantment of her mouth. Smiling, she pursed her lips, pantomiming a kiss. "It was wonderful, my darling. *You* were wonderful . . . sensational."

Rudely he snapped a sheet from the bunk, wrapped it around his middle. He could see his garments across the cabin, and he made a move to get at them. "Oliva, we've got to stop this."

"How quaint of you, Devin." She sat up, shook out the waterfall of her hair. With that movement, her bosom rippled seductively. He turned his eyes away. "You have needs, Devin — so have I. We might as well satisfy each other." Her eyes slanted up at him. "Which we seem to accomplish with great flair and imagination. Not many people can do that. It's obvious you were — shall we say, ready? — last night. And from that I judge you certainly aren't pleasuring yourself with that maiden you're escorting to Trois Îlets. She's rather prudish, or haven't you noticed that she actually wears two dresses at a time, one over the other?" Oliva giggled.

His jaw set and the planes of his face grew threateningly dark with annoyance as he pulled on his breeches. "I've got to get back to my quarters before it's light. Listen to me, Oliva!" He straightened, fastening the top button. "We'll be in Fort-de-France in the morning. You'll be met there by your new husband, and you'll be starting a fine, new life."

She shrugged, watching him. "Go on."

"A much better existence than you've ever had before."

"And better than I deserve?" She yawned.

"No. You deserve more, much more, Oliva. Think back. You've told me how Arakcheev treated you before you returned to Poland from St. Petersburg, and about the prince who left you pregnant with a son you lost. Back in Pulawy it was never easy in your father's house. I remember that enormous old castle—miserably cold. It might as well have been built of ice as of stone. All those morose servants skulking about and on the point of revolt. No money. Eventually you might have learned to love Valinski; he might have made the difference. But there were the wars that he was sent to fight, and then you were widowed."

"Spare me." It was said cooly, haughtily, but he knew by the expression in her eyes that she was listening.

"You deserve good things, Oliva, for the rest of your life. You have a wonderful heart, a great capacity for tenderness and passion; there is so much generosity in you. You give of yourself so freely; you hold nothing back. A man who knows you is indeed fortunate. If you let him, Anton Russo will be a devoted husband." Devin hoped this would turn out to be true. "You'll have sufficient wealth, which you've always lacked before. And you'll move in the best circles of island society; for this reason there should never be any scandal attached to you. They're far more straitlaced here than in Paris. But you'll travel; the Russos are originally a Florentine family, and with the troubles there drawing to a close, he'll take you to see Italy if you should so desire."

"You forget I'm a Slav, and I wish to stay put."

"Not always." He grinned at her. "Be sensible, dear Oliva." He knelt beside her, shaking her bare shoulder, but when he did this there was another exquisite movement of her tawny breasts. He forced his gaze away. Noting this, she laughed at him. Annoyed, he grabbed a roll of the silk material unfurled it and tossed it around her nakedness.

"I may stay on the island for a while, and look into the state of the old house on my family's plantation. It's been all but abandoned. You and I have to forget that we've shared some lovely times. Do you understand, my Oliva?"

She nodded tiredly. "I understand too well, Devin." She curled the long piece of silken material around her shoulders, and moved sideways, closer to his knees, looking up at him as he stood slowly fastening his shirt. "Tell me, why is it so impossible for you to love me? I mean to love me enough to want to share your life with me. It could have happened in the past. I thought we were suited—it would have been so perfect. What's wrong with us . . . me?"

He had never seen her face so delicately beautiful and appealing, nor had she ever spoken out quite so candidly before. Oh, she'd come close, she'd hinted—but she was proud and, heretofore, had been fairly accepting of their situation.

He looked thoughtful. His hands paused in the lacing of his shirt. "It isn't you. And it may be my problem." He knew, though, that she deserved more honesty than this halfhearted shading of the truth. Was he saving himself? Yes, of course he was. He closed his eyes, and when he opened them, this time he drew her look, smoldering and intense, into his own.

Truth?

So, all right—truth. He had always felt that she wanted to lure him into her womb and claim him forever—his manhood, his being, his thoughts, himself. She had a way of probing, questioning—his motives, his reasoning, his feelings. He was not that complicated, for God's sake. And he didn't want to discuss *why* he did certain things; so, for him, there was no privacy and no serenity with her. And if it were possible that fault did lie in his corner—after all, he hadn't tried very hard to stay away from her—then guilt compounded the anxiety he felt when he

154

was with her.

What a terrible thing to say to a woman. He couldn't. He wasn't brave enough.

So, instead, he reached down and plucked her up into his arms, cradling her against his chest, knowing once again the delight of her bare breasts pointing against his own. He kissed her deeply, surrendering himself into her mouth though he would not surrender his life to her.

When he released her, and she stood swaying beside him, he reached for his boots, not wanting to look into her eyes. He wouldn't have been surprised it they'd held ridicule for him because he wasn't courageous enough to tell the truth. With curious ambivalence, he amended that estimation: that is, the truth as it seemed to him.

"You will come back to me," she pronounced, standing before him, her arms folded across her breasts. The sweep of red hair fell to her hips, and her pelvis thrust insolently forward, its badge of tight red curls aflame.

Quietly he closed the door to her cabin, then stood for a moment, heartsick, his forehead pressed against the wood. He hadn't liked what he'd just seen of himself. He had eagerly pursued all manner of erotic experience with Oliva, but it all had had a brackish taste; for love had eluded him. No, he would never go back to her.

He turned, boots in hand, and walked stealthily along the passageway. If he met someone he'd brazen it out. Upon reaching his own corridor he turned back, and climbed the companion ladder to the deck.

The crewmen's hammocks were gone. He was alone, and the sea was a great silver platter with only the thin edge of dawn beginning to pale the sky.

He knew the truth; he'd known it all along.

He'd given his love, and would give his life—if she'd have him—to Antoinette de Cavanac, that rakish Gypsy of a girl who rode like the wind, who'd worked in the fields when necessary. Her allegiance was to the Bona-

155

partes, and like a young princess, she'd sat at the dining table of that ancient château. As such things go, he barely knew her. But he knew enough.

He wanted them to belong together—their bodies, their souls. He decided, despite the massive odds he'd reviewed earlier—part of those being his failed relationships with Clare and with Oliva—he would win her. The battles and the scars didn't matter. He wasn't too old, she wasn't too young. He whistled for courage as the sun's disc brightened the sea before him.

She would be his.

# Chapter Sixteen

It was extraordinary, Nanon mused as she leaned out over the balcony of the Hôtel Beaux Jours. She did miss the dark mysterious forest surrounding her family's château, but she was enchanted by the scenes below her.

In the three weeks she'd been here, she no longer scanned the harbor daily for sight of the ship that would return her to France. It would come in good time. For the present, she was enjoying the exotic sights, sounds, and smells of this alluring island. Even from her second-floor balcony, she could breathe in the scents of honeysuckle and amaryllis rising from the garden below.

A butterfly, velvety-yellow, jeweled with tones of brown and green, landed on her sleeve; perched, fluttering; and then flew off into the hibiscus bush. Her attention remained on the sleeve with its delicate embroidery. She was still bemused by the fact that this tasteful, new wardrobe of hers had come into being. And so much else had happened. She put a hand to her temple in wry remembrance; it literally made her dizzy to think about these events.

They had started the day following her arrival on the island. D'Amboise had alerted the de la Pageries, and an invitation had been sent her by messenger, requesting that she visit Trois Îlets immediately.

For this occasion she'd dressed with great care in the least revealing of Joséphine's frocks, a high-waisted muslin with puffed sleeves, broad collar, and pale lavender sash.

It was with relief that she'd watched the hotel laundress remove the clothing she'd worn on shipboard. When the woman promised to return it promptly, she had told her there was no hurry.

Feeling at ease, Nanon had joined D'Amboise in his open carriage in the street below. Her smile, almost generous in its warmth, had provoked an immediate response in him.

He'd murmured. "You look ravishing today, Nanon." She'd made a modest disclaimer, and he'd followed with, "No, it is true." She hoped so, for no one had ever told her this before.

A sidelong look at him revealed he was at his dapper best in a well-cut gray coat and white linen vest, his white cravat emphasizing his sun-bronzed skin and thick, black hair — still worn a bit too long. The light gray trousers that shaped his muscular thighs — and hugged him intimately elsewhere — were so snug that she'd turned her eyes away.

Draping his arm along the seat rim above her shoulders, he'd inclined his head toward hers. His confidential murmur had stirred those wisps of curls escaping the ringlets that crowned the top of her head. "Nanon, let me assure you I'll not overlook a single opportunity to see that you have all that you need." Tactfully he'd added, "While you are here."

His soft breath had tickled her ear in a rather thrilling fashion, and aware of her own self-consciousness at this, she'd moved along the seat to put distance between them. But then her attention had been, almost immediately, captured by her surroundings. She'd gazed about her at the pastel-colored town rising into the dark green hills above the magnificent bay. And she'd leaned forward in anticipation, opening the parasol provided her by the hotel clerk as protection against the blazing sunshine.

This, then, had been the beginning of the spell. . . .

The carriage had rolled on in cadence to the swaying of the stately plumes of the giant bamboo, while D'Amboise had related the island's history, naming for her the unfamiliar flowers. Scarlet petals from the flambeau trees were strewn, like a fiery necklace, along the wayside. Everywhere there were lush bougainvilleas and the tall palms whose silver fronds were tossed about by the insistent tradewinds.

The sight of the many gardens adrift with tropical flowers — gaudy orchids, jasmine, anthurium — had reminded Nanon of her godmother's fascination with the greenhouse at Malmaison. It had contained many of these same exotic blooms that had been part of her island girlhood.

She'd listened eagerly to D'Amboise; but after a while the heat of the sunshine, the languorous air, and the steady, rhythmic pace of the horses had lulled her into a dreamy lassitude.

Then, all at once, she'd shot upright, twirled her parasol briskly to one side, and peered at the man beside her. "Will you kindly repeat what you just said!"

He had done so, and she'd been shocked.

"I have arranged for Minette who is Fort-de-France's premier dressmaker to call upon you tomorrow. She'll bring with her fabrics, patterns, designs — whatever is needed. Choose what you will, and her workshop will quickly make up the garments for you."

Stunned by his offer, Nanon told him firmly that she required nothing other than the clothing she already had. Except, perhaps, one sensible outfit to wear aboard ship when she sailed back to France.

Coldly she'd concluded. "I must tell you that I strongly object to you having summoned this woman to sew for me."

There had been silence then, save for the shuffling of hooves on the dusty road. Finally, he'd glanced at her with a calm authority that plucked at her nerves and set her teeth on edge. "There was no opportunity to discuss this with you first, Nanon. The woman is talented and knows her business; she is in great demand. You may dispose of the clothing Minette will design for you in any manner that you wish, but I would be exceedingly remiss in my responsibility toward you if I didn't see to it that you possess a proper wardrobe while you're here, no matter how brief a time!"

As she had stared straight ahead he'd studied her stubborn profile. "You will be invited to parties at the plantations, and you'll discover that the people here have not forgotten how to dress, that they live as elegantly as they did in their native France."

She'd turned on him, an abrupt retort on her lips. "How does it happen that you know so much about the seamstresses on this island? It is said you've never married, and I also hear that you've not resided in Martinique for many years."

"Since you've been listening to shipboard gossip about me, I suppose I should be flattered. Chastise me all you wish, Nanon—I accept the reproof."

"But you're still going to have your own way?"

"Only know that I intend to make your stay here as easeful as possible."

"And I do thank you for that!" She'd underscored the words.

"Oh Nanon . . ." He'd sighed. "Let's not waste this day. I believe it the estimable Joséphine who said, 'It's easy to love, it's not easy to get along.'"

"It was one of her favorite sayings—yes! But she meant the loving and getting along *with the same person.*"

"Well, then . . . ?" he'd prompted wickedly.

She'd stared at him, but after a moment's puzzlement as to his meaning, she'd burst out laughing.

His amusement had joined hers, which had made for

160

good-natured camaraderie between them. But looking into his eyes, greened by the sea beyond, Nanon had felt an odd and treacherous thrill deep inside her. Shifting uneasily, she'd been distinctly aware that his arm was resting idly on the leather rim behind her. And she'd thought confusedly, What is the matter with me?

Certainly once she'd believed he might be her love . . . but that aberration, since it had nothing to do with reality — only with an impassioned kiss or two — had been settled and was long buried, and forgotten.

While she was thinking this, the carriage had wound smoothly into a long, oleander-shaded driveway. The horses had accelerated their pace from a trot to a gallop, cane fields had flashed by, and in the distance the diamond-studded sea had glistened beneath the sun. With a flourish they'd arrived at Trois Îlets.


All the de la Pageries had assembled on the wide veranda, and Nanon had been warmly welcomed by Joséphine's relatives. After being shown around the gardens, and escorted through the big, solid-stone sugar refinery, she had sat down to a luncheon of many courses. For the first time her tongue had tasted the fruits of papaya and mango trees. Next she'd savored an excellent fish chowder, that was followed by a startling array of broiled langoustes, rice and conch, clams in piquant sauce, and pineapple braised with vegetables. The dessert, fruit ice and crème caramel, had been followed, thankfully, by a steaming cup of full-bodied island coffee.

When the time had come to depart, Nanon had paused behind the others to gaze into the gilt-frame mirror near the double doors that opened from the reception hall onto the veranda. It had not been her own pensive expression that she'd seen reflected in the glass, but the face of a young Joséphine, dreams in her eyes. How many of those bright hopes had been dashed! And yet, that young girl had become Empress of France.

Nanon had been saddened at realizing she couldn't accept further hospitality from these people. Neither she nor D'Amboise had informed the Pageries that she was the product of a bungled abduction, that it should have been a member of their own family they welcomed instead of Antoinette de Cavanac.

Then, just before she'd glanced away, over her shoulder in the mirror's reflection, she'd perceived him staring at her from the veranda's green depths. His look had been so brooding and intent, so passionately absorbed, that it had seemed as though she were being watched by some powerfully primitive creature lying in wait for her in this strange land.

Her cheeks as red as the blossoms on the scarlet flambeau tree, Nanon felt a surge of response. Her lips parting in wonder, her hands beginning to tremble, she had dragged her gaze away from his image in the glass and had whirled about to face him.

But then, outside on the veranda, his back had been turned to her and he'd been bidding the others good-bye. Her heartbeat had paused in its ragged rhythm and, suddenly, she'd been herself again. And wondering . . . had she partaken of some exotic food or drink that could create such a fantastical imagery. The wine . . . ? She was not really accustomed to it, though she'd drunk sparingly . . . .

As he'd handed her into the carriage, she'd managed to present an unruffled appearance while unfurling her parasol and smiling and waving to the Pageries who had again gathered on the wide veranda.

During the return to Fort-de-France, Nanon had been relieved that neither of them had seemed inclined to engage in conversation except in desultory fashion. Yes, she had enjoyed herself. No, she had not reconsidered her refusal to remain as a guest at the Pagerie plantation. She would feel like an interloper. Every now and then, she'd sent him a swift questioning glance, but he had maintained a somewhat preoccupied air, as though his thoughts were on many other matters. The mirror had played her tricks, then; that had to be the answer.

Upon reaching the hotel, as he had assisted her from the carriage, their fingertips had barely touched. He had bowed and assured her in businesslike fashion that he would round up the widowed Madame Arnaud to companion her in her suite for the remainder of her stay, since it was evident that she would persist in her plan to reside at the Hôtel Beaux Jours.

At this Nanon had raised her brows and had sent him a mocking look from beneath the veil of her lashes. "Very well, D'Amboise. I see we both have taken a stand, and that there's no moving you from that noble pedestal of yours. So . . . do as you please about the woman. But remember, I, too, do as I please."

"I'm not likely to forget that about you, Antoinette." He'd raised her hand and lightly touched her fingertips with his lips. But then she'd been astonished to hear him growl. "I should like to do more than this, but unfortunately I have your reputation to consider."

Had she heard him rightly? "Devin . . . ?"

He'd paused. "Yes, Nanon?"

She'd swallowed, fixed her gaze on his left eyebrow, and thought, Why not say it? Be honest.

"When your Madame Arnaud is established here, I hope you will come to call upon us."

"And *I* hope you will both dine with me tomorrow night. Would you like that?"

She'd felt tiny shocks of excitement as their gazes merged. "Oh yes, I would . . . I mean . . ." At least she'd finished with dignity. "It will be very pleasant to dine with you and to see something of the town at night."

163

His lips had curved to a whimsical smile as he'd studied her. "And it will be very pleasant to show it all to you, Nanon."

So, today—three weeks later—Nanon looked once more at the sea, then stepped back as a bird with brilliant plumage flashed by her. In the room behind her, the jalousied shutters cast grids of yellow light across the dark planks of the wooden floor. She turned and walked through the golden bars, thinking that this enforced stay on Martinique was not an imprisonment at all, it was the most glorious freedom she'd ever known.

In the sitting room of the two-bedroom suite, Madame Arnaud was attending to her constant needlework, embroidering pillow shams, bureau scarfs and hand towels for her five daughters and for the hope chests of her female grandchildren. She was an energetic woman of sixty or so, and her relationship with Nanon was an easy one since she did not attempt to go along on her charge's daily strolls through the shops and markets.

Instead, she like to regale Nanon with arch tales of beautiful thirteen- and fourteen-year-old girls, all from Martinique society, who were married to rich planters. Nanon smiled to herself, correctly guessing that Madame, learning she was nearly nineteen and unmarried, had relegated her to a state of elderly maidenhood.

Except, of course, there were those daily visits of Monsieur Devin D'Amboise, which the older woman watched with great interest. In his absence she never tired of remarking that he was a fine, rich gentleman, respected, handsome, virile, and unmarried. Quite a suitable match for you, my dear, her brightly curious eyes seemed to say.

And now Devin will be here shortly, she thought, glancing into her mirror and knowing dreamy satisfaction at what the dressmaker had wrought.

That had been another experience; for from the day Minette had arrived Nanon had been unable to oppose her. A tall, severe-looking woman, all white teeth and golden eyelids, the dressmaker had swept into these rooms and taken charge like the remarkably talented general she was.

When Nanon, not yet realizing the futility of opposing her, had resisted the tape measure, protesting that she neither needed nor desired a new wardrobe, Minette had responded with outrageous honesty.

"Mademoiselle! If you refuse to accept the clothing that has been ordered for you by Monsieur D'Amboise, I and my seamstresses will be cheated out of a fine commission that will keep our children in food, and our workshop prosperous, for the better part of a year. Would you do that to us, would you so deprive us? Every beautiful young woman likes proper clothing, though I must say that it is unusual for one's fiancé to supply such a wardrobe. However, in your case, I am sure there is nothing *outré* about the matter."

Nanon, recovering from the impact of this attack, had suppressed a smile. "We are *not* affianced!" Minette's ebony brows had swooped at this while Nanon had continued. "Nor am I beautiful! I, too, can be honest with you, and tell you that I detest such compliments when I know them to be purely deferential."

Minette, a proud woman, had appeared furious at this. "If you had dared to use the word *obsequious, mademoiselle*, I should have left this room on the instant!"

Nanon had gauged the other woman's temperament correctly. The two had continued to stare at each other in challenge, and then, quite suddenly, Minette had tossed back her head and laughed ferociously, her white teeth square and gleaming, her gold-hued eyelids curving over her great, black eyes.

Nanon had shrugged permissively. "Very well, do your best. I shall wear your dresses here, but I shall not take the garments with me when I leave your island."

Now she wished that she could. The gown she was wearing for the drive with Devin to the Farrar plantation was beautifully crafted of lightweight silk, the waistline fitting very high, the subtly-draped skirt inset with gores in the new A-line, which gave willowy movement to each step Nanon took. Of course she liked this outfit. Of course she was pleased. She couldn't deny that she enjoyed the admiration and that "something else" in D'Amboise's gaze when he took her to dine, to visit his friends to take tea, or to share the best times of all—the drives in the afternoon along the seawall. Then Madame A. remained at the hotel, and there were just the two of them. And dare she remember more . . . those times on leave-taking when he'd tilted her cheek toward him and gently, fleetingly, shaped her mouth to his?

There was a knock on the door, and when Madame admitted him, to Nanon it was as though his presence filled the room, warmed her blood, excited her senses until she was attuned to the palest bar of light in the farthest corner, to the barest nuance of a darting glance, to the tiniest chirp of a cricket in the tree outside.

It was as though the icy-white of the gardenias he offered to Madame scorched Nanon's bare flesh. And their perfume, drifting across to her, seemed to drench her parted lips like a mouth pressed against her own.

She was unable to drag her gaze from him as he placed her embroidered silk scarf around her shoulders. At the last moment, though, she did remember her wide-brimmed straw hat, and while Madame rushed to get it, the two stood smiling absorbedly at each other.

The older woman returned, set the hat straight upon Nanon's head, fussed at it, perked up an artificial flower, and tied the ribbon beneath her charge's chin. Then she frowned as she watched them leave.

They would return late from the Farrars', and she decided that this time she must remain up for them to see her charge safely returned for the night. Perhaps she had been shirking her responsibilities. Unless she had lived a long life for naught, she could recognize that desire had been almost tangible between the two of them. And if that girl were to marry Monsieur D'Amboise, as Madame devoutly hoped, there must be no slipup at all. Her maidenhead must not be sacrificed to a rake—and in her opinion all men were rakes—who might not be so eager to wed after the fact. . . .

# Chapter Seventeen

Amalie Farrar sat behind the tall, silver coffee urn, her china blue eyes darting, making certain that her liveried slaves were continuously at her guests' elbows with trays of cool drinks.

Out of everyone's sight, another of the house blacks was confined within a narrow hallway closet, sweat soaking his powerful frame, his expression frantic. Energetically, he jackknifed his body up and down, his fingers cramped tight around a rope hanging from the ceiling. Attached to a pulley, this served to spin the huge overhead fan that partially cooled the large room where the gentlemen and the ladies were assembled.

If the heavy wooden paddles didn't revolve properly, if the room became meltingly humid, then — with thirty lashes scoring his back — the unfortunate slave would be banished to field labor, which would considerably shorten his life. Though one circumstance seemed hardly preferable to the other.

As Amalie continued watchful, among her guests Oliva Russo was the center of a group that gossiped, mimicked others, and occasionally snickered softly while bandying about some choice tidbit. The clique surrounding Oliva appeared to the most amusing and select, Amalie mused, as she saw her friend disengage herself and drift closer to her hostess's position.

As Oliva paused beside her, Amalie's normally high

voice lowered to a sharp whisper. "Do you see who has just entered? Nanon de Cavanac and . . . your friend."

"My friend?"

But Oliva knew very well whom had just come into the room. She stared across at D'Amboise whom she thought ruggedly handsome and so much more impressive than the other men present. In his informal white coat—his black hair edging the collar—in his linen vest, light-colored trousers, and Hessian boots, he appeared stylish on this hot afternoon and very much at ease.

Oliva observed Nanon at his side, but dismissed her as she would an unfriendly gnat. True, the girl was said to be installed with a chaperone at the Hôtel Beaux Jours, a curious choice when one might expect to to be more likely that she'd be a guest at Trois Îlets. And why wasn't that chaperone with them *now?*

She frowned, studying the situation and the other woman's attire. The rumors were true, then. Minette had fashioned a wardrobe for Nanon. Certainly she was no longer wearing one transparent frock on top of another! Oliva recognized the subtlety of the day gown, and noted the sophisticated yet discreet manner in which it displayed Nanon's figure. She had a passable form, yes; but one not as seductively curved as Oliva's own, nor as bountiful in the bosom. Devin had always liked this last asset.

She purred at that last thought but decided to stand back and not immediately confront the two. Her lower lip fell into a pout as she entertained the notion that D'Amboise had known where to find her, for thus far he'd made no effort to call upon her. And they'd been on the island nearly a month.

Oliva quickly looked among the guests to search out her new husband. When she found him, her eyes narrowed speculatively. How long would he be engaged as he was at present? The whole bloody evening, she hoped!

Anton Russo, heavy-faced, sensual-lipped, and corpulent, stood among his male companions, a silver-stemmed goblet of cooled wine making rather too frequent trips to his lips. Piss on Anton—a drinker and, as she'd had occasion to learn, a failure in bed.

She returned her attention to D'Amboise, her appreciative gaze roaming the span of the wide shoulders that stretched the material of his white coat. She admired the length of his legs and of his splendid body—which had a certain splendid length elsewhere, too, she recalled.

The girl she could disregard. Though she had made an effort to befriend her on shipboard, that had been because she'd wanted to discover her connection with Devin. The answer to this had never been satisfactorily resolved. Yet she was said to be Josephine's goddaughter, and this might account for Devin's having known her previously. Ah well, since it was reliably rumored that Nanon would soon be returning to France, Oliva decided she would let the matter rest.

In the meantime from behind the coffee urn, Amalie had been glancing at her red-haired friend, disappointed that her expression disclosed so little of her feelings. She'd always suspected there'd been hanky-panky between her and D'Amboise, but Oliva had not been one to discuss the romantic escapades she'd indulged in. Amalie suspected there'd been quite a few. Since the marriage exercise with Anton Russo could hardly be other than boring, it was just as well Oliva had some provocative memories to call upon when additional stimulation was needed in the bedchamber.

Amalie rose, shaking out the hem of a skirt ornamented with puffs and swags. Daintily she touched a fingertip to each of her pearl earrings, making sure they were in place, and then she said to Oliva, "Will you be a dear chum and take my seat here behind the urn for a few minutes? I must find Charles and mingle a bit with

170

our guests."

Aware of her exact target, Amalie was off on the instant, alertly moving through the crowd. She avoided the flutterings of the women's ivory-and-lace fans, as well as the urgings of the men who begged her to pause and listen to whatever tale was being embellished. She'd heard all the stories twice over, but D'Amboise's presence here with the young de Cavanac was a fresh and original event—and might turn out to be a far more titillating one.

She halted at the room's threshold, glanced around to be certain she was unobserved, then swept into the hallway to peer into the tiny closet. "Faster . . . faster. . . . *Vitement!*" she bade the cringing servant; and was gratified to see the heavy wooden paddles spin at an even swifter, giddier clip, sending downdrafts of air onto the heads of her guests.

When she finally caught up with D'Amboise and Nanon, her greeting was profuse. "My dears, I'm so glad you've both arrived, although a trifle late. However, you've missed very little of our gay times, as you can see. Nanon, you look quite lovely. . . ."

"Thank you, Amalie. I'm delighted to be here and to see you again."

"Yes—our first reunion since we were together on shipboard. And where have you kept yourself, you sly one? Has this handsome man been showing you around Fort-de-France?"

D'Amboise, who was accustomed to Amalie's maneuverings, stood by with a cynical smile, wondering how Nanon would parry this. But before she could answer, they were joined by Charles Farrar.

"Ah, D'Amboise and his lady . . ." When Amalie demurred softly at this nomination, he proceeded. "I thought so, anyway—and more pity if it isn't true. Please present me." He beamed at Nanon. But then almost immediately began questioning Devin about the ancestral plantation he'd inherited.

Bored by the interrogation, whose purpose he understood, D'Amboise finally replied coolly. "I've not yet made any decision one way or another, Charles. True, the exterior of the manor house is badly in need of restoration but the interior's in fair condition. And my caretaker— you know Emil Terren—has kept the sugarcane fields going. The yield as you may have guessed is unimpressive."

Farrar was aware of all this but listened politely, hoping for a hint that D'Amboise might have some interest in selling the place. He would be more than willing to take it over if the price were advantageous. He'd get rid of that lazy Terren and whip up the even lazier blacks living in the slave quarters. By applying the sensible discipline that his own field manager used so well, at little cost he could make the sugarcane fields prosper once more.

However, no inkling of an inclination toward a sale was forthcoming. Instead, the discussion launched into ways of restoring the interior of the manor house.

Amalie drew Nanon aside from the men. "It's so good to see you again, my dear." Craftily she interjected, "And have you accompanied Monsieur D'Amboise on a visit to this fabulous old plantation house of his?" Amalie knew it was located more than an hour's drive outside the town, and much intrigue could occur between two people while alone in lush surroundings—especially when exploring ancient bedchambers. . . .

"No, I've not been invited there, Amalie. You see, except for infrequent visits to Trois Ilets, I must remain at my hotel near the harbor. With my companion Madame Arnaud, I watch daily for any ship that might be sailing to France."

Amalie sniffed. "I would assume the harbormaster

would be the first to inform you of such merchantmen sailings, Nanon. And, incidentally, why didn't your Madame Arnaud accompany you today? Charles and I would have been happy to receive her."

"She had previously arranged to visit an ill grandchild, but only briefly, Amalie. She's probably waiting for me now."

"Yes . . . ?" mused her hostess. "You must meet our other guests now. And, of course, Oliva is here and eager to see you." She glanced at Nanon's dress. "Most charming. One of Minette's designs?"

Nanon nodded, her eyes shining with amusement, the dimple in her cheek barely under control. Well aware that she was being quizzed, she was also somewhat perplexed as to how she would answer if Amalie questioned her as to the expense incurred. Certainly the older woman would not be so rash.

But she was! "I understand Minette's prices are very dear. For this reason Charles will not allow me to patronize her dressmaking establishment." It was said wistfully: "I have often wondered if some arrangement could be made for a lesser charge—if one promised to appear in her frocks at every social occasion on the island."

Nanon smiled sweetly. "One has only to ask, I suppose." This time the dimple was permitted full play.

Amalie's expression didn't change, only a tiny glint of chagrin appeared far back in her pale blue eyes. If her friend Oliva was considering D'Amboise as a lover with whom to pass the time while Russo was in his cups, then she must warn her that this girl was no simpleton. Something was brewing between these two—and Amalie suspected there might well be—then Nanon could prove to be a formidable obstacle.


The dinner, served in the early evening, was a merry

173

one, due in part to the long refectory table being so narrow in its crosswise span, that the diner seated opposite was almost as close as the partner in the next chair.

And Oliva had seen to it that she was seated directly opposite D'Amboise.

As he looked across the table to her, the tip of her tongue stole out to wet her lips seductively, while her fingers traced and rearranged the edging on her low-cut bodice.

Leaning far forward to speak to him, she was aware that her scooped neckline exposed the winsomely rounded beginnings of what D'Amboise knew to be a pair of magnificent, low-hung breasts with nipples so exquisite that he'd once likened them to purple grapes, and had acted accordingly.

Fiercely D'Amboise swore to himself, disgusted because these erotic memories persisted. With Nanon seated nearby, what a cad he was to recall Oliva's sensuality . . . and the extreme pleasures the two of them had engaged in. He wanted to make himself worthy of Antoinette de Cavanac, and here he was peering down into the opening of Olivia's bodice like some lascivious youth. . . .

The matter of achieving worthiness was becoming even more difficult, because Oliva was using humor to woo him. She looked at a morsel of fish posed precariously on the tines of her fork, her expression one of charmingly funny distaste. Then murmured across the table, "Have you tasted this pièce de résistance, Devin? It is so heavily-sauced. Does this bespeak a major lack of confidence, do you suppose?"

He managed to rein in his smile. "Restrain your quips, Oliva. You're not yet on solid enough ground socially that you can afford to offend your hostess's kitchen."

She pouted prettily. "And *you* are becoming quite a sobersides!"

He looked away from her, his glance taking him the length of the table. "Would that one could say the same of Anton."

She followed the direction of his gaze in time to see her new husband laugh uproariously and fling both arms into the air at the ribald cap of some joke. In so doing, he upset the enormous, ornamental flagon of wine that stood on the table in front of him.

The crimson liquid flooded slowly, inevitably, across the tablecloth, its progress attended by a momentary, embarrassed silence. There followed a quick spurt of conversation, a swift mopping up, and apologies and laughter all around.

Oliva observed all this while wrapped in her own silence. After reflection, she returned her green gaze to Devin's watchful eyes. He read her lips as they formed a frosty whisper. "At least, he married me! And he's not yet been as cruel to me as you have been. *I* may laugh at him, *you* may not!"

"That's understandable and fair, Oliva. But I do not laugh, nor do I make fun of him or you. Ever. And I am sorry that you feel I've been cruel. I don't remember our relationship in that light at all. I respect it, and you. But it *is* over, and both of us know it! I must tell you, Oliva, that I too plan to marry as you yourself have done."

"Congratulations! Have you yet informed whoever it is you've chosen to wed?"

He shook his head.

"How like you, Devin!"

With feigned indifference, she turned her attention to the eager gentleman to her right. She would stab D'Amboise if she could. Thinking this, she glanced along the table to perceive Nanon chatting gracefully with her dinner partner. Oliva's temper flamed. This girl had to be the one D'Amboise had chosen. Certainly he wasn't returning to London and that English Clare of his. . . .

This virgin! she thought with fierce hatred. She was nothing, she knew nothing. Would she appeal to a man of Devin's appetites if she were no longer virginal . . . ?

Of course, that was *it*. Oliva relaxed and smiled slowly, abstractedly, entranced with the prospect that lay ahead of her.

# Chapter Eighteen

With an accompaniment from Amalie at the pianoforte, a female guest, in lovely voice, sang an operatic aria, then gazed out over her appreciative audience. In mischievous answer to shouted requests, she began a lively song in the Creole patois. Murmurs of amusement rose at the sly suggestiveness in the words.

Enjoying the rhythm but not understanding the earthy dialect, Nanon sat back in the shadows, aware that D'Amboise was smiling at her from across the room. With a thrill of pleasure she thought, He wants to be with me as much as I want to be with him. Now he was indicating by a slight tilt of his head that he was on his way to join her.

Her deep breath became a sigh of delight, and she turned to look about her at the spacious, beautifully furnished salon. The unshuttered lengths of floor-to-ceiling windows admitted the stray breezes of mid-May. Multi-branched candelabras and silver wall sconces illuminated the room as twilight was fast fading into night.

There was movement near the entrance door in the hallway, and Nanon, craning upward from her chair, saw that Blanche Lecourlaix was among the new arrivals. Instead of rising to address her former shipmate, she decided to remain where she was for the time being. Doing so gave her an opportunity to observe D'Amboise, who had detoured from his path toward her to exchange greetings with the late guests.

So, to look—and look—at him. Yes; that was what she wanted. It was easier to fill her eyes with him when he was at a distance. Near at hand, the excitement his physical presence aroused invaded every nerve in her body, setting up a response that made her self-conscious. Whereas, looking at him from afar, she was freer of his hold over her senses. Thus, it was easier to perceive his worth, as well as his integrity where she was concerned.

He'd let her know he admired her. Even more importantly, his actions showed he had regard for her opinions. How else could they have shared long conversations during their afternoon strolls in the market place? Nanon was grateful for her father's insistence that she absorb European history as well as that of her own country and of its Revolution, whose terrors had occurred before she was born.

Because her views were not parochial, she and Devin could wander far in their discussions. Such debates frequently became lively, for in terms of wit, the discrepancy in their ages and experiences had never mattered.

Still . . . what? An imp of honesty danced within her amber-flecked eyes. For all the wide-ranging talk they'd shared, it was the physical reality of Devin beside her, his touch on her arm, his gaze looking deep into her own, that seemed to count the most. For her, this had made their past month together a constant wonderment.

In the old château in France, she'd been beguiled by him—she could admit that now. And on shipboard, too. Though at that time, disbelieving, she'd renounced the magic.

But now . . . *now*. In the midst of strangers in this strange house, how could she have guessed that she would finally acknowledge her love for him. And more than that, her need to be loved by him.

Her heart seemed to give a convulsive leap. *Listen to me, love.* . . . She wanted to run to him, place both palms on either side of his wonderful face, bring his lips

178

close to hers, and pour out all the fervor, the ardent, fiery intoxication sweeping through her. *Listen to me, love. I'm like a chalice overflowing and waiting to be brought to your lips. You have been patient, and it's taken me too long to know what you must have known from the beginning. You have been faithful in waiting for me to accept that I love you with all my heart, and always shall. Tonight and forever . . .*

Her hands clasped tightly in her lap, Nanon sat as though dazed, staring straight ahead, unseeing—only perceiving love.

"I have been watching you." The heated murmur, faintly scented with wine, breathed into her ear.

Confused, Nanon glanced upward. Oliva was leaning close, both of her hands resting on the chair back.

"I see who's caught your attention. You're entranced by him. I'll tell you a secret." It was said with a giggle. "There's only one way, dear girl, to win him to you forever."

Nanon whispered back distractedly. "I don't understand what it is you're trying to tell me, Oliva."

"No . . . ? I think you do. Hear me out. I am on your side, Antoinette. I want to help you." She stepped around in front of Nanon and extended both her hands. By the force of her personality, and by the mesmerizing stare of green eyes set in a delicately beautiful face, she drew the younger girl to her feet. With insistent strength, she urged her toward the open window. "Step out here; then we can talk. . . ."

"Wait . . . please." Nanon's effort to hold back was unsuccessful, and she stumbled over the sill's threshold onto the wide porch. The swift-falling tropical night and the perfume of the garden assailed her, while the social clatter from the room behind her faded. She was alone, trapped by the odd intensity in Oliva's manner. She straightened. "I do not care to discuss—"

Oliva's interruption was silken. "Ah, but you must." Her fingers, bracelets of steel, gripped Nanon's wrists.

179

"Give yourself to him, Nanon! You know that you want to. And you've thought about it. *Haven't you?* Tell me."

Nanon was attempting to free her wrists by twisting them out of the other woman's grasp. But at hearing Oliva's utterance, it seemed her blood stopped running and she was helpless. This was an attack of the most incredible proportion. It was insulting, base. She must get away from the outrage of Oliva's words.

"You're white, bloodless—totally without passion. You've never known sexual love, and because of that, you will lose him if you hold him off as you've been doing. I know what I'm talking about!" One hand dropped from Nanon's wrist, and pointed to her breast. "Do you know what it is to have a man caress you . . . *here?*"

Before she moved away, Oliva gripped her other wrist more firmly.

"Do you know what it is to have him suckle your teats like a babe until your insides writhe and you scream for him to do more, to fondle you . . . between your sweet thighs."

Nanon's face flamed with anger as she fought to free herself of Oliva's implacable grip. The strength that she had earned in fields and vineyards seemed to have deserted her.

Oliva's words continued to scourge her, and there was no way to shut out her sensual whisperings. A vein in her temple throbbing, Oliva panted. "And then, he'll plunge his length into you when you're wet and waiting for him, and he will break your maidenhead." Her voice rose. "But it will be a *joy*, Nanon, for he'll carry you along with him into paradise. Do you hear? You want that, don't you? If you want him to be yours, this is how you must win him, by the favor of your body."

Then Oliva's strength—or was it her purpose?—seemed to weaken. She looked shaken, and a swirl of red hair cascaded from its tortoiseshell pin. Eluding her swiftly

Nanon stood back at a safe distance. "You must be mad to think I'd give credence to such scurrilous talk!"

"Advice, Nanon—advice!"

Oliva lunged as she turned to flee, twirling her around by the shoulder. "You *have* listened! So now ask your question of me, Nanon. I see the query in your eyes, and I see it lingering on the tip of your tongue. You want to know how *I* know all this about Devin—how *I* know how enjoyable it can be when he strips a woman of her clothing and puts himself inside her."

"Let me go!" Nanon tried to shrug away, but Oliva's fingers clamped tightly down and Nanon realized they were very near her throat.

"*I know* because it is what the two of us did together while we were on board that ship. While you were hiding in your cabin, a good little virgin, he and I lay in each other's arms . . . every one of those nights! And I was gratifying him in a way a man sometimes likes; in special little ways, with my lips pleasuring his body. . . ."

With full force, Nanon's palm slashed across Oliva's mouth. A thin spurt of blood traced through the air. Nanon stared, horrified, at what she had done. She was in pain—Oliva's words had lacerated her—but was that a reason to strike out so violently?

A moment's stark silence passed as the two women stared at each other. Finally, Oliva shrugged, her fingertip lightly blotting the corner of her mouth. "I have told you the sure way to win him. I say it again: give yourself to him, Nanon. Why are you delaying? You'll thank me when you're in his arms . . . when you're a woman, no longer an ignorant girl."

Certain that she would be sick at any moment, Nanon turned and fled along the porch. Oliva's triumphant gaze followed her. When the girl recovered from shock, she'd do precisely what Oliva had suggested. All she'd been waiting for was a push like this. Devin was a man; he'd take her willingly—but then, after a time, he'd no longer think of marriage with his deflowered Antoinette.

Nanon knew she would never enter this house again. Somewhere on the garden circle, she'd find the carriage and driver that had brought Devin and herself here. She'd have the man take her to Fort-de-France. And once there she'd not step outside the hotel until the ship arrived that would carry her home.

She would never see any of these people again. How they must have laughed, seeing her moon about this past month with D'Amboise while they were all privy to the ongoing liaison between himself and Oliva. Her mirthless laugh raked over her as she recalled what a dreary romantic she'd been, whining to herself about her faithful love waiting for her.

And how quickly she'd forgotten her godmother's caution. *We easily believe what we ardently desire to be true.*

She rushed down the driveway searching for the carriage. One of the bays—she'd fed the horse carrots—recognized her approach and whinnied loudly. She shook the sleeping driver awake, ordering him to take her back to town. He looked at her, astonished. "But should we not wait for Monsieur?"

Without replying, Nanon sprang into the open carriage and impatiently urged the man on. While the horses galloped at full tilt, the coach careening through the night, she sat rigid and upright, bleak misery drenching her heart, tears streaming down her face. Yes, he was faithless, still she mourned him, mourned what might have been, and what was now lost forever. . . .

Nanon would have rushed past the clerk at the desk, but he stopped her, handed her the key to the suite.

"What is this . . . ?" She looked at it numbly.

"Madame Arnaud left it for you. She said there is a

message upstairs that will explain."

"Very well." She hesitated. "Thank you."

Her step slowed, and by the time she reached the top of the stairway, she was clinging to the banister, barely able to mount one stair tread at a time. The clerk who had always admired her youthful exuberance looked after her in surprise.

A lamp was lighted and waiting for her. Propped against it was a sheet of paper on which Madame's apologies were inscribed. The grandchild's illness was worse. She must remain the night and spell her daughter in sponging the little body with alcohol and cold compresses. She would return by dawn.

So Nanon would be alone tonight. She was sorry about the grandchild, but it was just as well that Madame A. was absent. It would have been impossible to hide from her the blow she had received.

Opening the jalousied door that led to the balcony, Nanon stared out into the black night. The tears that had been so shattering were now dried and her body was drained of all emotion. As difficult as it had been to accept the truth, she had to admit that Devin's amorous intrigue with Oliva was not perfidy on his part. He had not betrayed her; there had been nothing—no promise—to betray. She had no claim upon him.

It was just that it had all seemed so perfect. And too easily she'd believed only what she wanted to believe.

The shock would remain with her for a long time, and so, unfortunately, would those passionate images conjured up by Oliva's words. She huddled back inside the sitting room, covering her eyes with her hands in an attempt to shut out the memories. But the eye of the mind remained alert, and she continued to see Oliva and Devin together in those seductively erotic acts each had performed upon the other.

With deliberation she marched across the room into Madame's bedchamber, found the decanter, and poured

183

herself a glass of the good lady's nightcap rum. She knew Madame used it to invite sleep; and at this point she, too, sought sleep and its blanket of immediate unconsciousness.

But three sips only set her to a bout of explosive coughing. Hastily she put the glass down. And then came the familiar surge of homesickness, a longing to see her father and the château and her mare Dominique. Again, Nanon began to weep, this time uncontrollably.

After a while, with only an occasional sob jolting through her, she lay on the chaise, a wet cloth covering her eyes. She had no idea how much time had passed, but she'd rest here a bit longer, gather her strength, and then hide herself away in her bedroom. She hoped that Madame A., mindful of the late-night party at the Farrar's, would not expect her to make an appearance until midday tomorrow.

Oh . . . The devil take her luck! There was a softly insistent rap on the door of the suite. Who . . . at this time of night . . . ? She pulled herself up from the chaise, her face crumpled, still sniffling.

Why hadn't the man at the desk halted whoever this was? Possibly it was the desk clerk with another message. Well, devil take him . . . she was not answering the door.

But wait. Having given up her key, Madame might be returning early from her grandchild's bedside? On stockinged feet Nanon walked to the door and listened.

At hearing a familiar sound of impatience in the corridor outside, she stiffened, and then slowly backed away from the closed door.

But from where she stood, halfway across the room, she heard his voice. "Nanon, are you all right? I must speak to you. What happened? Why in God's name did you leave the Farrars' so suddenly? Are you ill? Is Madame A. caring for you?"

In sudden fury, she crossed the room and flung open

184

the door. "So, it's you, D'Amboise, sounding as though you really care about what happens to me! What a mask you've been wearing, and what a fool you must think me!"

Then, to her great chagrin, Nanon burst into tears. . . .

# Chapter Nineteen

Unprepared for the sight of tears, D'Amboise halted. "I've never seen you cry." Stunned, he edged closer. "Antoinette, what is it?"

Her tear-clouded face stared up into his. She was wondering if the disdain she felt was for her own weakness or for his duplicity.

"Is it something I've done . . . or failed to do?"

"No. What has happened is of no importance."

"Everything is important between us. You know that. Tell me, why did you run away? And what mask have I been wearing?"

He did seem totally bewildered, standing there with that ridiculous froufrou of a hat clutched in his powerful fist, along with the trailing scarf she'd left behind at the Farrars'. That was a man for you . . . innocent, without guilt of any kind, eyes guileless as a babe's.

Tentatively he reached out to touch her shoulder; but she drew back and, in answer to the fresh doubt in his face, cried out, "Nothing that you've done matters one whit to me. I may have spoken as though you've caused my injury, but you really haven't. You can put down that silly scarf and hat—and leave!"

He dropped both items on the chaise. This time he replied coldly. "I will not leave, Nanon, until you tell me what I'm supposed to have done and let me know who it was, and what it was, that sent you running from the

Farrars'. I looked for you as discreetly as possible; then my driver returned to say he'd delivered you here."

He glanced toward the closed door of the bedchamber. "Call Madame A. Ask her to come in here at once. I want her to be witness to your litany against me."

Shaking back her curls and forgetting she was no longer wearing her shoes, Nanon padded close to him. She peered into his face with a fierceness that astonished him. "You do . . .? You really do? It's your wish that Madame Arnaud hear that all this time you've been calling upon us, arousing *her* foolish and romantic hopes that she was playing *duègne* to a match between you and me — *her* hopes, you understand, *not mine!* — all this while, you've been making love to another man's wife right here in Fort-de-France!"

With the unexpected accusation, the blood drained from his face and the skin over his cheekbones grew taut, a groove deepening beneath each.

"You refer to Oliva Russo." A muscle rippled along his jawline.

"Why yes." She spoke airily, pivoting away from him. "My friend Oliva. And how quickly you guessed!"

"Nanon! Stop it!"

This time, when he reached for her, she was caught off guard and stumbled back against him. She attempted to push away, but he held her captive to his body, locked in a grip that compelled as well as immobilized her.

Her head slanting sideways, her cheek profiled against his chest, she could hear his heart's angry thunder. And it recalled that lone tigerish image of him reflected in the mirror at Trois Îlets. . . .

She'd never known the impact of a male strength that she could not outmaneuver. Théo had attempted to restrain her in the loft on that awful night, but it had never occurred to her that she couldn't break free from

187

him.

This was different.

Looming above her, wide-chested and hard-muscled, D'Amboise was truly a massive force, an unyielding rock.

"I'll answer any question. But ask it straight out. Sarcasm and roundabout ways are not like you, Nanon."

Within his iron grip she was unable to move. Once again tears were close to brimming, and she hated this—she'd never been a tearful sort. But how dare he dictate to her what her response should be. When it was he who was in the wrong. She began to tremble, looking away from him, her thick lashes wet. "Madame Arnaud is not here tonight. You had better go."

"Where is that lady?" he roared, staring down at her. "Never mind! Later, you can tell me the reason for her defection. Let's settle our present difficulty. Who told you this tale at the Farrars'? Was it Amalie or her husband? Or any one of a half-dozen others? Who? And what exactly was said? It's my right to know so that I may defend myself."

She shook her head, making one more attempt to struggle free. It was then he appeared to realize with what bruising force he held her.

He stepped back, releasing her but cautiously. Though he retreated, she was still cornered. It was impossible to bolt to the left and barricade herself in her room. Nor could she circle in another direction and head toward the exit to the corridor. Behind her there was only the balcony—and a long drop to the garden.

So she faced him, as icy in demeanor as he. "There's no need to defend yourself, D'Amboise, since I've no claim upon you. What you did with Madame Russo is of no matter to me."

Instinctively then, he knew the tale bearer's identity. "It was Oliva who spoke to you." He made it a flat

188

statement without emphasis or emotion.

She matched it by merely nodding.

"Look at me!" He made no attempt to touch her, but his voice was commanding and reluctantly she lifted her gaze to his. "I shan't ask you to repeat whatever it is that she told you."

"I wouldn't ask if I were you," Nanon interjected.

He paid no attention. "It's over between Oliva and me. And has been for a long time. We have not met in Fort-de-France until tonight at the Farrars'."

"And on board ship?"

His brow rose in faint amusement. "Remember, it doesn't matter to you. Look, Nanon, I don't deny that I have loved women. Would you prefer that I pursued an alternative passion like hunting, the senseless butchery of animals? Or that I love another man?"

She was so impassive, he wanted to shake her, awaken feelings in her—distaste, disgust, amazement, shock . . . anything.

"You say what I've done is of no import to you; still, Madame Russo's words must have been effective. It was her intent to hurt you, and she succeeded or I would not have found you here with those tears on your cheeks."

"You're mistaken. The tears were not occasioned by any disillusionment at hearing the details of your liaison. I . . . was homesick." She turned from him. "I'm very tired now—and I want you to go so that I can be alone."

"You will be, my dear, unless Madame returns soon." He'd glanced at the paper lying on the table. Now he picked up the note and read it. When he looked up from it, his eyes searched hers, but this time his regard was gentle. "I know how much you miss your home and your familiar life. I do understand, believe me. . . ."

His voice held so tender a note that she found herself

succumbing to another wave of homesickness. Overwrought from the allurements of the day's entertainment, and still cringing from Oliva's explicit account of her nightly couplings on board ship with Devin, to her dismay Nanon was unable to restrain fresh tears. She covered her face with her hands, mumbling. "Please go."

"God's sake, Nanon—what have I done to you? It would seem I'm little better than a murderer!"

She was weeping pitifully now, and he knew that though she was too proud to admit it, it was he who was making her suffer. He shuddered, realizing the extent of what Oliva might have said to his bright, courageous Nanon. A jumble of incoherent thoughts whirled about in his mind.

Long before this, he should have asked her to marry him; he should have spoken of his love for her much, much sooner. She had touched his soul, invaded his being. But he had waited too long, torturing himself with his own inadequacies—and thinking only to give her time. . . .

"Nanon, don't . . . my most sweet . . ." He reached out and swept her up into his arms, holding her close to his heart. For a moment he stood so, then, lowering his face to hers, he breathed in the perfume of her silken hair while his lips roamed her damp forehead, rounding the curves of her eyelids to nuzzle her cheek, which had the aroma of day lilies. His lips trailed her cheek's outline to the corner of her mouth.

A pause . . . and then he knew a surge of pure joy. She was turning toward him in shy response.


Only moments before, with her head against his shoulder and her senses in confusion, Nanon had asked herself why she was struggling with these fierce proddings of anger and resentment. Did any of it really count—her tension, the perceived unfairness, Oliva's confession? Perhaps. But now she was being overwhelmed by sudden wild excitement as his lips slowly traced the contours of her face to send delight shivering through her veins.

With a sigh, knowing there was no purpose in resisting, Nanon turned her mouth to meet his. This was what she wanted to do more than anything in the world. If she was being coerced, it was by her own greedy desire.

Without breaking stride, he began to walk across the room, still carrying her in his arms. She was now only conscious of his mouth never leaving hers, and of the lightly sensual stroking of his tongue as it ripened her lips, coaxing them apart.

Using his shoulder to edge open the door to her bedchamber, he carried her as easily as though there were no weight to her at all. But she was no disembodied spirit, and each searched the other's mouth in flagrant delight until he put her down against the tall pillows with their fancy embroidered shams—which made her think of Madame.

She spoke breathlessly. "She'll come back, Devin. We mustn't . . ."

"Yes, we must. I adore you, Nanon. I have from the time I first set eyes on you in that old carriage in the Paris alleyway. There you were, lovely and indignant, and pretending that brother of yours was your coachman. And there I was—my uniform bloodied and my hand in its stained bandage—hoping you didn't think me too large and ungainly and awkward."

*"You?"* It was a hoot of disbelief. "Devin, you were gorgeous!"

"My God, Nanon, you always speak the truth, don't you?" He grinned at her.

"I do?" Her eyes were merry, but she was breathing so

191

hard that she was fearful her bosom would strain through her bodice. Moments earlier, he had run his hand teasingly around her throat, then down her spine, allowing his palm to linger seductively just above her buttocks. His hand, pressing her so intimately down there, sent thrills of anticipation through her.

"You see, we feel the same about each other. There is no way to conceal love, my darling." He withdrew his hand and lay down beside her.

But then alerted by the tension he felt in her, he raised his head to study her face. "You're still thinking about Madame A., aren't you? Well, don't. I know the lady and her family. A sick child is her happy excuse to play infirmary nurse, and seldom is it anything serious. And if she should return here at an inauspicious time, then she'll know she's failed as your chaperone." He smiled whimsically. "Or, better yet, succeeded. Didn't you tell me that she was hopeful concerning our impending romance? We won't disappoint her, will we?"

"Ah, Devin . . ." Her fingers tangled in his thick, dark hair. She'd been tempted to do that for a long time!

He gave a tiger's purr of pleasure and, stretched beside her on the bed, began to trifle with the lacings on her bodice. Before she recovered from one languid delight, Nanon was plunged into another.

His fingers slid inside the confining silk, wandering beneath her chemise until his palm curved caressingly to cradle her breast. She gave a throaty gasp which turned to a voluptuous moan as he massaged the bud of each nipple, seducing and titillating in turn until she cried out softly. "We mustn't, Devin . . . Oh!"

"Sweet Nanon . . . please."

He raised up, his weight supported on one elbow, and pulled aside Minette's elegant lace-and-embroidery handiwork to release her straining breasts. Naked, except for

192

# ── FREE ──

# B O O K  C E R T I F I C A T E

## ZEBRA HOME SUBSCRIPTION SERVICE, INC.

**YES!** Please start my subscription to Zebra Historical Romances and send me my free Zebra Novel along with my first month's Romances. I understand that I may preview these four new Zebra Historical Romances Free for 10 days. If I'm not satisfied with them I may return the four books within 10 days and owe nothing. Otherwise I will pay just $3.50 each, a total of $14.00 (a $15.80 value—I save $1.80). Then each month I will receive the 4 newest titles as soon as they come off the press for the same 10 day Free preview and low price. I may return any shipment and I may cancel this arrangement at any time. There is no minimum number of books to buy and there are no shipping, handling or postage charges. Regardless of what I do, the **FREE** book is mine to keep.

Name _____

               (Please Print)

Address _____

City _____ State _____ Zip _____

Telephone ( ) _____

Signature _____

      (if under 18, parent or guardian must sign)

Terms and offer subject to change without notice.      11-89

---

## MAIL IN THE COUPON BELOW TODAY

**GET FREE GIFT**

To get your Free **ZEBRA HISTORICAL ROMANCE** fill out the coupon below and send it in today. As soon as we receive the coupon, we'll send your first month's books to preview Free for 10 days along with your **FREE NOVEL.**

# ACCEPT YOUR FREE GIFT
## AND EXPERIENCE MORE OF
### THE PASSION AND ADVENTURE
### YOU LIKE IN A
### HISTORICAL ROMANCE

Zebra Romances are the finest novels of their kind and are written with the adult woman in mind. All of our books are written by authors who really know how to weave tales of romantic adventure in the historical settings you love.

Because our readers tell us these books sell out very fast in the stores, Zebra has made arrangements for you to receive at home the four newest titles published each month. You'll never miss a title and home delivery is so convenient. With your first shipment we'll even send you a FREE Zebra Historical Romance as our gift just for trying our home subscription service. No obligation.

## BIG SAVINGS
### AND **FREE** HOME DELIVERY

Each month, the Zebra Home Subscription Service will send you the four newest titles as soon as they are published. (We ship these books to our subscribers even before we send them to the stores.) You may preview them *Free* for 10 days. If you like them as much as we think you will, you'll pay just *$3.50 each and save $1.80 each month off the cover price. AND you'll also get FREE HOME DELIVERY. There is never a charge for shipping, handling or postage and there is no minimum you must buy.* If you decide not to keep any shipment, simply return it within 10 days, no questions asked, and owe nothing.

the filmy chemise, they thrust upward beguilingly, their tightened tips crimson and delectable. He groaned as though his breath would burst from his lungs and, thirsty with desire, lifted the transparent material that partly covered their impudent outline. Then he laved them with kisses, surrounding them with his lips and drank from each moist bud.

Raw sensation whipped like lightening along Nanon's nerves. Was this she, Antoinette, her body vibrating with desire, lying here and wanting more. . . . Of what, she wasn't quite sure. Should she be permitting him to do these exquisite things to her?

Suddenly there was no question of what she should do or should not do. She closed her eyes, for almost without help from her, except for one minor wriggle to raise her hips a bit, he was relieving her of the need to decide — and of her fancy dress and petticoats as well.

But not my chemise, she thought in unexplainable alarm; not . . . my pantaloons.

But yes, that happened too. Her underclothing was drawn swiftly from her recumbent body, her silken stockings stripped away; all of her clothing abandoned on the floor. She lay there looking cool as a lily, but with her flesh on fire — knowing herself to be beautiful. Because he'd told her so.

He rose, stepping away from her to the long balcony window. He opened its slatted jalousies, and the flambeau in the garden below sent its soft glow across the ceiling of the bedchamber.

Somehow, during his few strides back across the room to her, he had divested himself of his own garment. A haphazard trail of masculine attire lay strewn along chairs, day couch, and the floor beside her bed.

She wondered if she should behave in some maidenly fashion, but it seemed so natural to open her arms to him without pretense. Suddenly she closed her eyes in

193

panic. As he approached her in the shadows, she'd filled herself with the sight of his perfect body, wide-shouldered and deep-chested, with an interesting pelt of dark hair spreading from chest to navel to loin . . . but here her gaze had veered away.

She'd squeezed her eyes tight shut; now she slowly opened them.

# Chapter Twenty

But that part of him was now cast in shadow as he knelt above her. With one knee nudging her side, his other leg astride, he captured her body beneath his. Ripples of desire shuddered through her as she dug her fingers into his shoulders. Her breath came quickly. Would she suffocate, could she breath at all . . . *did it matter?* She could die like this, and gladly!

Her fingers laced together at the back of his neck and tangled in his hair's unruly length. She tugged his face down close to hers, aware of the trembling of both their hearts, and of the torment in their breathing.

His arms were holding her, and as her head tipped back, he forced his tongue past her lips, moistening their surface with its rough strokes. As he plunged deep into her mouth, she could only cling to him, dizzied with sensation. But she was learning, and she began to follow his lead, sealing their deep kiss with a seductive search of her own.

"Gypsy . . ." he growled. "Wild gypsy . . . do your will!"

Answering his challenge, she cradled his face between her palms, her tongue tantalizing his, exploring the hungry demand of his mouth. With amorous daring, she teased her tongue across his, probing and curling its tip into the sensitive places. She could hear his low groan of delight as their mouths clasped in mutually drugged surrender.

Then, boldly possessive, her lips traced the powerful line of his throat with small, ravenous kisses — as she had once yearned to do in the ship's passageway. Her mouth, continuing to explore, discovered his nipples within the curling hair on his chest. Her tongue circled the small nubs while her hands trailed down his body, and she could feel his powerful muscles tighten, his breath explode.

She was innocent, untutored, but instinctively passionate; thus, her response to him had aroused D'Amboise's hungry urgency. He had intended to be less than immediate in his lovemaking, to act as prudent guide and cautious lover to this wonderful Nanon of his. But he forgot all that, the way a man does when he throws his cap over the mill wheel to gamble away his fortune. He could no longer restrain his passions, nor rein in the true ardor of his nature.

Lowering his head, he greedily tasted her breasts, his lips molding their crests, his tongue licking and tightening their eager nipples.

The heat of his mouth, and of his seeking tongue, which now roamed across her stomach, sent an exquisitely stinging sensation into her belly's small inverted button. He was linking her to him with chains of ecstasy. She was his, bound to him forever. There was no way to escape this plundering possession of her body.

Nor did she want to!

A shock raced through her as she felt him thick and throbbing against her leg. What was he saying . . . ? "Gently, my darling . . . gently." In husky answer she cried "Yes!" and gasped aloud as he spread her legs apart, tenderly claiming the soft inside of her thighs.

The darkness between their bodies grew hot and moist. And this time she cried "No . . ." Yet all the while she desired him — she was flowering for him as his fingers parted the rosy petals of her entry. And stimulated by slow strokings, by slower kisses, she was wet and waiting, and wanting . . .

The pain was quick and sharp—frightening.

But he eased all that with the splendor of what came later between them. And later still, it was his words she listened to—and remembered.

"I can never deserve you, Nanon, but I will love you and take care of you. Will you live with me always—will you be my wife, beloved Nanon?"

She responded, "Always, Devin, I will love you and be wife to you."

And dawn crept into the room before he left her.


Now, in her bed, she slowly turned over to watch the morning arrive. To see the sheer curtains that covered the shutters billow toward her. To smell the breeze bearing its scent of cinnamon and spice. To feel the silken sheet beneath her naked skin.

In farewell, he'd kissed her eyelids closed and told her to sleep. Of course she had not slept. She'd lain there recreating the passion imprinted in her heart and on her body. It seemed she could still hear the urgent whisperings they'd exchanged in the night. . . .

Sighing, she stretched her arms ceilingward. She would not dwell upon the one flaw in the diamond radiance of their love . . . that faint echo of Oliva's onetime presence in his life.


Four weeks had passed since the announcement of the impending marriage of Antoinette de Cavanac and Devin D'Amboise. During this time the betrothed pair had become the focus of the island's social life. It was not what either of them had planned or desired, but they both knew it was important to follow the conventions of Martinique society.

There were the invitations, the social events, the trousseau fittings with Minette and her seamstresses; and the meetings, first with the priest, then with the bishop. And always there was the constant hovering of Madame Arnaud who was observing her duties with even greater seriousness than she had before.

And, finally, there was the Pageries' insistence that Nanon abandon her suite at the Hôtel Beaux Jours. It was unusual for no member of the bride-to-be's family to be present when the nuptial vows were taken. Therefore, residing at their plantation until the wedding took place seemed more circumspect for the fiancée of their cousin than staying at a harbor inn.

Nanon had, perforce, agreed to this move, and Madame A. was in the process of packing boxes and trunks with Nanon's new wardrobe.

Mid-June brought summer's increasing heat, and life in Fort-de-France moved at a somnolent pace. It was also the season for hurricanes, and few ships were sailing into the harbor. Martinique appeared isolated from the outside world. For this reason there was little news of what was occurring on the continent.

When the seas became safer, the married pair would return to France to visit Nanon's father. Then they would make their way to Ireland and Devin's ancestral holdings.

But their hope was that they could reside some few months of each year at the D'Amboise plantation house, which was being refurbished—though this, too, proceeded at a slow pace.

Their first journeys of inspection had been made in Devin's carriage in company with Madame A. However, when Nanon expressed a desire to ride a horse once again, Devin's polite suggestion of a gentle mare to transport Madame was refused.

Today, with the trade winds blowing stubbornly and the unyielding sun gilding the town's roofs, the two set out alone for the plantation. Madame had decided that nothing untoward could possibly happen on horseback.

Thus, she remained behind to receive last minute deliveries of Minette's hand-sewn wares.

Devin was astride his bay, while Nanon, demurely riding sidesaddle, was mounted on the black mare he'd picked out for her. The road turning into the mountains led through a tropical rain forest before reaching groves of bananas and shimmering green fields of cultivated sugarcane. As they rode along occasionally a carriage passed them, as did several riders who bowed courteously and exchanged greetings.

And always there were those others—the anonymous black men and women. Some in donkey-drawn carts, but more on foot. The women, their heads swathed in bright cloths—magenta, pink, and orange—never glanced up; the men, lean and ragged, kept their mournful eyes cast down as they shuffled through the roadway's yellow dust.

Nanon had not been able to accustom herself to the sight of slaves. Their subservience and their obvious ill treatment saddened her. Having recently passed a group even more decrepit looking than those she'd observed earlier, she guided her mare in to a walk and glanced meaningfully at D'Amboise, who was riding his bay beside her. "There's a matter I'm most concerned about, Devin. I'd like to discuss it with you."

He inched his horse close to hers and, shifting his reins, reached his free hand across the space dividing them. "What is it, my darling?"

"It's the cruel use of human beings that I see here. As though they're merely work beasts."

After a thoughtful moment he responded. "It's true that your *Liberté, Égalité, Fraternité* has little meaning here. Whatever I might say in defense of Martinique's custom and tradition would sound feeble. There seems to be no other way for the plantation owners to raise their crops productively than to use slave labor. Certainly I share your revulsion—but change can come about only slowly."

"That's a conscience-saving remark, Devin. It's unperceptive. Of human life and its value."

"And less than courageous, I agree." He shrugged. "But
look at France herself. It took a groundswell of Sun
Kings behaving decadently to bring about your Revolution. Blood flowed during that savage time. We can't
allow that to happen here."

If she said another word, they might quarrel. So
Nanon touched her horse's flank and the mare sprang
forward. She called back over her shoulder. "When we
reach the house, let's talk further about this."

He raced his mount beside her. "You mean . . . together we're to settle the island's fate. Is that it? Let me
be the one to take up this matter."

She heard his challenge. Or was it his promise?

She was reminded by this, as perhaps he had intended
her to be, that his influence could be powerful. If he
chose, he could plead a case properly in the Royal Court
itself.

Now both were subdued. No news had been received
from Paris in many weeks. No one on the island knew
what was happening on the continent. Was Napoléon still
in power, or was he in exile?

They reached the road leading into the plantation and
passed between gateposts once askew but now reinforced
and newly whitewashed. They cantered side by side,
Nanon's gaze fixed ahead on her future home. Devin
could not take his eyes from her. It seemed to him she
rode with such grace and spirit, her breasts moving delicately with the motion of her horse.

He longed to take her in his arms, crush those tempting lips to his, breathe in the provocative scent of her
skin and hair, make ardent love to her. Instead, he cautioned himself to behave in a proper manner. No scandal
must touch her.

Such restraint was not easy considering what had already taken place between them. Still he was determined
there would be no stain on their alliance. Their situation

was curious enough. The uncertainty concerning the outcome of the wars, as well as the vast distance between this island and France, explained why they had not returned to her family château to celebrate their marriage vows.

Martinique society, outwardly conventional as he had once warned Oliva, adored its titillating gossip. There might be private speculation concerning their relationship, but in public no one would dare be critical due to his illustrious name and to the influence his fortune could have on the island's future.

When Devin thought about Oliva, it was thankfully. She was behaving with circumspection as she played her new role as Anton Russo's wife.

He'd been able to convince Nanon of the truth—that he'd been only twice with Madame Russo while they were aboard ship. It had not been a nightly occurrence.

And Nanon had proven to be wise beyond her years. She'd refused to listen to any other confessions. Indeed, she'd stopped her ears with flattened palms and a mischievous smile, and had told him that, no matter what, they were destined for each other and his previous experiences did not matter.

The sympathy he'd read in her amber eyes, and the solace of her approach to him, lightened his conscience considerably. He could not have been happier, or more fulfilled, than he was at the moment they approached the sweeping veranda of the island house that was to be their home for a time.

They dismounted, tied the horses to a rail, and hand-in-hand mounted the wide steps. The long-uninhabited, two-storied residence was handsomely constructed of masonry, and had been recently whitewashed. Large containers holding fresh plantings of shrubs and flowers had been placed around the bases of its supporting columns.

Devin produced a key, then unlocked and swung wide the carved mahogany double doors. He paused for a moment to inspect one of the side window's iron grilles. "These will all have to be replaced," he muttered.

"Let's not stop here, please. I'm so eager to see what's been done since we came the last time with Madame A."

Nanon rushed ahead of him, then exclaimed in delight. "Devin! The drawing-room floor has been repaired, and it's beautiful. Look at these planks! They positively gleam. . . . And the dining room—over here." She danced across the wide foyer that separated the two rooms. "Its panels have been exquisitely finished with real artistry, rubbed and painted that pale gray shade you requested. Who did you say was responsible . . . your overseer, Emil Terren?"

"Not he, never Terren. No, it's a black man called Jean Henri. He's been here a long time."

He came up behind her, wanting to nuzzle the back of that delicious neck of hers, to touch her impudent breasts outlined beneath that thin blouse, but he didn't dare. Instead he murmured, "It's *your* slaves, *mademoiselle,* who have completed the decoration here as *you* suggested."

"That's not fair." She spun around to face him, her expression serious as she studied his. "Devin, I know you'll see to it that conditions are bettered here."

"With your help, yes." He sighed. "We two will do what we can. But I fear, my dearest, that despite all the good will the two of us own to, what we accomplish will be too little. And do we really want to incur the enmity of our neighbors by attempting to set an example that they will never agree to follow?"

"Why not?" Her eyes flashed somberly. "Perhaps they'll learn by what we do here."

"Oh, Nanon." He shook his head at her, and ran his finger along the cord of lace at her wrist. "I fear all of this sounds too oversimple, my dear one. You've much to learn about life here. Island society regards field slaves as animal-like creatures without souls. And those blacks they take into their houses and train for service fare little

202

better."

Moodily she looked away from him. His finger beneath her chin turned her face back to his. "Believe me, it is the common view that slaves do not feel heat or hunger or thirst—only the lash makes its impression. This is all wrong, of course. But tell me, if you had been born here instead of into an enlightened family in France, would you feel differently than our neighbors?"

"Yes. Yes. Yes!"

"Very well. We shall partner each other in this effort to investigate conditions in our slave quarters." With a faint smile he concluded. "As well as partnering each other in more intimate ways."

"I regard this as a serious problem," she declared, "and one not to be treated lightly—with quips." Then she wondered if she'd been too harsh. After all, he had understood her feelings—and she didn't want to spoil this day for either of them. Stepping back a pace, she scrutinized him, her tongue tipping the center of her upper lip.

She had not told him this was a special day for her. It had remained her secret. . . .

# Chapter Twenty-one

Then, too, by this time Nanon was otherwise involved
. . . in noting how his raven black hair, slicked by the
dampness of perspiration, curled against the column of
his strong throat. And, through the thin fabric of his
shirt, she was aware of the outline of his muscular chest,
which narrowed to his taut waist circled by that familiar
silver-buckled belt. Below, tailored breeches snugly fit
long legs. She drew a ragged breath and moved a step
backward.

He heard the unevenness of her indrawn breath in that
quiet hall. And he could see in her eyes that she remembered . . . everything.

"Would you . . . ?" He paused. He must phrase this
carefully. "Would you care to give your approval to what
the workmen have done . . . upstairs?"

Her voice quavered. "They've finished?"

"I believe so. Terren was at my house in town the
other day, and he indicated the furniture had been moved
in. Shall we see to it?" He could not believe how calm he
sounded.

But suddenly better instincts took hold! What was the
matter with him? Where had all his fine resolve gone?
The color rose in his face; his eyes dilated and darkened.
He was nothing but a whoring sensualist, lusting to put
himself inside her. Well, he could control the stiff desire
in his groin, that shuddering excitement that made him
want to pull her close against his body, fondle her

breasts, and thrust his hand between her legs until she was hot and wet for him.

In sudden fierce denial of his own arousal, he shouted at her. "We'll see what they've done upstairs another time. "We'll visit the overseer's house now. I've told you about Emil Terren, but you haven't met him or his wife. I don't intend to keep him on, but I . . ." It seemed he couldn't stop this inane palaver; the sentences kept flowing out of him.

"Hush!" She walked up close to him and placed her finger across his lips. Her mouth shaped into a mocking smile. "Devin, I love you. I want to share your life and your thoughts—all of them. And I mean those you're having now. I understand what they are at this moment."

He brushed her hand aside. "Oh no, you don't! Nanon, you have no idea—"

"I have something to tell you." Amused, she still watched him closely. "Nineteen years ago today I was born in the château near Malmaison, and your cousin Joséphine was at my mother's side."

Dumbfounded, he stared at her. "You are telling me today is your birthday? But why didn't you say so earlier? We could have had a gala celebration."

She shrugged charmingly. "We still can. I was waiting to choose the proper moment. And now I do think it's arrived. I'd like to celebrate in a special way."

Shaken, he stared at her, and then was unable to stop his eyes from roving toward the elegant staircase that swept up to the second floor. He hesitated, unsure of her meaning. "You mean . . . up there?"

She nodded, her eyes gleaming back at him.

"Great God, girl!" He ripped back his head and let out a bellow of laughter. Then, before she could anticipate his next move, he bent forward and slung an arm under her hips. Supporting her shoulders, he lifted her high and started up the staircase. Taking the steps two at a time, he grinned. "I have a present for you!"

She appeared shocked at the baldness of his words. "Devin!" she remonstrated.

He let out another great roar of pleasure. He was enjoying himself hugely. "Your mind, my dear wife-to-be, seems not as elevated as a maiden's should be."

She turned a bright crimson and shook her head. "Some things you simply should not say," she chided.

He paused at the top of the stairs, his smoky gray eyes abrim with humor. "I have been saving this for a special time. You're telling me the truth? It *is* your birthday?"

She nodded her head, shyly this time.

The hand supporting the curve of her buttock tightened. "My gift to you is a painting I found here, one that resembles you in a sense. There. Are you disappointed . . . with your gift, that is?"

From behind the wisps of curls scattered across her forehead, she peered at him, abashed. Her arms curled more tightly around his neck. "No . . . not exactly. But you've made me curious. When will you let me see it?"

Holding her in his arms, he stared down at her, at the sweet curve of her eyelids, at the lashes almost touching the crest of her cheek. The hand that held her shoulder lifted slightly to allow his thumb to rub the silken skin of that cheek, stroking close to her warm red mouth until her lips opened for a breath and her tongue tip teased at his thumb.

"Now!" he answered. And he whirled her along the hallway, beneath a chandelier whose prisms winked in the sunshine, and on into a large, sunlit bedchamber.

He set her down. "And now for your present." She blushed, the pink in her cheeks deepening as she watched him go to a large armoire, open it, and bring out a small, unframed canvas, which he offered to her.

She held it in her hands and looked up at him while he explained. "It was done by a great-aunt of mine . . . you can see her signature and the date on the back."

Her eyes returned to the painting, and she nodded

pensively. "I like it very much, Devin. It has delicacy; that's difficult to achieve with oils. She was skillful."

"She must have copied it, probably from the original Watteau that once hung in the library. I found it there—wrapped and protected from the damp. Somehow, it seems to belong in this room."

Nanon looked around at the large chamber he'd carried her into moments earlier. "It does. There's light here, and color. I like this room. And I like the manner in which you carried me over the threshold." Her eyes were mischievous. "I like my birthday."

"We'll see that you do. Is this chamber truly suitable?"

She nodded. The walls were freshly painted, the white panels trimmed in vivid green, it still smelled of beeswax and lemon. Dust sheets had been removed from chests and side table. A wide bed facing the balcony was covered with a puffed quilt, its swirling design a mixture of brilliant greens and blues.

"This room is like the island—full of bright sunshine and the shades of the sea and the mountains. Tell me, did your Jean Henri do this, too?"

"He and his woman Mathilde together." Devin's brows flexed upward in concern. "Is there anything you'd like to change? I'd hoped it would be to your taste—I wanted to surprise you."

"It's beautiful, Devin. I should like to meet them and thank them both, personally. And I thank you for all of this—and for my birthday gift. I shall cherish it."

Her eyes glistening with emotion, Nanon quickly turned back to the picture she held. That he'd rescued it at all showed her another side of him. She had much to learn concerning his nature. He was so many things—soldier, diplomat, swordsman, man of wealth, man of nature, horseman, and landowner . . . her lover, too.

Thinking this, she flushed as she concentrated on the lady in the pastoral scene, whose ringlets had the darkly-fired hue of autumn leaves. Though the woman reclined against a traditional background, a wooded park in which sheep grazed, she had a lively and licentious air. Her satinlike skirt was hoisted well above bare and sprawling thighs, her bodice was carelessly pulled open, and her naked breasts were lushly displayed. A young man, fully clothed, yet passionately inclined, knelt beside her.

"But . . . how does she resemble me?"

His lips twitched in an amused smile. "Perhaps not in her *déshabillé*, my darling—though, believe me, I do not disapprove. But you must remember that artists in the decadent days of Louis were mirroring court life as it was in that period. Do you see the fine brush stroke that curves our lady's cheek, and that glorious hair that's spun around her face like bright coins? She's *you*, my gypsy queen, but, I trust, as no one except me shall ever see you."

Nanon placed the canvas on the bedside table, regarding it with a kind of reverie. Her smile grew thoughtful, and then secretive. Slowly she turned back to him. He stood watchful, studying her face in the hot, white sunlight. The silence between them tensed, swelled, became alive—steamy and arousing. Her expression glazed with desire, and wordlessly she extended her arms to him.

One step forward and he'd caught her, molding her to him until he could feel her heart pounding against his. The past several weeks' restraint, the pent-up fire in his loins, blazed through the armor of his control. Hard, predatory, his hands etched down her flanks to harshly covet her buttocks and then possessively fit her between his legs.

Their mouths met and blended with molten violence, their tongues swirling and interlacing with impatient passion. Meanwhile their hands explored each other with a kind of aching lust until he gathered her hand in his, guided it down their heated bodies to the discernible desire that swelled from his groin.

Excitement convulsed somewhere deep in her belly as she touched him, mysterious and male, his hard erectness straining to reach her through the check of his clothing. Whispering amorous phrases, unlearned but instinctive, she brought her fingers upward to his belt in an attempt to release its buckle so he could come to her.

She heard his low and dusky laugh, seeming to come from far away. "May I offer you assistance? I think I know the procedure a bit better than my sweet Nanon."

She looked up with a kind of muted surprise. He was already freeing one broad shoulder. Quickly he discarded shirt, breeches, and underclothing. Above the thundering of her heart, Nanon heard the boots hitting the floor; using his heel, he'd scuffed each one off behind him.

The burning sunlight that filled the room showed her his sculptured body — the muscles smoothly powerful, rippling as he touched her; his waist and hips narrow and tautened, his maleness huge and hard. Her eyes widened. He laughed and swung her close to his naked chest, muffled her face against his own, licked fevered kisses onto her throat and into her mouth.

He had shocked himself with his own wild reaction. He'd know passion with other women — but never this savage surge, this sublime resolve to possess this one woman forever, to claim her as his before the world, to penetrate the hotness within her and infuse his seed inside her.

Shaking with fierce desire, and an even fiercer proprietary love, he stripped the thin blouse from her shoulders. Her silk chemise split, rended to her hips.

The force of his action staggered her backward onto the bed, into the path of the sunshine. She could feel skirts and pantalets being swept down to her ankles. The hot sun caressed her skin with fire. No . . . it was *his* mouth, *his* lips imprinting her body with kisses and swirling her into a nebula of light.

As his tongue trailed a slow and fervid passage between her breasts, pausing at their peaks to draw sweetness from her taut nipples, she thought there was no more quivering ecstasy to be endured. But his mouth continued to seek her sensitive places until the triangle of tight curls between her legs yielded to him and her limbs opened and he found her swelling bud.

From another far distance she seemed to hear his words tremble on the air: "Oh my love . . ." And she enfolded him as he thrust deep into her hot and throbbing center. Penetrating her, he was aware that his rhythm had quickened her immediate response. He was astonished, wondering if she realized the good fortune they shared. In her naïveté, she might assume it was always this way. Let her never learn otherwise! And then he thought no more. . . .


They had fallen asleep in the sunlight, their bodies moist, entangled; the air surrounding them hazed with motes of gold. Nanon awakened to the sensation that she was in a place strange to her, but the protective arm thrown across her breasts was familiar. She stared at the ceiling, and then her gaze traveled around the room, remembering.

He lay beside her, his sleeping face profiled against the pillow, his sword arm guarding her. How thick his lashes were, shadowing the rim of his high cheekbone closest to her. She wriggled her hand out from beneath his wrist and, with her fingertip, soothed back the lock of hair that touched his lips. His mouth was firm, strong even in the relaxation of sleep. She longed to caress the corner of his sensual lower lip, to fit her own to its fullness.

His gray eyes opened with a suddenness that surprised her. He sent her an instant smile and turning over, lazily reached out for her. Before his hand could capture hers, they both heard it — prolonged and intense, a shrill screaming.

Nanon was the first to jolt upright, piling the quilt around her nakedness, believing she recognized the sound—that long, drawn-out cry as though for help.

"Peacocks! Did your family bring them here from France? What a romantic idea." She loved their iridescent, fantailed appearance, hated their strident cries.

A motion of his hand demanded silence. It came again, this time almost human, frighteningly tortured—diminished but still there, and real.

He leaped to his feet, and she stared at him as he pulled on his clothes. He was at the door, stopping only to adjust his belt with its sheathed dagger.

He told her. "There are no peacocks! Stay here!" And he was gone.

# Chapter Twenty-two

The door banged shut behind him, and Nanon listened in alarm to his footsteps rushing down the hall and the stairs. Another crash signaled the slam of the front doors. She wanted to follow him, and knew she would even though he'd told her to remain where she was.

She rescued her garments, and was momentarily dismayed as she held up her torn chemise. Pulling on her crumpled blouse and riding skirt, she combed through her hair with her fingers while she ran to the balcony. Devin had disappeared. But there were sounds of quarreling and tumult coming from the other side of the house. At least, she knew where to go.

Pausing for a fraction of a second, she stared down at the railing beneath the trees where their horses had been tied. Both mounts were gone.

Outside, she flinched under the searing sun. Even then she might have halted and turned back to look for her straw hat, thus obeying Devin's order to remain in the house, but she told herself the disappearance of their horses made it imperative that she find him.

The rumble of voices rising to high pitches of anger directed her along an overgrown path. But, thank God, the brief, anguished screaming had stopped. She rounded the side of the house and quickly stepped behind a massive oleander bush.

Devin and another man, lean and hard-browed, stood in the midst of a knot of black men and women. Her shocked gaze went to the man lying on the ground near Devin's booted leg. It was obvious the man could not rise. There were purplish bruises on his face, an open gash on his head. His arms, limbs, and back bore the marks of a chain thrashing, while his chest was criss-crossed with whip lashes.

Her impulse was to run forward and assist the brutally beaten slave, but hearing the fury in Devin's voice, she stopped herself in time. It was just as well, for there was a look of solid menace in the dark faces that surrounded him and the thin-faced man he was confronting.

"Terren, against my express orders to go easy here, you've had this man whipped. You've had him strung up by the thumbs. And before this? How many others have you kept in stocks for days at a time? Goddammit, I should flog you myself, give you a bloody taste of the chain! Instead, I'll deal more fairly than you ever have. You and your wife have one day to pack and get your-selves off this property."

With hands outspread placatingly, the overseer whined. "How else could I get a decent day's work out of these lazy bastards? Give me another chance, Monsieur D'Amboise. Haven't I handed you a fair accounting of every-thing—crops, acreage, livestock—even down to the last ox and mule? I've told you the troubles we've had here— fires started in the cane fields by . . . who knows? . . . no rain, two years of drought. Runaway slaves in the hills—thieving bastards they are!—who come down in the night to steal! How am I supposed to deal with all this unless I show them a bit of discipline?"

"God knows *I've* been remiss, but you, Terren, you are an indecency and a blight. You're full of excuses; but there's misery, hopelessness, and fear here—that can't be disguised. You were in charge, and these people are starving. Look at this man, barely alive after what you've done to him. I'll stay and look after matters myself. I want you off this place!"

*"Monsieur,* I will do better. . . ." The whining voice droned on.

No longer listening, D'Amboise remained stunned and thoughtful until he announced. "Send for your wife. She's a good enough woman, as I recall. You two can stay a day longer than I've decreed, but only because I want food prepared for the slaves who are sick in their quarters. Get some able-bodied men and women in from the fields to help you. I'll send for others. They'll come here from Fort-de-France. And where is Jean Henri? He should be here."

"He ran off to the hills last week when his woman was sold to the Deschamps on the other side of the island," Terren whimpered, his eyes cast down. "They needed a house slave, and I got you an excellent price in gold for Mathilde. The bill of sale's in the house safe along with the money. You'll see the accounting in the ledger."

The overseer read the expression of outrage on D'Amboise's face and fell back a pace, complaining. "But the interior of the house is finished, and the two of them are no good working the cane fields."

Upon seeing Devin's reaction, Nanon raised her hands to her lips to stifle a cry. His face was so white she ached for him.

He stepped over the injured slave to advance on the cringing overseer, the words being ground out from between his clenched teeth. "You deserve to be strung up yourself, Terren!"

*"Monsieur, monsieur* . . ." The man winced away, but there was hatred in his eyes. "You've said nothing of all this up until now, *patron.*"

Thus reminded of his responsibility toward the plantation and its slaves, D'Amboise glared skyward in an attempt to regain control. Then he groaned. "That's it, exactly! As *patron* I said nothing! You're right about that, at least. I didn't pay enough attention — which is no excuse at all." His face still drenched with pallor, he re-

214

peated. "No excuse . . ."

He was shattered, and Nanon knew it by the beaten hang of his shoulders, by the knife lines of defeat that grooved his cheeks as though he himself had been flogged.

In her heart she knew more. Their light and happy days here had ended. With the painful situation just uncovered, whose origin she had not yet learned, Devin could rightly accuse himself of terrible negligence in having overlooked the pitiful conditions here. The slaves, who'd been listening with brooding expressions and smoldering eyes, began to stir and grumble.

Suddenly Devin straightened, wheeled, and reached down to take the injured man up in his arms. He held him as carefully as though he were a babe and spoke to the faces around him, faces that were no long impassive. "Clear the way . . . we'll bring him to the house."

Nanon shrank farther into the bushes in an attempt to make herself invisible. He was in control now, and the presence of a female stranger might prove a distraction and hinder matters.

She heard Devin give orders. "Stir yourselves. Help me to help your brother. We'll bed him in a ground-floor room near the kitchen, where he can be cared for."

As though coming out of a long stupor, the blacks raced to do his bidding. He walked slowly with his burden, shouting after them. "There's a charcoal brazier . . . heat some water. Tear the towels you find into strips. And there's rum to cleanse his wounds." As he disappeared into the house, his voice faded.

Nanon was about to peer from the bushes when a yellow-haired woman came hurrying from a house near the stables. She came up behind Terren and delivered a brisk cuff to his shoulder. He jumped around to face her.

The woman gave him an additional swat. "Now, you can see what's happened, husband. I warned you. You'd better look to it and send Abou to find Jean Henri in the hills. He can't have gone far; he's too frail. Oh, you wouldn't listen to me, Terren! Oh no!"

Emil Terren sullenly cursed his wife, but her voice rose even higher. "And there's the gold. Before he asks to see it, put it back in the safe, and be quick. Don't dally. The *patron* is different than you thought he would be, eh? He'll get that Mathilde back, you'll see. And you and I are done for; I heard what he said." She gave him a rap across his nose and then turned away, continuing on a run to the house and up the kitchen steps, all the while calling. *"Monsieur, monsieur* . . . I am here. I can be of help."

. Hearing taken in the entire scene, Nanon was shocked by the venality of the pair. She watched Terren as he started off, supposedly to do his wife's bidding.

From her hiding place, she stepped, on tiptoe, back onto the path. But the man halted—as did she. He had shifted to stare spitefully in the direction of the house. Taking care, Nanon moved back within the protection of the oleander bush, but not swiftly enough.

From the corner of his angry eye, Terren had caught the fleeting movement. Abruptly he lurched toward her place of concealment, and with a bullying hand he reached into the depths of the greenery. "Who do we have hiding here?" he rasped. "Somebody's whore?"

When she eluded his rude grasp and stepped out to face him, he looked her over from head to foot, then released a sound that was like a whimper of penitence. *"Do* forgive me, *mademoiselle!* Ah, you must be the patron's fine lady from France. My most humble regrets for my ill-chosen words." His vindictive eyes watching her closely, he continued to mumble apologies, hissing and whining and bowing but standing squarely in her path.

Nanon knew he was aware that she had heard his wife's accusations. But why should she care about *that?* Terren was a mean and dangerous man, but Devin was ridding himself of the overseer. And he was within hearing distance should there be a need to call for help. Which she would not do. He had enough woes to occupy him.

She sidled past the man, tilting her nose up in disgust since the oaf was making it necessary for her to brush against him before she could reach the path.

"I beg you, do not go until you tell me that you pardon me, *mademoiselle*."

He was fishing, trying to find out what she knew; and his humility was so false it set Nanon's teeth atingle. She would like to have smacked that skinny, rat face, instead she measured him coldly. When she spoke, her voice was low and convincingly steady.

"You know I have knowledge of what passed between you and your wife. I shall see to it that Monsieur D'Amboise receives this information. As your wife suggested, you'd better set matters straight. You do recall what she advised you to do?"

The man's sharp face grew crimson with rage which, somehow, he managed to swallow. He bowed low; to Nanon's relief this gesture concealed the nastiness of his expression. She walked away with careful dignity, not looking back because she didn't dare show further revulsion. Instinct told her this man was capable of violence, and it was better to get him off the place before he could plot a revenge.

When she was out of sight, she ran — around the side of the house and up the front steps to land, breathless, in the foyer. Hearing footsteps approaching along the corridor, she sent up a hope that it was Devin, and no one else.

It was he. Seeming not at all surprised to find her there, he took her in his arms and crooned softly. "It's as though you belong here, waiting for me. You are my heart and my conscience, Antoinette. Whatever good I can do here — now and in the future — will be because of you. How much I love you! Will you be patient with me

217

and with what I'm going to ask of you?"

"Devin, what is it?"

"Will you return to town without me? There's no transportation here other than a horse cart, but I've arranged for it to take you to Fort-de-France. You can't ride the mare back alone."

"But why should I have to go? What about you?"

"I can't leave just yet. Tomorrow, perhaps. But then I must return here until some proper arrangements are made. You see, a great injustice has been done, and there are deep wounds which I perceive will take time to heal. No, I don't mean the man in the kitchen . . . I mean all of them. I'll need you—and very soon—but it's better that you leave now."

"I want to stay here and help you."

He shook his head and gathered her closer to him. "I want you back in Fort-de-France, and safe. This dispute with Emil Terren could deepen. You've been outside, haven't you? What did you see?"

"I saw enough, Devin. But the horses are gone."

"I know that. They were frightened off by someone or something when the melee began. We'll get them back. The cart I ordered should be in the driveway now. The man who'll take you into town can be trusted. He was freed long ago. His name is Christophe. I'll be there with you tomorrow at the latest, I promise."

She placed her hands against his chest and looked up at him. "There's something you must know. I did go outside. I hid and I saw what happened. After you left, Terren's wife came. She accused him of taking the gold that was received for the sale of Mathilde. They are terrible people, Devin—malicious and scheming."

"I know, I know. And right now I don't want to think of what else that scoundrel Terren may have done, what tricks he may have been up to. Now, will you go? Will you do this for me?"

Gratefully, she huddled next to him, and then, standing on tiptoe, she raised her face to receive his kiss. As their lips parted, she told him, "Your kiss gives me courage."

"I need *your* courage. But I'm the *patron,* and I must stay here and resolve this. As a result of the quarrel between myself and that wretch Terren, these poor people mustn't suffer any more than they already have."

"Can he be saved—the man you carried inside just now?"

"I don't know whether you were aware of the drums calling in the hills . . .?" She shook her head. "Someone will soon come here who understands what to do, a black man who's a physician of sorts. There will be incantations, dancing, some form of sacrifice. One does not inquire too closely into the special arts of this man, but he is a healer."

"How do you know these things?"

"I was here as a child. I have come here enough. I know."

He took her hand, and together they walked to the veranda. The look she gave him was searching. She was remembering how with his long stride he had approached her for the first time in the Paris alleyway, with Boru, the powerful gray who matched him well, at his shoulder.

She recalled the sculpted cheekbones; the clean, wind-scoured look of him; the direct gaze of eyes the color of slate, eyes that had dazzled her with their candor; the quirk of his sensual lips. And she recalled more—the hunger with which that morning he'd probed her mouth, the hard drive of his passion that had brought her womanhood to climax and sent her on to shuddering release.

She shivered, tightening her arm around his. Turning to him, she let her head fall against his chest, relishing its protection and pressing her lips to his heart. If she should ever lose him. . . .

"What is it, my darling?" he asked, concerned.

How could she possibly tell him what she was thinking, feeling, fearing—when at this moment he had to deal with so much that was harsh and threatening. "It's nothing," she murmured. "Simply that I shall miss you."

She placed her straw hat squarely upon her head, then walked down the steps to the cart. He assisted her up onto the seat next to Christophe, and she stared straight ahead. One downward glance and she would have retreated into his arms never to leave them.

Only when they were halfway down the lane did she gaze over her shoulder. He was standing on the terrace watching after her. He stood so until the cart disappeared from his view as it turned onto the main road.

The drive through the groves, past the cane fields, and into the dense rain forest was eerily silent. For long stretches there were only a few passing horsemen to be seen. Little conversation was exchanged between herself and Christophe, except when he occasionally pointed out to her the exotic birds nesting in the tree branches overhanging the road.

A curious lull appeared to have settled over the landscape, and as they came in sight of the sea and the town, the oddly depressing quietude continued. In Fort-de-France itself, the colorful Creole population, always genial and smiling, appeared to have undergone a muted transformation. On this twilight afternoon, an almost shroudlike hush prevailed. From atop the cart Nanon looked around, wondering what event could have quelled the spirit of the town.

As they neared the Hôtel Beaux Jours, Christophe pointed with his whip in the direction of a newly arrived sailing ship anchored at some distance from the confusion of fishing boats and small tugs.

Somberly he remarked. "The currents of the sea no longer move in opposite directions to the winds . . . so I think it is safe for the world to visit our island once more."

Her own words were less poetic than his when she smilingly replied. "It *is* good to see that shipping's returned to our harbor."

The arrival meant long-delayed news, packets of letters to be opened, as well as fresh supplies from the continent. Even a coterie of disembarking passengers. Living on an island, it was too easy to feel cut off from civilization.

The horse cart stopped in front of the hotel. As Christophe helped her down over the high wooden wheel, Nanon bade him good-bye. She would have liked to send a message for Devin with him, but he seemed eager to start the return trip and she didn't want to detain him further.

She watched him depart then took off her hat and shook out her hair, letting its lengthening strands flow with the persistent wind. She glanced up at her balcony, wondering if Madame was upstairs packing still—she herself was looking forward to a hot bath. Once again glancing at the silent street, Nanon was curious anew as to the reason for the town's lassitude.

She entered the lobby. As usual, it was quiet, dark and cool; redolent with the scent of the ginger flower, the ceiling fans turning slowly. . . .

The man behind the desk greeted her with his usual look of devotion, but then, surprisingly, he rolled his eyes and cocked his head in the direction of the pergola. "Over there, *mademoiselle*. The gentleman's been waiting for a long time. It's been a half-day since the French ship came. And you have heard the sad news . . . ?"

But she was already gazing at the place he had indicated, her eyes narrowing to adjust from the bright sunlight outside. Who could possibly be here to see her, from the French ship? And waiting all this time? It must be a mistake. . . .

But then suddenly she knew, and she felt faint from a great wash of terrified anticipation. Could it be news of the de Cavanac family, news of her father?

The high-backed rattan chair faced toward an open arch leading to the outside pergola. Its occupant was rising as she timorously approached. He turned toward her; she could not see his face, with the strong sun behind it.

And then she could.

She halted, stunned.

"Nanon, my dear, dear Nanon . . ." He advanced, limping slightly. And caught her in his arms as she swayed, her eyes closed in fierce denial of what she was certain he had crossed the sea to tell her . . .

# Chapter Twenty-three

It was dark now. They were seated side by side on a marble bench in the garden outside the pergola. Flame from a torch lit Georges Degrelle's face as he held her ice-cold hand in his, trying to chafe it to warmth.

In soothing litany he repeated. "Your father went courageously to meet death as he had met life. He slept in a coma last week. He did not even know . . ." He hesitated, biting his lip beneath the new, pale moustache he wore.

"He didn't know . . .?" She took up the burden of his tale. "He didn't know that Josephine had gone . . . before him?"

Georges sighed and continued stroking her hand. "It's just as I've told you."

"I can accept Father's death with my mind—though not with my emotions. As painful as it is to lose him, I knew it was inevitable—the wounds he suffered were too severe. Yet, I'd always hoped—no, I'd *expected* to be at his side to comfort him, to hold his hand in mine at the end so that he wouldn't be . . . alone. Or afraid."

Pain suffused her voice, and for a time she could not go on. Then, she straightened abruptly, removed her hand from Degrelle's but only to press it hard against her side as though attempting to stop the pain that wracked her at his news. "No . . ." she cried. "I don't believe he was ever afraid, even at the moment of his death."

Degrelle shrugged as though in gentle assent. He would let her talk, reassure herself in this manner.

She looked at him despairingly. "But Joséphine, too? Georges, this is tragic!"

She placed her hand over her eyes, and he drew her to his waiting shoulder while she murmured. "She was so brave, so strong—perhaps not strong in her physical person, but strong in her spirit. Think of what she had to face in her lifetime—escape from the shadow of the guillotine and the rise to the throne of France. Then, like that, it is over. She truly loved Napoléon. And he did love her." Her hand fell from her eyes, and she looked directly into Degrelle's face. "With what grace she was able to surmount tragedy."

"One never surmounts the final tragedy, Nanon. Still, we must remember not everyone regards death as such."

After a moment, Nanon added pensively. "And what was Father told of me?"

"He believed that at the last moment a decision was made that you should accompany Joséphine to Navarre. That you were with her was a comfort to him—and he was told you would soon return."

After that they were both silent, until she sighed and said, "Tell me once more how it was with her?"

Patiently he began. "The Empress caught a chill driving in an open carriage in the forest. Ten days later she was still ill, but she opened a ball for the Russian visitors at Malmaison. She danced frequently with the Tsar; it was obvious to all that Alexander was quite taken with her."

At this, Nanon smiled faintly while he continued. "It is reported that in her filmy gown she walked out with him from the overheated ballroom into the night air of the gardens."

Nanon nodded. "She wished him to intercede on Napoléon's behalf."

"Yes, undoubtedly that is so. But a day later she was feverish, her throat badly inflamed. Alexander was expected to dine with her, but could not keep the engagement. When he heard of her indisposition, he sent his personal physician who was joined by two doctors from Paris. Nothing could be done. Two more days passed, and . . . she was gone. They say at the end she looked . . . beyond, and had a most astonishing expression of happiness upon her face."

Nanon slowly nodded, then stared into the dark garden. "And Napoléon . . . what of him?"

Degrelle glanced at her with a look of surprise. "You've heard no news at all, then? Bonaparte was forced to abdicate. At present, he's in exile on an island called Elba."

"It's finished." Nanon's voice sank sorrowfully.

He took her hand in his. "You must have seen the misery that's come over this town. When my ship arrived at midday, the people here in Fort-de-France learned for the first time that their own Joséphine of Trois Îlets was dead."

She rose slowly. "I thank you for coming this long distance to tell me. It would have been even more difficult had I learned of these grievous happenings from strangers. Georges, I do appreciate your . . . your presence." Again she sighed deeply. "Now. Tell me about my brother."

Degrelle, too, had risen. He picked up the cape he'd dropped beside the bench. It was almost a delaying ploy. "Nanon, there *is* still more." He paused, looked about as though for escape, then went on in a rush. "By now, Théo must have arrived in Italy."

"*Italy* . . . ? Why Italy?" Her eyes, enormous in their accusation, accosted his. "What have you not told me?"

"After your father died, anti-Bonapartists stormed out

225

of Paris to assault the country villages and the estates of those who'd been loyal to Napoléon's regime. No one was spared, and the de Cavanac château was sacked and partly burned. The Royalists had disbanded Théo's secret assembly and he'd already fled to Northern Italy, to the lakeside villa of a friend."

Dazed by this additional blow, Nanon was barely aware that he'd placed an arm around her shoulder and had pressed his lips to her brow. Blindly she began to pace forward, but he stepped in front of her, grasping her arms. "Nanon, *we* shall join him there! The three of us will establish a family once more, until it's safe to return to France. Believe me, the new King Louis will recognize your father's valiant service to his country, and your lands will not be confiscated. If we're patient, all will be settled in good time."

She could only shake her head at this while letting him lead her into the lobby. The young man behind the counter, taken aback by her tearful condition, raced to her side.

"Mademoiselle de Cavanac, what has happened? Allow me to call Madame Arnaud." He whirled to face Degrelle. "What did you say to mademoiselle?"

The clerk was a frail man, but at this instant he would have done ferocious battle for her. Even in her stunned state, Nanon realized this and put out a shaking hand. "Robert, I've had sad news from my home. This gentleman has come a long way to make it easier for me."

She took a deep breath, and released herself from Degrelle's sheltering arm. "Georges, why not arrange to stay here for a few days? There's much we have to discuss. And I, too, have something to tell you."

This was not the time to inform Degrelle of her coming marriage. First, she must go upstairs, see Madame A., bathe, and make herself presentable. She was

226

aware that in the hotel's lamplight Degrelle was studying her with some dismay, taking in the disarray of her garments and her hair. She wanted to reassure him that she was safe and content in her present life.

She thought quickly in answer to the question she saw in his eyes and provided him with part of the truth. "I've been riding in the countryside. I'll go now and change, and we'll dine together. Is that satisfactory? Oh—I've just thought. What of my Dominique? I cannot bear to hear that she, too, is gone."

"This is one piece of good news I have for you, Nanon. You see, the Royalists still considered Joséphine one of theirs due to her aristocratic birth and the fact that Napoléon had divorced her. Malmaison has been left untouched, and your mare is safe in its stable. The caretaker there is a good fellow who'll keep her for you. The time we spend in Italy may not be too lengthy, so there's no need to send for her."

There would be no time at all in Italy—but she would save this for later. She listened as he said "I shall look forward to dining with you."

"Until then," she murmured, and turning away from his keen gaze, she walked slowly up the stairs, sorrowfully conscious that his eyes followed her until she was out of sight.

Clad in black in respect for Nanon's loss, Madame Arnaud accompanied the two to the hotel dining room. Since there were no drab garments in the trousseau, Madame had insisted that Nanon's dark gray traveling dress would be appropriate for a period of mourning. To Nanon it didn't matter. This was an evening she wanted to end quickly.

During the course of dinner she learned that Théo and Edmond had followed her trail to Brest, to the ship

227

that had sailed at dawn carrying her off to Martinique. But they were unaware that Devin D'Amboise had sailed at the same time.

Later, sitting together in a private corner of the lobby with Madame ensconced at a distance, out of earshot, Nanon unfolded her story to Degrelle. The time had come to tell him, as gently as possible, that she was to be married.

"To Colonel D'Amboise?" From the shock of what she had just said, he paled, the thin, lavender-hued scar standing out in scarlet detail on his classically-featured face.

She placed a soothing hand on his sleeve. "You see why I cannot accompany you to Italy, though you've so gallantly offered me escort there."

"Nanon, I came prepared to offer you far more than that. I came to ask you to marry me."

"Are you doing this because I'm without family or estate? I do appreciate your chivalry, Georges—as much as I appreciate the care you gave my father all these years. You alone understood the use of the drugs he needed to sedate his pain."

"The care I gave your father and my feelings for you are not quite the same. And it was not mere protection that I was—and am—prepared to offer you. I love you. I always have. I always shall." He could not hide his bitterness. "This D'Amboise is a very rich man, so the loss of your property in France cannot matter to you now. Except for sentimental reasons."

"That's not true." Nanon understood the tension and the unhappiness in his expression, but she was now so exhausted from the day's earlier happenings and from the sorrowful news she'd so recently received, that she could think of no words to assuage his hurt. Not at the moment, certainly.

"Please. Let us talk further tomorrow. I repeat, I'm

deeply touched by your devotion to me and to my family. And I'm greatly complimented by your offer of marriage, though I cannot accept it. When Monsieur D'Amboise returns, will you do me the favor of meeting with him? It will make me somewhat content if you two come together in a friendly manner."

A flicker of a sardonic smile touched Degrelle's lips, for he knew both of them remembered the final scene in the library of the old château. And their discussion concerning the proper dosage of laudanum in brandy.

She looked with understanding into his lynxlike eyes. "Some things are better left unsaid, Georges, isn't that true?"

"I agree, Nanon."

She rose, and he bowed over her hand, watching thoughtfully while she and Madame A. swept out of the lobby and up the staircase.


Sometime later, as Georges Degrelle walked swiftly to the harbor to find the longboat that would carry him back to his cabin aboard the anchored sailing ship, he considered what he must do next.

That Nanon and D'Amboise were betrothed was a shock, but it did not disturb the flintiness of his purpose. He had laid his plans too well, he had invested too much of his strength, will, and imagination in his scheme to allow it to be destroyed by a young woman's fanciful illusion that she loved another. That his rival was rich and powerful presented a problem. But in Degrelle's plotting, no barrier seemed impossible to surmount. Though it was true, the circumstances of his plan might need to be altered.

Now, peering through the summer mist that rolled in across the waters of the harbor, Degrelle could guess that an intimate connection might have been formed between Nanon and D'Amboise. He had already ascertained that the dragon of a woman, that chaperone, had not been present on the long sea voyage from France to Martinique.

And then there was the man's curious heritage. His lip curled as he pondered the bastard background of this Anglo-Irishman with his intermingled French blood. Unfortunately it did not add up to any signs of cowardice as one might suppose. D'Amboise's reputation was unassailable.

Nevertheless, with single-minded ferocity, Degrelle dismissed D'Amboise, his reputation, and his riches. Matters might be a great deal more difficult than they had seemed at first, but he was prepared to cope with this. Somehow, he'd spirit her away to Italy.

The longboat was wedged against the jetty, its two seamen half-asleep at the oars. He hailed them and stepped into the craft as the fellows bestirred themselves and prepared to row him out to the ship which was partly obscured by mist.

Degrelle wrapped himself in his cape and settled back. A worldly man, he was well aware that Théo's affection for his sister was significantly deeper than it should be. He had no intention of joining forces with him, for long ago, he'd decided that the brother must never return from exile to claim the de Cavanac estate.

A shooting accident should do it, or perhaps a boat capsized on a lake. Easy treachery . . . Nanon would inherit under the new French law. Then the two of them would marry and rebuild their lives and the château.

After climbing the ship's ladder he went directly to his cabin to open his apothecary's bag and remove the thin envelope inside. Shortly thereafter, he explored a feeling of extraordinary and powerful elation. Leaning back against the pillows on his bunk, he knew that he was comfortable with his duplicitous plan, and that he'd sleep well on it, though the hand he now held was not the same one originally dealt him.

# Chapter Twenty-four

Each of these last three mornings Nanon had awakened early, anticipating this might be the day Devin would return to his house in Fort-de-France—and to her.

On the fourth day, seeing the horse cart pull up beneath her balcony, she raced down the stairway, through the lobby, and outside to the street. Leaning over the wooden wheel, Christophe waved a missive at her, then quickly dropped it into her outstretched hands.

She read its contents, her gaze rushing down the open page once, and then twice. She looked up, her eyes sparkling. "They coaxed Jean Henri down from the hills! But . . . the Deschamps have promised to take him into their household staff along with Mathilde? How is that?"

Christophe's mellow voice replied. "They will not sell Mathilde back to the *patron,* even at double the price. The *patron* believes it wise to be patient in these matters. So, he will bide his time."

Her fingertips tingled at touching the paper Devin had held in his hands that very morning. She folded the letter into its envelope and slid that into her pocket, while Christophe continued. "The drums tell us sad news of our Empress." He looked closely at her. "And they tell us, too, that the Bishop says there will be no celebrations within church walls until the mourning period has passed." A sly smile rimmed his lips. "On our island, this should be a mere matter of a week or so."

She could guess that this was Christophe's oblique way

of referring to the delay in her wedding ceremony. The Pageries, in somber dress, had already visited her to commiserate concerning the postponement.

Now Nanon was anxious to return to her room to reread that final, deliciously loving paragraph written in Devin's hand: *My own dearest — I feel your lips on mine as I write this . . . your breath is my being . . . and I ask what my life would be like without you. I do not deserve you and your goodness. You have inspired me to do my best, and I shall love you more than anyone has ever loved before. Until we're together — soon, and forever — I am yours.*

Nevertheless, she quelled her impatience and running her fingers through the cart horse's sandy-colored mane, she inquired. "Tell me, how is the poor man who was beaten by Terren?"

"Zachée recovers nicely, *mademoiselle.*" But Christophe's clear gaze flickered away from hers.

"Something is troubling you."

He jumped over the high wheel and down into the street to stand beside her. His voice lowered, he said, "The new overseer has not yet arrived. For this reason Terren remains, though he's sent away his packed goods and his wife. I do not like these circumstances. An evil spirit dwells in that man!"

She was about to reply when he looked up and over her shoulder. "There is someone here for you, *mademoiselle.*"

Nanon bade Christophe good-bye, and turned to face Georges, who had strolled up from the harbor for his daily rendezvous with her.

He bent over her hand, his attentive gaze following Christophe's retreating cart. Since she said nothing in response to his obvious curiosity, he announced, "My dear Nanon, this is the first day since I arrived here bearing my sad tidings that I've seen you looking serene. Have you just received propitious news — is that it?"

"Oh . . . news of a sort," she answered cryptically, not

really willing to share her happiness at the letter which rested inside her pocket against her thigh.

This day, Georges was wearing stylish Parisian attire — white frock coat with tails, abbreviated across the waist-line in front; and long, tight white trousers — his panama hat set at a rakish angle. He asked, "May I?" And she nodded as he lit his slender cigarillo. They strolled inside the hotel grounds, she walking slowly to accommodate the unevenness in his pace.

Her heart began to soften toward him as she recalled his devotion to her father — in battle and in the invalid years that had followed. She was sorry for her reluctance to trust him; thus, she began to confide the reasons behind D'Amboise's delay in returning to Fort-de-France.

When she'd concluded her tale, Degrelle brought them both to a halt, inquiring sympathetically. "You're worried about this man Terren staying on at the plantation since he and the Colonel have had disagreements in the past. You feel an even nastier quarrel might be brewing?"

"You put it more strongly than I might have. After all, Devin can take care of these matters; I've full confidence in him. It's just that I'd hoped it would all be resolved and that he'd be here much sooner, so that the two of you could meet again."

"I don't think this will be possible, Nanon. You saw the ship that sailed into the harbor the day before yester-day? It will be returning to Genoa as soon as it can be provisioned and loaded with trade goods from this island. I've spent most of the morning seeing to it that my travel chests are moved on board." He hesitated. "You're still determined that I'm to sail alone? I can do nothing to dissuade you? This decision of yours is a great disap-pointment to me, you know that."

"You've been so kind, Georges. Patient, understanding."

As they began to stroll once more, he shook his head at her reprovingly. "This is a most circuitous compliment you've just paid me. In the old days, you would have said it bluntly, like this: 'Enough, Georges. My mind is made up!'"

She paused beneath a flambeau tree. A scarlet petal fell, catching in her hair as she laughingly repeated his words to him. "Enough, Georges. My mind is made up! There, does that satisfy you?"

He removed the blossom from her curls and pressing it suggestively to his lips, replied, "Certainly not. I can think of a far more poignant satisfaction than a phrase of dismissal."

Disregarding his advance, she allowed her humor to vanish. "I am serious now. Devin and I love each other, and, believe me, I'm not making a mistake in my desire to share my life with him."

"I see I've no choice but to believe you—since I can't convince you otherwise." He dropped his cigarillo onto the path, stubbed it out with his boot. "Tell me again about this ancestral plantation where D'Amboise is at present. Describe to me those sugarcane fields, the road winding through the rain forest, the dark slave quarters, and the wicked overseer. It does sound barbaric."

"To someone like yourself who has never lived here, I suppose it does. But not to us in Martinique."

"Ah . . . spoken like a native." He laughed softly and looked into her eyes with tenderness. "'Not to us in Martinique' you say. It sounds as though you are quite at home here." He gestured with both hands and smiled broadly. "You are as set in your ways as you ever were, young lady. Shall we find your Madame Arnaud so that the three of us may enjoy luncheon at some exotic spot? We may be coming close to the time when I must bid you farewell."

But then he stopped, seemingly stricken. "No! How stupid of me to forget. I've business with the Consul that must be consummated this morning. It may take time. May I call on you this evening?"

"Of course. *Addio*, Georges." She sent him a mischievous grin, hoping it was not too apparent that she was in a wild rush to get away and read her letter once again.

But he lingered. "You wished me farewell . . . in Italian? Do I detect a note of encouragement?"

"You do not," she explained hastily while shooing him down the pathway. "It's the only word I know in that lovely language. Now, don't be late for your appointment."

"No, indeed! That would never do." With a flourish, he placed his panama hat on his head, his gleaming eyes almost as golden as his fair hair.

She watched him walk off, only his gait impeding his jaunty air. She had disliked him when they'd lived under the same roof, but he was different now, amusing, kindly, consoling. Wasn't he?

She scolded herself, wondering at the ambivalence in her attitude toward him when she should be feeling grateful because he'd so generously undertaken a long voyage on her behalf.


While putting away the slender chain with its unobtrusive garnet—she'd worn them at dinner with Madame A.—Nanon folded Devin's letter and placed it in her jewel case as well. Just now, she'd felt peaceful on rereading his words, but glancing into her mirror, she knew that her reddened eyes attested to the sorrow that remained with her.

It was difficult to believe she would never see her father again. Nor share womanly confidences with Joséphine. She—Nanon—was still living on this planet; sadly, those two to whom she'd been so close were gone from it forever.

From outside her bedroom door, a voice spoke. "My dear, the porter tells me that Monsieur Degrelle is waiting downstairs. I suppose he's here to say good-bye, since Robert informs me the Italian ship will be sailing tomorrow or the next day."

Nanon opened her door to the older woman, who appeared more fretful than usual. Madame A. went on. "As soon as he concludes his evening visit, I must go to my daughter's, Nanon. One of the grandchildren is ill again."

"I'm sorry about the little one. I hope it isn't serious. But why not go there immediately? Surely one unsupervised visit with an old friend in the reception room downstairs will not stain my reputation." She could not resist adding, "After all, I am finally affianced, so it's not as though I'll be losing out on the main chance by my adventurous action."

Madame favored her with a shocked stare. "You do make such impossibly risqué statements at times, Antoinette. However, I shall take you at your word, and I'll leave at once. There are a number of guests in the public rooms downstairs; and Robert is there to look after matters, so there can be no hint of indiscretion. I can trust you to behave with judiciousness?" There was wavering indecision in Madame's sharp black eyes. It would be a terrible blow if this exceedingly advantageous marriage came a cropper, as the English would say, at this late hour.

"Wait, Madame. I have a much better thought. Why don't you send word to Monsieur Degrelle that I can't come downstairs at all. I can assure you, this would suit *me* much better."

"Perhaps . . . perhaps . . ." Madame pondered, then shook her head. "No, it would not be kind — you know that. Your eyes are puffy still; you must put tea leaves on the lids when you go to bed. I had hoped you'd grow resigned to your loss by this time. It is God's will, *ma chérie*. We all must go one day."

"Yes, yes. Now go, *please*, Madame. And I do pray all will be well at your daughter's house."

She closed the door on Madame's raised eyebrows and

leaned against it, wishing that it were Devin waiting for her instead of Degrelle. Then, she dressed again in the dove gray traveling gown. Georges had been difficult these last few days, pressing her more than once to change her mind and sail with him to Genoa. He was not one to give up easily. *If only Devin were here . . .*

Georges was waiting for her on the pergola, and though she urged him to retire to the main room so they could converse under the watchful gaze of the other guests, he refused. She decided to humor him and he led her to the marble bench near the darkened garden.

"Let me have this last hour alone with you," he protested. "If the tide is full and the winds are with us, we shall sail tomorrow." His voice sank to a meaningful level. "You heard what I said . . . *we'll* sail, you and I!"

She thought quickly, almost desperately. "Why won't you accept the truth, Georges? It's almost perverse of you, this insistence. Why will you not believe that I love Monsieur D'Amboise and that I shall become his wife? If the town were not in mourning these days, you could have met our friends, and perhaps that would have convinced you." She emphasized her next words. "People here are kind. They've entertained us, and everyone is aware of—and happy for—our coming marriage. Had there been time you would have been welcomed as our friend."

He interrupted fiercely. "I don't need people to welcome me, Nanon. *Your* welcome is all that I require. I know what you're trying to do now. You're trying to impress upon me that it's a fait accompli, and this entire island knows you and D'Amboise are considering marriage."

"*Considering?* Devils and demons! It *is arranged,* Georges." She was angry with herself for going back to those girlish oaths. She straightened. "We shall marry! Again I ask you, why won't you accept this? Truly, your refusal to believe is . . . well, it's tiresome." She started to rise.

With surprising strength, his arm encircled her waist, and he jerked her down beside him, murmuring against her cheek, "I won't accept it because I've known you since you were fourteen years of age, and I've loved you all this time . . . *adored you, Nanon!*" She could almost hear his heart beat madly. "What do you really know of D'Amboise? Have you forgotten he has been an enemy of France? Would your father have approved of this — whatever he is! Englishman, Irishman. What small drop of French blood can this mongrel fellow lay claim to?"

"Georges!" Nanon was stunned. "I despise you for what you have just said!"

Savagely, and this time with both arms, he wrenched her around, hurtfully straining her body into his own. She cried out, but he muffled her plea with the flat of his hand and deftly he forced her down on the length of the bench until she lay crumpled beneath his weight. Her head banged hard against marble. Through the silk material of her gown, she could feel his mouth burn as it groped toward her breasts, then moved upward to capture her throat, and higher still until his lips were grinding into hers.

Since he'd fallen heavily upon her, Nanon could make no sound. She was strangled by his mouth, entrapped by his torso. With one arm, he pinned her close, while his other roamed beneath her skirt to slide up her thigh.

For an instant more they grappled, and then as he twisted, seeking to keep her from freeing her arms, she was able to double her legs and thrust herself sideways against him. Off balance, they both might have fallen, but he recovered first and quickly righted her. At the same time, with belated gallantry, he dusted her skirt down with his hand.

Dazedly, she held her gown together at the neckline as she glared at him. But before she could rake him with some choice phrases she'd learned from Théo, he was on his knees in front of her. His face buried in the folds of

239

her skirt, he implored. "Nanon . . . forgive me! Forgive my love, my passion for you. Forgive—"

"For pity's sake, Georges, get up!" Now Nanon was standing, peering over her shoulder at the arches that led into the lobby. She was no longer intimidated by him. The situation had become ridiculous. She could have boxed his ears, smacked his face hard. But she knew that, for all their sakes, she must control the untidiness of this stupid scene.

She whirled on him. "I don't want anyone to know I've displayed so little sense as to allow an undignified assault of this kind. No real harm has been done, but this could be blown into a scandal. I want you to stop all this mewling talk about love and passion. Pull yourself together, and let's see if we can both walk inside with some decorum. Is that understood?"

Seeing the fury in her eyes, he stepped back hastily. "Will you ever forgive me?"

"No." She straightened her dress and set out along the pergola at a fast clip.

He rushed to keep up with her. "Think, Nanon! When a man loves a woman as I love you, when he has loved as long as I have with single-minded devotion, and when he sees that woman considering marriage with another— then he loses all restraint. I should not have used force, but then . . ."

Over her shoulder she flung him an angry retort. "No, you shouldn't have—you foolish man!" She was in the doorway, the lamplight from the reception room shining on her face. When she hastened past Robert's station and saw him looking at her with his usual grave devotion, she knew she had passed muster.

She glanced behind her to discover Degrelle, seemingly as composed as herself, pacing along in dignified fashion. For an instant their gazes clashed. Seeing his sedate expression, his benign deportment, Nanon could barely repress an hysterical titter.

He came closer to mutter, "Are we to part forever as enemies?"

She glanced around her. No one seemed to be observing them, so she faced him, speaking reluctantly. "You did journey a long way to find me. Always I come back to that when judging you, so I suppose I have to say I understand. It's not wholehearted understanding, and it's not without reservations."

"Such an extreme lapse on my part will never occur again. I give you my gentleman's oath. You may trust me on this, Antoinette. If I sail tomorrow, will you see me off so that I may swear on my officer's sword?"

"I'm not all that foolish, Georges. We'll say our good-byes right here. And right now. You may swear on your sword without me!"

He was facing the entrance to the hotel, and as he looked across her shoulder, she saw the tide of color rise in his fair skin. Fascinated, she watched the line of scar tissue on his cheek deepen to a ghoulish slash of crimson, saw his pale eyes darken ominously. Caught by Degrelle's almost murderous expression, her own heart raced in fear and she turned around.

He was standing there in the doorway, his eyes on her alone. All at once, she felt herself go soft and yielding; she was adrift in rapture, borne along on tender desire. Astonished by her own emotion, she gazed at him, her eyes filled with awe, with wonder and with love. . . .

# Chapter Twenty-five

Other heads had turned as well as her own; other eyes watched. And though it seemed her heart would soar like a ship's rocket, Nanon managed to control her excitement. In front of the hotel's guests, she behaved with aplomb.

As he raised her hand to his lips in greeting, she exclaimed. "Ah, Devin. We're fortunate that your arrival is so timely. You do remember my father's aide, Captain Georges Degrelle? He's come this long way to bring me news of home."

"Captain Degrelle." Devin bowed in acknowledgement, though he was finding it difficult to wrench his attention from Nanon's glowing countenance.

She glanced at Georges, relieved that his face was no longer contorted by jealous fury. Perhaps no one but herself had noticed.

But as she turned back to Devin, her heart sank. The slight smile with which he favored Degrelle did not reach his eyes. His gaze was steely. Worse, it seemed to Nanon it was knowledgeable. She sensed that in his alertness he'd already searched out the flaw in the man behind her.

Degrelle's shoulders straightened as though in mock salute. Had he been in uniform, he might have clicked his heels. "I have brought certain painful information concerning her family to Antoinette. There's much else that has happened; she will tell you." He waited, feelers attuned.

D'Amboise was blunt. "In that case, I'd like to speak to Mademoiselle de Cavanac in private. You will excuse us?"

"The longboat is waiting for me. I'll not intrude further on your time." Degrelle looked meaningfully at Nanon. "You know my plans for the future." He bowed to D'Amboise. "Good night, *monsieur*."

D'Amboise's nod was cursory. He'd detested the fellow when they'd first met months earlier and he saw no reason to change his mind about him. There was something sleek, unctuous, and untrustworthy about Degrelle. And, definitely, the man had a lecherous eye for Nanon.

The hotel guests were aware of the potential here for an interesting encounter and now feeling deprived of one, settled back to their cards and conversation. Some of their talk was whispered, centering on the fashionably dressed Frenchman with the intimidating scar. The gossipers were mindful that he and the young lady had just come in from the dark garden — at almost the same moment her impressive-looking fiancé had made his appearance.

Earlier, Robert had not missed a chance to hint at the identity as well as the background of these illustrious visitors to the Hôtel Beaux Jours. He now bustled to the couple's side to speak confidentially to them. "Madame Arnaud has departed for the evening, but the library is at your disposal."

The inference was plain. Convention decreed it would be unsuitable for them to go upstairs with Nanon's companion absent. The two forebode to exchange amused glances as Robert waved them in the direction of the nearby annex to the main rooms.

As they stepped around a corner into a small alcove lined with shelves of books, D'Amboise remarked wryly. "This is the best we can hope for, I suppose."

Nanon's heart hammered wildly as she stared up at

him. "What does it matter what they think? Can't we go somewhere private? There's so much to be said."

He reconnoitered, then turned back to her, his shoulder shielding her from view. "For the moment we have seclusion," he said, and took her in his arms.

Passion flamed between them as his fingertips, trembling with desire, caressed her forehead, her cheekbones, her lips while he pressed urgent kisses upon her mouth and throat. The thrilling sensation that laced through her, as the back of his hand unintentionally brushed the outline of her breasts beneath the gray silk, was so powerful that she could not help gasping aloud.

He muffled her faint outcry with his lips, and her arms curled tightly around his neck, her fingers twisting through the thick locks of his hair, still damp from the sea mist outside. Her flesh hungered for his flesh in the most intimate way, and she shivered uncontrollably as she felt his passion hard and throbbing against her leg.

He groaned. "How can I leave you now?"

Her breath seemed to stop in her throat. Finally it emerged in a choked whisper. "You don't have to. Let me come with you."

"I'm on my way to my house here in town, to spend the night. My carriage is waiting outside; we could . . ." But then, in an abrupt release that seemed to surprise him as much as it did her, his hands dropped away from her waist. "I can't . . . we can't."

Questioningly she stared up at him. He cupped her head in his hands and murmured against her lips. "God knows I've never considered myself a beacon of righteousness—even the idea is absurd. But I want to take care of you. I don't want people to whisper about us, to gossip and to create scandal. And there is something else."

Slowly she drew back from him. "I think I know."

"You remember what we talked of and planned together? It was *you* who taught me how much there is to be accomplished here. We are not the only ones to be

244

considered. . . ."

She read zeal in his face—and knew that she was responsible. He was reaching for the dream she'd wanted them both to share. They'd not only made love in the hot sunlight of that upstairs chamber in the plantation house; afterward, away from the world, they had talked long. About themselves, of course, but also about the workings of justice.

Her lips curved in an enigmatic smile. "I do remember. Let me quote: If the peasants in France, little better than slaves themselves, have found freedom, why is it so impossible for Martinique's slaves?"

"Exactly. And we have to rely on the use of example—slow and tiring, perhaps—but only in this way can we convince the other owners."

"Therefore," she finished, "we must never undermine our reputation in their eyes. Nor our mission."

"*My* mission would be to convince the Court."

With her arms around his neck, it was too easy to forget that he was an important man, that he did have great influence. The riddle is answered, she thought. He is English, truly, with the Englishman's great understanding of freedom. And he carries the blood of the Irish, with their vast and wild dreams. And I . . . I am French. I want to be in his arms; I don't want to lead a crusade.

"What are you thinking?" he demanded.

She shook her head and touched his mouth with her fingertips, tracing the curve of his lower lip, then leaning forward to tease it with the tip of her tongue.

He whispered in her ear. "Ah, but I do love you so much, Nanon. I want you so much. If you say what I think is in your heart, we'll leave for my house at once."

"No, you're right." She tried to smile. "Admittedly, I hate it that you're right, but you are. We'll stay here. And behave."

It was difficult to restrain himself from touching her

245

lips and her hair, but he did. Instead, he stared at her, pondering. "That man Degrelle—tell me everything he said to you."

She did, but in the telling it became apparent to D'Amboise that she seemed unaware of the man's duplicity. Degrelle was not so generous-hearted that he would woo her away to Italy, to the side of her brother Théo, and then see them installed once again in the château near Malmaison. No. Not expecting nothing in return. Of this, D'Amboise was certain.

"I don't trust him. Believe me, I was fully aware there were plottings against me that night I stayed under your father's roof." He paused, studying her with bemused concentration.

So, he knew, she thought.

He turned serious. "I want you away from Fort-de-France. The Pageries are in mourning for their Josephine, nevertheless, I'll take you there. Will you finish your packing and wait until I return? In the morning I have to go back to the plantation and have it out with Terren, but later in the day we'll go down island to Trois Îlets."

Then, as though he had time at his disposal, he moved them farther back among the shelves of books. Threading his fingers through her hair, he kissed the autumnal-shaded tendrils that curled around them, breathing in her perfumed scent. Then he looked deep into her eyes before languorously probing her mouth. With his tongue coaxing hers to eagerness, their lips clung, the closeness and female scent of her woman's body almost weakening his resolve.

Nanon's own will to resist was shaky as she let her flattened palms glide down and around his flanks until he gripped her remorselessly, urging her lower body between the stance of his legs. Feeling the shudderings in the deep core of him, she gave a tiny moan and swayed away.

At her resistance, his smile was bittersweet. "Until to-morrow, my own darling."

The next day not even the tradewinds stirred. The very air was oppressive and sultry. She could not bear to put on the gray silk so, wearing a simply made white dress of thin batiste, she sat near the balcony, alternately fanning herself and then wiping the film of perspiration from her neck and from between her breasts.

Lifting her curls, she swirled them up and twisted the russety mass high on top of her head, anchoring it with two tortoiseshell combs. She took off her coral eardrops and removed her matching bracelets, dropping them in her reticule. Unadorned, she felt cooler.

With the move to Trois Îlets, Madame Arnaud's services were no longer needed; nevertheless, she'd been in and out of the suite with a siege of last-minute counselings. This time she'd disappeared for almost an hour. Nanon's travel bags were on the floor, and on a nearby table a low-crowned, wide-brimmed summer hat perched alongside silk gloves.

From the balcony, Nanon had been watching the harbor and idly wondering when the Italian ship in the distance would depart. Certainly in this weather, with no stirrings of wind, it would lie at anchor for an indeterminate time.

Her eyebrows narrowed thoughtfully. Was Degrelle already aboard? A great mass of blossoms had arrived with his card, and a note which had sounded a wistful farewell. Perhaps he'd really given up and she could expect not to see him again. Yet, somehow she didn't think so. Was this a nagging premonition, or simply a consequence of his having been so insistent these last few days?

She was keeping a far more ardent watch for Devin, and she smiled at the delicious thought that inside the closed carriage he certainly couldn't care a fig for their reputations. Secure from everyone's eyes, he could at least hold her in his arms. *That* warmth would be exceedingly agreeable. She grinned and, with a dainty finger, flicked a drop of perspiration from beneath the wispy curls on her forehead.

Then she glanced at the one piece of jewelry she still wore—the superb emerald Devin had placed on her finger when their betrothal was announced. Briefly she held it to her lips as though it were Devin himself. Then she stretched her arms high above her head before leaning back and falling into a misty reverie.

Nanon was dreaming, romantically anticipating that Devin had arrived and they were off on the road to Trois Îlets . . . and the flowers were nodding and the sunlight sparkled and his lips were coming closer . . . closer to hers. Ah, sweet and tempting . . .

The door to the suite was flung open with a burst of sound that brought her dizzily alert, and to her feet. "Madame Arnaud! What is it?"

The woman's face was chalk white. Her mouth strained, but her words at first seemed unintelligible.

A distressed Nanon was instantly at her side. "Is it one of the grandchildren? Sit down, please. Let me get you a glass of water. No!" She sped into Madame's bedroom. "A bit of rum . . . where is it?"

"Brandy will do," gasped Madame Arnaud. "Oh, never mind! There isn't any. Wait, let me catch my breath." And finally she did. "It's such deplorable news. My dear, dear girl, prepare yourself!"

Kneeling beside Madame's chair, Nanon rocked backward on her heels. She had already heard the worst with her father's death and Joséphine's, so what could this woman be talking about?

Suddenly she sprang up to stand over her. Was that her own voice keening. "Devin . . . ?"

"Yes. Yes, that's it. It seems your fiancé has shot his overseer. What is his name? I can't remember. But he was a man of bad repute, cruel they say. Nevertheless, that doesn't excuse . . ." She stopped, bit her lip, stared up at Nanon. "The *patron's* pistol was found next to the body."

*Her* body, her emotions, seemed locked in paralyzing numbness. Still, even in shock, she made herself speak slowly. "Madame, please compose yourself. What you've just said to me cannot be so. There's been a misunderstanding. I know who Emil Terren is. But it must be someone else's plantation, someone else's overseer."

Madame interrupted. "That's the name. Emil Terren. I've seen his wife in town, a yellow-haired flirtatious wench. She has all the men panting after her."

Nanon could not move, she could not feel. But her mind was working, though slowly. "If Terren is shot, and if what you say about his wife is true, then it must be some jealous dispute. It can have nothing to do with . . . us."

Madame Arnaud's expression had calmed somewhat, but her eyes were shining. Nanon had the awful thought that the woman might be enjoying the excitement.

"The pistol belongs to Monsieur D'Amboise, Nanon. This has definitely been established by the investigating authority, my dear. And he himself admits it is his. My son-in-law is with the court and he heard the news immediately."

Upon receiving this new information, Nanon grasped the back of the chair. Her heart was thudding, and she could barely swallow. "It's not the way it seems . . . it can't be. You must have it wrong."

Madame's lips tightened resentfully. Was this chit calling her a liar? Rising from the chair, she fished inside the beaded bag hanging by a cord from her wrist and brought out a small, dark green bottle. Uncorking it beneath Nanon's nose, she ordered, "Sniff this, a deep whiff."

Nanon choked as the fumes from the smelling salts

seemed to penetrate her brain. She heard Madame conclude. "Now, you listen to me. Whatever Monsieur D'Amboise did, he probably had very good reason for doing it. I should not speak ill of the dead, but that Terren was considered to be a very bad character. So, as I said, whatever caused Monsieur to act as he did—"

"He did nothing! There has to be an explanation."

Madame shrugged and forged on. "That's to be seen. Allow me to finish. Monsieur is a very rich man, and therefore his fortune is regarded as a support to the island economy. In addition, he possesses the D'Amboise name which makes him a member of an old, respected Martinique family. Quite enough to make one forget the rest of his lineage." This she said dryly. "I grant that his relationship to this branch of the family is a distant one and, except for the Pageries, none of the relatives are left. But he has inherited property here, and he and you will return from time to time." She leaned forward. "He'll neither be charged nor prosecuted."

"But you spoke of an investigation . . . ?"

"Yes, but it's being hushed up right now. Oh, there'll be a hearing of sorts. It works that way. But it will be easily accepted that this Terren was shot by some harbor drifter. The pistol stolen from the house, that sort of thing."

"Then that must have been what happened." Nanon's face brightened.

Madame Arnaud smiled cryptically. "You see? It is easy to believe, isn't it? Of course, a shooting suppressed makes for a juicy scandal." This was added out of spite; Madame's feathers were still ruffled.

Nanon released the chair and started to turn away. She supposed the woman intended to allay her distress, but her cynical words had only increased it. She put a hand to her forehead where a dull ache was beginning.

Finally she replied. "I cannot believe . . ." She stopped. Madame was facing the open door to the corridor, her expression one of startled disbelief. "Why, Monsieur . . . !"

D'Amboise strode into the room. "Will you leave us, please, madame."

"But I don't think . . ." She hesitated, glancing at Nanon who stood in front of the balcony shutters, her back to the light, her face in shadow. Resolutely Madame Arnaud returned her gaze to D'Amboise. "No, monsieur, I don't think it is appropriate at this time. The situation is . . . well, delicate," she stated by way of rebuke.

"I am the proper judge of that. Leave us." He looked dangerous.

# Chapter Twenty-six

Madame's head went up starchily, and her shoulders jerked with indignation as she walked out of the room. He waited, his eyes on the door until it closed with a small bang. He turned to Nanon, but she was already across the room, flinging her arms around him, crying, "Devin! Oh, I'm so glad you're here. Surely Madame's mistaken in what she's been telling me."

The rage went out of him as he held her close to murmur in her ear. "There, there, my dearest one . . . I know. I won't deny what she's probably told you is fairly close to the truth—as she has heard it. As everyone has heard it," he concluded bitterly.

"You were annoyed with her?"

"I've never minded her presence before, but for her to lean on protocol at a time like this . . ." His face darkened with returning anger. Setting her from him, he spoke starkly. "Terren is dead . . . shot. She told you that?"

Nanon nodded. "Devin . . . *was* it your pistol?"

"That, too? News does travel fast, I see. Quickly . . . let me tell you what happened. I returned to the plantation on horseback this morning, to tell Terren that the new overseer would be there later today, that he had to move on immediately. But when I got there, his body had been discovered in the cane stalks near the house, and the local *agent de police* had been called."

He reached for Nanon's hands, covered them with his own, and held them against his heart. She could hear its solid, slow thumping, and she pressed her lips to his shirt front.

He went on, looking down at her bright curls. "There's no easy way to say this. They hadn't moved him yet, and when the local man questioned me, it was obvious that he believed I could have ridden off, then circled back to arrive when I did. He showed me the pistol he'd picked up near the body—and I told him yes, it was mine."

A muscle jumped in his cheek; she tried to put her comforting arms around him, but he held her fingers in his, staring down at them. "I asked why I would have left it there, if what he was thinking was true? He was quick to agree with me—too quick." He glanced at her. Their eyes held.

"Then he *did* believe you!"

"No . . . he didn't, you see. Everyone knew Terren and I were on bad terms. The authorities will merely believe what they choose to. And though it's the truth that I had nothing to do with this killing, the *purported* belief that I'm innocent is exactly where the difficulty lies."

"I don't understand you, Devin. Oh!" As she recalled Madame's words, her eyes were so clear with comprehension that he hardly needed to ask what she was thinking. She muttered. "Madame said that you would never be accused of Terren's death, no matter what the evidence was. Devin, why can't you accept this?"

He regarded her with a faint smile. "I suppose she also told you the reasons?"

"Yes, she did. Your distinguished name, your powerful position in England as well as here, and the financial boon the island can expect to receive from your presence. She said people will look the other way . . . never at you."

"The lady is correct." He brooded. "And no matter what story is concocted to cover up this suspicious affair,

253

I'll refuse to go along with it. Nanon, I have to explain. I know it's a difficult time for you. You're sorrowing over the loss of your father . . . and this happens. It's no longer the time for celebrations. I refer to our marriage. It will have to wait."

"Do you mean . . . even after the mourning period for Joséphine ends?"

"The rumors surrounding Terren's murder will follow us like a spreading bloodstain. There will always be whisperings — I know these people. I can't let this happen to us. To the children we may have. I *must* discover the truth. I must be completely vindicated before we marry."

He looked searchingly at her. She did not speak. He waited for her to, then sighed. "I'll take you to Trois Îlets. You must stay there."

"For however long it takes? Oh no, Devin! We need each other . . . we must be together during this time."

He shook his head, his gray eyes cooling; and she feared that already she could see a distance between them. He said stiffly, "I will not have *you* the subject of scandal, as well as myself."

"Devin, I don't want to stay with the Pageries! They don't know me. I don't know them. You and I belong together. I'm heartsick, but I'm not going to sit around doing nothing and letting my heart break when you need me."

"We mustn't be selfish, Nanon. We have our future, our family name, to consider. And there is something else. Though no one seems to have witnessed whatever occurred there in the field, Zachée has talked to me."

"The slave who was flogged? Might *he* have killed Terren?" She was ashamed to sound so hopeful.

"Not likely, he's still bedded from the beating he received, but he tells me the drums say Terren had been threatened by the hill blacks with the *magie noire*. I know this isn't Haiti, the voodoo island; still, the overseer had a reputation as a superstitious man. There are slaves hiding in the hills who bear him a grudge. He might have taken my pistol from the house to protect himself."

Nanon shuddered. "Devin, this is all frightening. What is it you think might have happened?"

"Whomever he met—quarreled, and struggled with—could have turned the pistol on him and then tossed it away. It's far-fetched, I admit . . . but I'm clutching at suppositions. I have to start someplace." He drew her close into his arms and rested his chin on her head. But it was intended as a comforting gesture only. She knew by his moody gaze that his thoughts were back there in the cane field.

"A man like Terren would have his own guns. Why should he have taken one of yours?"

"Because he was a thief. He couldn't resist stealing anything he could lay his sticky fingers on." Sighing, Devin released her. "I was far away in England, and I learned of his character too late."

"What about his wife? Madame said she is known to be a flirt. There could be cause for jealousy there."

"I'll explore that, but it seems she's been staying at Saint-Pierre across the harbor from Mont Pelée. It's too far."

"And what happens now?" Nanon queried bitterly. "Do we ask the drums?"

Grim-faced, he left her, promising to return once again to try to convince her to stay with the Pageries. She remained on the balcony, watching as he descended to his waiting carriage.

Madame A. had been lurking in the main rooms downstairs until he departed. And a few minutes after he'd gone, she appeared bearing a pretty tray containing a plate of salad greens and curried shrimp and rice. "Nanon, let us make peace," she said. "You must eat. Here is food for us to share."

Later in the day it was still hot, but the tradewinds had begun to blow again, rattling the palm fronds and rippling the sea grasses they flattened to the sand. And the harbor below was coming alive in a bustling manner. Heavily laden carts drawn by oxen, sleek carriages, and men and women carrying parasols swarmed across the esplanade that led to the jetty. It had begun to look like a sailing day.

Watching from the balcony, Madame clutched Nanon's arm. "Look there — below. Isn't that your friend, the gentleman who sent you the beautiful bouquet?"

It was Degrelle approaching, but this time not on foot. An open carriage drawn by two matching grays waited as he stepped out and glanced up at the hotel's second floor. It was too late to step back and out of sight, so Nanon was forced to wave to him, then was embarrassed to see the pure delight on his face. Madame Arnaud, too, was observant.

"It's pitiful how devoted that poor man is to you. He came all this distance to bring you the news of your father's death. And now he goes alone to Italy to join your brother. How faithful he is to your family."

Nanon observed the older woman's concerned expression. "It's not entirely like that, Madame. I mean, he does have other things in mind."

"Well, of course, I'm sure he *likes* you, dear — and perhaps even a bit more than that. But he's been very discreet, behaving well, always seeing to it that I was included whenever he escorted you. Besides, he knows of your engagement." Her eyes went to the emerald ring Nanon was wearing, and her brows knitted as she adjusted a loose swirl of her high coiffure. "I must say I was disappointed in Monsieur D'Amboise's attitude toward me a little earlier. I hope the plans for you to go to

256

Trois Îlets have not changed. It's exactly where you should be at a time like this. But now, let us prepare to receive our guest."

They both walked inside, Madame Arnaud teasingly breaking off a rose from the bouquet in the tall vase and tucking its stem under the narrow ribbon at Nanon's waistline. At that precise moment, and before Nanon could remove the flower, Georges knocked at the door.

When he entered, he immediately commiserated with Nanon, news of the mysterious shooting having already reached him aboard the Italian ship. Then he beamed at the flower she wore and, without drawing a breath, added that it was definite his ship would sail at midafternoon.

"The tide will be full and the wind at its most favorable." He rushed on. "There's to be a farewell gathering on the pier, a surprise leave-taking for a lady who was children's governess to a member of the Russo clan."

Madame interrupted happily. "Mademoiselle Duvall is sailing?" She turned to Nanon. "It's so romantic! The young woman accepted an offer of marriage from the owner of a glassblowing factory in Florence—a brilliant match for her. He's a much older man, a widower. They met when he sought refuge with his relatives on Martinique during the wars." She turned to Degrelle. "Who will be there?" Her eyes were shining.

"All the Russos, I understand. And a gaggle of their friends as well, I'm told." Forlornly he looked at Nanon. "Am I to sail alone with no one to wish *me* Godspeed? For old times' sake, will you and Madame Arnaud find it in your hearts to attend my solitary departure? Or wait, Nanon! Perhaps I should remain in Fort-de-France. These are trying days for you. If you need me . . . ?"

In haste, she gasped. "No, Georges! I wouldn't think of your changing plans. There's no way of knowing when another ship to Genoa will again enter the harbor."

Touched by his offer, though still mistrustful of him, Nanon admitted reluctantly, "I do know the feeling of being alone as you are, far from one's country and loved ones. But I can't come to the ship to see you off. Monsieur D'Amboise may soon return; I must remain here." It was a reminder to him that she was about to be married—a fact which he stubbornly refused to accept.

Madame A., clearly disappointed with Nanon's decision, sighed lengthily. "It *is* sad to say good-bye, particularly when Monsieur Degrelle is so devoted to your family. It's the severing of a last link, isn't it, Nanon?"

Nanon looked sharply at her, but her countenance was all innocence. She guessed that the older woman was eager to join the party on the pier, to hear all the latest gossip, the frivolous talebearing that would be going on.

She wavered, glancing back at Degrelle. Today his skin was paler than usual, his heroic scar more pronounced; and he had dressed somberly. Somehow, minus his fashionable attire, he appeared less the man who had clumsily assaulted her on the pergola, more the faithful aide she remembered. He had soothed her father's pain with his medications, had attended to all the raw and intimate details of the sick room.

"Very well, Georges. Madame Arnaud and I shall accompany you as far as the pier. We can't let you leave without your own little clique to bid you bon voyage."

A quarter of an hour later, while getting into the carriage, Nanon could hear Madame burbling. "How fortunate for us that today you have this conveyance, monsieur."

Seating himself on the small seat opposite the ladies, Degrelle murmured. "Dear madame, the time was short, I thought to hire it since I was in a great hurry."

Nanon gave him a keen glance, wondering why she felt the faintest nudge of uneasiness. Had he expected—no, planned—that they would come to the pier with him? He was a surprisingly obstinate man, this persistence being a side of his character rarely seen in former days. She was thankful that only this brief time remained for him to continue to be a puzzle to her.

Stepping from the carriage at the far end of the wharf, they quickly found themselves surrounded by a merry-making group of well-dressed men and women. Nanon recognized that several of them belonged to the island's elite.

She was amused to see that Madame Arnaud was ecstatic. It was apparent that Madame knew some of these people, and she would have liked to know more of them. Nanon was pleased, not only for her sake but because the overly buoyant spirits of the crowd would make it easier to bid Georges a quick and impersonal farewell.

She was about to do just that, when her arm was caught in a less than gentle grip. Startled, she turned around to stare straight into the pale green eyes of Oliva Russo. Recalling their final encounter at the Farrars', Nanon knew it was malice rather than the hot sun that narrowed the other woman's gaze.

With a tight smile on her face, Oliva spoke. "What a delight to see you again, Nanon. Will you join a few of us aboard ship with your friend there?" She nodded toward Georges who, with a worried expression, was peering over the heads that separated them. "I understand he's the gentleman that brought Martinique the sad news of the former empress's demise. And that he's sailing today."

Nanon didn't reply. She had once slapped that elegant face, a loss of temper which she still regretted — even with the memory of those lacerating words Oliva had spoken that night on the porch flooding back.

But an insistent Oliva linked her arm through Nanon's. "Let's let bygones be. You *must* come — a few of us are going aboard with Mademoiselle Duvall. Some of the men are a bit too convivial, perhaps." She winked broadly.

Nanon's reply was brief, not at all courteous. "I think not, Oliva."

She was silently furious as she attempted to pry herself free and move away from the confusion and the jests. The festive group milled about; the men — those in their rum cups — overly gallant, the women uttering teasing squeals. It was as though released from their households and the formality of plantation life, they were set to have a rollicking time wharfside at Fort-de-France.

Defying a wharfman's warning, the more adventurous began a rush to the edge of the wooden jetty where a short rope ladder, with its accompanying safety net, reached down to a waiting longboat that would hold perhaps thirty persons.

Carried along in concert with the others, Nanon could look down and see the Italian sailors, oars poised, ready to push off. Several men had already clambered down the ladder to assist the departure of the pretty governess who now looked up, waggling her fingers at those above.

Suddenly, Georges was once again at Nanon's side. "Madame Russo tells me she's been urging you to come aboard as well."

She shook her head. "That wasn't part of our bargain." She tried to smile. "Madame Arnaud and I will wave to you from here."

He gave her a smoldering look. "Madame Russo says you will never marry D'Amboise."

"How dare she say such a thing! And how is it you know her well enough to receive such a confidence?"

His face darkened and he started down the rope ladder without a reply. It was at that point, with an audacity that could only be called *courage fou,* that a kind of mass sortie began. With a series of inebriated yelps, the more reckless who'd taken hold of the rope ladder, loosed their grip and plunged down its length to slide to an awkward landing in the dangerously tipping boat.

A shocked Nanon hung back, staring at the giddy passengers below, but some movement behind prodded her forward. And in a flash she found herself off balance, looking up at a piece of hot, blue sky and then down at the bluer sea beneath. Flailing forward, with arms outstretched she seemed to be falling into that blue, blue sea . . .

# Chapter Twenty-seven

She closed her eyes, her head cracking hard against the wooden gunnel as she landed inside the boat. There was a second's blanking of consciousness — a *pavé* of stars exploding. And then pain, fright, humiliation, and dizziness — replaced by anger. Had someone pushed her? Deliberately?

A din of voices shouted concern. She reached up unsteadily to catch the dangling ladder but it eluded her grasp and slapped against the piles. Shocked faces looked down at her from the jetty above.

Other hands were hauling her back inside the longboat as the scowling Italian sailors raised impatient oars, sliced them into the current, and, with a heave, the boat shot forward.

Someone was stroking the damp strands of Nanon's hair, and there was a murmuring in her ear, her name repeated. "Nanon . . . Nanon . . ." She looked up into Georges' face and saw it scarlet with apology as he placed himself between her and the others who were trying to peer over his shoulder.

"By God, someone will pay for this! These drunken louts are Martinique's *beau monde?* It cannot be."

She struggled upright, pulled down her thin skirts and pushed aside Georges' hovering hands. "It *is* . . . obviously." She ordered herself to stay in control.

"Dammit . . . where is Madame Arnaud?" He was searching the boat with a worried gaze.

Nanon touched her temple and winced. "Probably in a state of shock. Hers was the last face I saw as I fell down the ladder."

"I am to blame," he declared.

"No, you're not, Georges. The crowd pushed, and somehow I slipped. I don't want to hear any more about it, and you're not to worry." She felt she should reassure him. In truth, he looked wretched, the flush in his face having faded to a dull tallow color.

She turned to look toward the looming ship they were fast approaching and noticed that its sails were being set. "Your Italian captain will send the longboat, and everyone in it back to the wharf immediately. Except you and Mademoiselle Duvall, of course. He won't allow this particular bon voyage to continue."

They nudged alongside, and to Nanon's astonishment from among the still-noisy revelers in the bow of the longboat a familiar figure was being assisted up the ship's ladder by willing male hands.

Her skirts wrapped tightly around her slender, perfect form, Oliva raised her beautiful face to accept the welcome of the Italian captain. He leaned over the rail, obviously enchanted by her bosom and the length of her legs. *"Buon giorno, signora!"*

Within minutes of arriving on deck under the cold regard of the crew, the wellwishers did appear sobered. Standing close to the rail, and with departure imminent, they watched Oliva. Hanging back from the others, she was chatting flirtatiously with the captain who seemed captivated by the red-haired Polish beauty.

Degrelle smiled cynically. "It's apparent the good captain didn't expect to find an exotic like Madame Russo in Martinique's harbor."

"Georges . . . how do *you* know her?"

"But I don't. Oh, you mean because I quoted her remark that you and D'Amboise would never marry?" He shrugged. "The truth is, I overheard her say it to someone else." His pale-lashed eyes sent her an insinuating look. "All's fair in love, you know."

Suddenly he slapped his hand to his brow. "How could I forget? The medal . . . your father's award! It was his wish that you have it."

She eyed him skeptically. "What are you saying? A medal of valor intended for me, not for Théo?"

"I'm sorry . . . sorry. I'll fetch it immediately. Wait here . . . it's in my cabin."

She watched him set off at a rapid pace, concerned that he looked unwell as though her fall from the jetty into the boat still affected him. If he didn't return in time, medal or no, she'd leave with the others—and thankfully. She was still bruised and sore. Now, anxious to return to the hotel, she gazed longingly in the direction of the shore and its houses, yellow-, pink-, and lime-colored with red-tiled roofs. In the distance the cathedral spires pierced upward, and on the slant of the hill the Hôtel Beaux Jours settled against the sky, its vine-covered walls enclosing scented gardens. Whether they would be married soon or not didn't really matter—Devin awaited her there.

The day was still hot, but the sea, blue-green and translucent, looked cool. The tradewinds blew strongly, steadily; and she was aware of the remembered sensation of a deck bucking beneath her feet. She knew that the ship, its sails spread like some giant white-winged bird, was eager to be off. How strange her life had become, the turns it had taken. She'd learned of ships and sails, and latitudes and winds. She'd learned of love . . . and of love's passionate consummation. How far along the road she'd come. . . .

Hearing the skirl of a ship's whistle, she hastened to take her place in the departing line of now-subdued merrymakers. One final time, she glanced toward the companionway.

He was there.

He was standing very straight in his soldierly fashion, except that the hand, with which he held the doorjamb, for support, had begun to slide downward in an awkward manner. From where she was, Nanon could see the pallor in that waxen face. His eyes seemed to be looking directly into hers as his body slowly collapsed backward like a puppet's, falling into the shadowy companionway. Startled, she looked around to see who else might have observed. Instinctively starting toward the yawning doorway, Nanon halted to call for help. A soft voice speaking her own tongue stopped her.

It came from a burly man in sailor's garb. "Quiet, *mademoiselle*. I am here. A friend. It's better not to call attention. We can assist him below . . . help me, please."

She wavered. Still, she felt she must help. "Is it a seizure of some kind? Perhaps we should call someone else. Where are you taking him?"

"To his cabin, *mademoiselle*. In such matters, one must be discreet. I'll find the officer who acts as ship's doctor. Could you remain with him until I do?"

She answered uncertainly. "I'm not a passenger on this ship, you understand. I must leave. But, yes, I suppose . . ."

"Settled, then!"

Bewildered, she followed the big man as he bore Degrelle ahead of him, padding down the dark steps to the passageway below. Alarmed by George's sudden illness, Nanon knew she couldn't desert him.

The cabin was dim as she entered and tripped over an apothecary's bag on the deck by the bunk; the quarters were eerily reminiscent of her father's sick room. The sailor bent over the bunk to deposit his burden. With no further word to her, and with unexpected agility, he hustled around her and out of the cabin, sharply slamming the door.

It was indeed a brusque exit, and wonderingly Nanon turned to the bunk, anxious to help but more than a little afraid of what she might find. Its occupant was no longer lying supine in a seemingly unconscious state. Instead, he was sitting up and regarding her with a healthily speculative look. "My dear Nanon, we must talk. . . ."

The tone of voice was normal, but his lynx-gold eyes blazed with excitement. He no longer appeared physically undone . . . what was happening here? He stood—and she knew an instinctive rush of terror.

"Talk . . . ?" To her shame, her voice quavered. "There's no time. And since you have made an amazingly immediate recovery, I must leave with the longboat. Now."

"I don't think so. Not when I've so recently recovered from my indisposition."

She took a shaky step backward, her hand groping for the door latch. Another step. And she lurched, off-balanced having again made contact with the black bag on the floor. Swiftly he moved behind her, and she could hear the grate of a key being twisted in the lock.

He was still behind her—close behind her—the heat of his breath making the small hairs at the back of her neck quiver. A petal-light fingertip stroked her earlobe to the sensitive curve of her throat. At his touch she recoiled inwardly.

"Don't!" She snapped out the one word. Its harsh sound, like a blow to the heart, stopped him. Taking advantage of the stilled moment, she whirled on him. "What is your ploy, *monsieur?* You can't mean to keep me here. This ship will sail!"

"Exactly. How bright of you, Nanon. Ships sail; that's the nature of ships. And you'll sail to Genoa. Listen to me . . . if you remain in this Caribbean backwater with these roistering Creoles, and with that murdering fiancé of yours, you'll be in no state to make a decision that will affect the rest of your life. A few weeks at sea will clear your mind. Attended by a man of your own background, who truly loves you, you'll come to your senses."

"Have you taken leave of yours?" She was thunder-struck.

He went on as though she hadn't spoken, his eyes fiery. "You'll see your life as it's meant to be lived, in the France of your ancestors. You will bear children of French blood undiluted by bastard strains. Nanon! Why are you laughing?"

"Don't you understand, Degrelle? This is what happened to me once before. A ship sailed from France with me as an unwilling prisoner."

He gave her a brilliant smile. "And what occurred then, Nanon? You fell in love with your captor. Isn't that right?"

"This is not the same, you ridiculous man. I detest you. You must know I always have, though temporarily you didn't seem such an imbecile to me. Nothing you can do will ever change this. Now, move aside. Since you're recovered from your faked fainting spell, tell your accomplice I couldn't wait for him to bring a ship's officer."

They stared at each other, his gaze uncertain but menacing, hers belligerent. But then her eyes widened in sudden panic, just as his half closed in satisfaction.

"What is that . . . ?"

"What do you suppose it is, my dear?"

She could feel the shudderings of the ship, sense the wash of its movement. Knowing that far above them ropes had been released and canvas freed, she rushed past him to the porthole. Looking out, she could see one blue swell rising to collapse upon the next one. They were under way! The sailing ship was moving with the wind and the currents of the sea. . . .

He had prepared a speech for this moment, and he gave it now. "Antoinette, I shall spend my life earning your forgiveness and your respect. My love for you has overwhelmed me and dictated my actions. It was no charade I acted out. I *was* ill, fearful for your well-being

267

. . . ill for the love of you!" He amended this with, "I am sure you can't mean what you said to me, that you have always detested me . . . ?"

He came up to her as she stood at the porthole staring in disbelief at the shore they were leaving behind. Fitting his body to hers, Degrelle spread his legs to encompass the slenderness of her hips. She stood rigid, aware of her nausea at his touch. His arms began to encircle her, his hands creeping upward across her bosom, his fingers cupping the roundness of her breasts. But with his head slumping against the back of her neck, he began to weep hot tears that she could feel staining her flesh through her gossamer-thin frock.

The captain was in fierce dudgeon, raking his fingers through his tight-curled black hair. He sprang to his feet, swept his map books across his desk, mashed his gold-braided cap upon his head. "You inform me *now* about this? Show him in, Giametti. Do not leave us alone, otherwise I might be tempted to strangle him with these hands of mine!" He curled his fingers ferociously and thumped his fists on the desk. "I tell you these Frenchmen — from Napoléon on down they bring nothing but trouble."

The younger man started for the door while the captain continued to shout. "I have no time, no inclination, to perform the marriage ceremony for him and his whore!"

"My captain . . . she is a lady. And I understand she is another man's intended bride brought aboard this ship against her will. The Frenchman Degrelle does say she is ill and it will be necessary that she spend the voyage abed in their cabin."

"Oh? Is this truly the case, Giametti?" The captain appeared to ponder. "Oh no, this fellow must mean abed in her *own* cabin, not his. See to it that she is moved in with Mademoiselle Duvall, who has the good sense to be sailing to Italy to marry a Florentine. Now, you may show this Degrelle in — but remember, do not leave us alone. I may not be responsible. And you say you've found his friend, that other Frenchman? Good, put him below in chains. *I* captain this ship, not the French!"

# Chapter Twenty-eight

Both horses broke over the crest of the hill at a gallop. As they were reined in by their riders, pounding hooves slid to a halt, and the two men reached across intervening space to shake hands.

"My friend, here I leave you," said one.

Glancing at the scattered orange and lilac-colored rooftops of Fort-de-France lying beneath them, D'Amboise replied with bitterness. "The winds are blowing us close to the reef, Nicholas. Even that investigator Leblanc politely masked his disbelief in what I told him. You must have sensed his deep suspicion, and I thank you for standing with me. Prudence will dictate society's belief in my innocence, but that kind of lip service is not enough."

The other man's troubled expression eased, but he spoke with irony. "As a longtime acquaintance of the Pagerie family, and as your lawyer in this present matter, I can do little else but support you."

In reply to D'Amboise's raised brow and quizzical look at this remark, he gave him a harsh smile. "During that one winter you visited here on our island, you and I were youths together, Devin. I was your friend then, and I am your friend now."

"I recall it well . . . my first winter of sun in contrast to the gray chill of London. Warmth, honeysuckle, the spice-scented air, the full lips of the Creole girls. You know, Nicholas, that early memory helped convince me to plan to spend time here after Nanon and I are wed. I want to provide similar memories for my children, God willing that we are blessed with them. Now, I wonder if it will be possible for us to return to the plantation."

"It could be possible if your pride will allow you to accept the politic verdict on Terren's death. Let's say . . . an assailant, name and motive unknown. It's not unrealistic. The authorities will be satisfied with a random tale of a stranger, perhaps a drunken seaman on an island prowl from the docks. And they could be satisfied even more by the wounded Zachée's story of the sentence of *magie noire* pronounced by the hill people who bore Terren a grudge."

"I'll have none of that! I must discover the truth. I'll not allow whisperings of guilt to follow Antoinette and me."

Nicholas Jorry released his friend's hand, then clapped Devin's shoulder, exhibiting a confidence he didn't feel. "If you won't let the matter go, that's it, then. We'll get to the bottom of it. Even though you've been champing at the bit to return to your fiancée, you were patient enough with that investigator who again questioned the slaves who found Terren's body. *And* your gun." Saying that last, Jorry shook his head.

"I had to stay; there might have been evidence that could be of use to us."

The lawyer mused. "The appearance of that black man was helpful — a most impressive fellow. What was his name — Christophe? I listened closely — and so, I think, did Leblanc — when he told of the roadside workers who'd observed a stranger riding in the direction of your plantation. They noticed him particularly because he kept to the path beneath the trees, and because his manner of looking about as though unsure of his bearings was most peculiar."

Listening to this summing up, Devin shrugged and spoke with cynicism. "You're speaking of black men's testimony, Nicholas. Such would be considered of little import even if these same workmen could be found and convinced to talk. And remember, we have no description of this outsider."

"On this, regretfully I must agree, my friend. Still, I'll pursue it. Not much information that was solid could be gleaned from this second round of interviews. Though I saw that your loyal slaves were reluctant to admit that you and the overseer had quarreled."

"There's no disguising the bad temper between us."

"We know that Emil Terren was disliked. No, hated and loathed. His enemies may have been many, but unfortunately they now seem to be merely shadowy presences." Jorry sighed. "Even the widow Terren, in her admission of her husband's bilking of your estate, claimed it was a matter of careless bookkeeping. With this slippery Terren fellow, there's nothing you can quite hang on to."

"And my gun?"

"As to that, I shall seek permission of the Deschamps to speak to your former slaves Jean Henri and his wife Mathilde. We'll bring all that out later in the courtroom, if you insist. This Christophe informs me the pair were in your house doing refurbishing when they observed Terren at your desk drawer. They've already said they believe it was at this time that he took out your gun for his own use. You didn't notice its absence?"

"No . . . there was no reason to." Devin had always been in the house in the company of Nanon and Madame Arnaud. And, at the last, with Nanon alone, when she had told him it was her birthday. Certainly there was no thought of guns *that* afternoon.

Thoughtfully the lawyer continued. "And mud from the cane field on its handle." He looked questioningly at D'Amboise. "The man Christophe is an invaluable friend to you, it seems. Is there something here I should know?"

Devin shook his head. "I've pondered his situation myself. He's a man of intelligence, brave, trustworthy. For reasons I've never learned, the last member of the D'Amboise family to live here provided him with an instrument of manumission. It seems his gratitude for this far exceeds whatever generosity was shown him. After all, his freedom was little enough to grant him. It is only what the rest of us on this island should be thinking of granting to our slaves."

"Give slaves their freedom?" Jorry looked shocked. "I wouldn't let it be known among the plantation owners that you've become an advocate of such humanitarian principles. It wouldn't go down well at all. Temper your impulse in this, D'Amboise."

Devin smiled and idled his hand across his horse's mane. "It's not caprice. And in this grave matter I can't follow your advice, Nicki. It shall be known soon enough what my true beliefs are." Suddenly Devin's face came alive as though touched by some gladsome memory. Amusement shone in his gray eyes, reminding Jorry of a quick track of summer lightning.

"You have met my fiancée, but you must learn to know her better, and soon. Soon, Nicholas! Antoinette is my wellspring for all that is good and fine which I might espouse in the future. She sustains me, she is my illumination, my teacher if you will — this young and lovely and forthright girl. The best of me is crystallized in her person."

"Ah, a man in love! Next, he will be describing the shape of her eyes, the contour of her pert nose, her winsome grace, her lithe form, her . . . her . . . Save me! I've been through it all myself. Enough of this. Go and find your angel at once. She must be languishing these three days you've been gone, which, as you've told me countless times, is far longer than you promised. I know you must escort the young lady to the protection of the de la Pageries, so off with you!"

Feeling as ridiculous, as fatuous, as a lovestruck youth,

D'Amboise motioned a farewell to his friend, then wheeled his horse to canter along the downward path that led to his house in town. Nicholas Jorry watched for a moment. Shaking his head soberly, he set off in an opposite direction, toward his own estate north of Fort-de-France.

Freshly bathed, clean shaven, and dressed with the greatest care, D'Amboise ordered the closed carriage and the team of four to be brought around. At least he would have some privacy with his Nanon. While waiting, he asked his valet to send a groom to the Hôtel Beaux Jours to inform Mademoiselle de Cavanac that he would present himself within the hour.

The man looked at him strangely, but D'Amboise passed it off and entered his library to glance at the post that had been left on his desk during his absence. One of the communications on the mahogany surface was imposing. It was enclosed in heavy parchment cover set off with ribbons and a scarlet seal.

The valet was still at his side. D'Amboise glanced at him impatiently. "Have you sent the fellow on the errand as I required?"

The man did not answer directly, instead he murmured, "Sir, a special messenger from the frigate that entered the harbor yesterday brought this to the house." He departed hastily.

Devin ripped open the envelope, slowly read its contents, then stood for several minutes while perusing its pages a second time. Calmly and without expression, he carefully placed the missive within a desk drawer. He turned the key and secreted it in his vest pocket.

It was only then that he clenched his fist, rammed it onto the desk top in fury, and then whirled about to stare at his image reflected in the great mirror on the opposite wall. He saw a man immaculately clothed in white, with black hair in need of a trim. A man from whose face the earlier bright expectation seemed to have fled. Now, his brow thunderously dark, he swore a brief and pungent oath, which seemed to make him feel better.

"To hell with it!" he muttered. "And so be it. That's the way it is and one has to accept such things. Maybe . . . just maybe . . . it's for the best!" He straightened his shoulders and strode to the door. A small smile momentarily lifted his lips as he shouted for his valet.

In the corridor outside the man trembled. *What next?* he thought. *I'm not the one to tell the master what has happened!*

But Devin was giving orders, "I want you to make immediate preparations to close the house. Have Renaldo go over the accounts, pay the bills, and see to the servants. You pack my gear. Everything. I'll explain later; that is, if you'll wipe that look of stupefaction off your face." Abruptly, Devin grinned.

The man watched in awe as his employer marched outside to the waiting carriage with a step that made him think he heard bugles blowing.


Robert, the hotel clerk, saw D'Amboise enter and tried to slip into a back room. Madame Arnaud, having returned to retrieve some bolts of material promised her by Minette, spied him in the doorway and made a cautiously swift exit by way of the pergola.

Only the few hotel guests in the lobby watched the entrance of the tall, wide-shouldered man who, at the moment, presented a somewhat swashbuckling appearance.

D'Amboise felt wonderful. He didn't own the world yet—but almost. First, he was about to race upstairs, take Nanon in his arms, and let his kisses wander where they might in all manner of pleasant places. Next, he would tell her the visit to the Pageries was off. The whole bloody mess was out of their hands and was being re-solved—probably in their best interests—by a power greater than either of them.

Though initially he'd regarded the official communication as a fierce blow, it was not that at all. Temporarily it made the whole business of Emil Terren fade into the background. Until the time came when he could ferret out the truth of what had occurred at the plantation, he'd swallow his damn pride and accept the island's cynical verdict of his innocence.

He knew when to fall back—not in surrender but to bide his time. Now, since he'd been recalled once more to the Service, and to Paris and the Royal Court this time, he'd take Nanon to France with him on that frigate. They'd be married properly there in the cathedral . . . they'd . . .

But the small hairs rose on the back of his neck as a familiar, mocking voice accosted him, and he turned slowly to face Oliva Russo.

She whispered breathlessly, "I must speak to you in private."

"No. Not while I stand upright!" He quickly realized this was an unfortunate remark to make, so he amended it. "Not while I draw breath."

"Don't expire just yet. I mean you no harm. It's not by coincidence that I am here."

"I didn't think it was," he almost shouted. Then he hastily looked about and lowered his voice.

"Let's go upstairs so we can talk. I'm a respectable matron. Hah!" She seemed to chortle at that. "So, it doesn't matter what these people think. Come. That sniveling desk clerk won't stop us."

"Where in hell is *upstairs?* Are you crazy?"

"Upstairs is Nanon's former suite, of course."

"You *are* mad! Listen to me, you've caused enough trouble between Antoinette de Cavanac and me. Do you want to try and seduce me in front of her?"

"You're being loud again, Devin—and rather conceited. Your Nanon is not there. She is, in fact, on her way to Italy."

With that last outrage he grasped Oliva's arm. Not caring that interested eyes were now following their every move, he pulled her up the stairs, pushed her along the hall, and pushed open the door to Nanon's suite.

The afternoon sun streamed from the balcony, displaying the emptiness of the rooms. Only faded flowers remained in a tall vase on a table in the center of the room. Disbelieving what his eyes told him, Devin raced to the closets in Nanon's bedchamber, with Oliva's voice trilling after him.

"Her apparel was already packed by Madame Arnaud for your stay at Trois Îlets. However, look behind those doors there. You'll find her trunks and boxes filled with the clothing you had Minette design for her. God knows what she'll wear on that sailing ship."

He strode back into the main room and again he seized her by the arms. This time he shook her hard until she clasped at her straw hat edged with silken rosebuds to keep it from whirling away. His eyes kindled with dark menace. *"Where is she?"*

"I told you."

A whitefaced Robert suddenly stood in the open doorway, causing them both to turn. "Monsieur! Madame! This is causing a great scandal to the Hôtel Beaux Jours." He stepped inside the room, closing the door behind him. "Please . . . !"

"Then, *you* tell him, Robert! He does not believe me. With my dear husband who's waiting below in our carriage, I've maintained a watch outside Monsieur D'Amboise's house. Our intent was to gently break the news to him that his fiancée has fled aboard ship and sailed to Italy with her old friend Georges Degrelle. See . . . "

She hastened to the balcony. Throwing open the shutters, she stepped outside. D'Amboise, attended by

277

Robert, stalked after her. Both men looked down to the street. Behind D'Amboise's carriage, there was another, an open one in which Oliva's corpulent husband was seated looking sweaty and uncomfortable beneath the summer sun.

Robert took a deep breath. "This is all very well, madame. But I have heard a very different version. I was told that Mademoiselle de Cavanac boarded the ship with a number of people to say farewell to Monsieur Degrelle, but the ship sailed with her as an inadvertent passenger."

"A likely story, my dear Robert. From whom did you hear that — Madame Arnaud? Well, it's probably much kinder than the truth. But it did seem to all of us *who were there* that she did not truly love her fiancée and she simply could not face marriage to a man accused of murder. . . ."

"Oliva!" Devin grasped her arm with a kind of aching fury. "Tell me everything you know!"

# Chapter Twenty-nine

*Genoa*

Nanon had traveled an ocean and two seas—the length of the Atlantic to the Caribbean and then across the Atlantic to the Mediterranean. With Captain Patrese, she now stood on the shore. Intrigued by her background, by her courage, and by the tale of her romance with D'Amboise, he'd sworn he would see that the villain Degrelle was conveniently lost—overboard. She'd dissuaded him from that rash act, asking only that he help her to return to Martinique.

This he could not do. And today on Genoa's shore, the impasse continued. "I've told you, *signorina*, I can do anything but this. You know that you've won my respect and my admiration. Have I not kept you safe—and separate—from the Frenchman the entire voyage?"

"Yes. And I am grateful to you for that, Captain. And grateful as well to Mademoiselle Duvall. We had her connivance, and certainly her patience, during the time I shared her cabin."

"She has good sense, that young woman. She's marrying a Florentine. Now, back to your problem. I tell you again that with Napoléon in exile, conditions are too unstable for you to attempt to return to an island belonging to France. The allies have been lenient, but true peace will only be decided in Vienna in September. Until then, as we've discussed, your only recourse is to remain with my family in northern Italy. My wife and children will welcome you. But we have other matters to discuss. See what I have for you."

She stared down at the fat leather purse he'd pulled from an inside pocket.

"Open it," he ordered. Amusement glistened in his dark green eyes.

"Gold florins?" She was astonished. "Captain Patrese, I cannot accept these from you."

"Oh yes, you can. No one can exist long without gold. I say this, perhaps cynically; but gold can provide one with backbone and courage. Not that you lack these requisites, *signorina*. I've been impressed with you—with your intelligence and spirit, that is. This has been my sole reason for championing you. My good friend, the merchant Giovanni Marsicano, will explain this to my wife when he delivers you to my house."

"I cannot accept your gold." Nanon spoke firmly, handing back the purse.

But the captain refused to take it, closed her fingers over its heavy clasp, and smiled wryly. "It is not *my* gold, *signorina*. I extracted it from your abductor when he changed his gold pieces into florins. Today, he's being detained by a ruse—hadn't you guessed?"

"When I left the ship I did wonder what had been arranged. . . ." Thoughtfully she hefted the purse. It would surely hasten her return to Martinique . . . and to Devin. She would keep it.

"Signorina Duvall is already on her way to Florence. And now you are to join my friends, the Marsicano family. No, no, don't argue with me, please. It's arranged. They are people of substance who travel with retainers; so there will be an armed escort to protect your caravan against the brigands who hide in the hills."

Gently he kissed the back of her hand. "I am allowed this liberty, one that I've never taken before. I do feel affection for you, my dear, and a fondness for the spirit you've displayed under these most trying circumstances." His dark eyes moistened with emotion. He straightened, cleared his throat. "You have your instructions, your gold, and you have a head start from here. Go immediately. I shall deal with the Frenchman. He'll be held under guard a day and a night, and then turned over to the authorities at the port. Kidnapping at sea is a grave offense, but since he is a citizen of France, we cannot detain him long. Ah, there's something else . . . that emerald of yours. You have the ring safely on the chain I gave you?"

"I have it around my neck." He glanced at the bosom of the highnecked shirt Nanon had gotten from Mademoiselle Duvall's modest wardrobe. Then, politely, he withdrew his gaze.

She would like to have thrown her arms around him in a hug of gratitude. But better not, she thought. The captain, a most attractive man, had behaved toward her with circumspection, yet she was aware that the temptation to be more familiar frequently hovered behind his warm contemplation of her. As it was though, he had even restrained himself from asking pertinent questions about Oliva Russo. Nanon knew he was curious about the siren of Fort-de-France, but she felt it was better the topic of sex did not come up in any guise.

When he bade her farewell, Nanon felt very alone as she watched him descend the path that would take him into the town. His ship lay at anchor in the harbor below, where the port handlers were already unloading its cargo. Yes, she was on her own again!

Securing the purse inside the belt of her long, full skirt, Nanon picked up the bag containing the few clothes and necessities given her by Madeleine Duvall. She would place herself under the Marsicano family's protection only until she could make quiet inquiry as to which ships might be sailing, in the immediate future, from Genoa in the direction of Martinique. When she'd secured this information, she would slip away to rent a room in a tavern near the port.

She had not counted on the warmth of her reception by Signore and Signora Marsicano. Nor had she anticipated being immediately put in charge of their only son, the ten-year-old Carlo—a blue-eyed, handsome boy, lively and articulate, and tall for his age.

The family was temporarily staying in a large house that belonged to their Genoese relatives, and Nanon found herself assigned to share Carlo's upstairs room. Settled beside her during dinner, the boy regaled her with tales of his dogs, his riding horse, and his treehouse in Milan. It was then she realized that his parents must have confused her with the captain's other female passenger, the French governess, and she knew this was to be her role until they reached the villa in Milan.

She was further startled to find that as soon as the repast ended, she was escorted upstairs by Carlo and his mother. Signora Marsicano tenderly kissed her son and then smiled at Nanon. "Bedtime is early because we leave at dawn tomorrow to take advantage of the long summer day. We must be safely settled in our next hostelry by nightfall. Captain Patrese must have told you that, with the collapse of Napoléon's empire, there's been a breakdown in law and order. Hill bandits are everywhere. These ruffians prey on unescorted travelers."

Again, she kissed her son. "But we will be safe, won't we, Carlo?" She glanced at Nanon, ready to change the subject. "Tell me, *mademoiselle*, is my French speech better than Captain Patrese's? *I* have had the advantage of an education in a convent school with French nuns. And you, on your voyage from Martinique, you seem to have gained some facility in our language."

"Signora Marsicano, you are indeed fluent," Nanon declared, trying to control the alarm in her expression. "You say . . . we leave at dawn?" She had not expected such an immediate departure; the captain having indicated to her that the Marsicanos would be several days in Genoa before setting out for the north.

"We leave sooner than planned—and secretly—to prevent servants and others from carrying news of our departure. We also lock our doors securely. I shall lock Carlo's now, and awaken you early, in time to breakfast. There, to the side, is a small washroom where you can undress. Carlo, say your prayers for Mademoiselle de Cavanac, and practice your French grammar with her, my darling."

Nanon stared dispiritedly at the closing door, then listened to the clanking as the key turned in the lock.

Carlo was already rustling around, undressing. "Do not fear, *signorina* . . . I mean, *mademoiselle* . . . I shall protect you from the brigands." The words were declared stoutly as he pointed her toward her side of the chamber where her bag lay.

Nanon noted that her bed was far from the window, or any other possible exit. And when she ventured to look out, she saw that this room was facing the sea but many feet above the ground. She guessed there would be nothing for it but to try to slip away tomorrow during the dawn departure.

She closed her eyes, thinking of Devin and the loving safety of his arms, and knew that she would dare any danger to reach his side. She asked herself—and certainly not for the first time—what he could be thinking now? Madame Arnaud would have described to him her fall down the ladder into the longboat. But what explanation could there be for her not returning with the others from the Italian ship? Surely he must realize that when it sailed it had carried her off against her will.

"Will you hear me say my prayers, *mademoiselle?*"

She looked down at the eager face so near the height of her own shoulder, and sighed. "Will you say a prayer for me, Carlo?"

"Yes, indeed. I shall pray that you'll stay with us forever in Milan."

Which wasn't quite what she had in mind . . .


The next morning it was barely light when everyone met in the seclusion of the courtyard. There were several handsome coaches assembled, and the equally fine teams of horses nickered softly. As always, this familiar sound awakened in Nanon a wistful pang. Dominique . . . if only she could run her palm down that satiny nose and once more watch the mare's nostrils flare with spirit as she tossed her beautiful head and mane at her mistress's touch.

"*Signorina!*" It was Riccardo, the red-haired leader of the escort, who approached and motioned her to an open coach door. "*Per favore . . .*"

She was pulled back from memory while he pitched in her bag and then assisted her inside. She was pleased to see this coach was several vehicles behind the Marsicanos', and that she would be seated with two elderly aunts and a cousin, all returning to Milan. This would make escape much easier.

Discreetly Nanon tried the handle on the opposite door. In the excitement of the muted farewells being exchanged, she planned to wait until the aunts' heads were turned and then step out the other side of the coach, the one shadowed by cypress. If need be, she could elude detection by mingling with the family members and servants being left behind, none of whom knew her. When these people returned to the house, she would make her solitary way out of the courtyard and down into the city.

She hunched farther into the corner, watching the aunts who were already beginning to doze. She did entertain a regret at the thought of deserting Carlo who, only minutes before in the dining room, had been told to stop talking to his new friend and finish his breakfast.

He was a stalwart youngster, with a feeling akin to her

own for horses, and he had showed her much the same devotion as had Claude the cabin boy on the long sea voyage from Brest.

His brightness and quickness had already captivated her, and she was amused to note that his bronze curls were much the same color and texture as her own. She'd guessed that his blue-eyed, olive-skinned appearance stemmed from his northern Italian ancestry, for it betrayed the Norman strain of those who had once invaded his country. Someday she would have a son like him.

The coach door slammed shut, and craftily her fingers sought the opposite handle. The aunts were actually snoring. How easy this was going to be. The cousin, seated across from her, was staring out the window toward the large house that loomed in the shadows.

Suddenly this maiden lady screamed. "Carlo! Carlo, no!"

Nanon stiffened, and her hand fell away from the far door as she gripped the edge of the seat. A stream of Italian invective, so rapid that she couldn't follow it, filled the coach. The old aunts came awake with a jolt, adding their voices to the cacophony of sound. The carriage wheels that had begun to roll slowed as the door was flung open.

There was a moment of silence as the boy peered inside, hands gripping either side of the door, feet half-running to keep up with the pace of the barely turning wheels.

"I have permission, aunties," he shouted as he landed inside the coach next to the indignant cousin and opposite Nanon. His eyes were merry, and he looked very pleased with himself.

"A spoilt boy . . . indulged by foolish parents," hissed the cousin. "Given everything his heart desires. With five sisters at home, and himself the heir and young rooster cock!"

"Hush your words and yourself, Cousin Lucia!" The

boy's blue eyes were as fierce-looking and insolent as an adult's.

"Carlo . . . you must apologize for speaking so rudely to your cousin." Nanon was stern, but as she spoke, her heart had sunk into her boots. She was once more fulfilling her role as governess. But immediate escape was foiled, for the splendid horses were beginning to race along the road. The landscape was flying by.

Carlo was looking at her with grown-up amusement, but then he turned and apologized in such a graceful and heartwarming manner that his elderly cousin, Lucia, seemed quite smitten with him again and the old aunts clucked in praise of their fine grandnephew.

The image of a haloed cherub, Carlo looked gravely across at Nanon. She shook her head at him in censure. "Did your parents say you could ride in this coach with me instead of with them? *Truly*, Carlo?"

"I am to practice my French grammar with you, *mademoiselle*." He grinned persuasively at her.

To keep from smiling back at him in return, she looked out the window at the Italian countryside flowing by. The boy had made her planned flight from the caravan doubly difficult. She saw him as being too full of life and of himself. She doubted he would ever curl up into a proper, cozy sleep. For a fact, he looked as alert as though he had never napped in his short ten years on earth. He would be formidable to elude. Also—and what an impossible thought, for what did she know of children?—she was becoming quite fond of him!

A confetti of white blossoms was blowing through the orchards they passed . . . the air was fragrant and warm, with the sun coming up over the hills they were fast approaching. Carlo began to ask her questions. She, in turn, closed her eyes feigning sleep.

They had made a stop for a picnic lunch, their party

well guarded by Riccardo and his men. A change of teams was possible here, since the escort riders who brought up the rear led several strings of fresh horses.

Proudly Carlo pointed out to her a rangy black gelding he had once ridden while on a secret foray to the Marsicano stables. Since then he had stolen away to feed the black horse now and then.

"He threw me that time, *mademoiselle*, but no one knew. And he is my friend, even though he's not been trained as a riding horse. Still . . . it is possible."

"They're all a fine-looking lot, but are you sure, Carlo, that he's the one you rode, even briefly?" The boy could be boasting. The animal was striking in appearance, and spirited.

The youth stood up. She disguised her smile, for he seemed to have grown in stature and manliness since early morning. He pursed his lips, gave three short, sharp whistles. The gelding threw up its head, looked away from its teammates, bent a fiery eye on Carlo, and pawed at the clods of earth.

"You believe me now, don't you?" The boy had a child's complacency at finding her out. She could have taken him in her arms and hugged him. But she wouldn't — she planned on leaving him too soon.


Late afternoon, and the long shadows were creeping across the folds of the darkening and deserted hills. Nine well-armed riders pounded ahead while Riccardo and three of his men brought up the rear of the line of five coaches.

The stop scheduled for rest and water was forgone, since the travelers had need to hasten through the canyons ahead in order to reach the next village inn by nightfall.

The aunts and cousin appeared comatose in their fatigue, and even Carlo's curly head bounced against her arm as he slept. Nanon, too, was tired, but, reminded by the Italian landscape of the vineyards and fields of her home, she was once again grateful for the hard work she'd done and for the muscles she'd earned—the muscles of which Théo had made so much fun.

Mustn't think about Théo. She must bury the thought of her brother's lips wetly invading hers, of his hands trying to explore her body. She must hide that memory far away in the deep recesses of her consciousness, never to be taken out, never to trouble her again. Nor would she think of how it might be if she were forced to face him one day. Oh, let the future take care of itself . . . now, *now*, she must plot to get out of this coach.

Temptations of Hades! She had begun to revert to these ridiculously youthful exclamations of hers as she edged slowly to the coach door, letting Carlo's head fall against the back of the seat.

She had reasoned it was better to leave now, rather than upon arrival at their stop for the night. The other four occupants of the coach had been sleeping through the late afternoon. Thus, upon reaching the village inn, they were sure to be wide awake and *watchful* . . . even the old ladies, and particularly the young boy.

She'd observed boulders as large as small huts beside the road, and she decided to hide behind them. In tomorrow's early light, she'd start walking back to that last settlement they'd galloped through, perhaps five or six kilometers away. Surely there, for gold, she could hire a cart and donkey to take her back to Genoa. If need be, she'd buy both!

She felt the satisfactory weight of the purse and was again grateful for Georges Degrelle's gold, lent her unwittingly. A worrying thought did occur to her: she must be cautious for Degrelle might already have been released and he might be following her north to Lombardy.

Surely the coach horses must slow as they entered that labyrinth of defiles just ahead. That should be her opportunity to leap to freedom and quickly hide herself in the approaching dusk.

Of course the elderly relatives and Carlo would instantly awaken, but by that time she would be off, running in the dark to hide behind the boulders. It would be too late, too dangerous, to halt and make a search for her. She'd be labeled an hysterical woman and since none of them really knew her — and with their own lives and possessions to preserve — her absence would matter only to Carlo. But that would be for a short time, as she judged children's memories.

If this plan of hers was somewhat tenuous, still she'd chance it. For Devin! From the coach window, Nanon stared ahead as the ravines seemed to approach rapidly. Soon they were within the high, sand-colored walls, their pace slowing noticeably as the horses negotiated the horseshoe turns along the circuitous and narrow road.

When they were at a walk, with a wide place in the road ahead where the pace might pick up, Nanon knew the time had come. She closed her eyes, her fingers moving instinctively to the defined hardness of the emerald beneath her shirt front — her betrothal ring, a talisman of Devin's love.

Here . . . now . . . she was ready.

She opened her eyes and took a deep breath; her fingers, quiveringly alert, resting on the door handle.

But in the next instant she found herself in a daze, confused. Had she actually thrown open the coach door? No. There was a crash — and she was pitching forward, but not lying outside on the ground. Instead, she was still *inside* the coach, huddled in a tangle of bodies, her ears smote by screams and the sounds of gunfire.

Beside her, Carlo, showing both fear and courage, cried, "What is happening to us?" His voice cracked. "*Signorina*, are you and my aunts unhurt? I shall look out for you."

He was speaking in his own language, but she could

understand. Tears welled in her eyes. How could she so easily have thought of leaving this boy?

She swallowed hard, summoned her own courage, and said soothingly, "It's all right, Carlo."

She wondered if he believed the platitude that came so swiftly to her lips. She raised her head, fighting fear as the coach door was yanked open and a face, with the glittering eyes of something that had escaped from the deepest depths, looked in on them. A dangerous face, a murderous face. And Nanon could hear the old ladies weeping in terror. . . .

# Chapter Thirty

The guttural voice matched the man who possessed it, and understanding this much of his command by its angry sound, Nanon stumbled from the coach.

As her feet slammed to the ground, she reached back to aid the old ladies and Carlo. It was a vain attempt. A second man, equally menacing, joined the first and cuffed her smartly. The blow across the back of her neck sent Nanon reeling. As she fell, rough hands pinioned her wrists, a rope tightening around them; there was a knee in her back, a twist of pain, and then numbness as she and the others were dragged a little way up the hill.

Thrust face downward on the ground, Nanon was aware of the harsh surface bruising her cheekbones and filling her nostrils with summer dust. Yet, something squirming and alive beneath her had pillowed her fall, and she realized that her own body was resting on top of Carlo's, shielding his. She lay very still. Stunned, frightened for the others, she waited for that ransacking of her clothing and person that seemed inevitable.

Her betrothal ring . . . She stifled a moan. It would be torn from its chain around her neck, this symbol of Devin's love that mattered as much to her as life itself. She would no longer have gold with which to bargain as she had planned—she was at the mercy of the bandits.

She waited, barely daring to breathe, but the physical assault she'd expected did not occur. Slowly, then, she raised her head, finally sitting up awkwardly because her

291

hands were bound behind her. Carlo was warm beneath her, but his elderly relatives lay, bloodied and too silent, on the ground next to her. And the men had fled to join in the combat below.

Remarkably like a scene in a play, the melee below them continued. Riccardo and his men were still fighting hand to hand against an attack that had been launched with stealth and skill, and by bandits with an intimate knowledge of this terrain.

Men and horses milled about; and snarling cries, the clash of daggers, and the brief snap of gunshots came to Nanon's ears. She could see that traveling cases were being plundered, while coaches sat at mad angles across the road. The Marsicano family was huddled behind one that was overturned. Perhaps that was to the good. Nanon's coach, the last in line, seemed to be the only one waylaid, its passengers dragged forth.

She could hear Carlo snuffling beneath her, weeping for his mother and his father. After all, there were limits to a ten-year-old's manly courage.

But not to his quick-wittedness.

As his choking sobs subsided, he whispered, "My hands are untied. He made the loops too big."

Rolling aside from him, Nanon whispered back. "Loosen my bonds."

He did so, and on hands and knees, the two of them scuttled up and away from the clashing action going on beneath them.

"My aunts . . . my cousin?" His voice faltered.

She left him and crept down a few feet to touch a wrist, but then she drew back. Was it death she felt? Or with the shock of the attack were the women unconscious, in a faint? To her eyes they seemed to lie much too quietly.

She spoke determinedly. "By ourselves we can neither lift nor revive your relatives, Carlo. You and I must get away from here. I don't know whether Riccardo and the escort will prevail against these ruffians. But your parents are down there, and we must believe they're still safe. If we could only ride from here, that last village is not too far behind, we could try to find help. . . ."

The boy's eyes narrowed. She could almost see the flash of their blue in the night shadow. "I can ride anything . . . in any manner . . . and without a saddle."

She looked at him. What could he be thinking? "I, too," she whispered back. Once more they looked down into the ravine. Two of the coach teams had broken loose from their traces, in another few minutes they would be galloping to freedom in the hills above. She turned questioningly to Carlo. "Do you think we can?"

The child, no longer weeping and bewildered, understood and grasped her arm. "Down there, look. . . . The black is starting to make a break with the others. I think I can head him off, distract him somehow."

"You're counting on a miracle!" Nanon gasped. "My Dominique would come to me at the snap of a finger, but not that horse. He doesn't really know you. We'll have to try and run for it." She looked up the hill, gauging the distance to the crest, hoping they could escape unseen by those below.

But Carlo, still tugging at her arm, had already whistled his sharp command. Next, he was pulling her after him toward the gelding who'd stopped short. With a slow turn of its head, the horse looked through the darkness in their direction, examining them with grave curiosity.

Nanon thought her heart would stop as Carlo ran ahead of her to grasp that flowing mane, and while he crooned softly, she saw him bring out what seemed to be a twist of hard candy from his jacket pocket.

The big black first nuzzled, then chomped the sweet. Caught by excitement and fear, torn between laughing and crying at the sight, Nanon ran forward and quickly pushed the boy up onto the animal's back. She stood still, ready; fully expecting the horse would rear and

Carlo would come flying off into her arms. Instead, though the creature shivered almost convulsively, the boy gripped its mane with both hands and stretched his body along its neck, half singing into those nervous ears pricked back at him.

With this quieting maneuver, he prevented the horse from bolting. At least right then. When Carlo straightened, he looked down at her triumphantly. "You see!"

Standing beneath him, she sighed. "Without a stirrup to give me a boost, or a rock big enough for me to stand on, he's too tall for me to mount. *You* ride away, Carlo — keep as safe as you can. There's moonlight now . . . go back down along the road to the settlement. Tell them what has happened."

"I will not. I'll not leave you. *Signorina,* try!" he commanded, and he held the trembling beast steady with the pressure of his knees while he continued to make soothing, coaxing sounds.

Now he was speaking rapidly in his own language, to her and to the horse, but Nanon could make out only every other word.

Still, listening to that reassuring voice, the gelding seemed to understand, and he stood there, concentrating on running the toffee between two rows of big teeth, testing, tasting, enjoying his treat.

Nanon told herself this was not the time to lose courage and be cautious. She never had before. Hadn't she practiced wild tricks in the fields with Dom? She recalled, too, that Paris alley when, upon first spying D'Amboise in the Allied ranks, she'd rejoined Théo on the run — and careened upward to land inside their old coach with that one mighty leap.

She turned and gained the upper slope, lifted her impeding skirts and tucked them at her waist the way the peasants did in the field. Then, taking a deep breath and gritting her teeth, she set out on a short, fleet run. At the end she flexed her knees, tightened her muscles, and assayed a great leap into the air. Her arms flailed to give her balance, and she did reach her target, arriving hard and a bit hurtfully just behind Carlo on the animal's back.

The astonished horse grunted, then shuddered in anger and surprise. There was no time for Nanon to groan or rub her backside. She gripped Carlo's shoulders, steadying herself and him as the creature spun, reared, and whirled in one spiraling movement.

Anguished, she closed her eyes. Surely the two of them would soar into the air, and the noise and impact of their landing would bring part of the robber band up here to search them out. But Carlo was able to control the great beast, and when Nanon opened her eyes they were still atop that quivering back. Her legs dangled, her knees gripped the animal's girth, her full skirts were somewhere up around her waist.

She managed to tug them down. Then her arms encircled the boy and her hands sought the fifteen inches or so of leather trace that still remained attached to the bridle.

"Help me find what's left of the strap," she murmured. "I can use it as a rein. Someone's ridden him at some time, he does seem to understand."

Carlo spoke bravely over his shoulder. "I told you. *I* have."

"Once, Carlo. And you fell off."

"Never mind that . . . I'm older now. Here's the strap end. Are you ready? I'll give him a little kick to start him off. Hold on. . . . Do you pray?"

"There's no time, Carlo. And will you try to speak in my language—at least part of the time? It will make it easier for me."

He nodded briskly. *"Allons.* We depart. *Courage!"*

Leaving the turmoil below them on the road, they mounted the hill. Using the broken trace and the pressure of her knees, Nanon was able to guide the animal.

Almost at once, her confidence returned. Riding minus a saddle was a freedom she'd enjoyed in the fields at home, yet she knew if the creature stepped into a hole or was frightened and broke into a gallop along this dark, unknown terrain, they were done for. The two of them would be thrown and seriously injured—or worse.

"Listen to me, Carlo," she whispered rapidly as they jogged. "You go ahead and pray if you want to. For all three of us. Pray the horse doesn't stumble."

"Rest reassured," he told her nimbly. "God will hear."

And she knew that she loved this child. . . .


Their eyes adjusted to the half-dark as their mount picked his way among rushes, trees, and boulders to gain the crest of the hill. But they came to an even sharper rise of land before Nanon realized their danger. The clearly defined shape of the horse bearing Carlo and herself had become a black silhouette against a sky paled by stars and the light from a distant half-moon.

They halted, and as she felt the tension in the shoulders of the boy in front of her, Nanon knew that he had heard it, too. He continued to look straight ahead, sounding older than his ten years. "The sound of hoofbeats travels. Is it a coach and horses on the road below . . . could my parents have escaped and be traveling down there?"

He turned to her, and again she caught that flash of blue in the moonlight. As ages go, she felt thrice her own nineteen years. Less hopeful than he, she replied. "Perhaps it is, but wait. Ah, no . . . ah, God no!"

They both were aware that the black had pricked up its ears, and then it came—the soft whinny.

"Carlo. There's another horse up here somewhere. And that sound of hooves is coming closer."

"A rider that's not a friend?"

She didn't answer but pulled the short rein sharply to

the left, toward what she believed to be the shadowed side of the next ravine. Here they could hide beneath a dark shoulder of land, in some place where moonlight could not reach them.

"Here the descent may be tricky," she told Carlo. "Hang on tightly to his mane."

She guided their mount so that, with instinctive care, he took his first steps down the couloir, but when the real plunge downward came, they proceeded at a giddier pace than she had anticipated. The sides of the canyon were steeper, more difficult to traverse than she'd realized. Hooves skidded on rock, and slowly she and Carlo began to slide sideways on that sleek back. Both tried to shift upright, to regain their balance. It was no use.

At the last, Nanon wrapped her arms around the boy, hoping to cushion the impact as their bodies slid backward off the animal's haunches and jarred onto the ground. They hit the earth together, tumbling and then rolling over and over into a wild tangle of bushes. Out of breath, unhurt, they sat up, while ahead of them the black horse disappeared, picking its own way down the canyon's side with equine grace.

Carlo pursed his mouth to whistle the creature back, but Nanon's hand on his lips stopped him. "Listen!"

The boy was silent. A horse neighed above them, and from somewhere down below, the black whinnied in return. She pulled Carlo into the place where the bushes were thick and tunneled into the side of the ravine.

He protested. "I could get him back again."

She answered grimly, "The first time was luck. You've emptied your pockets of candy . . . he won't come back."

The strange voice that accosted them from above their hiding place was almost lighthearted. "I can wait you out until morning. It will be easier for me then, young fellows. I'll round up your horse . . . and wait. But step one foot from where you are, and it will be your last passage."

Nanon was terrified, but she would not let Carlo know it. She gestured stubbornly with the flat of her palm, whispering. "It's all right . . . we're safe until light, Carlo. And we will be gone long before then."

Quite reasonably, the child asked, "How, *mademoiselle?*" He is too trusting, she thought. How, indeed!

# Chapter Thirty-one

Carlo had fallen asleep, his curly head resting in the crook of her elbow. She'd become so accustomed to thinking of him as a sturdy comrade, almost a peer, that, glancing down at the boy's handsome face, it was with urgent surprise that she saw him now as he really was; childlike and vulnerable, as innocent-appearing as a cherub.

In the absence of his parents, it was she who was responsible for his well-being. Possibly his life. She raised her head with pride. *Allons. Courage!* she told herself, recalling the boy's staunch words of support. Then she twined her fingers around the chain that held the emerald as though this ring, this magic talisman, could call Devin to her. . . .

She and Carlo had tumbled into these bushes to find refuge in the canyon's side. But this safety would last only until daybreak. Soon they must attempt to climb down the ravine in the darkness, braving the threat of the man who watched from the ridge above. Or they could stay here until it grew light in the hope that he'd become tired of waiting and ride off.

Possibly it was the black horse he'd been after all along. He might have thought its riders were poor village lads astride a valuable mount, probably stolen. Perhaps he was not part of the band that had attacked the caravan of coaches.

Ruminating thus, Nanon slept briefly, then awakened

to take up the thread of her previous thought. There was only one man above them . . . but one man or twelve, it didn't matter. He was armed and full of malice, and they were on foot and helpless. Still, she had the gold.

She felt along her belt for the purse, weighing its heft with her fingers and feeling better for it. The ruffian could probably be bought off, for he'd sounded more jaunty and carefree than vicious. Except that he had assumed the two hiding below him were youths. Carlo was safe enough, but how might the man regard a young woman alone and unprotected?

With gentle hands, Nanon let the boy's head slide onto a soft mound of twigs, and not wanting to disturb him, she carefully pulled the folds of her skirt from beneath his limp body. He was deeply asleep, fortunately. She was aching and stiff, bruised from her recent fall; but after a stretch and a kneading of taut shoulder and leg muscles, she stood with some degree of ease and peered from their shelter.

It seemed quiet on the ridge above, but this was no time to relax her guard. Cautiously Nanon angled herself along, feeling her way, her fingers scrabbling at the bushes that grew out of the steep, rocky sides of the canyon. Pulling herself along in this manner, she half crawled a few feet upward along the ravine.

At some distance from the place where Carlo slept, the ground sloped more gently and she found a ledge on which she could stand. Looking skyward through the paling light, she strained for sight of horse or rider. Her ears listened with such acuteness that, finally, the only sound she was conscious of was the hammering of her own heart. The morning world around her seemed quiet and reasonably safe, yet all she could hear was the pulse and pounding within her own body.

She was unaware of the excited swoop of birds who'd been disturbed, unaware of the silent footfall that had caused their alarm.

The hand pressed across her lower face muffled her instinctive exclamation, then her attempt to scream. The muscular arm that encircled her from behind was a girdle of steel around her waist, knocking the breath from her.

The attacker's voice, at her ear, was sarcastic, surprisingly rich with self-mockery. "I have never misjudged a person's sex before, which is a worrisome thought to me. Have I been away so long soldiering that I cannot tell the difference between a youth and a young woman?" He breathed into her ear. "I'd best remedy that lack in me—and right now! Let me look at you . . . let me feel . . . let me taste. . . ."

His palm still across her lips, he pivoted her to face him. "So, *you* are one of the two youths I've been following—and out of curiosity only."

With this, he bore her down onto the ground, ran his hands down her torso, and then sat lightly astride her.

Shocked by this quick attack, Nanon stared up at him as, in one sinewy hand, he clenched both her wrists. He lowered his face to hers, and his mouth now stopped her from further outcry. But she would not have made a sound in any case, so fearful was she of alerting Carlo who, if he came to her defense, might meet injury or death.

With sensual and skillful possession, the stranger silenced her. And when Nanon arched her body to throw off his weight, his free hand traced the swell of her bosom, lingeringly and with a palpable pleasure that she sensed with disgust. His fingers, inserted between the buttons of her modest shirtwaist, now pushed aside the cotton chemise underneath, to tease across her flesh.

In despair, Nanon bit the lips still riveted upon hers. With an oath he released her lips, and she panted. "I have gold to give you. Let me go. . . . I'll not make a sound, not cause you trouble, I promise."

Unthinkingly she had spoken in her own tongue, not

in his, and she was astonished to see his head rise and his black brows wing upward.

Then he answered her in kind, though with an awkward accent. "Stay tranquil, *mademoiselle*. I will not hurt you. I have fought under your Napoléon. I am from Piedmont, impressed into the army, first by the Austrians and then by the French. Influence might have saved me, but I chose my way."

He was inclined to be talkative, she could certainly tell that. If she could somehow keep him conversing, she thought, she might with cleverness free herself and Carlo.

But as his fingers continued to probe beneath her shirtwaist, Nanon heard his deep sexual sigh, the erratic pounding of his heart. Even the faint shuddering in his lower limbs hinted at his needs. "Later . . . we'll talk of gold," he concluded.

Adeptly he had found and brought erect the tender points of her nipples. The tantalizing, raking motion of his nail tips across each sensitive bud sent an involuntary and sensual shiver through Nanon's core. She hated him blackly for this; but kneeling astride her hips while confining her arms above her head, he had rendered her powerless to resist him.

By the fast-quickening light she could see that this brute on top of her was not much older than she. The eyes looking deep into hers were almond shaped and very black, the savagery in them curiously softened by seductively long lashes.

Ah God, she hated him . . . hated that face, so thin and bearded and eager, with saliva twitching at the corners of its mouth. The only thing in his favor was that his look was more sardonic than lascivious—as though there were a joke here someplace. But how could any man want to take a woman unknown to him, one who'd just happened along at the break of day—there was no sense to it!

He was moistening his lips with his tongue, bending

close to whisper into her ear with such passionate emphasis that, though she did not comprehend the full meaning of his erotic language, there was no mistaking its lustful fervor.

Then he leaned back on his haunches. Relaxed, he watched her eyes and her lips, slyly amused as though enjoying her reaction to his words. She tried to shift her hips away from his, while her gaze secretly searched along his belt for a hidden weapon or dagger. There appeared to be a scabbard at the back . . . if only she could grasp it.

"Ah, that feels good. . . . Writhe more, and still more, *mademoiselle*," he ordered. "You do excite me, moving your body in that manner beneath me. Ah, yes."

Instantly, Nanon lay still as death.

With tongue in cheek, he continued. "Is it possible someone like you was part of the caravan that was attacked by bandits while traveling from Genoa last night? It was a rich merchant's, I understand. Does he need ladies to dally with while making such a move? What is your name, and tell me the truth, what were you doing with those people—a Frenchwoman like you?"

Eyeing her modest blouse still unbuttoned for his pleasure, he released one of her hands and studied its palm as well as her slender fingers. "You're not a servant, though I can see a telltale callous here and there. And what about that horse you were riding as fleetly as any man along with that small comrade of yours?"

She looked at him icily, without answering.

"You refuse me? Well then, when we are in more intimate circumstances, perhaps you *will* unburden yourself." He shrugged and smiled amiably; then his hand once more assaulted her bosom. This time, instead of touching her breasts, his fingers curled around the hidden chain. When he brought forth the dangling emerald ring, she stifled a cry. He heard, and grinned. "Stolen . . . ? Never mind, I shan't turn you in to the gaoler." He flipped it back inside the neck of her blouse. "I'll look at it later and tell you if it's real," he promised.

Springing to his feet like an acrobat, he extended his hand and pulled her upright. With a suggestive intimacy, he then bent forward and rearranged the fullness of her skirts, straightening their length to her boot tips.

Frantically, Nanon looked around. The sun was brilliant above them, promising heat, and painting with ocher and gold the tops of the hills that encircled them. Could their black horse be grazing nearby? No, miracles didn't happen.

In a conversational tone, he explained. "During the night I obtained two horses so that you and your friend can come with me. Call him . . . or her . . . whoever it is, to join you here." From the back of his belt, he removed a heretofore hidden weapon. "I shall not let you out of my sight, lovely one. And remember, I could have taken you at will right here, but I don't like to fornicate on hard ground. You and I will be more comfortable in the bed at my villa near the palazzo."

At his words, Nanon tried to remain impassive. She told herself that he seemed to talk so much, she no longer felt as threatened as she had earlier. "Why do you choose me?" she asked curiously. She knew she was plainly dressed, her hair tangled and her face dirty. Indeed, she was completely unkempt, hardly a prize of femininity—besides, she was quite sweaty.

"You want compliments?"

"No! It's just that I do think someone like yourself must not entirely lack for female companions."

"Maybe I told you the truth. Maybe it's been a long time and I worry about myself when I confuse you with a youth. Oh, Lord!" His laughter was full of swagger. "The lady does want to be told she's attractive. Actually, I wasn't going to have anything to do with you, untidy creature that you are. But I spied a welcome dimple, and when you smile your eyes light up. And . . . your hair is

304

like Bernini's bronze, and I want to see your body naked. You're a beauty that way, I can tell."

Nanon's face was crimson. What had she gotten herself into? "Shut up!" she said coldly.

He was still laughing at her; then suddenly he was astonished at the approach of a sullen and downcast Carlo, who regarded him warily. "But what a beautiful boy . . . you didn't tell me this." He looked from Nanon to the blue-eyed child. "There are some who would not be able to agree as to which of you two is the tastier. . . ."

He rode just ahead of them, holding the ropes with which he led their two mounts. They were proceeding at a sedate pace because, with rightful mistrust, he'd tied their wrists to their saddles.

Even to Nanon's dejected gaze, the countryside that now surrounded them appeared beautiful. Having left the dry hills and ravines behind, they now rode across a vast plain broken by a swift-running river and spectacular, sparkling lakes. She constantly exchanged looks with Carlo, shaking her head at him each time he might have spoken out. It was important that he keep silent, for intuition told her that her own purse with its gold florins was insignificant, that real wealth might change hands if her eccentric captor were to learn that this young boy was the sole heir to the Marsicano fortune.

She was unprepared for the remarkable beauty of Palazzo Alessio. They came upon it suddenly at the end of a lengthy avenue lined with cypress. The gardens, filled with rhododendrons and azaleas, and alternately shaded by ilex trees or open to the sun, were extraordinary, terraced on either side of the palazzo itself and interspersed with statues and obelisks.

Behind the palazzo's magnificence rose a gentle incline, and on its crest stood a small building of exquisite design. Their guide glanced at Nanon with amusement as her eyes widened.

"You are impressed, I see. That is a temple dedicated to Bacchus," he told her. "My own villa is to the rear of it, and this is where we shall go, you and I. I can show a woman like yourself matters of a more intriguing nature than you'd experience in the palazzo itself. I can assure you of that!" He glanced at Carlo. "A bath and proper clothing for that enchanting boy there, and he shall be brought to the Duke."

His gaze held hers meaningfully, and she frowned in some dismay. What on earth was he talking about? It really didn't matter, she told herself. Let him ramble on; she and Carlo would escape this impossible situation before too long. The Duke must be lord of the surrounding territories. Such a man would uphold the laws of the province. She would demand that both she and Carlo be taken to him so he could hear their story and return them forthwith to Milan.

The amorous couplings of nubile nymphs and lecherous satyrs must have had particular appeal for the artist who had created the frescoes and several of the large paintings in the open corridors leading to the salon of the villa they had entered. She turned her eyes away from the florid canvases while Carlo, marching at her side, was clearly startled, yet fascinated, by such explicitly sexual revelations.

A valet appeared, and before Nanon could protest their separation, he took Carlo by the hand and led him down a high-ceilinged corridor.

When she would have followed, her host stopped her, explaining that a bath and a rest were in order for both herself and Carlo.

"Now that we have the time to relax appropriately, my name is Cesare." He confided this as they entered a private apartment, its stucco ceiling gilded and painted in soft sea green shades, its furniture upholstered in velvets

306

matching the blues and greens of the sea, its walls mirrored with pier glass. It was a cocooned world of seascape within enclosed walls.

Nanon's self-proclaimed *amante* appeared completely at home in this rococo splendor, and though in the turmoil of their first meeting she had not noticed his clothing, she now could see that his breeches and his full shirt with flowing sleeves were of exquisite silken weave and his boots were of the finest Italian leather.

"Tell me your name, and let us be civilized." He came close to her, his smile thin-lipped and scarlet through the well-groomed black beard that followed the lines of cheek and jaw.

"Antoinette . . ." There was no purpose in lying, for very soon she would be explaining to the Duke the importance of her father, the late General de Cavanac, and would make clear her close relationship to the former Empress of France. Ah, Joséphine. Nanon sighed. What unhappily strange events had been fated to occur when, at her godmother's insistence, she had taken her place in the campaign coach.

And yet out of all of this had been born the eternal love between herself and Devin D'Amboise. *Devin* . . . But it was too cruel to think of him at this moment, for the creature was approaching her with a wine glass in his hand.

She was about to disdain his offer when he murmured. "This is not for you . . . you've not eaten food today. The wine would go to your head and make you giddy. I do not propose this for you. It's for the pretty boy to drink before we send him to the palazzo."

Cesare leaned toward a mirror and regarded his image while running a finger along the distinguished contour of his neatly trimmed beard. "He is being groomed and bathed at present—as you will be. But you will have the entire morning to rest and to look about, with proper chaperonage, of course, so that you do not get any ideas about unlocked doors."

She stared at him starkly. For the first time she was beginning to comprehend his shadowy intimations concerning the Duke and the boy.

Her face paled almost to the bone as she spoke obliquely but with rigid emphasis. "I cannot believe what my faint understanding of your insinuations is beginning to tell me, *signore*. I hope that my thoughts are merely evil minded and mine alone, and that they do not match what I perceive—again, wrongly I hope—to be *your* implication of what awaits my young friend in the palazzo of your Duke."

Cesare sent her a sidelong glance, then strolled to a nearby chest, picked up a crystal decanter, and poured another glass of wine. He twirled the goblet, studying its ruby content, not looking up again until at a chosen and precise moment he glanced slyly at her.

He cleared his throat, examined a fingernail. "I shall be completely forthright. My distant relative the Duke of Allesio is handsomely corrupt—an elderly pedophiliac, if you will. I do not mind since I am his heir, and I do expect he will soon kill himself with his dissolute excesses. Which is all to the good, wouldn't you say? Let us rid the earth of his decay. And anyway, what is the boy to you?"

At the impact of his words, the sea green room seemed to swirl around Nanon. Before she tumbled into its floating depths, she knew what she must do. "Cesare . . ." she implored. *"Help me. . . ."*

# Chapter Thirty-two

Cesare leaped instantly to her side, solicitously bending over her. "Antoinette . . . what is it?"

She let him assist her to a gilded settee. As though seeking support, she placed her arm around his muscular waist. And her fingers felt along the braided leather belt.

The scabbard was there, she was right about that. It was empty.

Defeated, she sank back upon the settee.

But could she truly have done it?

Even to save the innocent Carlo from defilement, could she have plucked the dagger from its sheath and plunged it into Cesare's back? Picturing the act itself, Nanon closed her eyes, struck with horror. Torn flesh, spurting blood, a man falling unconscious. Dead. By her hand.

She recoiled now from a further memory. The day in the Champs Élysées, the knife attack against the Tsar, the frightened young man trampled beneath Cossacks' hooves . . .

She opened her eyes. He was watching her. "Are you better . . . has the faintness passed? Tell me, how can I help you?"

Somehow, she must find the boy and escape with him from this treacherous place. She spoke urgently. "Cesare, you must *not* take him to the palazzo today . . . you must wait!"

Seating himself at her side, he quirked his brow at her, bemused. "Will you rephrase that sentence? As a question, not a command. Speaking as you just have can only raise the hackles of a man and make him obstinate."

He smiled. No, it was not exactly a smile. His lips showed only the faintest crinkle of humor, his eyes none at all. She knew she must be very, very careful. He was so young—volatile and completely undependable.

Her dimple deepened, and as the expression in her eyes warmed to dark amber, she tried to lift the corners of her mouth in a merry pout. *"Please,* Cesare, it can't matter all that much if you delay a little longer in sending Carlo to your relative's house. Perhaps we can discuss the problem, you and I. The boy *does* matter to me. I'm very fond of him."

"You are?" He twisted a bronze-colored strand of her hair around his index finger, intently shaping it into a fat curl. Then, leaning close, his brow almost touching her forehead, he inhaled deeply. "Your female body scent is seductive, Antoinette—even unwashed as you are. Now, tell me what you have in mind. I know what *I* have in mind."

Grateful that he could not read her violent thoughts at that moment, Nanon decided to shift to a safer, less personal topic. She looked around at the rich furnishings in the room.

"It was foolish of me to believe that you planned to kidnap us for ransom. I see by your surroundings that I was mistaken. You're not a bandit, but exactly what you say you are—a member of a ducal family."

She shivered. Men with the wicked propensities of the Duke did not have families. They had only a clan, only relatives like Cesare waiting for their demise.

She continued, striving for lightness. "Though it's apparent that you do ride out at night—and sometimes bring home travelers."

"Yes, for my own amusement. How perceptive of you." He was diverted.

She went on. "Carlo is the only son of the merchant

family that was ambushed. I'm hopeful that the armed escort did prevail and that they're all safe now. But they must be mourning, not knowing the whereabouts of their child. You see, the family has been kind to me, and I'm the boy's governess."

He'd leaned forward to sniff beneath her ear and nuzzle his lips along the curve of her throat, but at her words he drew back, an expression of puzzlement on his face. "A French governess in an Italian merchant's household? A peculiar arrangement."

"They wished him to become proficient in my language. To prepare him for the time when he will head the family's trade and carry it across the continent. This is sure to happen one day when the wars are settled." Close enough to the truth, though a bit embroidered.

"I'm aware that some of these Milanese merchants are industrious and ambitious. So . . . you taught the brat?"

"He's become very dear to me. Cesare, I beg you, is there some way he can be saved from this . . . viciousness you've described to me? I have a purse filled with gold. It's yours, or do I offend you by offering it?"

"You do offend me. I have no need of your money. You realize, of course, that you have attributes other than gold, and I prefer to claim them."

His hand gliding to her waist, Cesare halted it at the purse's hiding place. When she stirred uneasily, his fingers slipped inside her blouse and splayed across her stomach to rub it in a gently suggestive manner.

Nervously Nanon sprang up from the settee. "Then it's decided? The boy will stay here in this villa tonight . . . is that right? Now, please allow me to excuse myself. I would like to bathe and freshen my clothing. And . . . and I am hungry."

"I, too." He leaned back, crossing his legs in cavalier fashion and smiling insinuatingly at her.

She reprimanded him. "My hunger is for food, Cesare! I've not eaten since yesterday."

"Forgive my misunderstanding you, Antoinette!" He grinned roguishly. "A repast will be served you." With a swift change of mood, he narrowed his sloe-black eyes thoughtfully. "I'm not quite sure why you seem to think I've agreed to your wish concerning the little chap. Why shouldn't I provide my relative with a morsel as attractive as this boy? Such a gift will mean a rewarding boost in my inheritance. And that is something *you* cannot provide, my lovely one." He rose, scowling. "You seem to regard my delay in sending the lad to the pleasure palazzo as a fait accompli."

"Well, isn't it?" she retorted saucily, her heart jolting with panic at her own effrontery.

Audacious in her desire to bargain for Carlo's freedom, Nanon stepped closer to the man facing her. Placing both hands, in seductive petition, upon his breast, she implored prettily. "It's a small favor for you to grant me, isn't it? Especially since your inheritance is already so substantial."

"No matter what prospect of riches one has . . . one always wants more!" he shot back at her. Then he looked down at the hands positioned so appealingly upon his chest. When he again glanced at her, the pupils of his black eyes had expanded alarmingly.

"It seems that you're trying to compel me to grant you a favor. Female wiles don't work well with me."

"They don't?" she asked sweetly, and her fingertips moved in an entreating pattern on the silk of his shirt.

Her curiosity was stirred. She'd sensed in his bravado a strain of ambivalence. For all his swagger, his open sexual gestures, there did seem to exist in him a certain pettishness—even a lack of assurance—that she found surprising.

But then, her standards of masculine conduct had been shaped by the much older D'Amboise, and that could make a difference in her perception of other men. Moreover, she was surprised that she had recognized this in-

312

consistency in the youthful Cesare, considering her own lack of experience.

Still, she had had one triumphant womanly experience. She smiled inwardly, then shivered lustfully. How she longed for Devin, longed to be enfolded by his strong arms, to feel his loins tauten, his vitality throbbing inside her.

Color had risen in her face, but as the flush of memory receded, she replied quietly. "Very well, Cesare. I understand what you're saying to me, and I shall remember it. I shall not presume further."

She was about to withdraw her fingertips, but he grasped her wrists. With his hands covering hers, he pressed her palms firmly against him, forcibly sliding them across his chest. She could feel its surface then, his hard nipples.

"Antoinette, it's *my* will—remember that! It's what *I* say!"

In dismay, she attempted to drag her hands free. But, refusing to yield her, he compelled the pads of her fingertips to massage his tiny nubs. Her face crimsoned as they came erect. Her breathing was as agitated as his own, but for a different reason. She was furious while he was bemused by his own arousal.

"You're demeaning us both." The scorn in her voice was like the flick of a whip.

But he lowered his face to hers, swirling his tongue between her lips in a kiss that smothered while his hands, hot as a fired hearth, began to mold the bodice of her blouse.

Adroitly Nanon snapped her head aside. Gasping for breath, she pulled free with a burst of strength and quickly put the settee between them.

Thinking fast, she cried. "You've spoiled everything."

His empty arms dropped, and he looked at her with almost comical astonishment. She knew she mustn't infuriate him—for Carlo's sake. She could not insult his male pride as he stood there breathing hard, with that telltale bulge in the front of his silken riding breeches. "What are you talking about?" he demanded.

"I'm talking about what we're both *thinking* about. To make love with any degree of amatory skill when one is hot and sweaty and tired . . . well, it could be so much more pleasurable the other way around."

She licked her lips and then pursed them alluringly. Returning his startled look, she sent him a drowsy smile.

And then he, too, smiled with such a brilliant flash of even, white teeth that she was reminded of a certain stallion in the château's stable, one she'd had to gentle down after a mad gallop. She'd stroked his neck, talked softly, and while circling him watchfully had kept a wary hand on his check strap.

"Why the devil are you laughing?" The words exploded from him.

She made no attempt to conceal her provocative downward glance at his lust. "You Piedmontese are truly outstanding in your fervor."

"*What* . . . ?" Could he believe what this brazen woman had said?

"Outstandingly handsome and brave." The tip of her pink tongue scorched the scarlet rim of her upper lip.

He decided that matters of *amore* had gotten a bit out of his control. He stalked behind a high-backed chair to conceal his rising excitement at the thought of the amatory skills she promised to offer him. She was, after all, a Frenchwoman.

His heart pumping with anticipation, his breath uneven, he concluded. "Cornelio will show you to your chamber. We shall meet . . . soon."

Shortly thereafter the valet brought her a note. It announced that Cesare had been called forth on estate business. She was to bathe, feast without him, and nap. He

314

would attend on her later.

Reading the next line, Nanon's heart bounded with exaltation. She had won. He had written that Carlo was to remain in the villa, at least for that day and night.

She realized that she would have to pay for such a dispensation. But then, she had always known she would probably have little choice. Unless . . . unless . . . She raised her hands to her temples, pressed hard to concentrate, and began to pace.

It was dusk, and she sat across from him in the small salon in which they'd dined, served only by the single servant Cornelio. Twilight's first stars twinkled in at them as she twisted the stem of her glass, its contents untouched. Finally she looked up, studying him.

Only a hairbreadth taller than she, and wearing impeccable evening garb which added to his graceful bearing, he was quite handsome tonight. His Vandyke beard was a trim point of ebony against his pale, almost polished-looking skin. His almond-shaped eyes, shadowed by those long lashes, gazed amorously into hers.

Though it was unintentional, Nanon knew that she, too, looked her best in the gown that, earlier, Cornelio had brought to her room. It was a frock as lovely as any that Minette had created for her in Martinique, and it fitted her extraordinarily well, shaping itself to her lissome waist and bosom.

With unhappy wit, she'd deduced that Cesare's taste in women must run to those of an exact height, weight, and form. But some thought must have been given to this finery loaned her, for its peach color complemented the warm tones of her complexion as well as the mass of autumn-bright hair she'd twirled carelessly into a pouf at the crown of her head. The result was appealing, though again not planned. Nor had Nanon planned the flattering effect of the few disengaged curls that wisped above her neckline.

Now, unobtrusively, her fingers felt for and discovered the gold chain bearing Devin's emerald—she'd slipped it inside her bodice while dressing—her talisman.

Cesare reached across the table's white cloth to place his hand over hers. "You have extracted a promise from me—one that I'd never thought to give." She tried to withdraw her hand, but he only held it more firmly.

"And what is that?" she asked, her mind busily contemplating all avenues of escape that would not lead through her host's bedchamber.

"I speak of my promise concerning the boy who's still here—and not there." He nodded in the direction of the palazzo whose looming shadows hovered, like some waiting malevolence, beyond the temple of Bacchus.

Gazing at her meaningfully, the Duke's nephew continued. "And you, too, are here and responsible for that promise. I feel a certain impatience." He placed his hand over his heart with a flourish. "Here. And . . . elsewhere."

Coolly Nanon raised her brows at him, as though requesting he be discreet in his dinner-table remarks. In turn, he winked slyly at her. "Now, finish this fine brandy. It's from your own country. Do you recognize the aroma?"

She shook her head and was about to admit that she had no taste for liqueurs, but decided he might then force her to drink.

Suddenly, she blurted out, "How do I know Carlo is here, and safe. Could I . . . see him?"

He pretended surprise. "You don't believe me? I have integrity, Antoinette. When you and I awaken tomorrow . . . together"—still holding her hand in his, he raised it to his lips, and repeated— "*together,* you have my word I shall invite your charge to join us for an intimate *petit déjeuner.*"

# Chapter Thirty-three

The candles had again burned low, though before his dismissal at midnight, Cornelio had replenished the candelabras on the side chests.

Nanon had watched Cesare steadily consume brandy in the manner of her brother Théo, while she merely touched her lips to the rim of her own glass, grateful that he hadn't noticed this dissemblance of hers.

Nor did he seem aware of her attention to this room, and her observation of the window openings that led to a terrace — and freedom. Not even her contemplation of the huge armoire in which a person could hide if need be.

Earlier, at his request, she'd described her life at the château. He'd seemed fascinated by her tales of the wartime days when she'd worked in the family's dairy and scythed wheat in the fields. But she doubted his assurance to her that he was familiar with the exploits of General de Cavanac at Wagram.

She learned that Cesare was barely two years older than she, with only scant knowledge of geography and with little historical perspective to draw on. Soon, she began to question the soldiering he'd laid claim to, thinking it more than likely he'd never ranged farther afield than the properties belonging to the Duke. Still, it was apparent a tutor had attended to his education, and that the man had been proficient in her own language.

At this late hour conversation between them had ceased. Since he, too, had spent the preceding night on the ravine's edge waiting for dawn—and for Carlo and herself to come out of hiding—Nanon was hopeful that his growing tipsiness would send him to sleep rather than to seduction.

But without warning, Cesare rose and threw down his linen square with which he'd dabbed at his mustache. Impatiently he summoned her. "I am ready . . . let us go."

She sprang to her feet, her eyes frantically searching for a path to the outside terrace. When he seized her, his arm locking her to his side, his tread was firm and not drunken as she'd hoped. And, step by step, he dragged her with him down the corridor, up a stairway.

In front of a closed door he paused, his hand gliding from her waist to clasp one satin-sheathed breast. Wrapped tightly in his arms, she was forced to endure his possession of her and, worse, the indignity of his thumb brushing back and forth across a nipple that was veiled by peach satin. It turned traitor to her, blossoming under his lightly erotic touch. She wanted, and intended, to die right there, but she wouldn't because dying had nothing to do with revenge.

He brought his face close to hers. "Delicious," he breathed into her ear. "This rosy bud shall be my dessert—but before that I shall love you *dessus dessous* . . . in front and behind. Shall you like that, my darling?"

When she didn't respond, he smirked. "Such pleasures will put you in the mood to enjoy your own feast. No answer to this? Then, I'll tell you. You may feast on *me*, I give you permission."

Nanon reminded herself that she was a general's daughter, she would not show weakness. She gritted her teeth, entertaining chaotic thoughts. *There's always the dagger. And this time I'll not hesitate. I will use it—or whatever I can find.*

Beneath the sheen of his superbly fitted frock coat, it was impossible for a weapon to be hidden. But a bedchamber would contain a bed, and next to the bed a night table, and surely concealed within its drawer . . . a knife, a gun. . . . It made no difference, she would use whatever came to hand.

He pushed open the door and ushered her through the opening in a rush. Once again he wound his arms around her, and his kisses glided, hotly ravishing, from her temple to her cheekbone to the corner of her mouth.

Rebellion gave Nanon strength. Turning her face away from his, by calling upon work-hardened muscles, she fended him off. But she knew it was a mere postponement. He would despoil her in brutal and eccentric ways, unless . . . someone could work a miracle in her behalf. But Nanon knew few prayers. She was not among the faithful who could ask for miracles!

No matter the insolent charm of this man's face, she'd begun to sense that he was one of those few who could only be fulfilled by sexually degrading another human. By herself it was doubtful she would have realized this. But when her engagement to D'Amboise had supposedly added a layer of sophistication to her youth, Madame Arnaud had passed on a scandalous tale of a plantation owner who engaged in just such decadent behavior.

Closing her eyes, Nanon uttered a silent plea to the person she knew best in the world, loved the most. Forgive me, Devin, forgive me, love, for what outrage may befall me. And save me if you can. . . .

Capriciously Cesare released her, and she faced him, even more fearful of what was to come. But he lifted one of her arms high above her head, holding her fingertips lightly with his own. It was, she thought in confusion, as though they were about to dance a minuet from a century past.

Instead, almost gloatingly, he twirled her several times in front of him. "This gown does fit you to perfection. Here . . . there . . ." He twitched at its material from the low neckline of her bosom to her narrow waist.

"Lovely, lovely . . . It looks almost as well on you as it does on . . ." He halted, his lips seamed of a sudden. After stepping back for a full view, he lingeringly adjusted the folds that fell from her slender hips to the hem of her skirt.

When he took another step backward and staggered slightly, Nanon knew a surging hope. It dissipated with his next words.

"Disrobe . . ." he muttered thickly.

In the flickering candlelight, her eyes questioned him. Here? In the very center of this room . . . ?

She shrank back a pace, her mind racing in quick alarm. "Wouldn't it be a happier surprise if you were to find me . . . there?"

She glanced in the direction of the bed that stood across the room, curtained on its four sides. If she could reach it, and get herself around it swiftly enough, there was a balcony on its far side. No matter the drop to the garden below, she'd gladly risk it. He, in his half-drunken state, might not find her. But then, there was Carlo. . . .

Still, before he could answer, she gathered up her skirts and fled. Instinctively pursuing, he raced behind, caught her up under one arm and, with the other, gave a yank to the curtain pull.

The bed draperies parted with a swoosh of sound and, dragging her with him, Cesare toppled them both onto a great puffed quilt. Gasping for breath that had been knocked out of her, Nanon slid across his body, face-first, into a mound of pillows.

Heart racing, she came swiftly to her knees, to strike with doubled fists at his shoulders and at that darkly handsome face. He gave a howl, sounding like the wolves in Malmaison's forests, and in the next instant he was above her, overpowering her, settling her beneath him, his knees athwart her hips as though to complete the act of ravishment begun in the ravine.

Her heartbeats almost suffocating her, Nanon momentarily lay quiescent while, using both hands, Cesare pulled the satin gown up and over her shoulders, over her head. Her hair fell across her eyes as she tried to save her gold chain and ring. Though her fingers scrabbled for them, they were torn from her.

Then, to Nanon's surprise, Cesare carefully flung the gown wide of the bed. From the corner of her eye, she saw it balloon upward, catch a puff of air, and settle like a limp butterfly onto a chair back.

He glared back at her. "You're a damn bitch, Antoinette. Why are you so difficult with me? Where are the Frenchwoman's wiles, the skills, I've been promised?"

Cleverness deserted her, and she could make no answer except to revert to her girlhood fury and call down imprecations on him—the most sinister of which she'd overheard Théo use in privacy behind closed doors.

But he proceeded, with her petticoats and camisole drawers taking no care at all, and as he ripped them down her front, they came apart with a knife-splitting sound. He stared down at her, studying every luscious, lunging move she made to defy him. But he'd had enough of struggle. He grunted. "You are a crazy woman to resist me!"

With a sharp rap of the knuckles to the side of her head, he left her dazed. Quickly he lowered his face to her throat and bosom and he licked at her heaving breasts. Dizzied by the blow, Nanon was faintly aware that he was laughing and inserting the tip of his tongue into the slit of her navel.

He raised his head, still grinning. "Ah, such a fruity taste, my dear—like tart apples in autumn. You should try it . . . well, it will soon be *your* turn."

She knew she must recover her wits, must summon strength to resist. Now he was sliding over the length of her body, his gold buttons, the stiff seam of his coat, the small jeweled buckle on his trousers leaving welts across her flesh.

Suddenly, holding her imprisoned once again between the vise of his knees, he pulled off coat and ruffled shirt, then stripped down the lacings of his breeches.

Not yet fully unclothed, he fell upon her, but when she made an effort to thrust him away from her, he grasped her fingers in his.

"So you won those little roughened palms of yours by working in the fields, did you?" He was panting now, trapping her hand in his and forcing her fingers low on his body to hold and intimately surround him. "There . . . it feels good, good. You have a man's grip, Antoinette — if not a man's technique. Go on, lovely . . . do it as I tell you to!"

Hatred for this base humiliation rose like the product of sickness in her throat. With her free hand she clawed at his body, attempting to free herself, but his strength was overpowering and she could feel him beginning to push apart her thighs. . . .

She cried out in rage. "No! I will see you to your death . . . I will kill you!"

It was a vain threat, she knew; but suddenly, there ensued a terrible and total silence. It was as though the air were suddenly heavy and filled with a strange desolation. She stared, as before her eyes his lustful drive diminished and, his passion sagging, he collapsed.

Above his kneeling, sleek, and sweating body, his head bowed, his black eyes closed as though in weary despair. The triumphant slash of his red lips crumpled. His voice faltered. "I wanted to make love to you . . . I wanted to! But it's happened to me again. What kind of man am I?"

Nanon was still terrified. Though she'd sensed what had happened to him, she was not sure that she was safe from him, not sure there was no longer evil and blight in this room, no matter what he had said. She didn't ask *why* he could not perform as he'd intended, even though she was grateful that his passion had deserted him.

322

But he told her, as though hoping she might understand, as though unburdening himself in a confessional of the flesh.

She listened, her arms clasped around her breasts and shoulders, though that still did not quiet her shivering. Her legs drawn up tightly to her belly, she rolled over onto her side. She could not shut out that voice, that tale of depravity, and she listened to him . . . the Duke's first victim. She could not close her ears to his voice, so, shuddering as though she were lost in some wintry and desolate clime, she heard what had been done to him when he was a child younger than Carlo.

Finally she heard him say with deep remorse. "I can't go through with this anymore. Get dressed. There will be proper clothing for you and the boy. A coach and horses as well. Go to Milan, take the boy with you. . . ."

She didn't look over her shoulder as the door closed softly behind him. After long minutes had gone by, she sat up, spent, weary to the bone. Hardly aware of what she was doing, Nanon ran her fingers among the quilts, feeling for and, after a time, finding the broken gold chain. Numbly she held it up, looking at it, letting it slide across her palm. Then she continued to search, at first without hope. What was the use? It was gone. . . .

No, that couldn't be! It was her talisman.

She came alive, concentrating on her task, tearing aside pillows and quilts and silk sheets . . . and when she found it and closed her fingers over the glittering green fire of her ring, she began to weep long, exhausting sobs.

# Chapter Thirty-four

*Milan*

His hand held tight in his father's, Carlo looked up a
her and said cheerfully. "I told Papa when the man sen
us away he gave us a light coach and six good horses s
we could travel fast." Sudden tears welled in the boy':
blue eyes. "Mama and Papa are safe, and we're here—
all of us."

Manfully the lad brushed aside his tears and ther
turned to his mother, who knelt beside him. "It was a
adventure, Mama—you mustn't cry. I'm sorry that ou
own black horse ran away. Nanon, why did the mar
finally let us go when he wasn't nice to us in the begin
ning?"

Her own eyes brimming with tears and love, hi
mother reprimanded him gently. "Carlito, you forget . .
you must call her *mademoiselle*."

"But we're best friends now, Mama. You remember
when you said so, Nanon, when our hands were tied tc
the saddle before we reached the villa." He finished stur
dily. "When they separated us and took you away, .
would have found you the next day, but you found m
first."

His parents exchanged distressed looks while Nanor
spoke. "You're a brave boy, Carlo. Whatever his reason:
for acting as he did in the beginning, the young mar
wanted us to be safe. That's why he sent us away."

In private, Nanon had revealed the sordid truth to the Marsicanos, but only as it pertained to their son. Signore Marsicano's face darkened with fury as he recalled what he had told them.

He met her gaze while the boy continued. "That servant Cornelio said I was going to the palazzo to meet the Duke who lives there. And that he had fine ponies to show me, and animals of all kinds. But we didn't go. I wanted to."

Still barely controlling his anger, the father patted his son's cheek and lovingly ruffled his hair. "Let's try to forget what has happened, son, since we're all together now. We'll only remember when we say our prayers for your great-aunts who were so wantonly slain. Now we must visit Cousin Lucia who is recovering from the ordeal, but slowly. Afterward, we'll rejoin *your* good friend—and ours—Mademoiselle Nanon."

As they left their guest's bedchamber, Signora Marsicano gave Nanon an impulsive hug. "Tomorrow night we've prepared a celebration of the miraculous return of our son. For your return, too. No, no—it's all planned. Say no more! You *must* be present. We have a special surprise for you, my dear!"

There was no surprise Nanon would relish except finding herself miraculously transported back to Martinique and Devin. But the Marsicanos departed before she could beg off being included in the festivities.

Walking slowly through the handsome suite assigned to her, she mused that she still had her small hoard of gold. She'd learned well the lesson Captain Patrese had sought to teach her. Purpose, courage and desire were all very fine, but a heavy purse was an extra advantage, a wherewithal not to be lightly dismissed.

For Carlo's sake, his parents might try to dissuade her from leaving. She had enough gold to ensure her passage to Martinique, but she would have to ask for their assistance in hiring transportation to Genoa. The driver who'd brought her to Milan at Cesare's behest had long since disappeared, along with his coach and horses.

Broodingly, Nanon looked out over the slopes of the garden surrounding the villa. She would never understand what had prompted Cesare's outpouring of that terrible story. Perhaps he'd had to ease a burden he'd found intolerable when confronted by herself and Carlo. As if they were mother and son, she and Carlo together must have had some poignant and tragic meaning for Cesare. They must have recalled to the unhappy man his own lost childhood.

Nanon shivered. She must not think again of those frightening moments in Cesare's bed. Instead, she folded the fingers of her right hand over her left, and was reassured by the feel of her emerald ring.

There was a knock on the door, and the maid the Marsicanos had provided entered. *"Signorina,* is there anything you need?" The woman's dark eyes rolled admiringly. "You are the heroine of the household."

Hardly that, thought Nanon. And I would not be if you knew how anxious I am to escape all this. Only Carlo tugs at my heart, but my duty to him is finished.

"Thank you, Serafina—but there's nothing you can do for me at the moment. No . . . wait. There is something. Could you tell me a little of what's being planned for tomorrow night? I confess I have a woman's curiosity as to what I should wear for the occasion." It was a reasonable request since Carlo's mother had seen to it that a small but suitable wardrobe, for Nanon's use, was hanging in the armoire.

The maid's smile was radiant. "The evening will be wonderful, *signorina.* All of Milan will turn out for it. There will be a great ball, dancing, music, fireworks, and the finest foods. Suckling pig, goose, venison—"

Nanon spoke hastily. "Oh no, let me be surprised by the menu. But I do wonder what else has been planned that's so special. Do you know?"

Serafina could not resist this appeal to exchange a confidence. She came close, half-whispering. "I think this must be it. There are many of your countrymen gathered here, though I'm not quite sure of the reason for this." She looked perplexed.

Nanon nodded encouragingly. "You must be referring to those followers of Napoléon who were forced into exile when the Bourbons returned to power."

The maid's bafflement lessened. "Yes, I suppose that may be the reason why some French had to flee over the Alps to settle in this region, though they haven't been too well received. Their customs and airs are so different from ours." Her eyes began to twinkle. "Anyway, as many as can be found have been invited because of *you, signorina*. I think that is the special surprise."

Nanon was ashamed of her own lack of excitement at this news. And even more ashamed of her guile. "Thank you, Serafina. Now, I shall know what gown to wear."

"May I dress your hair for the event? I'm competent in the new styles."

Nanon nodded absently. "That's kind of you . . . we'll see."

"If I hear further, shall I bring you information, *signorina?*"

"Oh my, yes. I appreciate these tidbits of talk between us." Nanon returned from the dressing table to press a gold coin into the woman's hand. When the maid shook her head, Nanon insisted. "Take this as a token between us. It is good to have a confidante."

She could see that she had Serafina's full attention. The other woman's eyes grew large as she studied the gold piece; finally, she pocketed it. "There's nothing I wouldn't do for such a lady as you," she said. "You have brought back to this family its only son." Her voice lowered as she added, "There will never be another child— you understand?"

"I'm sorry to hear this."

"It is God's will."

"Perhaps. Now, I do think I'll rest awhile. Could you return, later?" Nanon knew she was being not only guileful but calculating. At least, Captain Patrese would approve.

Serafina dipped a curtsey and disappeared. Nanon watched as the door shut behind her. She felt stifled by the luxury of this merchant's house, and by the extent of the planned celebration—no matter how well-intentioned. She longed to travel the road to Genoa, to sail the seas to Martinique. Her passion for Devin D'Amboise, who was never out of her thoughts, seemed to have turned her into a wanderer . . . and a deceptive one at that.

To think of Devin was exquisite pain. For without the presence of one's love, memory was a thorn that could pierce the heart. Not knowing what had happened to him in Fort-de-France was desolating. *He* might need *her* as badly as she needed him at this moment.

Anxiously she began to pace. Once again she seemed to hear her godmother's lilting voice assuring her that for the grandeur of true love, one must wait. She *had* waited, and she had been swept up in that promised golden storm. But now there were no sun's rays. There was nothing that would foretell the end of turmoil.

Nanon's pacing grew languid as she looked at the great puff of a bed in the corner. Promising herself a brief nap, she plumped down inside the quilts. After all, there *was* something to be said for the comfort of her surroundings.

It was Serafina shaking her shoulder that brought Nanon awake. "Oh *signorina* . . . I am sorry to call you this way, but it's already late afternoon. I knocked. You were so heavily asleep. . . . I have heard something."

Nanon sat up, her eyes wide as she took in the expression of anticipation on the other woman's face. "What

328

have you heard?"

"A gentleman from France has just arrived from outside the city. He sent his manservant to inquire for you."

Nanon's brows rose in uneasy question. "Someone who knows *me?*" Even as the maid nodded, Nanon's dismay and fear receded somewhat. It had to be a mistake. "Did you learn his name?"

Serafina shook her head. Thoughtfully, Nanon rose and walked to the window to look out at the approaching dusk. Degrelle could have learned from seamen's talk that the captain had arranged for her to go to Milan with the merchant family. It would be easy for him to follow her since he was already heading north to rejoin her brother. Due to her having been waylaid by Cesare, it was even possible that Degrelle might have arrived in Milan ahead of her.

But in this short time how could he have established himself and engaged a manservant? And, as a field soldier, that was not Georges' style. Yet, pondering this, she recalled his recent grand airs and his fashionable attire while on Martinique.

She looked over her shoulder at Serafina. "Where is this lake country of which I've heard?"

"To the north, *signorina*. There is the beautiful *lago di* Como in Lombardy, and the even more beautiful Maggiore on the Piedmont boundary."

Her own brother could be anywhere in that region. Nanon wished she'd quizzed Degrelle as to Théo's exact location. But she'd been so shaken, so disgusted by his proposal that she become part of a family composed also of himself and Théo, that she had not wanted to inquire. She did not care to face her brother after the terrible thing that had happened between them in the inn at Brest.

Controlling a quiver of fear, she spoke briskly. "Serafina, it's important that I learn who this person is. Could you find out for me?"

Nanon had read correctly the curiosity in Serafina's open gaze, so she continued. "You see, it might be a friend of my late father's. If so" — she shrugged pensively — "it will mean a great deal to me to be prepared for such a meeting."

She crossed the room and returned to press another coin into Serafina's no longer reluctant fingers. "I know you help me out of friendship, but please take this. You might have some unforeseen expense while on an errand for me."

The door shut so quickly on Serafina's bright blue skirt that, despite her distress, Nanon couldn't help indulging in a clandestine smile. Degrelle's own gold would enable her to avoid him, if this were he. Of late Fate had been so malicious toward her, it might well be.


It was not until late the next afternoon that Serafina brought her colorful gossip concerning the betrothal of a very young and madly-in-love Austrian heiress and the Frenchman. Upon hearing this, Nanon decided there could be nothing to the story that this particular gentleman had inquired about her.

Someone her father's age could hardly be the object of such romantic adulation. And as for Degrelle, fickle though men were said to be, he couldn't possibly have found himself a very young heiress in so brief a time.

Nanon thanked Serafina for her efforts, and the two of them set about selecting a gown for the night's festivities. Later, with good grace she would permit the maid to structure her wayward curls. No longer did she fear an unpleasant encounter.

# Chapter Thirty-five

*Paris*

D'Amboise had not wanted to attend the gathering at which he found himself that night — or any other for that matter. The only element in this one's favor was that it was to be informal. Therefore, none of the august members of the Paris Conference would be present. Castlereagh, Metternich, and the others would not attend, but Liane had promised that Talleyrand, France's foreign minister, would put in an appearance.

"Why are you so certain of this?" D'Amboise had asked her several days earlier. He'd been lounging in the purple and gold salon in her large house on the Rue St.-Florentin, garbed in an open-throated white linen shirt, a dark green riding coat, and buff breeches. His long Hessian boots crafted of shiny patent leather were carelessly planted atop one of Liane's velvet footstools. His handsome mane of black hair was trimmed but, nevertheless, unruly. Without realizing it, he presented a larger-than-life enticement to the vulnerable female eye.

Liane, Countess de Morens-Charents, an exceptionally pretty woman, had snapped out her ivory fan. Grinning at him over its fluted edge, she'd winked seductively. "He will be there because he adores me, and can only be in my company at small affairs such as this one that I myself will give. If you wish to speak to him — privately — this is your opportunity . . . my darling." She'd drawled that last endearment.

Idly Devin had noted that the hue of her fan matched

her flawless skin. But he was not her darling, nor anyone's except Nanon's. Not that Nanon had seemed to want him. *No! He mustn't think of her at this moment!* It was not flattering to either woman.

"Then, I shall be there. And I do appreciate your assistance in this matter." He had risen and had bowed over the Countess's scented hand while he'd sent her a grave and impersonal look.

Liane, too, had risen, whipping her skirts flirtatiously about her hips in a manner that called attention to her rather spectacular *derrière*. "Devin, my dear one," she'd purred, "you may escort whomever you wish to my soirée."

"Testing me again? You know I prefer to arrive alone."

"Alone as usual." She'd pouted. "And why is that? Do none of our Parisian ladies enchant you. Or even amuse you?"

Studying her, he'd shrugged. "I am totally preoccupied with political affairs, my dear Liane. You, of all people, should understand this aspect of *all* our lives as we're being forced to live them in the Paris of today."

"Mmm . . . yes, I suppose I do. I comprehend, somewhat. Yes, perhaps I do." She'd moved closer to him and had tapped her velvety lips with her fan, murmuring. "Yet, why are you so ardent in your attempt to solve the problem of . . . slavery? It doesn't make for an attractive subject when one thinks about it. France promised to abolish the slave trade when the Treaty of Paris was signed the end of May. Why not let matters rest there?"

"But that's it, Liane!" He'd loomed above her with a look of impatience. "It's only a *promise* thus far. I was called to Paris to help sway the Court by my firsthand testimony to slavery's evils—and to make certain this so-called promise is fulfilled. After all, it is a matter of treaty. Talleyrand has the power to see that it's put into effect immediately. His influence with Louis XVIII is great."

"Of course it is, and that's why he intrigues me. It was Talleyrand who put that stupid fellow on the throne. And

you know how he did it?" She'd looked up at him provocatively, the pink tip of her tongue lazily moistening her rosy
upper lip.

At this point Devin had begun to move toward the door,
musing that any man other than himself might have
watched Liane, fascinated by her wiles. And any other
man would have taken her into his arms, since the offer
was so clearly there.

He'd sighed and answered her. "I do know, certainly.
Your admirer did it by clever maneuvering and by persuading the Sénat to declare that Napoléon had forfeited
the throne. They are all wolves yapping around France's
onetime beloved hero."

"Yes . . ." Liane was happily concentrating on Talleyrand's bold moves and Machiavellian vision. "I like the
notion that our great French statesman is not to be trusted
by either side. A small warning to you, my sweet." She'd
tapped D'Amboise's stubborn chin with a playful gesture of
her fan.

Immediately he'd reached out and caught her hand in
his large one. "I must leave you now, Comtesse. We shall
meet soon, I hope." His thoughts had not been on their
banter, but on the hours that lay ahead of him, hours of
reading and of writing reports.

She'd pursed her lips at him sweetly. "When the others
depart, you have my permission to remain. Later we'll
talk. . . . Perhaps."

He'd kissed her fingers and then released her small,
warm hand. "I understand."

"Then, why don't you act on your . . . understanding?"
Her tone had grown a mite sharp. "Are you not a man?"

"I am. But there are times I don't feel like proving it."
His gray glance kindled dangerously. "Though the temptation you offer would definitely be worth it."

He owed her that much.

Yet, hadn't it been she who had pursued *him?* In time,
and on his own, he could have netted Talleyrand. Still,

Liane's suggestion of the social evening was a quicker way of doing it.

"*Zut!* my friend," she'd cried, rather inelegantly. "Off you go—before I withdraw my invitation! For if I do that, you will not catch your big fish."

In conspiratorial fashion they'd gazed into each other's eyes and cozily laughed together. Quietly then, he'd closed the door to her salon behind him, and had halted in the corridor outside to take a deep breath. Nanon, his love, might well have betrayed him—which he didn't truly believe—but there was still no other woman who could walk in her shadow. The female goods displayed for his choice had mattered little to him.

It was some nights later, while he'd been dressing for this evening at Liane's, that the old uncertainties had returned. In actuality he'd not believed Oliva's story of Nanon's defection. Yet, occasionally he'd wavered in this.

Nanon was a young woman to whom family was dear. She had been devoted to her father, and to the memory of her mother and her two dead brothers. Her relationship to the Empress Joséphine had meant a great deal to her. The Château de Cavanac, its fields and forests, her mare Dominique—even Théophile, the one brother that remained alive—were part of her heritage.

She'd been ruthlessly torn from all this in a most terrifying manner. Beneath the surface of their passion for each other, could she have harbored a deep resentment toward him for being instrumental in bringing about her losses?

True, they'd loved—and grandly. She'd even seemed to accept and forgive the cruel entrance of Oliva Russo into their lives—Oliva who had almost torn apart the fabric of his and Nanon's love! Or, at the end, had she succeeded?

Now, here at Liane's gathering, he would seek Talleyrand's assistance in hastening the resolution of part five of the treaty—the abolishment of the slave trade. But he was still troubled. He didn't believe Oliva's tale of what had occurred on the Italian ship. He couldn't. His Nanon would never leave of her own accord with the detestable Georges Degrelle, no matter how close the man's ties to her family. Her mistrust and dislike for Degrelle was real. Equally real—and exceedingly powerful—was her love for Devin himself. He'd bank his life on that!

And yet, was it possible she *had* deserted him? He tried to thrust anger and suspicion aside. It was difficult to do, especially when he recalled Madame Arnaud's ambivalence as to why Nanon had not returned to the wharf in the longboat with the others.

When he was free to leave Paris, which should be very soon if he were as successful tonight as he planned to be, he would be to go to Italy and attempt to find Nanon. He tried to convince himself that somehow she might be held there against her will.

Boru had been brought to him from Ireland, and he had already ridden the horse eight miles outside Paris to the old château that had belonged to Nanon's father. He had found it ruined and empty—a house without life.

But this was tonight. He must forge on, yet for all his challenges to himself, he continued to wander morosely through the chambers of this elegant residence while searching out his hostess.

The Countess de Morens-Charents was in the drawing room with her escort of the evening, Count Edmond de Périgord, the sixty-year-old Talleyrand's nephew—and a most convenient mask for the occasion. Devin planned to head in their direction, but he was distracted by the sight of a youthful man in impeccable evening clothes, whose well-groomed hair beneath the candlelight appeared to be of an unusual pewter shade for one so young. It was certainly not powdered, an affectation assumed by some who tried to cling to the old ways.

D'Amboise's trained memory was dredging up certain facts about the man. This was de Laval, a member of the Montmorency clan. A former officer in Napoléon's army, Devin recalled, and considered by some loyal Bonapartists to be disloyal to his past and to his rank. But there was more. . . .

Devin's eyes narrowed icily as he moved closer, through a scattering of guests, recalling much that he had learned from his department's files. The Secret Assembly—that was it! This man, and certainly Nanon's brother, Théophile de Cavanac, had been part of the now-disbanded group. Was it possible this de Laval might have knowledge of the other man? There were rumors—and hadn't Degrelle told Nanon this?—that the heir to the de Cavanac estate was in exile in the north of Italy? If the two were keeping in clandestine touch, this might provide a clue to Nanon's whereabouts.

But as Devin approached, closely studying the other man, there was a softly insistent pressure on his arm. He halted and looked down into the hazel eyes of his hostess. She smiled up at him with serene confidence.

Her gaze challenging his, she spoke over her shoulder to a presence behind her. "You see before you, dear Prince Talleyrand, the brave and elusive Colonel D'Amboise, present tonight at my personal invitation—and for a reason. He is a most difficult man to pin down, surrounded as he is by British secrecy and power. I shall leave you now, for I can see an interesting discussion is about to take place between the two of you. I've not been subtle, have I? I believe in coming right to the point. You may enjoy the privacy of the balcony behind that swag of curtains. You will find chairs and a table there and I shall have a waiter bring champagne."

"But am I to be deprived of the pleasure of your company so soon?" The softly murmured complaint came from the surprised, yet amused, Talleyrand.

"I think it's the other way around, Prince Talleyrand," Liane declared. "Never fear. I shall claim you within the hour." She nodded at Devin, making certain that the expression in her eyes was cool. "Please do not keep the prince too long, Colonel."

Both men bowed and watched Liane saunter away. She half turned to cast a mischievous glance over her shoulder, well aware that both men were gazing at her delightfully sinuous backside. She returned the older man's ardent glance with a winsome smile. "The evening will be far more pleasant when you rejoin me, Prince. But now, do listen to what Colonel D'Amboise has to say to you."

Devin's tone was more heartfelt than he had intended it to be as he bowed very low and said, "Thank you, Comtesse. You do me an honor by this introduction."

"See that you remember it!" was her pert response. At the same time she dazzled Talleyrand with her smile before swaying away from the two men and back to her other guests.

Talleyrand turned to Devin. "We've met before, of course, on state occasions. But never in this manner, in private. I am well aware of your eloquence in damning the iniquitous slave trade, Colonel. I have heard you speak. Now, let me hear what you wish to tell me personally. But first I must inform you that I'm on your side, so I'm well disposed to assist you by my influence, if this is what you desire of me."

With that, Talleyrand parted the heavy velvet drapery, and the two men walked out onto the balcony overlooking the city. Beyond some rooftops, a dark upthrust of trees could be seen in the distance.

Devin appeared reflective, but inwardly he was recalling a wild shout . . . *We have succeeded, Nanon. Of this, at last I am sure! We have won! But, my Nanon, where are you? Why can't we share our victory?*

And, in counterpoint, he began to grow angry with her. Because she wasn't with him. Because she couldn't share this triumph . . .

# Chapter Thirty-six

The clement weather of this early summer evening made it possible for the Marsicano family to throw wide the double doors of the reception hall that served as a ballroom for the celebration of their son's return. The gardens were filled with women in fluttering dresses, accompanied by well-groomed men wearing the finest clothing. The cream of Milan's mercantile society was present, as were the dignified town officials for whom it was expedient to put in an appearance.

As Serafina had promised, the buffet was elegant and the music merry. And later fireworks would explode against the night sky.

Carlo stood between his mother and father, wearing a velvet suit and looking quite grown-up as he assisted in receiving their guests. Watching him, Nanon felt both proud and sad. In the morning she knew she must speak to Signore Marsicano and arrange an immediate leave-taking.

Tonight . . . well, tonight she would dance with any man who asked her, she would listen to the music, and she would enjoy herself as she had during those few summer events held at Malmaison. She would not put on a long face. No, she would keep a smile on her lips as her godmother had urged. . . .

Waves of guests surrounded her, praising her for rescuing Carlo and begging to hear her account of how she and the heir to the Marsicano fortune had survived in the hills. Amused by her newfound ability to be evasive, Nanon parried questions when they grew too personal concerning her strategy during the escape.

With the assistance of Carlo's mother, she soon found herself at the center of a group that was more somber of mien than the Milanese. These were her own countrymen, present out of politeness and to meet this young woman of whom they knew little, except that she was the daughter of the esteemed General de Cavanac. A brief introduction, a spate of animated talk, and the French were soon engaged in their private preoccupations, discussing the politics of France and their own hoped-for return from exile.

Attempting an inconspicuous exit, Nanon edged her way out of the reception hall, stepping behind huge pots decorated with miniature orange trees. On the polished floor beyond, couples were swinging around and around in time to the music's lively beat. It was dark now. Soon rockets and flares would light the night sky, and everyone would be drawn outside into the garden.

Her plan was to watch for a while from her bedchamber window and then to begin collecting her few belongings so she would be downstairs in the early morning, thus giving the household little time to rally for her leave-taking.

Whether Carlo's parents assisted her or not, she was prepared to set out for Genoa. If she must purchase a horse and saddle, disguise herself as a youth, and ride south alone, she would. Not exactly a sensible notion, she admitted to herself as she fled along a corridor, rounded a stairway's newel post, and started up the steps. Desperate as she was, though, she felt she could carry it off.

"Little sister . . ."

That familiar name, those well-known, deep tones!

Nanon remained rigid, staring up into the dark of the landing, her back to its owner. Finally, with a sinking heart, and with both hands clutching the banister, she slowly turned around.

He was leaning against the newel post, arms folded, and looking up at her with a wry smile that twisted the well-remembered contours of his lips. Though his expression was as unreadable as ever, Nanon knew he was studying every trace of emotion on her face. In her astonishment, she was powerless to control her fear, disdain, and disbelief.

"Yes, it's I, little sister. Since I have the advantage, I shall give you a few moments to recover. You see, I knew *you* would be here."

He looked the same and yet . . . not. Always a strikingly handsome man—tall, imperious, his sensual features chiseled like a Greek statue's, his eyes shadowed—now he appeared changed. The once-youthful bearing, the definition in his countenance, appeared subtly altered. His thick, dark bronze hair was no longer worn in military fashion; his handsome garments were somewhat dandified. He seemed to have aged in the few months since their last meeting, become harsher in expression, more cynical—if that were possible.

Sounding both affrighted and defensive, Nanon was at last able to mutter in reply, "You . . . needn't."

"Good, then. In that case, don't shrink away so. Let's go where we can talk privately. We've much to tell each other, and there's little time." His black brows unaccountably scowling, he announced abruptly. "I am betrothed."

Intense surprise staggered her. She wondered how this could happen. Was this his apology, his explanation . . . ? Did he believe this new commitment of his would make everything right between them?

"Aren't you going to offer me congratulations?"

She spoke coldly. "You have my congratulations—as a matter of form."

"No warmer words than that, little sister? Aren't you curious as to how it all occurred? You're not angry with me—are you?—because I've changed my allegiance from you to my darling Louisa? Oh, I know what you're thinking. I can read what's in those eyes of yours. Believe me, the world did not end back then, because I stole a kiss from you in an unbrotherly fashion. I was a drunken sot that night . . . there was no more to it than that."

"Théophile!" She was shocked by his candor, and more shocked to hear him laugh uproariously.

"And you were so beguiling." He lowered his voice, "Find it in your heart to forgive me. Dammit, Nanon— you were always a difficult little prude. Come along with me." He grabbed her hand and pulled her down the remaining steps into the hallway. "You know this house. Find us a quiet place so we can talk."

Still shaking with anxiety over this extraordinary re- union, she stumbled ahead of him into the small li- brary—the scene of her interview with Carlo's parents three days earlier.

Théo indicated a chair, but she shook her head, prefer- ring to stand while he spoke. "I knew you were in Marti- nique, kidnapped in place of Joséphine. Edmond and I waylaid that Englishman, Andrew St. Giles. By the time we caught up with him he was full of drink and talk. So, later on, I sent Degrelle to Martinique to find you. What happened to him? Did he see you?" She nodded. "Then, where is he now?" She shook her head. "For God's sake, girl—talk!"

Angrily he strode across the room, and back. "We don't have time for you to be coy. And it was not bright of you to give your real name, though it enabled me to find you. The de Cavanacs are too well known. I use our uncle's name . . . de Rhoulac. Only sweet Louisa knows the truth." He grinned at the thought of her. "She is a beauty, fresh of face and body, all of sixteen years and actually intelligent, and she adores me."

"She's that intelligent, then?"

He shrugged. "We still have a caustic tongue, I see."

341

"I suppose *she* is the Austrian heiress I've heard about, and *you* are the French gentleman who is said to know me."

"How did that get about? But yes, it's so. Louisa and I—with a covey of chaperones we manage to elude now and then—have come down from Como expressly to see you. You must return with us."

"Must I? I say no!"

"No? How is this, Antoinette? Are you still cherishing a grudge against me?"

*A grudge? Dearest God, what did the man think? Oh, what was the use!* He was going on again, and she was forced to listen. "Tell me now, did you see Degrelle? Is that why you came to Genoa?"

She debated whether she should disclose the truth about the manner in which Degrelle had tricked her into boarding the ship. But Théo was striding toward the door to peer into the empty corridor. The distant sound of music faded as he closed it once more.

He looked back at her. "Another time we'll talk about that rascal. Still, I do wonder where he is at this very moment."

"I don't know his whereabouts, Théo, though he arrived in Genoa at the same time I did. He was in some kind of trouble, and the captain kept him secluded in his cabin. I didn't see him while we were at sea." She was being evasive once more.

"That's strange. I'll find out if it was his usual chicanery. I've never trusted the fellow, and I don't want him sneaking up behind me. When he left here at my direction to return to Paris, he didn't know about Louisa and me. I had not met the girl when he sailed to Martinique to look for you."

She spoke thoughtfully. "I find I do wish you well in your betrothal, Théo."

"That's kind of you. Now, since we are at truce, what have you to say for yourself?"

She swiftly detailed to him her plan to return to Martinique and to Devin. "He needs me because he is in a special difficulty which I won't speak of, now. If I don't see him soon . . . Well, Théo, I shall die—I do love him so!"

"That's dramatic enough! I see you have a surprise of your own. Has he asked you to marry him?"

She nodded and extended the hand upon which the emerald ring now rested.

"You do what you please—you always have—but Martinique is a fool's errand. If you must, I shall help you to return to France, but only to Malmaison where they'll take you in. Our château has been ransacked; it's not livable. But when I'm free to return there, Louisa and I—thanks to the considerable fortune she inherits in less than a year's time—will restore the house and the estate. I expect my recall from exile to occur soon, if my source of information is correct."

He seized her arms and though she resisted, he dragged her to the mantel, to stand beneath the glowing candelabra. As its light shone down on her face, he murmured. "Look into my eyes. Will you trust me? I have my source as I've told you. Now I want you to prepare yourself. . . . It's been nearly two months since you've seen D'Amboise. Is that not so?"

She was beginning to panic as she nodded. "What . . . has happened to him?"

"I thought my latest news of him was of no particular moment until now when I learned of your . . . attachment to the man."

"You've had news of Devin? Théo, I don't believe you!"

"Since you have so little faith in me, believe or not, it doesn't matter. I don't want to go to the trouble or the expense of sending you across the Alps, but, remember, in July the coach roads are fast. You can be on Malmaison's doorstep in less than twelve days. And that will

343

appeal to you, I'm sure, after you hear what I have to tell you. Will you listen to me further or will you walk out that door?"

"Speak plainly to me, and I'll judge your truth. What is it you have to say?"

"Mind your tongue with me, Antoinette! I should leave you now, make you dangle. But the time we have together is running short. So, I'll tell you. My friend de Laval has made an opportunistic peace with the new regime. Edmond has been trolling around Paris in his usual, inimitable style, and he has learned much. Ask him when you see him, and he'll give you the news of your Colonel D'Amboise."

"Colonel . . . ?"

"Stop staring at me in that big-eyed, benighted way. I *did* say colonel. I understand he's once again in uniform, as an attaché with the British who seem to admire the man. I can't guess why. At any rate, your Devin is no longer in the West Indies but in Paris." He raised a wicked eyebrow at her.

"Devin is in Paris?" Nanon was thunderstruck.

"Precisely. And since he's at the court of the new King Louis, wouldn't you say that's about eight miles or so from Malmaison? Doesn't that news give you a thrill of pleasure?" Amused, he pinched her cheek.

She was beginning to believe him, and especially so since Edmond was involved in the telling. Her amber eyes widened, deepened with wonder and delight. Agitatedly she began to plan, and to run her fingers through her hair, almost dismantling the entire stylish arrangement that Serafina had contrived.

"Stop that!" He seized her hands, pulling them away from her curls. "You'll resemble a wild woman and tonight, right now, you must speak to your host. That is, if you want to leave with Louisa and me. She refuses to remain longer in this town of merchants and traders. It has something to do with our lake being more conducive to civilized living—and to romance, of course. She's quite an enthralling young lady, never tires of loving."

Only half listening to her brother, Nanon was ready to leave Milan—even tonight! Suddenly, and to her own amazement, she reached up on tiptoe and gave Théo a hasty kiss on the cheek.

"That's very nice," he said. But his eyes, so like her own, turned strangely cold. "You always did have a delectable smile, Nanon. I'm glad you've become a charmer and have finally found yourself a husband. That is, if D'Amboise is still of a mind to make you his bride."


The good-byes had been difficult, especially when Carlo had put his arms around her neck and had wept on her shoulder. Then, his courage restored, he had promised her that in a very few years, he would follow her across the Alps to France and would spend a long summer holiday with her.

"I shall look forward to that," she had told him gravely. "I shall watch for you, and you will be all grown-up by that time. I shall be proud of you then, as I am proud of you now. But, Carlo, do not forget the French verbs."

He had beamed at her and, standing between his parents, had waved good-bye. And that had been it. She and Théo and his pretty Austrian had left early that morning for Como.


For Nanon the two weeks on the mountain roads that wound over the passes to France went by in a long mixture of thought, exhaustion, sleep, scenery, and remembrance. She recalled what Joséphine had once told her: *Make room in your mind for miracles. With hope one never feels abandoned.* She had repeated these words to herself like a litany. At the same time, she had turned the emerald stone on her ring finger until it was clenched tightly

345

against her palm.

And when she crossed the border and stepped into the next-to-last traveling coach for the final run to Paris, to become absorbed in the sight of the familiar forests and fields of France, she knew this must be the beginning of the miracle.

The traveling coach had finally let her out on the road at the edge of the woods, at the start of a long driveway. Valise in hand, she had walked its length alongside the yew hedge, gazing at gardens, grape trellises, and the greenhouse in the distance while ahead loomed the château Malmaison.

Marcel would probably be in his caretaker's house. Nevertheless, on an off chance, Nanon bounded up the familiar front steps to the double doors and gave a lusty pull on the clanging knocker. She was brimming with energy, spiced with happiness, and her heart was soaring as though she were coming home to her father's house. Malmaison was near enough.

Minutes went by. Nanon was almost ready to turn and walk to the rear of the château when she heard footsteps on the other side of the door. Tears rose to her happiness-filled eyes and streamed down her glowing cheeks. It was thus Marcel found her when he pulled wide the double doors. His eyes started in astonished recognition.

"Mam'selle de Cavanac . . . it is you! I do not believe it, but it *is* you! A miracle, *mam'selle!*"

Hearing Marcel's fervent whisper of that word, Nanon stopped crying as suddenly as she had started.

"Yes, truly it is!" she answered.

"Welcome! Welcome to Malmaison. I thought never to see you again. And here you are! A de Cavanac come home . . . a miracle! Only one more miracle do we need, and that is the return of our beloved Empress from above." He rolled his eyes heavenward and crossed himself, forgetting for the moment that he was a son of the Revolution and an unbeliever.

He took her valise, and with both of them asking and answering questions, they entered the foyer of Joséphine's house.

"Wait, *mam'selle!*" Marcel exclaimed, on his face the look of a mischievous and aging pixie. "There is someone who is longing to see you. Come with me!"

She knew!

She raced ahead of Marcel, through the silent, echoing house, past the big deserted kitchens, down the back steps into the vegetable garden, and on through the turfy meadow to the stables. Into the dusky shadows of the great barn she hastened, Marcel lagging behind but doing his best to keep up.

From the hay trough, the chestnut mare alertly whipped up her head, her dark eyes straining to see the breathless young woman who now approached quietly. Suddenly she reared, her front legs knocking violently at the boards of her stall, and letting out a keening whinny, she lashed her head up and down, sending her silky mane flying like a banner.

Nanon swung open the door to the stall and with a murmur of joy, threw her arms around the mare's rapidly bobbing neck. Her face pressed against Dominique's, she wept again and listened to whinnies of delight as Dom nibbled her hand with a wet, snuffling, velvet-lipped welcome.

# Chapter Thirty-seven

During this first week, late in the afternoon Nanon habitually sat on the rock wall surrounding the garden, looking up at her birthplace. She chose to return when the light was kinder to the old château whose turrets still loomed, intact and eagle-proud, above the massive, stone outer walls.

Her single venture into the ransacked interior of the first floor had sent her stumbling outside in tear-choked misery. The yellow-paneled walls in her father's downstairs bedchamber had been blackened by a wantonly set fire. The books in the library—her own retreat—had been destroyed, the wall maps defaced. And the green marble of the fireplace—she'd stood by it the night the three of them had plotted against D'Amboise—had been marred by blows from an ax.

The dining hall, too, was gutted. Seeing this Nanon had trembled and had recalled the warm gray depths of the eyes that had gazed into hers through the candlelight, their glance akin to the most intimate of caresses.

Finally, before fleeing the house, she'd looked up at the staircase they'd mounted side by side, his hand resting on her shoulder. Even now, she remembered her flush of excitement, the thrill within her most private self, at knowing for the first time that she was sexually desirable.

Now a muffled sound penetrated her thoughts, bringing her back to the present. She listened, recognizing the persistent tread of a horse's hooves on pine needles . . .

coming closer. Dominique, nibbling grass at a distance, raised her head with a nicker of anticipation.

*Should I stay? Run?*

Nanon remained.

From the solitary path to Malmaison, known only to the intimates of the Cavanac family, a splendidly-garbed horseman rode out of the woods. He stared at her alertly, and then, jauntily reining in his mount, swept off his hat, uncovering a silvered thatch of hair above a young man's face.

With shining eyes, Nanon returned his amused gaze. "Edmond . . . it is you!"

He leaned forward across the extravagance of his saddle's silver-studded pommel. "Yes, it's I. And what do I see here . . . the child grown into blazing beauty. I suppose a few months of sailing the seas, and a bit of fancy living and loving, can do this to a simple country girl. Nanon, your brother only prepared me in part."

"I shall not flatter you in return. But you've come into riches, I see."

"There are certain advantages to being a turncoat."

"You would say that only if it were not true. I don't believe that betrayal is your destiny. Tell me, you've had word from Théo?"

"That's why I'm here, pet."

He trotted nearer, swung down from his horse, then cast her a sly look. "I received his message in a roundabout manner not to be disclosed, and came from Court as soon as I could escape watching eyes. Just now at Malmaison, Marcel said you were here—as you've been every day. Brooding, I take it." He glanced at the château. "Never mind. One day it will all be set to rights."

She followed his gaze, then repeated with bitterness, "One day . . . Yes, I suppose. But I am glad to see you, Edmond. We've so much to say to each other."

He placed a comforting arm around her shoulder, a gesture of sympathy that brought tears to her eyes. Patting her cheek, he lightly kissed her brow and pushed back her tousled curls. "Much of it has to do with D'Amboise, doesn't it? And what happened when he swept you away to Martinique after we thought we'd rescued you."

Wordlessly she held out her hand to display the gleaming emerald.

His eyebrows rose. "Tell me."

She spoke with the directness he'd always remembered. "We fell in love. We are betrothed. But against my will I was forced to sail from Martinique for Genoa. Edmond, an explanation of the reasons for that will have to wait. I must see Devin at once. Can you reach him for me?"

"He's a remote figure these days, but I'll do my best."

"Yes, I know you will." Nanon continued thoughtfully. "It's difficult for me to believe he's here in Paris. You see, he was deeply enmeshed in a troubling circumstance in Fort-de-France. He said he couldn't leave the island, nor could we marry, until it was resolved." She added slowly. "So he led me to believe."

"Do I detect misgiving on your part, Nanon?" Edmond waited. "I don't understand. . . ."

Her lips curved in a forced smile. "When Devin learns I'm here, I am sure it will all be explained."

His next words were reflective. "You still have faith in your affianced, which is good and very like the Nanon I remember. But since you've not seen him for a time, there's something you must know. D'Amboise is considered rather a hero in diplomatic circles. By the British, not the French. It was due to his personal conviction, as well as his vigorous testimony, that the Allies have induced our country to adhere to the fifth part of the Treaty of Paris, which had been a sticking point. For the abolishment of the slave trade, he's spoken out knowingly and with great passion. Surprising—isn't it?—since he's a man of property himself."

While he'd spoken Nanon had remained very still, her expression of incredulity gradually being replaced by radiance. Eyes alight, she now exclaimed. "But this is wonderful news!"

He shrugged. "Not to the West Indian planters. To them, this is an economic blow and they predict calamity. But since the Allies have triumphed over our genius Napoléon, we must bow to their edict if we want the treaty to work. And it must."

A sudden bewilderment consumed Nanon. Devin had been a constant in her thoughts, but as he was when they were together on Martinique. Of this other side of his life — participation in the spheres of power and diplomacy — she had no experience or knowledge.

Still in some confusion, she murmured. "You say Devin has been in Paris a month? He must have sailed from Martinique at almost the same time I did." She paused awkwardly, entertaining an uneasy premonition. "Has anything been said about . . . an unsavory involvement on the island?"

Edmond quirked a brow quizzically. "What an odd question. And oddly put. There's been no hint of anything."

She lowered her eyes, uncertain whether to reveal that D'Amboise was suspected of his overseer's murder. If she did, it would entail a complex of explanation for which she was not ready.

But then Edmond chuckled. "Ah, you're not referring to the rumors concerning a beautiful Polish lady on one of those Martinique plantations? She knew D'Amboise, and rather well I take it, from their youth. There can be nothing to such gossip, now that you've told me you're betrothed to the man. But one does hear rumors, speculation. . . . To evaluate innuendo is one of my duties. Let me see, how did it go? Yes . . . She was staying near Paris with her new husband's relatives, but when the Allies entered the city, she sailed to rejoin her spouse who's said privately to be a rake and a drunkard. The men some women choose!"

Seeing Nanon's face crimson, he caught her chin in his cupped hand and murmured. "I've touched the quick, somehow . . . forgive me!"

She drew back with dignity. "It's nothing like that. And, Edmond, you've repeated what I already know."

A curious Dominique had wandered closer. Nanon retrieved the mare's reins and looped them over her arm. "Will you return to Malmaison and dine with me tonight? It will be simple fare, but I promise you the wine and the *pot-au-feu* will be excellent." A smile touched the corners of her lips. "I prepared the venison myself."

"I'm tempted, I assure you. But with the new regime in full cry these days, I walk carefully. If I'm not present tonight at a certain gathering at the Montmorencys', suspicions may well be raised. Oh no, pet, it's not a lady's jealousy of which I speak. Not this time."

"I believe you, Edmond. And I think you're more seriously engaged behind the opulent screen of Court life than you will admit. I'm grateful to you for coming to find me."

He kissed her gently. "I must leave you now. From here I'll follow through the woods and on to the main road to Paris. Your colonel may be a distant and almost unapproachable figure, surrounded as he is by the diplomats and the military, but I shall manage to send him word, in private."

Edmond remounted his horse and regarded her with playful humor. "I'm only sorry Devin found you all sweetly grown up before I did. Watch for him, Nanon. I vow he will return to claim you."

She nodded and saw him off with a bright smile that quickly faded. Watch for Devin? Edmond sounded very sure, yet she wondered. . . .

Though she would have been willing to stay in the caretaker's cottage, at his insistence she'd settled into quarters on Malmaison's second floor. It was lonely in this big house, but she walked about its hallways rapidly, summoning up courage, and tried very hard to go to sleep quickly so she would not hear the creaks and groans of old joints and timbers. Then, too, once asleep, she could dream of the comfort of Devin's arms, the warmth of his lips.

And from these rooms, she could see farther in the direction from which she was certain Devin would appear. Sometimes as she strayed down the abandoned corridors, a lovely ghost and a hauntingly familiar scent seemed to drift along beside her, eerily compelling her to think on the past and constantly straining her composure.

Each day of the week following Edmond's appearance, Nanon dressed with care in the more modest of the summer frocks left behind in the armoire. Marcel had told her that Hortense had come from her own exile in Switzerland to be with her mother at the end. Afterward, she'd removed all personal belongings, leaving these few simple dresses.

However, in the noon heat of this summer's day, Nanon was wearing a cotton blouse, a peasant skirt borrowed from the scullery, and one of Marcel's big aprons. Her face was red with exertion, her hair bunched in ringlets atop her head, unruly curls wisping at her nape. On the way from the wine cellar where she'd helped Marcel shelve and turn the bottles, she'd been surprised by a quartet of gaudy peacocks trespassing on the terrace.

They had half-flown along, spreading their fantails in a trail of iridescent color. She'd raced them across the stone while they'd screamed at her with the arrogance of their kind before vanishing down a garden slope and into the forest depths.

Then she'd halted to survey the landscape extending before her. It had a gentle beauty. Yellow and purple irises burgeoned at the edge of a quietly flowing stream, and with the peacocks' disappearance, birdsong swelled above the cool water. How pleasant it had been to wade here when she was a child! Now, with defiant amusement, she plumped herself down on the parapet, pulled her skirts above her knees and set about removing her footgear.

Suddenly she halted. Raising both hands to shield her gaze from the sun's glare, she looked toward the driveway. A bay horse stood alertly, its black-clad rider staring in her direction. She dropped her hands and hastily lowered her skirt.

A stranger, certainly. Perhaps a messenger?

She stood, then cautiously walked toward horse and rider.

As she came near, he called to her. "Young woman, is Mademoiselle de Cavanac within? If she is, will you call her out? I'd like a word with her."

Nanon advanced, a hint of merriment in her eyes. Quickly she removed Marcel's apron and thrust it behind her. "Call my mistress out, indeed! May I ask why you wish to see her in such informal fashion?"

"You may not. I'll say it again. Is your mistress here?"

"She is."

"Well then, do as I say."

He was obviously someone's aide and full of his own importance. Yet, she might be misjudging him. After all, he did think her a serving maid . . . and as such she would seldom be shown courtesy.

At this thought, Nanon flared at his rudeness. She was about to respond with hauteur when a coach drawn by a team of six rolled slowly through the gates from the main road. It came to a halt. The window curtain snapped open, and as the door was set slightly ajar, Nanon caught a glimpse of a booted male foot.

From the coach's darkened interior, a deep voice rich with humor called out. "Ask the young woman to come closer, Reynaud."

Reynaud turned, containing his stiff impatience beneath a show of utmost respect. "Sir, this country minx is being troublesome. I myself shall inquire at the château."

Upon hearing the voice coming from the coach, Nanon had begun to tremble, yet she made herself speak loudly. "I'll ask Mademoiselle de Cavanac to come to the salon. There she will receive whoever wishes to see her."

She knew the man inside the coach was probably immersed in a fit of laughter. But he knew that she would flee inside and, at the château's front door, would permit him to enter, thus drawing them both away from Reynaud's prying gaze.

She could hear stifled mirth when the coach's passenger spoke again. "Have the wench come here, Reynaud. I must teach her a lesson."

With disapproval, the aide said "Sir, I respectfully urge you not to—"

Nanon interrupted, her face flushed scarlet, thundering rhythms of excitement pulsing through her. "I shall obey your master," she snapped. "You need not interfere."

Her limbs were shaking so that she doubted they'd hold her upright long enough for her to run to the step of the carriage. But run she did.

Of what could he be thinking? He was obviously incognito. Would he take her away right now? Ah well, nothing mattered. She sped to the coach and tumbled through the door and into Devin's waiting arms.

# Chapter Thirty-eight

The coachman and the mounted rider watched without seeming to as the young woman leaped into the coach. As the door slammed behind her each man found it very strange that no angry roar rose from inside the vehicle. Their master was not an easy gentleman to deal with these days.

The driver continued to stare straight ahead, his hands, taut on the reins, holding the team in place. At a distance, the escort dismounted and, with a stoic demeanor, crossed his arms and waited beside his horse.

The hot sun beat down. Neither man glanced at the other. It was not their province to question, merely to observe and thereafter keep silent. Except for the inevitable report.

Inside the coach, the passenger reached out to check Nanon's flight, but she landed upon his long powerful frame in a flurry of skirts, a bounce of bosom, and a display of bare thighs. With her precipitate entrance, instinctively his arms closed around her, his lips moving soundlessly against sun-warmed hair that smelled of crushed grape leaves.

Joy swelled in him. Nanon, his lips seemed to say, my only love . . . my Nanon. The torment of these past weeks was forgotten. He'd found her, his lovely love. He could forgive her anything!

But the euphoria didn't last. Fury and hurt returned as Nanon sat up athwart his middle, laughing and straightening her clothing, pulling up on her bodice and down on her skirts. Why . . . the wench was *laughing!* And after all she'd put him through . . .

He straightened, almost dislodging her from his lap. "So, it's really you, Nanon! I was ready to disbelieve de Laval's message saying I'd find you here, that you'd been in Lombardy! I had to come and see for myself."

Her eyes widened in distress as she stared at him from her awkward perch. Where was the tenderness and humor she'd sensed in him only moments before when she was outside the coach?

He went on accusingly. "Why the hell did you leave without a word—to sail off to Genoa on the same ship with that detestable fellow? Was it so important that you meet with your brother? I would have tried to understand if you'd confided in me. Instead, you deceived me. You ran off. You destroyed everything there was between us."

Shock sent Nanon scrambling backward. Losing her balance, she sprawled across his legs and onto the seat opposite. Then, pulling herself to a sitting position, she drew a deep breath and studied his glowering face.

She noted how exceedingly rich and finely made his clothing was, how elegant the carriage. But Devin himself appeared primitive and dangerous. She could picture him astride Boru on a stark battlefield. The deep-set gray eyes that surveyed her were those of a warrior—but a desolate warrior.

She wanted to flee. Then she thought, he hasn't ordered his escort to put me out of this coach. And, after all, he did come here to find me, didn't he?

"Did you come all the way from Paris to castigate me, Devin D'Amboise? And do you truly believe I'd deceive you, deliberately leave Fort-de-France without telling you? You've thought this of me right along?"

"Damn it, Nanon, yes! What else could I think? When I questioned Madame Arnaud, she said that it seemed you'd decided to stay aboard the Italian ship after the farewells were over. She waited a long time for you on the wharf. The longboat came back with the others and you were not there. I remembered that I'd offended her earlier, and she can be spiteful, but I couldn't understand why you'd gone down to the harbor at all? Degrelle meant nothing to you. You'd already decided not to involve yourself with him and with that brother of yours. So you'd assured me."

Her amber eyes molten with anger, Nanon spoke slowly, carefully. "And what did the farewell party's hostess—*Madame Russo*—have to say about all this? I'm sure you must have asked her. Did she say that I'd entwined myself around Georges Degrelle and was unable to tear myself away before the ship sailed?"

His answer was terse. "She was only there to bid goodbye to that little governess of theirs. She did say the man became ill, had some sort of seizure—she saw him in a doorway—and that you appeared extremely concerned. She assumed it would have been wrenching for you to leave him in that condition, considering there were family ties not easily sundered."

"And how could she know that? Did you discuss the de Cavanac family with her? Oh, this is infuriating. Devin, you're presumed to be a man of intelligence, certainly a mature man and an experienced one. You've been given weighty responsibilities by your government. You're supposed to understand human nature and the deceptions often practiced. I shall say no more than *that* about Oliva Russo! How could you have believed such falsehoods? You know life, you know people . . . I thought you knew *me!*"

He countered coldly. "Nanon, *do* I have all those qualities you attribute to me? Sometimes I wonder, since I don't believe I'm wise in regard to you. Do you know what I actually am? I'll tell you. I'm a man who was deeply in love and therefore no better, no wiser, than any

358

other. And remember this: I was a man wrongfully accused of the crime of murder—a man in turmoil, wanting to clear his name for the sake of the family he would have. This very human man thought . . . he feared . . ." He had become less resolute.

"Feared *what*, Devin?" She leaned forward to speak with passion. "Did you think because you postponed our marriage I took umbrage? That I sailed off in a pique? How could you not have known me better! I was *tricked* into staying aboard that ship. For the love of God, it happened! You, of all people, should know that!"

"I . . . yes . . ." He faltered. Had he made a cruel mistake?

"The captain trusted and befriended me. He helped me escape the ignominy of Degrelle. And when we reached Genoa, he saw that I was put under the protection of his friends. But wait, Devin. You said . . . you *were* in love. *Were?*"

He perceived the lifeline and seized it. "Nanon, I still am! I will always love you. Never doubt that, though I have doubted you. Yes, I admit it . . . fully, freely, and with shame. I was jealous, miserable, and unmanly in my doubt of you. But when I was sent for by the British to return to Paris, though my problem on Martinique is still unresolved, I came with the thought that at least one thing could be salvaged from the pyre of what we had been to each other. At least, I could do what you had once asked of me."

She regarded him in thoughtful silence, then tentatively reached across the space between them. She could not help herself; her fingers sinuously, seductively, traced the jaw of his austere face, and without taking his eyes from hers, he caught her hand in his and brought her fingers to his lips. As his tongue tip strayed across them, she could feel its touch in the deepest part of her.

"What you asked of me, Nanon, became my mission."

"I once requested that you speak out in defense of

those poor people I saw on the island, so ill-treated and enslaved."

He nodded. "I did my best to convince the Court to seek an end to slavery in all of its possessions. Your King Louis has agreed in principle. Now we'll see what really happens."

She thought, Devin D'Amboise, I love you more than words can ever tell. Aloud she concluded gravely, "Edmond told me that you spoke out with passion and conviction, that you are the one responsible for the enforcement of the treaty—this time in all its parts—by France and England."

"Seeing what has happened on my own plantation, it was not so difficult, Nanon. I tried to convince the Court that slavery was a degradation no civilized people should visit on other human beings." A wry smile played across his lips. "I had some help from Talleyrand. I think my telling argument was that if the British were enlightened in this matter, the French should be. Ah well, the plantation owners who were my friends will hate me now. But tell me, what are the feelings of a certain Frenchwoman for me?"

Nanon leaned closer still, and with that movement the thin material of her blouse slipped down over one shoulder. His gaze fell from her face to linger on the swell of her bosom, and he sighed deeply, as he waited for her to answer.

"That woman is proud of you . . . she loves you very much."

Fiercely demanding, his mouth was upon hers, their lips, their tongues, surging together to explore deeply, feverishly. Opening her eyes, Nanon saw his—sensually hooded, burning silver—and she moaned softly, knowing she ached with an immediate, hungering need of him.

When the heat of his body suddenly seemed to become flame against her flesh, she realized that, as his flattened palms caressed the curves of her breasts, he had pushed her blouse and camisole to her waist. Now she sat asprawl him, half-naked, her legs dangling on either side of his.

She looked down at his black hair, at the neck bared to her as he licked and sweetly tormented the peaks of her breasts until she was athrob with wanting him. She could sense his body, demanding as her own, his aroused desire hard against her through the smooth material of his trousers.

His lightly sweating forehead was just beneath her own lips. She slowly lowered her head to let her lips trace each sable winged brow before nibbling at the slant of a cheekbone. A hand swept downward to close hesitantly on that seductive bulge whose outlines were now so extraordinarily apparent to her shaking fingers.

As he groaned in pleasure, she murmured against his closed eyelids. "I am shameless! I wish we were not in this conveyance with those men outside, but in my bedchamber. We could lie together and you could take me as . . . *Oh!*" She'd cried out in delicious panic.

The hand pushing her skirts even farther above her knees was gliding slowly between her legs in a lazy caress that gently pressed apart her thighs. The teasing hand was coming closer and with some almost-forgotten modesty, Nanon tried to wriggle away. At hearing the crotch of her cotton pantalets rip, she tensed.

She wanted to scream aloud at the torment of his next compelling touch. Instead, she muffled her face against his, her heart thudding hard against her rib cage, her breath seeming to explode and then stop, terrifying her with the thought she might never breathe again.

"Relax, my darling . . ." He was murmuring against her lips. Assaulted by tremors that rippled through her in tiny waves, she surrendered to the magic of that touch, allowing herself to open to the tender demand of his fingers as they slipped through the tight whorls of her hair and tipped inside her. A stab of exquisite sensation, like none she had ever felt, split starlike through her body.

At that instant their mouths hungrily plunged together, sucking and drawing sustenance, while she let herself move without shame beneath the resourceful fingers that were taking her from almost unbearable excitement up to and over ecstasy's edge and into a boundless beyond. . . .

She would have slept against his chest, but he kissed her, muttering. "Listen to me, my beautiful one, those men outside, the driver and escort, are far from being my friends. They are good Cornishmen and faithful spies for the British. In their eyes, I am more an Irishman than anything else. They know I've served a purpose with the Foreign Office. And that purpose is successfully concluded. To come here to Malmaison was perhaps not my wisest move. . . ."

"You are in danger!" She sat up abruptly.

"Nothing as dramatic as that, but I must return to Paris and explain why I took a trip to a country house that once belonged to enemies of the present regime. If I tell my superior the truth about my Frenchwoman, he'll extend a *congé* to me and then I can be off. I shall come for you within the week. I take it you're willing?"

She flushed and sent him a mischievous, sidelong glance. "Let me see. . . . Am I?"

"Oh ho . . ." He laughed softly and gathered her once more into his arms. "If you are not willing, my love, I shall see to it that you are eternally ravished by desire without fulfillment, by passion without release. . . . Now will you come with me?"

"Yes . . . *yes!*" Her lips, her hands, her body burned against his as she looked at him with smoldering eyes.

"Christ! How can I leave you? Well, I must. I'll come for you as soon as I can. We'll travel by coach — my own the next time, and with men who are loyal to me. When we reach the channel, Boru can be sent on by barge. . . ."

Real plans were being made at last. Incredible plans . . .

"My Dominique is here at Malmaison's stable. I cannot leave her again, Devin."

He hesitated, weighed the problem. "You don't have to. We'll manage. Kiss me, and then slip out of this carriage and run for the gardens at the rear. My keen-eyed friends outside will think I've been dallying with the maidservant and have forgotten, or no longer care, to call on Mademoiselle de Cavanac. One more kiss, Antoinette, one more sweet intimacy, my darling . . ." Once more she felt his lips, his touch.

Nanon was ready.

She had wandered the corridors and gardens of Malmaison for the last time. She had said good-bye to Joséphine's ghost. Her godmother had been loving and solicitous yet, in the end, a mite cruel. Still, if she'd not agreed to take Joséphine's place in the campaign coach, she might never have come to know Devin, her love, other than in that one careless kiss outside the door of his chamber.

She'd also paid a final visit to her family's château. This time she had ventured inside, promising the wounded house that either Théophile and his new wife, or she — as Antoinette D'Amboise — would return to restore it to gracefulness if not to splendor. After all, why splendor? To her, her home had always been a shabby, comfortable, and safe retreat.

She'd cast a cool farewell glance at the swamp pond in the nearby woods. For her, it had never been associated with a sinister act as Degrelle had hinted that night in the library; instead, it had been a pretend moat for the children, the huge rocks surrounding it were imaginary castles.

She'd ridden Dom into the village to see Sylvie, she

who had the adept hand at spun-sugar confections. Sylvie had married the apothecary and had opened her own sweet shop.

Finally, Nanon had had a long talk with Marcel in the caretaker's cottage. He'd promised that he would watch while in the fields and he'd alert her if he was the first to see puffs of summer dust rising above the hedgerows, which would mean a coach was traveling in their direction.

So she was ready. A small bag was packed with necessities. And near at hand in the stable were Dom's saddle and bridle and lead rope; they were to be attached to the rear of the coach when Devin arrived.

Nanon had ticked off the slowly passing days. A week—and then more than a week—had gone by. Today it was hot. And she thought this might be the day. But then, she'd thought that each morning upon rising. Yet, this day *was* different. Strange and expectant, it had arrived under a blank white sky, with thunder to the north. The sultriness in the atmosphere was sending little trickles of perspiration down between Nanon's breasts.

Using the hand basin, she'd twice sponged herself off. Twice she'd changed her undergarments, and twice she'd smoothed her sun-washed hair that glittered like fire due to the days she'd spent riding Dominique through summer fields.

The next time she gazed from her window across the far landscape, her vigilance was rewarded! Clouds of yellow dust were rolling along the by-road beyond the yew hedge. Joyfully Nanon did a half-pirouette. Then she picked up her bag and raced through the corridor, down the rear staircase to the kitchens, and onto the pathway to the stable.

Marcel was there ahead of her. He'd already saddled the mare and was leading her to the front of the house, to a hitching post over which he looped the reins. He returned on the run and seized Nanon's hands. Looking deep into her eyes, he mumbled cautions that she must keep herself alert to dangers and must not be too trusting for man was unscrupulous. Then, his face reddened and he turned and fled, as if embarrassed at revealing his concern for her.

Astonished and troubled, Nanon looked after him. He'd known her since she was a child, and crotchety as he'd been with her at times, it was plain from the expression on his lean, melancholic face that he was worried for her safety. However, the future she discussed was upon her; there was no time to reassure him further.

The hoofbeats were much closer now, which meant the coach was about to turn into the long driveway leading to Malmaison. She ran back to the shuttered house and up its rear steps. Hastening along the center corridor, past silent rooms, she entered the wide, high-ceilinged foyer.

She could hear the clatter of hooves outside and the screeching of carriage wheels being braked. Someone was coming, in great powerful leaps, up to the outer steps. Her face alight, she threw open the massive doors.

She would remember this moment always — the tremulous heave of breast, her heart slamming with undignified thuds as though she were some nubile girl having her first rendezvous.

And she would remember the silver-white day, the faint rumbles of thunder in the sullen distance, the heat clinging to her damp skin like a silken cobweb.

A figure blocked the pale sunlight in front of her, and her cry of greeting froze in her throat. . . .

# Chapter Thirty-nine

The impetus of that limping, headlong entrance threw Nanon back against the stairway's newel post. A scream for help would have been useless. From no corner of this lonely house would help come. Stunned by pain that jarred both head and body, she slipped down onto the lower step.

A face hovered close to her own. She focused hazily on gold, lynxlike eyes, the pupils dilated by some powerful elation.

As sight and brain began to clear, Nanon clutched at a banister rung to hoist herself upright while conceits scurried through her consciousness. It couldn't be. . . . It was too implausible. Try again, her mind said. *After all, he did tell you he would never give up*.

The ache in her head was disastrous. She closed her eyes, and when she opened them, the apparition was still there looking down at her with a kind of sardonic amusement. He stood with his fists knotted against his thighs, his legs set wide apart in a bullying stance. Gone was the fine Parisian-style clothing he'd worn in Fort-de-France. His dusty garments looked as though he'd come a long way under harsh circumstances.

"Believe what you see, Nanon!" He was responding to her expression of incredulity. "I told you I was not one to give up easily."

She shrank from the hand he extended to her. When he shrugged at this, she looked into his face again, belat-

366

:dly recognizing that the thin scar etched from his brow to his jaw must always have been a kind of physical barometer. Today, profiled in crimson, it appeared to warn of danger.

Determined to keep at bay both her fear and the painful weakness due to the blow she'd received, Nanon spoke coldly. "How did you find me?"

"Do you really care, or are you giving yourself time to think?"

Oh, he was watchful and cunning! She sensed he'd heard the tremor in her voice. Remaining silent, she gazed proudly at him.

His cat's eyes narrowed. "No answer to that?" He waited. "Well then, I have questions to ask *you*, Nanon. What occurred during our sea voyage while we were separated? Was the captain's cabin better than mine—his bed better than mine?"

His accusation infuriated her, and anger lent her unexpected strength. "What a despicable insinuation, Georges Degrelle! Captain Patrese is an honorable man. I shall long cherish his safeguarding of me, both on shipboard and when we reached Genoa. He knew you played me a contemptible trick by forcing me to stay aboard his ship." Her mouth twisted in wrath, and she hissed. "How is it that Fate should decree that I must see your face again . . . here, today?"

Degrelle's brow darkened. Instinctively Nanon glanced through the open doors to the sullen sky outside. He leaned close to prod at her bosom with a furious finger. "I don't relish your insults, *mademoiselle!* Nevertheless, I shall answer you, if only for my own pleasure. Remember, I hold the reins here, not you. Let us start with Genoa. The town knew of the bandits' assault on the rich merchant's caravan, and that two members of his family were murdered, several of his escort riders maimed. Do you follow?"

She stared at him with icy disgust. Meanwhile, she

nimbly placed her heel behind her so she might push herself upward against the banister. Somehow, she must outwit him, foil whatever it was he had in mind.

"But here's the interesting part! It seems a young Frenchwoman saved a boy's life, and she was fêted by the boy's parents in Milan. It wasn't difficult for me to deduce that this Frenchwoman must be the paramour of the captain of my ship. The merchant being a friend of his, I supposed the two merely traded the lady's favors. Thus, I was able to trace you."

*What advantage does this creature believe he possesses that I will allow him to speak in this manner?* The Degrelle Nanon knew would not dare imply these untruths unless he held some private knowledge that could do her in. Instantly her thoughts flew to Devin in Paris. Tender feelings for him and worries for his safety rushed through her.

She spoke curtly. "Believe me, sir, you'll suffer for what you've just said to me. But do continue. However, watch your tongue."

He bowed mockingly. "I arrived in Milan too late to invite myself to the celebration. I followed you from there to Théophile's love nest on that Italian lake." He paused and looked at her searchingly. Noting his manner, Nanon felt dread. He went on after a moment's silence. "There I was able to convince him and that silly Louisa of his that I meant you no harm. So he told me you'd come here to Malmaison to remain awhile so you might be near your family's abandoned château."

He was standing directly in front of her, and she cringed at seeing the malevolence in his pale eyes. There was something else . . . something he was holding back. She was not quite sure of the direction in which suspicion was leading her, but it was strange that he had not mentioned D'Amboise. . . .

He was glancing around, apprising the closed rooms, the lonely silence that surrounded them. His gaze, yellow and crafty, traveled up the staircase that led to empty rooms, empty corridors . . . and came back to rest upon her.

His next words, spoken in a tight voice, reinforced her foreboding. "I see that Malmaison, too, is an abandoned country place, or it might as well be. If I recall the caretaker rightly, the man spends most of his time with the wine vats."

Her thoughts darted. For the most part, he was unfamiliar with this house. If by some strategem she could dodge away from him, and hide . . . *If* she could reach Marcel in his cottage—or possibly the few men who labored in the fields . . .

Though the throbbing in her head was going on apace, Nanon continued to watch his eyes for any clue that would enable her to guess his next move. With some lucky pretext, she might make a run for it and escape through the kitchen area of the house.

But there was no time left for cleverness. It had to be now. . . . Now! She grasped the newel post, hurled herself around it, dived beneath his arm, and sliding around him, took him by surprise. That was it! Then she suddenly changed course.

She sprinted for the wide-open front doors, her goal the garden maze where Joséphine had once lost herself from pursuers. But the hard soles of her slippers sent her skidding on the oak floor. Pain cracked mercilessly across her instep, and then she was on her knees, trying to rise. But he confronted her, crouching there like a demon. His purposeful strength astounded her. Clutching her shoulders, he wrestled her to the floor and thrust himself on top of her.

His face only inches above hers, he snarled against her lips. "You need a mark put upon you, Nanon de Cavanac, burned deep to make you understand that you have no choice anymore! We're not yet wed, you and I, but everyone else has supped of you. Why not your future husband, the future master of your body and your lands! The brother who loved you more than his Louisa will not see you again. Three weeks ago the two set out in a frail bark and drowned in their Italian lake. A fitting end to an operatic tale. Tell me, why do you look so pallid, you who are now mistress of the Cavanac estate?"

"No! You're lying. Théo is alive. . . ."

"He is dead."

The horror of it was that suddenly she believed him. This was exactly where her terrible suspicion had been leading her.

In rage and in sorrow she clawed at him. There was an awesome gleam of emerald fire as her fingernails raked his face to leave bloody gashes on his cheek and his jaw. He howled, and his own retaliation was swift. His teeth clamped hard on her lower lip, and she could taste her own blood as well as his. Bitterly savaging her mouth with his teeth and tongue, Degrelle grappled with her clothing, pulling her skirts and petticoats up from beneath her hips.

Nanon had begun to weep, not from weakness but from desolation. His knee wedged roughly between her thighs, abrading her tender skin; and she could feel the sweep of his hand inside her skirts. She swore at him in fury, using Théo's oaths to damn him to hell, for her brother as well as for herself. She knew that somehow Degrelle was linked to that tragedy in the lake.

In an effort to twist herself from underneath his body, she gouged him with her elbow, first his chest and then his midriff. In her attempt to do greater harm to a more sensitive target, she was foiled as he groaned and rolled aside. She could hear profane oaths spew out along with the wind she'd knocked from his lungs. He was clutching his chest, his eyes distended in an effort to breathe.

Disregarding her painful foot, Nanon tried to rise, but his hand snaked out to clasp her ankle. Once more she was yanked down beside him. His next words came in a whisper, breathless and bizarre.

"You *will* do my bidding. Otherwise D'Amboise will never be cleared of having murdered his overseer. You don't want to see your erstwhile fiancé suffer this stain to his reputation, do you?"

Her heart had been torn with grief for Théo and Louisa. But now, what in the name of heaven was he saying? Listening in shock, she lay so motionless that he made no further move to seize her.

Instead, they both rose, as though at some silent cue, to face each other. He took a final gulp of air and stared at her with feverish eyes. "I can attest that I saw what happened—because I was there."

"I do not believe you." She lifted her chin.

"Think back and you will. You told me about Terren, about the past quarrels. You told me where to find the plantation. You recall, don't you? Along the road I came upon black workers who gave me further directions."

Nanon's amber eyes widened. At first she had thought this was a trap; now the truth became clear. *Dear Lord, Degrelle was there!*

"You went to the plantation after we spoke. Why would you do that?" How reasonable she sounded, yet she felt she was shattering inside with the exquisite relief.

He ignored her question. "The person who killed Terren used D'Amboise's gun—the one Terren took from the desk."

"Yes, yes, that's understood. But how could you know that, or have witnessed—?"

He was taut with impatience. "I didn't say I witnessed. I said I could attest to what happened. Without me, D'Amboise has no chance to prove he is innocent of having killed a man."

Nanon controlled her shaking with an effort. "You saw someone running away, is that it?"

He shrugged. "I will be believed whatever I choose to say. But it depends on you, my dear. You see what I am

371

getting at, Nanon?"

Silence surrounded them, and she began to wonder if she could force him to speak further. But while she pondered this, it seemed to her a change was coming over him. He was too quiet, and his eyes no longer showed elation. There was an opaque glaze to them that was even more frightening than their previous look of wild exhilaration. Watching him closely, Nanon suddenly asked herself if she had properly understood the words she'd heard him utter.

"I took care of Terren myself. No one will ever believe you if you try to tell them this. They'll say you're protecting D'Amboise because you were once engaged to marry the man. You and I share a secret between us now, don't we? It will bind us forever; isn't that right, Nanon? But of course you'll agree so that I'll exonerate D'Amboise."

Numbly she shook her head. "You . . . killed Emil Terren?"

"I'm not saying that straight out, am I? Oh yes, I've killed once or twice. More than that on the field of battle. That's all I shall say. Now . . . get out to my coach. Come along. I must—there's something I need, something I must do." He appeared to grow more alert, more agitated.

Beyond his shoulder, she saw the figure walking toward them along the corridor that led from the rear of the house. The steps grew longer as he came on at a faster pace.

"Marcel . . ." Her voice was low, urgent.

"An old trick." Degrelle laughed. "I'm surprised at you." Even so, he did look back. And halted.

Unexpectedly, Marcel, too, stopped. "Whose coach stands in front of this house? It cannot belong to Colonel D'Amboise."

She could see the sudden shock in his black eyes. "Stand away, *mam'selle*," he begged of her.

372

And then she understood. Almost by sleight of hand, Degrelle had drawn the small pistol from his belt. With all their scrambling about, why hadn't she been wary? How could she have missed that ridge of metal tucked away?

She called out. "Marcel . . . don't come any closer."

"That's right. Tell the fellow to hold off unless he wants a bullet between his eyes," Degrelle ordered. "I may practice my marksmanship anyway." He raised his right arm, aiming.

"No, Georges . . . please no!"

Wrapping his other arm around her waist, he half dragged her to the open doors. She screamed as he turned once, and fired.

# Chapter Forty

Pushed inside the small, shabby coach, Nanon tumbled onto the cracked leather seat while Degrelle grabbed for his single piece of luggage, the black apothecary bag she remembered from the days he'd tended her father. He sent her a murderous glare and, with an oath, slammed the door before she could recover and leap past him. She was startled to see him jump onto the driver's box and grasp the reins. Evidently, there was neither coachman nor groom.

As Degrelle whipped the tired-looking team of four into the driveway turn, Nanon looked back frantically. Marcel could not be seen. Only an excited Dominique was in view. She reared at the hitching post, then twisted her body and slashed down hard with her hooves in an attempt to break free.

They were away from the house now, and covering the ground at such a pace that Nanon knew if she opened the door and jumped, it would be her death. She must survive . . . she must bring Degrelle to his doom.

The horses were galloping along the country road that led to her family's château. Once more she looked back, this time to see Dom galloping after the coach! Chestnut mane flying, billows of summer dust rising from beneath her hooves, the mare was racing in a familiar direction, toward her home stable.

The coach swayed along the narrow, rutted road that led through the wood, and as she hung onto the seat bar, all manner of bewildering questions surged through Nanon's mind. If Paris was Degrelle's destination, why were they taking this circuitous route by way of the château? Was it to view the de Cavanac lands he intended to own? *Concentrate on what you must do*, she told herself. To round the circular driveway in front of the house, the team would have to slow its pace. Already Nanon could sense the uneven rhythm of their pounding hooves and she wondered how long the tiring animals could continue.

Looking back through the flimsy pane she could see that Dom, no longer following close behind the coach, was headed at a more docile trot in the direction of the old stable she'd occupied for so many years. Nanon's heart sank. She'd counted on the mare's legs. Well, she'd have to use her own to run for her life.

The coach neared the ruined steps of the front entrance, its team beginning to stumble, its speed slowing appreciably. Aware of what she must do, Nanon grasped the door handle. If she could reach the woods and the pond behind the château, she could get away; she was far more familiar with this territory than Degrelle was. She alone knew the many hiding places among the rock castles of her childhood.

Her wits were quicker than Degrelle's, and she was out of the coach before he could shout in surprise at seeing her jumping free of the slowly rolling wheels. She raced for the cover of the dense boughs and shadowy underbrush. He leaped from the driver's box but halted to furl the team's reins around an old hitching post.

By the time he again pounded after Nanon, she was at the edge of the swamp pond, quaking with fear. In his rage and excitement, would he try to kill her? He must still have that pistol he'd fired at Marcel. Her mind recoiled from the anguished thought that the caretaker lay dead because of her.

She shook away the numbing sorrow and made herself

assess the murky depths along the pond's edge. Sweeping up her skirt with both hands, she tucked the edges into her waistband. The petticoats drooped and dragged in the water, slowing her, as the muddy bottom sucked off her slippers and she pitched forward into a tangle of clammy weeds that grew underwater. But they, and fortune, were with her; quickly she ducked beneath the surface as Degrelle lurched to the side of the pond.

He was searching for her, but he appeared distracted as thunder rolled in the distance and the first spatters of summer rain began to fall, veiling the setting around him. Watching from behind the weedy growth, Nanon sensed his continuing anger at her and his bewilderment because she had seemed to vanish, leaving no trace. She knew the respite couldn't last, even though he had turned away, apparently intending to search among the trees and brush.

She pulled herself from the cold water and hastily clambered up the side of the nearest boulder. Even after the brief rain shower, its surface retained the summer's heat, and she clasped it thankfully even though this huge rock was less familiar than the others above her. Still, as though they had learned each crevice, her feet found easy purchase as she scrambled higher. She was as nimble as though a decade hadn't passed since she'd played here. But she was full-grown now, and a hiding place was more difficult to find.

Her shoulders were hunched to slide down into the protective cove she'd found when in the distance, she saw Degrelle stop short, glance back at the great rock, clench his fists and roar, "Nanon! You're there, I know you are! Come out . . . damn you, woman. You and I are not finished!"

Had he really seen her, or was he guessing at her hiding place? He might stalk her, but surely he wouldn't try to climb the slippery rocks. She could outwait him. Certainly, at dusk he'd turn away, perhaps go up to the house and watch for her from there. What did he want from her—some final submission to him? That he would never have while breath remained in her.

Again, sorrow assailed her as she dwelt on Théo and Louisa, picturing the drowning that Degrelle had described. It was terrifying to her that in this one thing she could believe him—for this made her acknowledge that the man who had nursed her father was capable of murder. She'd relied on his knowledge of drugs to ease an invalid's pain. Laudanum, she knew about, but what other draughts might he have prepared . . . tincture of opium, belladonna? There her knowledge ended. She shuddered, hoping she wasn't suspecting a sinister cause for her father's death. . . .

"Nanon, listen to me!" This time his tone was soft and conciliatory, and he seemed much closer. She didn't dare raise her head to peer over her rocky parapet and discover his exact location.

"Listen to me, I say . . . I was overwrought back there. I apologize to you. I am deeply sorry. Everything I've told you is the truth. It was a boating accident that took your brother and his fiancée. I was told about it when I arrived at their lake house."

Huddled in her hiding place, sore and aching, her hair dripping wet, Nanon listened to him in disbelief. Listened, too, to the stillness surrounding them. Under other circumstances, it would have been peaceful. No wind whispered among the pine needles, and the oaks with gold-green leaves were still. There was no rustle of birds, there were no sweet cries, even though the patter of rain had ceased. But there was something to be heard—her heartbeat, wild and racing with the desire to stay alive.

"I love you, Nanon. You and I can live together in the château. We've lived under the same roof since you were fourteen years. Did I frighten you then? No. Did I hurt you? Never. I loved you, always from a distance. And remember this, your father trusted me." He waited. There was no reply. "What of this D'Amboise? You cannot love him. You don't know him! Do you truly believe he will marry you . . . a Frenchwoman? He's too highly placed among the British. And how can you trust a man of such mongrel blood as his. You are France. He is England — with a smattering of Ireland and Martinique."

Listening to that eerie, wheedling voice that seemed to come ever closer, Nanon closed her eyes as though to shut out nightmares. Her mouth was dry with outrage, and her shaking hand bore Devin's ring to her lips, then held it against their softness. *I kiss you, Devin. I love you, Devin. . . . I will survive this, and we will find each other. . . .*

The triumph in Degrelle's shout nearly brought Nanon from her hiding place. Then, as his words penetrated, shockingly, she did stand up in horrified compliance to his command.

"Look . . . here's your damned mare. Come down here to me at once or the animal's dead. I have a bead on her. You've only seconds to make up your mind, *dear Nanon!*"

She half fell from the boulder's height, and her clothing torn, her arms purple with bruises, her bare knees scraped, she stood barefoot and panting beside Degrelle.

Dominique, having trotted past the abandoned stable, was now munching grass along the path leading to the pond. Pistol in hand, Degrelle was aiming at the mare's temple. He sent one evil glance over his shoulder at Nanon, and his brows raised as he took in her appearance. He mocked her. "I wonder by the look of you whether your surrender is worth it to me."

She answered him with contempt. "Nevertheless, I'm here as you demanded." But she knew she couldn't trust the man's cruel temper. Sensing what he planned, she swiftly stepped back a pace, her whistle to the mare sharp and clear in its imperative.

378

Dominique's golden-brown head came up like an un-furling banner. With a single snuffle of delight, she trot-ted forward, only to whirl aside the instant the man standing beside her mistress raised his arm and pointed toward her.

Degrelle had acted exactly as Nanon had expected. Still, the firing of the gun so close to her ear—and what the shot could have portended—made her frantic. She struck hard at his outstretched arm. The pistol flew in an arc toward the dank pond waters, and Nanon met Dom on the run. Grasping the mare's long mane, she pulled herself up into the saddle.

"Go, my darling." She breathed out, and bent low over Dom's neck. They were off and galloping the forest path toward the main road that led to Paris. With the occa-sional passing drays, Nanon would be safe even if De-grelle forced his tired team to follow her.

The woods had long since been left behind. They were now on the pathway that ran beside the main road. It had light traffic—carriages, wagons and horsemen. The day had again darkened; thunderheads, black and boil-ing, loomed in the distance. Nanon was exhausted, and she sensed Dominique's failing strength. The mare's swift gallop had easily covered the miles, but now she moved forward at a measured trot. And though she was going along steadily, an occasional stumble bespoke waning en-ergy.

Dom's head was drooping and her pace was uneven when Nanon halted her. Slowly, stiffly, she slid to the ground. After dismounting so awkwardly, she stood a moment, her eyes closed, wondering if she could ever move again. Then, sighing, she drew her tattered skirts about her and bent to tighten the loosened cinch strap around Dom's belly. Dom snorted in protest, but it had to be done since Nanon might be forced to remount quickly.

Next, she ran loving hands over her mare's withers, and resting her head against the animal's neck, she muttered, "Truth is, Dom, I couldn't summon strength to climb aboard you just yet even if the last judgment descended on us. We have to rest ourselves awhile."

Suddenly Dom turned her head to her mistress. Brown eyes glistening, ears pricked up alertly, she tossed her mane and whinnied softly. Nanon stood motionless, equally aware and listening. Animal and human together had caught the faint signal beneath their feet. Somewhere along the way they'd just come, distant hooves were rhythmically pounding the earth headed in their direction. Yet no one was in sight.

Nanon's shoulders sagged wearily. Covering her face with shaking hands, she murmured. "You don't really hear anything, do you, Dom? Please, no . . . Nor do I." She announced this last boldly with a defiant rise of her chin. But the denial wasn't working.

Degrelle's arrival would force her to climb into the saddle and spur on her tired mount. But she couldn't do it! She simply couldn't. She'd hail a passing dray and hope that her dirty and bedraggled appearance wouldn't startle even a good Samaritan into avoiding a mendicant female and her lame horse.

The August storm clouds rolled and clashed and thundered in the distance. Now Nanon could see no one coming along the road. As happens with flocks of birds, the warning dark in the sky had driven all passersby to seek cover.

Except for herself and Dominique.

And in the distance that tall figure astride a huge dapple-gray that came on with a slow and proud pacer's gait.

Nanon refused to look behind her at the single pathway. Shaken and distraught, she sank to the ground. Rest a moment, she thought. Rest for only a moment. . . .

Once more Dominique whinnied, louder this time.

Then there was a rush of sound, a thump of boots hitting the earth; and someone was kneeling beside her on the grass, someone large and warm and protective.

An arm enclosed her in an embrace that seemed to deliver fire to her soul. She didn't need to look up, for she felt herself transformed, alive once again, burning with joy and strength.

Finally, her eyes rising to meet his, Nanon saw that strong, rough-hewn face, on it love. It was as though his eyes were crystal and she could look through them to his soul, pure and ardent and adoring. Numbly she thought, I shall never forget this moment. . . .

"My own darling, did he hurt you?"

Lost in a whirl of emotion at discovering what it meant to be so loved, Nanon could only shake her head in reply.

"That's right. . . . Don't try to talk." Tenderly he lifted her in his arms.

Never taking her gaze from his, Nanon knew she must speak, must erase the terrible concern in those kind and loving eyes. She swallowed hard, and mumbled. "Devin . . . how did you find me? How did you know . . .?"

"I found the caretaker lying wounded in Malmaison's front hall. He told me what had happened so far as he knew it, that a man had forced you into his coach and drove off in the direction of Château de Cavanac."

"Then Marcel's alive! And you followed me?" Her voice was growing stronger.

"I did. On Boru here. I had a detail along with me, so I left some men and my coach behind to tend the caretaker. The others rode with me while we searched for you at your father's château. When you weren't there, we went along the road beyond that leads to this main highway. It was there in the woods that we found a broken-down coach. Next, we encountered Degrelle beating a fallen horse." His voice hardened. "I had to convince him—a bit too harshly I fear, but he'll live—to disclose the direction you'd taken."

She stared at him, her eyes brilliant with the tears she was holding back. "Where is he now?" she whispered.

"I left him with my men and came on alone to find you. Oh, my darling Nanon . . ." He buried his face in her thick, damp curls. "Thank God, you're safe. I couldn't have lived . . . I couldn't . . ." His voice broke. "If anything had happened to you . . ." He could not finish the words so bravely begun. Instead, he raised his head, studying her face; and his fingers gently touched the corners of her mouth, then smoothed the contour of her cheek.

She caught his hand and held it to her lips. "Devin, something even more terrible than this has happened! Is Degrelle still in the custody of your men? I pray God he is!"

"Yes. Why? I told them not to release him until I returned."

As rapidly as possible, she told Devin everything that had occurred from the moment Degrelle had surprised her in the doorway at Malmaison. "Devin, he has killed twice! First Terren, and then—oh, Devin!—he is responsible for the drowning of my brother and his fiancée. It was not a boating accident; it was murder!"

"Nanon, you've only this scoundrel's word that he did such a deed."

"No, Devin. He told the truth this one time. It was the circumstances of his telling of it that convinced me he *did* harm to Théo and Louisa. You have him now, and he can be brought back to Martinique. Your friend Christophe can find the workmen who will be able to identify him. Oh, why is my word not enough?" She began to sob uncontrollably, her face pressed against his shoulder.

"Hush . . ." he murmured, stroking her copper-bright hair that seemed to flame between his fingers. "Listen to ne, my love. I'm placing you up in Boru's saddle, and we'll lead your mare. Get ready." He hoisted her high in front of him, then quickly mounted.

She had never been on a horse so many hands high. But Boru is legendary," she protested. "I've been told no one has ever ridden him but you."

"The legend changes, my sweet. No one rides him except you and me. This is how it is, how it will be . . . forever. Have I told you I love you?" He was doing his best to distract her.

She nestled safely against the expanse of his chest, her head tucked beneath his chin. But she looked troubled. Yet, as Boru walked along in stately fashion bearing his double burden with ease, Dom trotting behind on a lead rope, Nanon raised a hand to gently stroke Devin's cheek. Tentatively her fingers touched his perfectly sculptured lips. "I don't even have to inquire where you're taking me. With you, I am safe. I love you. . . ." Her fingertips felt the smile on his lips.

It was after several minutes of riding in silence that he spoke again. "I had intended to sail with you across the channel, to Ireland, to my lands there. We have a small church in our village where the banns could be posted. And there we would be married. That is what I had planned for us."

"We can't?"

He shook his head.

She rested hers against his shoulder as she looked up at the sky. "I know. We must finish here what began here. But we don't have to return to Martinique, do we?"

"Not now. I do have influence. My solicitors and my highly placed friends will do what is necessary where Degrelle is concerned. But we must look into this matter concerning your brother. Therefore, we'll remain in France for a while. Do you mind? I can obtain permission for us to stay briefly at Malmaison since certain favors are owed me."

She spoke gravely. "If that is how it must be, I would like that very much." A faint smile touched her lips.

Neither had noticed that the storm clouds had turned to gold and had been blown beyond the distant hills. He twitched the reins to halt Boru, who bucked delicately in resignation. Devin bent his face down to hers, and with a sigh of happiness, they shared a long and exquisite kiss. This time she sensed the finality of it, and for some reason she repeated dreamily, "Antoinette-Élise D'Amboise," so softly he barely heard her.

In response to his inquiring look she said aloud, "I was thinking of the little church in Ireland."

"Nanon, we can be married in Paris! Would you like that?" He looked anxious, unsure, and yet hopeful, all at the same time. Not a bit like the somewhat intimidating Colonel Devin D'Amboise.

Nanon's laughter rippled forth. "Why yes, I'd like that very much." She held up her hand and gazed at her ring finger. She could have sworn its emerald fire winked back at her.